Acclaim for
**Amy Mason Doan's first novel**
*The Summer List*

Named a Best Book of Summer 2018 by
*Coastal Living* * *Family Circle* * *PopSugar* * *The Globe and Mail*

Named a Recommended Read by
*First for Women* * *Bustle* * **HelloGiggles** * **BuzzFeed** * *Brit + Co*

---

"A sparkling debut novel filled with nostalgia that will make you long for your childhood friends and carefree summer days."

—*PopSugar*

"This is a lovely debut by Doan, exploring themes of motherhood, daughterhood, and first love with tenderness and humor. The writing is fresh and charming, a perfect read for anyone who spent her teenage years reading the racy bits of cheap paperbacks out loud to her best friends."

—*Booklist* (starred review)

"If this Portland writer's debut novel were a beverage, it would be a glass of frosty sweet-tart lemonade, sipped with that one friend from way back who knows you better than you know yourself. It's an ideal summer read.... [A] compelling blend of love, betrayal, secrets and reconciliation."

—*The Oregonian*

"This accomplished debut novel from Doan cleverly blends a coming-of-age tale, the story of a long-simmering mystery, and a thoughtful study of relationships between childhood friends.... Doan's characters leap off the page, believably struggling with the conflict between resentment and tenderness. With lovable characters and a scenic small town, Doan's pleasant mix of mystery and high school nostalgia will please readers who grew up with the novels of Judy Blume."

—*Publishers Weekly*

"[An] engaging beach read about friends reconnecting.... This story made me realize that no matter where you are or how much time goes by, the important people will always find their way back into your heart."

—*First for Women*

"With a vivid sense of place and characters as real as your high school besties, this debut novel is sure to please fans of Kristin Hannah and Elin Hilderbrand."

—*Library Journal*

"One of the best books I've read all year, *The Summer List* by Amy Mason Doan is a tear-jerking story of the bonds that connect us, and the lies that tear us apart. From their joyful childhood memories to their current fractured friendship, readers are presented with a beautifully woven tale of nostalgia and suspense."

—*Arizona Foothills Magazine*

"There's not a word or plot line out of place in this fabulous debut about two girlhood friends from a small lakeside town who reunite as adults to try to salvage their broken relationship. Dive beneath the surface and you'll find a complex and finely wrought story as full of mystery and vitality as the lake itself. These characters and their stories are going to stick with you for a long, long time."

—Meg Mitchell Moore, author of *The Admissions* and *The Captain's Daughter*

"A trip down memory lane becomes a hunt for long-buried secrets in Amy Mason Doan's gripping and poignant debut about the bond between two compelling outsiders. *The Summer List* is an evocative tale of family, first love, and the unique and lasting gift of a friendship formed in girlhood."

—Meg Donohue, *USA TODAY* bestselling author

"A poignant tale of mothers and daughters finding their ways home to each other."

—*Kirkus Reviews*

"[A] character-rich tale about what could have been and the difficulty of facing what is makes for a satisfying beach-vacation read. A twist underscores what we already suspect: that life is too short for if-onlys."

—*Stanford Magazine*

"Fantastic. You'll stick with *The Summer List* until the very end."

—*San Francisco Book Review*

"In her mesmerizing debut, Amy Mason Doan challenges everything we think we know about family and forgiveness. Readers will be swept up in this haunting story of buried secrets and lost love."

—Lynda Cohen Loigman, author of *The Two-Family House*

"With its exquisite detail, *The Summer List* wouldn't let me go and the unexpected ending gave me chills. An irresistible novel of friendship and home."

—Jennifer S. Brown, author of *Modern Girls*

"A tender novel about friendship lost and rekindled and uncovering the truth of the past."

—Polly Dugan, author of *So Much a Part of You* and *The Sweetheart Deal*

"*The Summer List* is the perfect summer read. Impossible to put down!"

—Molly O'Keefe, *USA TODAY* bestselling author

# Summer Hours

Also by Amy Mason Doan

*The Summer List*

# Summer Hours

a novel

amy mason doan

GRAYDON
HOUSE

**GRAYDON
HOUSE**

Recycling programs
for this product may
not exist in your area.

ISBN-13: 978-1-525-82357-2

Summer Hours

GraydonHouseBooks.com
BookClubbish.com

**Printed in U.S.A.**

For my mom

# Summer Hours

Southern California, July
Early Thursday morning

We're in a rented convertible heading north on Pacific Coast Highway.

It's not yet dawn, so the ocean is only a string of white boat lights floating on darkness. Like a fallen constellation.

It's beautiful, but my passenger can't see it.

And I can't see him. Everything below his forehead is hidden by the gift wedged between our seats.

I didn't expect the box to be quite so big. I'd asked the eBay seller to pack it carefully, and she went to town on the Bubble Wrap. So this was the only way it would fit, the front end lashed to the cup holders with bungee cords to keep it in place.

"Seriously?" he murmured in the driveway before we left San Diego, laughing softly in the way I'd always loved. "Can we even get to the e-brake?"

"It'll be fine!" I assured him.

My words hover in the air over the convertible, zooming north with us: *It'll be fine!*

Not exactly an electrifying motto to launch a road trip. But I'm trying to embrace it.

Wrestling the giant wedding gift into the car last night, I'd said it to myself: *It'll be fine, Becc.*

I'd ticked reassuring items off my mental list:

The sporty red rental car. Hotel reservations for four nights. Big Sur tonight, then San Francisco, then Saturday and Sunday at the wedding venue, a gorgeous place on the beach in Oregon, just past the California border.

We'll have Sleep Number beds, robes, balconies. I found the perfect outfit to wear to the ceremony on the beach Sunday afternoon. The long blue, bias-cut sundress is rolled in tissue paper inside my suitcase, next to my travel steamer.

I brought wrapping paper, scissors, and tape for the present. I agonized over ribbon options, finally settling on something called a Bling Blossom—a $7.99 silver pouf bigger than a head of lettuce.

There's nothing left to do but drive.

Press my sandal on the slim, racing-style pedal, breathe in the chilly wind off the Pacific, and keep my expectations low.

But when we approach the off-ramp for Orange Park I can't help it. I want more. I want him to speak, to smile at me over our absurdly large present, to at least look out his window as we pass. Anything to prove the words on the green sign still matter.

Orange Park Road, 1 mile

I want him to show he remembers where we met, and how we used to escape together, years ago, when we were so sure we could steal time before it stole us.

But he faces forward, silent.

And I can't see his eyes when we fly past those familiar gold hills, the sun just beginning to rise behind them.

# 1

## Welcome to Orange Park

March 20, 1994

Dear Application Committee,

Thank you for considering me for the Francine Alice Haggermaker Scholarship for a University of California Undergraduate Pursuing a Media Career.

I have wanted to be a newspaper journalist ever since sixth grade, when I wrote a report about the fearless 1890s reporter Nellie Bly. She said of her legendary investigative work that "energy rightly applied and directed will accomplish anything." Her words stirred me when I was 11, and they still do.

As editor in chief of the Orange Park High *Squeeze*, I uncovered a $339 discrepancy in the South Field Astroturf Fund and wrote a three-part series on snack bar waste. Compared with Bly's undercover stories for the *New York World* about corruption at

Blackwell's Island Insane Asylum or her defiant trip around the world in seventy-two days, these articles may sound small. But Orange Park High has a new Beautification Committee chair who keeps detailed spending records. We started a partnership with a local food pantry, and fruit that would otherwise spoil is now donated over the weekend so that it can feed the homeless.

Is the truth ever small? Nellie Bly didn't think so. And neither do I. As Joseph Pulitzer, the owner of Bly's newspaper, said, "Our Republic and its press will rise or fall together!"

I know that you have a talented pool of applicants. But my 4.3 GPA, 99th-percentile SAT scores, extracurriculars, 100 percent attendance record, and passion for uncovering the truth show that I am a tireless worker who "applies my energy" every minute.

If you select me for this honor, I promise that I will live up to your expectations.

Sincerely,

Ms. Rebecca Reardon

June 10, 1994
One week before high school graduation
2:28 p.m.

WHERE I WAS SUPPOSED TO BE | Health and Human Behavior, back
corner window desk
WHERE I WAS | Health and Human Behavior, back corner window
desk

My seat overlooked the side parking lot, where I had a prime
view of kids sneaking off school grounds. Heading for pools,
the beach, blissfully chilly movie theaters.

Discreetly, I reached inside my drenched T-shirt sleeve and
tugged up my strapless bathing suit. I'd worn it under my clothes
to save time, but it only made me sweatier and reminded me
of my failure.

I was supposed to be out there.

The three of us had planned to ditch school together all year.
Just once, to prove we had it in us. For months, Eric and Serra
and I mapped exit routes and rendezvous points, calling Serra's
wood-paneled Pinto station wagon "the getaway car." The Stay

Wag had psoriasis-like patches of oxidation damage on its hood and shuddered if Serra drove over forty.

In our sketches it grew Pegasus wings.

But in April I won the Haggermaker Scholarship. Four years of tuition, housing, and books. Mrs. Haggermaker and her late husband were both Berkeley alums, and he'd made a fortune as a film studio head in the 1950s. So every four years, one lucky student became her six-figure pet.

She'd handed me the heavy bronze plaque herself at the Senior Awards ceremony, up on the auditorium stage. She'd leaned close, all seventy-five-year-old bony corners, and whispered, "I'm sure you'll do me great credit, my dear."

When the paperwork had come, my mom read the morals clause aloud. Stern paragraphs about "due regard to conventions" and "acts reflecting favorably on the Foundation."

"Really," she'd said, smiling over her mug of Sleepy Time tea. "As if they'd ever have to worry about you."

So I couldn't cut.

Not even one afternoon so close to summer, after eighteen years of good behavior. Tutoring and volunteering and racking up a perfect transcript.

I didn't feel perfect. Only stuck.

2:38 p.m.

"Rebecca, could you?" Mrs. Gaukroger held up the VHS tape of *Red Asphalt*, the gruesome drunk-driving movie we'd watched.

I was her girl Friday, trusted to return supplementary multimedia materials to the library. I was not a flight risk.

My flip-flops slapped the green linoleum in the empty hall as I passed the countdown-to-graduation banner, drawn in rainbow bubble letters (7 DAYS LEFT!!), a sign-up for the ten-year reunion committee (*no, thanks*), a poster advertising the bottomless sundae bar at Grad Party.

The door of the teacher's lounge swung open and Mr. Singleton emerged, popping a Coke can.

Coke was Mr. Singleton's thing. He swigged it all through AP Chem, sighing exaggerated *aahs*, and in October he did a whole week of Coke science experiments. He mixed it with Mentos mints, causing a reaction like a geyser, and in a less exciting one he dropped a nail into a beakerful of Coke so we could watch it decay. Once he pretended to sip from it, to a delighted chorus of *eews*.

He pointed the can at me, stopping an inch from my sternum. "It's the famous scholarship winner! You majoring in chem up at Berserk-ley?"

So he'd read the grad edition of the *Squeeze*. Eric, the only one going to an Ivy, had put that he planned to "ride the rails." His dad was pretty pissed.

"I don't have to declare yet, so—"

"Why aren't you in class? Don't tell me I have to write you up for truancy." He trilled the *r*, drew out the *oooo*. Everything he said had a faint tone of mockery. Even *mole* and *titration*—as if he'd have named them differently. I found him exhausting.

But I smiled. "I'm returning this for Mrs. Gaukroger."

"That's the Girl Scout way." He grinned, passing me with bouncy little steps and pivoting so he was still facing me. I turned, too, like we were dancing a reel. "Be good, now," he said, walking backward.

"Always."

My bantering-with-the-teacher smile collapsed as I dropped the tape on the faculty return cart in the library and checked the big silver-and-white wall clock. It was the centerpiece in a construction-paper design that said:

TIME IS PASSING. WILL YOU?
FOCUS!

The *O* in *focus* was the clock.

2:51. Nine minutes till the bell. Would Mrs. Haggermaker yank my award for a nine-minute transgression? Probably.

*You'll do me great credit, my dear.*

So I waited by a hall window, watching a distant figure cut across the baseball diamond. Loping walk, baggy jeans riding so low they must have been held up by invisible suspenders of cool: Donny Chambliss. He ditched all the time, as casually as if he held a pink dismissal slip for a teeth cleaning.

When Donny reached the old eucalyptus tree where our school grounds became the park, he jumped and hit a branch. Clocking out for the day.

Donny set his own hours, while I waited obediently for a bell to release me.

*2*

Floating

I was downtown by 3:03. I passed Kemper's Varia-T, where kids were already swarming in for Mountain Dews and Cheetos. I passed the poster of sundaes in mini plastic baseball caps at Baskin-Robbins, where Serra scooped ice cream. Bernadine's Closet, the "Fine Women's Shoppe." (Spangled, waistless getups, bridge mints, rose hand cream thick as bathroom caulk.) In seventh grade Serra and I invented a game called Least Hideous where we'd evaluate Bernadine's mannequins and pick the outfit we'd wear if forced.

A quick turn past the town square and there was the Stay Wag, right where they'd promised. They'd offered to stay behind with me, but I'd told them to stick with the plan. "Save yourselves, make me proud," I'd said.

I hopped in behind Eric, still in his green-and-white PE uniform. "How'd the escape go?"

He turned around and smiled over his headrest, growling, "We're such rebels." In his normal voice he continued, "Cops on our tail, Becc?"

"You're safe."

Serra pulled away from the curb. "I'm disappointed. I didn't even have to say I was going to the girls' room. Mr. Reynolds fucking *waved* at me when I left. He was helping someone with the lathe."

"Mrs. LeBaron was so busy collecting cones from the dribble drill I could've done back handsprings across the field and she wouldn't have noticed." Eric flipped on the radio. "Not that I can do a back handspring."

"At least you cut." I cranked down my window. The air was hot as a blow-dryer but I tilted my head into it, lifting my ponytail to dry the back of my neck. "I'm a tragic case. Every time I thought of you guys swimming I got sweatier."

Eric shook his overlong black hair so I could see it was dry. "Not so sure about your detective skills there, Becc."

"You waited?" I said. "I'm touched. So what'd you do instead?"

Serra shuddered. "Eric dragged me to see *The Fly*. I'm traumatized."

I laughed. "We watched *Red Asphalt*. Much scarier."

"Do one thing a day that scares you," Eric said. "Mr. California told me that's his life motto. Inspiring, huh?"

Serra and I exchanged a quick look in the rearview mirror.

Mr. California was Eric's mother's new live-in boyfriend. Six years younger and six shades blonder than her. His real last name was McCallister, and everyone called him Cal.

Mr. California: rich, expert sailor, casual investor in a fleet of tech startups, killer backhand. Possibly/probably the reason for the Logans' sudden split earlier this year, though Eric had been vague on the exact sequence of events.

Eric spent most of his free time at my house now, so I'd never met Mr. California. But I'd seen him in his convertible from my bedroom window.

Most residents of The Heights, the gated community where Eric lived, chose their Lexuses, Mercedes, and Porsches in dignified black or gray, or practical, heat-deflecting white. Mr. California's car was metallic turquoise blue, jeweled in chrome.

My house sat across the street from The Heights' gate, and from six until eight every morning, as I studied at my desk, a line of commuters descended the hill. Sometimes Mr. California's car appeared at 7:07 and sometimes at 7:58. I didn't catch it every day. But if I spotted that flashy vintage convertible heading toward me, I gave myself a study break so I could watch it. A drop of water sliding down the dry hill. Cool and smooth. I waited until its tanned, blond driver waved and smiled at the security guard—he always did, unlike most of his neighbors—before returning to my books.

It felt like a game, like a good luck start to my day. Nothing more than that.

But I'd never told Eric.

"Isn't he a wise papa?" Eric said. "Darling papa."

"He really said that, something scary every day?" I asked. "So he's jumping out of airplanes or cage fighting or whatever every day?"

"He does that Escape from Alcatraz triathlon," said Eric. "My role model." He punched the radio presets until he got KROQ. "Mr. Jones" was on.

"Not again," Serra moaned.

But I sang along under my breath as we left downtown.

We passed the turnoff for Orchard Hill, where the graceful old homes like Francine Haggermaker's hid behind mature trees. The new palaces, like The Heights, sprawled farther from town each year, secluded behind gates. Their expensive baby trees racing to catch up with the fully grown ones on Orchard Hill.

Orange Park was booming. Families came for our schools and low crime rate and gigantic empty lots. They built his-and-hers master closets bigger than my mom's whole bedroom, and bathrooms with two bidets, and slapped Italian tile on anything that didn't move.

When we were on Bird of Paradise Way, Serra asked, "Need to run in for your stuff?"

"No, I wore my suit." I gazed out the window to my left, at my dear, hopelessly unfashionable brown ranch house.

As we passed the gate to The Heights, Eric waved out the window at the guard in his little white booth.

Just like Mr. California.

To me, he was only a wave from a car, a drop of blue, a flash of light on white-blond hair. He seemed so sunny, such an unlikely villain.

I guess that only made Eric hate him more.

★

Serra pulled into the sagging carport of the LaSalle Villas. The apartments formed a rectangle around the mucky outdoor pool, which Serra called "divorcée soup" because most of her neighbors were in various stages of marital splittage.

"Last one in…" Eric slammed his car door and ran to the gate, peeling off his PE shirt. He didn't wait for Serra's key. We all knew how to get into the LaSalle Villas pool by reaching over and jiggling the latch. Before the gate clanged shut behind him, Eric hooted and splashed.

I shot off, calling, "Race you."

Serra yelled, "No fair, track star." My flip-flops and the gate slowed me down but Serra never stood a chance. I'd just run the 200 in 25.2 at the county meet.

When I got to the courtyard Eric was already underwater, gliding along the white concrete bottom, collecting rings left behind by someone's kid. Nobody else was there—no divorcée soup today. I stripped to my turquoise suit and jumped into the deep end.

Always, that panic in your confused belly as you fall, before the water catches you. Then sweet quiet.

Eric swam close to me and made a puffin face, his overgrown black hair floating around his head like when he'd touched the Van de Graaff generator on the science center field trip sophomore year. His long hairy legs kicked away and then Serra's smooth, rounder ones splashed down. She treaded water, like she was riding an invisible bicycle.

I stayed down in the cold and quiet until I couldn't stand it, until the pressure in my lungs got to me and I had to push off for the surface.

"Heaven," called Serra, back floating.

Eric sat in the shallow end, scooping dead bees out of the pool with cupped hands, flinging them to the bushes on jet trails of water.

For a long time the only sounds were Eric's splashes and a radio playing The Cranberries on the second floor.

Then Serra climbed out and dried herself with her T-shirt. "Snack time. Back in a sec."

I tipped off my raft and dipped under the handrail to join Eric on the steps.

"How's home, E?" I examined the inside of the plastic drain: a Band-Aid and more bee carcasses. I never looked at him when I asked about home.

"Dandy."

"Are your parents still using you as message boy?"

He pushed his wet hair off his forehead into a wall of absurd, spiky bangs.

"Can't you talk to them? Explain how it sucks for you?"

He shrugged. "I'm out of there in twelve days."

"Twelve? I thought you weren't leaving till September!"

"I decided to do early-start." He closed his eyes and sank into the pool.

It was Eric's last summer. Our last summer. And now we didn't even have July.

He couldn't wait to take off for Rhode Island, putting ten states between him and his parents, his role as go-between, the bad daytime drama of the past year. All the adult poison within the fancy iron gates of The Heights.

*The Heights.* It even sounded like a soap.

Eric's home made me appreciate mine. It was only me and my mom, and the only passion she indulged was for her latest shipment of seed packets from Gold Thumb Gardening Depot. My mom tended our flowers herself, unlike our neighbors in The Heights, who hired certified landscape engineers to present "design concepts."

Eric burst up, a skinny leviathan with wet hair pasted over his eyebrows.

I ran my hand in the water along the quivering oval shadow of his head. "I'm sorry, E."

"How can you feel sorry for someone who can do an underwater handstand like this? Time me." He shot away from the steps. His size-fourteen feet wiggled above the surface as he balanced on his hands, as confident as a Cirque du Soleil artist.

I started doing one-Mississippis in my head and lost count, drifting closer to him.

He fluttered his legs and tipped over, then bobbed up next to me, spitting water and cocking his head to clear his ears. "Well?"

"Fifteen seconds."

"Liar. You didn't time me."

"I'm feeling lazy."

"Too lazy to time me, hanging out with truants. Hardly behavior worthy of the Francine Haggermaker Scholar. Next you'll be injecting H with those guys behind the dumpsters in MacArthur Park."

"That's the plan for tomorrow."

"Sweet. I'll come with you. Blow off my mom's asinine grad barbecue."

"I think we have to make an appearance."

Eric shaped his wet hair into a '50s pompadour and raised his eyebrows like James Dean.

"I love it," I laughed.

"I know I won Best Hair."

Eric had *not* won Orange Park High 1994 Best Hair, Male. He often ran out the door without even pasting his hair down with water, resulting in a bouncing top layer propped up by cowlicks. I wouldn't change it. But I'd tallied Senior Superlative votes for the yearbook, and Best Hair, Male had gone to Chris Pettigrew, a snotty blond golf phenom.

"Don't be too bummed if you don't win." I swam away.

"Those bastards! Who got it?" he called, following me to the deep end.

"Not telling. You'll put gum in his hair."

Eric and I treaded water, facing each other. He batted at a yellow leaf floating between us. I batted it back. We sloshed it back and forth a few times. We figured out how, if you gently pushed the water from a few inches behind it, the leaf rode the waves like a mini surfer.

He swam closer, so close I could see how his long black eyelashes had clumped into triangles around his brown eyes. "How's Becc?" he asked quietly.

"Happy, now."

"What's that?" Eric touched my shoulder while his other hand carved fast figure eights to keep him afloat. That oddly quiet voice, again.

So serious for Eric.

His fingers rested lightly on my left shoulder, where the ribbon for hanging my bathing-suit top had come out.

"Oh, I keep forgetting to snip those," I said. His fingers stayed put, toying with the wet satin ribbon. "It's for hanging up my suit."

I ran on, panting harder, focusing on a spot two inches above his steady brown eyes. "I hate those suckers. I mean, I guess it's a nice gesture on the part of the apparel industry, but I wish I could tell them, 'Thanks, but no thanks.'"

"You've shown me encyclopedias of girl info," he said softly, caressing the ribbon. "How else would I learn about the courtesy hanger loops?"

"I'm the sister you never had."

"A sister. Let me get back to you on that one." He tugged the ribbon once and stared at me, unsmiling, while our heads bobbed up and down.

My face flushed. At the clang of the gate he removed his hand, slapping something on the water.

"A feast of junk food," Serra called. She had two more rafts under her arms, towels around her neck like Rocky, a green plastic mixing bowl brimming with snacks.

I swam over to inventory the food, grateful for something to do. Pringles and gummy candy from the Sweet Shed and lemonade Capri Sun bags from the freezer.

Shaky, I punctured the top of a silver bag with a straw and sipped hard. I got a few syrupy pulls, followed by chunks of bland slush. "Capri Suns make me feel like I'm in NASA. Bathroom?" I asked Serra, wrapping myself in a yellow beach towel.

"Door's unlocked," she called.

I felt Eric watching me as I fled, leaving wet footprints on the burning concrete.

Serra and her parents had a ground-floor unit set close to the street, so anyone on the sidewalk could see their high, rippled bathroom shower window. They could even make out the brands of shampoo and conditioner. That was about as poor as it got in Orange Park now. Serra's dad ran the mail room of a tech startup, and her mom worked as a part-time doctor's office receptionist.

Tyrant, her cat, leapt off the couch when I walked in. He crossed the living room to me, stretching every couple of steps, lordly and unhurried. I bent down to let him see my hand, waggling my fingers under his muzzle before scratching his ears, the way Serra had shown me years before. Serra said cats hate it when you descend on them with no warning, like an alien invader.

Tyrant followed me into Serra's room, winding himself around my legs. I sat on the bed and tucked the white satin ribbon into my bathing suit.

Serra had a picture on her nightstand. It was the same one I had on my dresser, the same one Eric had on his bulletin board. My mom had taken it after the Senior Awards ceremony and made copies for us.

Five-foot-one Serra in the middle, on tiptoe, her arms stretched to our shoulders. Eric and I hunching to even things out, the sun flashing off my glasses and the plaque in my hand. All three of us laughing.

My mom called us the Three Mouseketeers.

The three of us had been best friends for all four years of high school.

Eric spent so much time at my house his sweatshirts ended up in our wash. He and my mom had whole bits they'd do about me, my neatness and coconut addiction and the shredded scrap of pillowcase I'd slept with since I was four.

And now, two weeks before flying away, he was suddenly all eye contact and tender gestures.

★

When I came out Eric lay on a raft, hands over his stomach. "I really shouldn't have eaten that last rat, Becc," he said, as if everything was the same.

I forced a laugh. "You just wanted to say that." Translation: *Let's go back in time to twenty minutes ago, before you touched my naked shoulder.*

I jumped onto an orange raft. The three of us swam and floated and waited for the next song on the radio. Time fell away in four-minute increments, until the sun dropped below the roofline of Serra's building.

The radio ads came faster. It was almost commute time, and soon we wouldn't have the pool to ourselves.

# 3

## Truants

The next day

WHERE I WAS SUPPOSED TO BE | The grad barbecue at Eric's
WHERE I WAS | Consorting with the enemy

Eric's mom had gone for an Old West theme, with red-and-white-checked tablecloths and servers in bandanna neckerchiefs. But the faux down-home look had a hundred little flourishes that said *money.*

Warm, lemony finger towels waited by the rib station, and misters released a perfectly calibrated fog, cool enough to shield us from the ninety-eight-degree afternoon but light enough to preserve hairstyles. Silver goody bags held dark chocolate truffles shaped like graduation caps, custom-ordered from a store in Santa Monica. The food was delicious, the tiered backyard beautiful—everything snipped to perfection.

Behind our hostess's back, the sweating waiters tugged at their hokey red cravats. And if you didn't count Francine Haggermaker (and I didn't), the guests were Mrs. Logan's friends, not ours.

I wanted to jump into the cobalt-tiled pool nobody was using, or teleport up to Eric's room, where he'd fled with Serra ages ago, beckoning me to follow.

Mrs. Haggermaker's gray eyes had been tracking me, so I'd stayed. She sat in state under a mister, in a wicker armchair that seemed somehow more imposing than the others, while I attended her from the ottoman at her knees.

"How do you know the family?" She nodded at Eric's mom.

Mrs. Logan was laughing, surrounded by a visored group from the country club. She was hard to miss, even in a sea of other yoga-and-tennis-toned OC blondes, because she was even taller than me.

Mrs. Haggermaker's expression was inscrutable, but there was a micro pause between *the* and *family*; she knew about the divorce. Possibly the affair. She would still accept Mrs. Logan's invitations—she wouldn't have her booted from the garden club or hospital board; everyone involved was rich enough to ensure this level of gentility—but the minor scandal hadn't gone unnoticed.

"Eric Logan has been one of my best friends since we were fourteen."

"I see."

There was a long silence, so I scrambled for small talk. "That's a pretty pin. Is it a cornflower?"

She touched the stickpin on her chest. "Forget-me-not. My late husband's, from his lodge." She'd also worn the pin, gold topped with a five-petaled blue flower, the night of the awards ceremony. It was the same blue as the ever-present hair ribbon secured around her bun.

"And now you wear it to remember him? That's nice."

Another excruciating lull. Excruciating for me. Mrs. Haggermaker seemed perfectly comfortable.

"My mother's the gardener in our family," I said. "I don't know many flower names. I've been meaning to learn."

Silence.

"I know a few. Flower names. But only because of those plaques they have in the park. I wish they had more plaques in parks."

She narrowed her eyes.

*Plaques in parks?* If I were her I'd revoke my scholarship on the spot.

"Go mingle, dear."

Dismissed, I made the rounds, up and down the sloping flagstone paths, while she watched from her dewy lawn chair throne. When Mrs. Logan's friends introduced themselves, I shook hands with the right amount of pressure and smiled on cue at jokes about the beer kegs waiting for me at Berkeley. The USC and UCLA alums teased me about our Pac-10 football standings. Though I would probably spend those fall Saturday afternoons anywhere but in a stadium, I played along. It was easier.

I knew my part cold. When someone asked what I was going to study and I said I was leaning toward English, I added a line like "just what the world needs, another English major."

A guy in a Pebble Beach Pro-Am 1992 visor called me on that. He'd also majored in English, he said, "in the dark ages."

"Don't be defensive about our major." He clinked his beer against my lemonade and I felt a surge of kinship. Maybe we'd talk Yeats.

Then he said, "English is an excellent back door to business school. You'll stand out. Take some econ classes and you'll be fine."

I bolted from the visor guy, only to get trapped on the other side of the patio by a tall, ginger-haired hospital administrator, selling me on the benefits of her joint JD/MD—"You only need the *stamina* for it."

I nodded, smiling, though sweat had pasted my green cotton sundress to my back and the blisters on my heels stung from rubbing against my good sandals.

"Excuse me, I need to use the powder room." I called it a bathroom at home, but in The Heights I found myself using expressions like *powder room*.

I zigzagged and dodged and smiled without making eye contact and opened the first available door, escaping into the house.

The game room. Electronic blasts, yells, sweat, and beer smells. Doug Tilton and Jack Chang played Sega on the floor, verbally abusing each other and pounding it out through their proxies on the screen. Marcus Lochery watched, stuffing his red face with tortilla chips and shouting instructions. They were neighbor boys in The Heights, but Eric hadn't hung out with them in years, not since he'd met me and Serra.

"How's that feel, loser?"

"Puss move."

I padded to the hall as quietly as I could, but Marcus arched his back over the leather sectional to stare at me upside down. "Miss Scholarship. You got away."

"Yeah."

"Your crew left you behind," he said. "Not cool. I told them when they went upstairs. Santitas?" He rattled his jumbo tortilla chip bag at me.

"No, thanks."

"No man left behind," said Jack, his eyes locked on the robots. He punched his black controller maniacally. Louder—"No woman left behind!"

"It's fine," I said. "See you, guys."

"Oh, we will see you," Marcus singsonged over the battle sounds.

It didn't even make sense. They were messed up. Medicated to get through the party, with their parents just outside the glass French doors. Drunk or high on their Killer Green Buds. (They'd once snickered about their "KGB training" in front of me and I'd smiled, pretending I understood, but clueless until Eric explained.)

"Rebecca, play *Cyborg Justice* with us," Marcus yelled.

"No, thanks." Almost at the door.

"Hey, Rebecca," Doug said. "Will you go to all your classes at Berkeley naked? Like that Naked Guy in the paper?"

"See you guys," I said over my shoulder, hurrying into the hall.

"You've gotten hot," Doug said, laughing. "I remember the minute it happened. You had on white shorts and I thought, Eric's skinny brainiac friend has a nice—"

I slammed the door behind me, booking down the sunny hallway, away from the synthetic battle sounds. I slipped into the closest room and shut the door.

"Rebecca! We're just kidding!" Doug. I held my breath until his footsteps went away.

Finally, blessedly alone. I leaned against the door, pressing my forehead to the smooth wood. I'd wait a full minute, and when I was positive the coast was clear I'd sneak upstairs to Eric's room.

I'd do my Francine Haggermaker impression, mimicking the way she twitched the corners of her mouth a few stingy millimeters whenever she called me *my dear*. I'd describe the scene on the patio. How I'd fled from the game room boys as fast as their video game prey.

And the three of us would make the afternoon ours again by laughing at it.

College boys waited: legions of them. If they got red-faced it would be from arguing about Shakespeare, Heidegger. Not *Cyborg Justice*. I was sure of it.

"You hiding, too?"

I whipped around, knocking my elbow against the door. An excruciating, tuning-fork pain shot up my arm.

The puddling velvet drapes were shut so the only light came from the aqua glow of a fish tank.

Mr. California stood near the luminous water, awash in blue light, studying the drink in his hand. The ice made a silvery sound as he circled it around the glass. His voice was low, amused. "Sorry I scared you. Did you hurt yourself?"

"I'm okay."

"Rebecca, right? How is it out there?"

I was surprised that he knew my name. Eric's dad had never bothered to learn it. "It's a wonderful party. Thanks for inviting me."

"Donna does a good job on this stuff." His smile said, *You and I both know I didn't have a hand in the invites or anything else.* He flicked his head up just long enough for me to read sympathy in his eyes. "May I ask you something?"

"Of course." *Please don't ask about my major.*

He stared at his glass, running his index finger around the lip. "Will you do me a favor?"

"Sure."

"Sorry. I hate when people ask that before they say what the favor is. It's like asking someone if they have plans before you admit what god-awful social event you want to drag them to." He drained his drink.

"I hate that, too."

"The favor is, will you check in on Eric for me next year? Make sure he's okay?" He raised an eyebrow, biting a lip. As if bracing for me to say no to this small assignment.

"Of course."

"Do you have email?"

"I get an account from school."

"Good. His mom's worried about him. You hear about kids going off to college and getting depressed, you know. His dad moving out, me in the picture, staying here so often… It's a bit of a mess. Last week he…" He shook his head.

"What did he do?"

"Oh..." He chuckled. "He wrote me a note. A short but extremely heartfelt and...creative note. Let's put it that way."

*Oh, E.*

Eric didn't tell me everything. Mostly, I had to piece things together from jokes and nicknames, the moods he couldn't entirely hide from me. From the lateness of the hours when he appeared at my door, seeking political asylum with me and my gentle mom, who fussed over him.

But enough had slipped out over the years, and I could see the scenes at Eric's house playing like a film: the silence between his parents bursting into fights, his father camped out in the pool house with bottles of Belvedere. Then reappearing in the breakfast room behind his paper as if nothing had happened.

I knew it had gone on for ages. Silence, screaming, simmering, truce. And the in-between parts, when all three Logans were just bracing for the next cycle.

Until a few months ago, when Mr. Logan decamped to a penthouse condo in LA and Mr. California moved in. Though the official story was that Donna Logan's handsome new boyfriend was only "keeping a few things" there after selling his house up the street, because he also owned places in San Francisco and Mexico.

"So will you check in on him for me? I feel...responsible."

"Sure. We'll email and talk a lot, Mr. McCal—"

"Call me Cal. Everyone does. Easy to remember, because that's where you're going to college, right?"

I smiled at his little Berkeley joke, shocked that he'd taken note of my plans. "Cal. Eric and I will stay in touch as much as we can, from across the country."

"I'd be grateful. He's more...breakable than he seems. Don't you think?" He looked up at me, forehead creased in worry.

I nodded.

*Breakable.* This man the three of us had mocked all year, this walking postcard for California, had expressed perfectly with a single word what I'd feared watching Eric's bitterness grow. Eric was still only pretending he didn't care about his parents splitting up. But soon he might forget it was an act. You hardened, then you shattered. Like glass.

"Do you live in The Heights?" He waved his drink in the air, indicating the study, the pool, the flown-in palm trees, the chunky security guard who patrolled in a golf cart. He said *The Heights* with the same isn't-it-absurd inflection Eric used when he said *Mr. California*.

"We're just outside, facing the gate."

"That great old rancher? The brown one with the railroad ties?"

"Yeah."

"Then your family was there before they built all this."

"Yes, me and my mom. It's not her favorite topic."

"I'll bet. She must've been furious when it happened, literally outside your door. Did she chain herself to the bulldozers?"

When my mother bought our house, there was nothing on the hill across the street except scrub oaks. I used to play there. Now our place kind of looked like the carriage house for The Heights. An observation I would never share with her.

"She says it's better to accept reality and move on. She gets upset if I call it..." I shook my head. "Never mind."

"What?"

"Oh." I bit back a smile. "I have this secret nickname for The Heights."

"Out with it."

"You won't be insulted?"

"Not a chance."

"The Blights."

He laughed. "You let us off easy."

"Our road used to be called North Way, before the developments. But I guess that wasn't fancy enough, so when they paved it they changed it to Bird of Paradise. I still forget sometimes."

"So you haven't quite *accepted reality and moved on?*"

I smiled. "I guess not."

"An idealist, then. A vanishing breed." He smiled to himself, fidgeting with a blue model car on the desk. It was his car—a 1950s or '60s convertible with bright chrome flares.

I wondered what he'd say if I told him how I sometimes watched him in the real one. *You sang along to the radio last Tuesday, that song about two lost souls in a fishbowl. You really belted it out. Pounded that dash with every note.*

The urge to say it, to see if he'd laugh, hit so hard it startled me, warming my cheeks. "I should go."

"Of course. You'll want to be with your friends."

He walked me to the door, as if I'd come calling. His left hand floated behind the small of my back, touching only my thin cotton dress. I felt his fingers there somehow, sensed a subtle shift in the inch of air between the fabric and my skin.

When we passed the aquarium, he asked, "You have one?"

"No, but it's supposed to be good therapy, looking at fish. Not that I mean you need therapy. I just. I read an article about that." I didn't need a mirror to know my cheeks were a lost cause now, pink headed for scarlet.

He laughed. "I do like looking at the suckers. They are *excellent* little therapists."

"Where are they?"

"There are two...see. In that cave?"

He pointed, careful not to touch the glass. He was a lefty. The hairs on his left arm touched the skin of my right arm. He smelled like something clean and sharp and adult. Scotch or shaving cream or whatever rare mixture he used to polish the wood on his boat.

"Oh, yeah." Two narrow blue fish glowed in the toy cave.

"I think I'm becoming a hobbyist." He gestured at a small sailboat on the bottom, nestled against a curving plastic landmass, complete with trees and docks. Elfin red script on the side of the boat said *Summer Hours*. "Got it from a catalog. It's not a perfect replica of mine, but close. I picked the island because it's shaped like Catalina. My happy place."

"I've never gone there. I've always wanted to."

"Of course, it's closer to Atlantis in this setup."

I trailed my finger along the Plexiglas protecting the antique wooden table. Its perimeter curved up, in case of spills. Mrs. Logan's contribution to the hobby, I guessed.

"Have you named them?"

"That's Jack and that's Stephen. After these characters—"

"Jack Aubrey and Stephen Maturin. From Patrick O'Brian, right? I read those last summer."

He glanced up. His eyes were light blue, bright even against his golden skin.

"That's right. Didn't know anyone your age read him." He smiled, bit his lip, stared down thoughtfully at his fish tank again.

I clenched my hands together, digging my nails into my flesh, to resist clapping them on my cheeks to hide the redness.

"I should find Eric." I opened the door and stepped into the hall.

"Rebecca?"

I turned, but he was still looking down at the fish tank. "You take care of yourself, too."

★

I shut Eric's bedroom door behind me and collapsed on the carpet next to him.

Some guys taped dirty pictures on their ceiling; Eric had plastered his in movie posters. *Out of the Past* and *The Third Man* and *Metropolis*, *Freaks*, and *Nashville*. He'd run out of room on all the vertical surfaces.

Serra rolled to her side on the bed above us. "I saw you playing lady-in-waiting."

"You should've bailed when we did," Eric said. "They were like those ghosts in *Poltergeist* who fed on Carol Anne's life force."

"I may have a few drops of life force left."

Serra studied me. "You're sunburned, have you looked?"

"I'm just hot, it must be ninety still. We need music." I sat up and dragged the red plastic crate from under Eric's bed.

Music would drown out the party. It was still going strong without us, the clinking glasses and polite adult laughter amplifying as they rose from the yard, pressing into the room. Nobody seemed to have noticed that the guest of honor had gone AWOL.

"My mom knows how to throw an awkward party, huh?" Eric said. Watching me, trying to figure out why I was edgy. "I can't believe she invited Marcus and those guys. It's so fake."

"*I* can't believe Mrs. Haggermaker came out of her crypt twice in one month," said Serra. "She must be so *psyched* about your brilliant future, Becc."

"She knows Eric's mom from the gardening club." Francine Haggermaker was also on the charity board for my mom's hospital and donated money to the Berkeley art museum and the film preservation society at USC. The woman had her bony fingers everywhere.

"Are you going to have to, like, visit her all the time now?" Serra asked.

"No. Just write her once a year till I graduate. Fill her in on my classes and internships and whatever. Sort of a…scholarly update. I guess it's customary. My mom already bought me special stationery, it's so annoying."

"What does that come to, like thirty-thousand bucks a letter?" Serra said.

A twinge of guilt, because though Serra had a grant from the Latina Artists' Network, she was taking out a mint in loans. The least I could do was not grumble about my good fortune around her.

I pushed my glasses up my nose and hunted in Eric's mess of

CDs and tapes for the cassette I wanted: *Upstairs at Eric's*. So ancient we had to tighten the spools with a pencil after every use. I'd bought it at Goodwill for Eric's sixteenth birthday, along with a T-shirt of Alfred Hitchcock's plump, mocking face above a movie clacker. Both were intended as gag gifts, but he'd said they were his two favorite presents that year.

I slid the cassette into the chute, snapped it shut, and pushed the silver play button.

I lay back on the carpet, curled close to the speaker. Eric's long pianist's fingers tapped the top of the boom box from the other side, picking out the background synth. His nail beds were stained bloodred.

"E," I said. "Did you get in a fight with…you-know-who?"

The fingers stopped dancing. "Who?"

"You know. Your mom's… Cal. Did you leave him a mean letter or something?"

The hand disappeared from view. "You could say that," Eric snorted. "I left a little message on his boat, that's all. A little welcome-to-the-family note. In Krylon Firetruck."

"You didn't."

"What's this?" Serra peered down, delighted.

"Eric vandalized a certain sailboat."

She laughed. "What'd you write, *homewrecker*? No, *devil*? One letter off from his name."

"Give me *some* credit for originality." Eric peeked over at me. "Come on, he deserves it."

It wouldn't take much to show Eric I was on his side. *I know he deserved it, E. What a weirdo. What a jerk.*

*He thinks he's so charming, such a stud.*

"Did my mom say something?" Eric asked.

"Hmm."

"What? Was she grilling you? It's nothing, he already had it cleaned. I'll tell her to stop bugging you—"

"No. He told me. Cal."

I stared at the *Vertigo* poster on the ceiling, where a body spun into an orange-and-white vortex. I closed my eyes but still saw Jimmy Stewart floating in space, nothing to grab onto.

Eric had shown me the film in the walk-in closet he'd transformed into a home theater. He'd set up his TV and VCR in there because it was quiet and dark and had offered double protection from his parents when things got bad.

Not once, in four years, had Eric reached for my hand in that dark closet. Not even last summer, when he'd screened *Truly, Madly, Deeply* and I'd cried at the end, wiping my face on the mountain of throw pillows he'd constructed for us. He'd only nodded in the dim glow of the credits and said quietly, "Right? Just perfect."

"Tell me what you wrote on his boat, E," I said. "He didn't seem mad. Only...worried."

He wouldn't answer.

"I know you can hear me."

Nothing.

"Don't be like this."

He hid from me on the other side of his boom box, behind the low silver wall it made between us. My good, breakable friend.

The man he'd decided was his enemy hid directly below us, in his own bunker, staring at his happy place—a plastic version of Catalina Island.

Maybe he and Eric weren't so different.

But I couldn't explain that to Eric. It was easier for him to direct his anger at Mr. California than at his parents.

And he expected us to hate him, too.

# 4

## Pyramus & Thisbe

2008
Thursday, 8:00 a.m.
Newport Beach

The island is only a speck in my left eye's peripheral vision, no bigger than a grain of sand.

Like a piece of sand, I want it out. My foot tenses on the gas pedal, itching to test out the rental's fancy turbo motor, to go sixty, seventy, faster, until we're past Catalina.

But traffic's heavy with morning commuters, so we're stuck. Inching along behind a battered gold Datsun with a bumper sticker that says, I Was an Honor Student. I Don't Know What Happened.

I stare at the Datsun, willing the former honor student to pick up speed. But there must be a stall ahead.

I glance to my right: the brown cardboard wall of the gift between us.

The only other place to look is left.

I know I shouldn't. I always face forward on this stretch of PCH.

But I turn toward the bright blue water, the flotilla of white sails gliding out toward the low mass of the island.

Catalina. Once the sexiest, most exciting word in the world. *My happy place.*

That beautiful hideaway. Its only town, Avalon, population 3,000, named after the mythical island in King Arthur. No cars allowed. Only golf carts, like a movie set. At sunset, the light is an exquisite pinkish gold.

*Look at that color. It's the magic hour. The Impressionists thought they could only find that light on the Riviera, but it's not true.*

*Someday we'll go there together so you can see. We'll go to France, Spain, Italy.*

But now Catalina feels like a foreign country, our time there as far from real life as a long-ago vacation.

★

Finally, we speed up.

I check the tripometer, which I set to 0.00 miles before we left.

We've gone a hundred miles without talking.

I won't speak again until we hit two hundred.

Or until we pass another Denny's. Whichever comes first.

Scratching comes from the box, as if an animal is trapped inside, trying to claw its way out. He's trying to get comfortable, rearranging himself against the cardboard.

*Don't say anything. Let him be the one to break the silence.*

"How are you doing over there?" I immediately call out.

"What?"

I shout over the wind: "This is like Pyramus and Thisbe!"

"Pyramid what?"

"Pyramus and Thisbe! From Shakespeare? *A Midsummer Night's Dream!* That part where they're talking through the wall!"

"Oh, yeah!"

I remember, too late, that Pyramus and Thisbe were lovers.

The radio blares on and his finger taps through satellite channels. He rejects Nick Drake on *Morning Becomes Eclectic*, blows past Nina Simone. He loves them both but can't seem to get away fast enough.

He lands on Green Day.

"Is this station okay with you?" he shouts.

"Sure! I love this song!"

"Yeah, it's a classic!"

I've always hated this song. An indecipherable, jumpy tune—an instant headache. He taps the volume to seven before his hand vanishes behind the box.

He's silent again, but his Green Day says plenty.

It says, *I could have flown up to the wedding.*

*We could've gotten them a gift card.*

*How many hours until I can get back to life as usual?*

And worst of all—*Don't get any ideas about why I agreed to drive with you.*

I want to tap the radio to Ozzy Osbourne or Weird Al, crank it to level ten. It might blow out the speakers, but it would feel good.

Like yelling back, *Relax, damn it!*

Instead I breathe deep. In for five, out for ten.

Let him have every silver button and knob on the dash.

All I want is to make it to the wedding without a fight, without anything distracting from Serra's day.

I want to see Serra's face when we give her her present.

When we were in college, she had to explain to me what her triptych project was: artwork in three parts. Beginning, middle, and end.

It's the perfect gift, or will be once we pick up the last piece.

The idea for the present was a lark at first, a goof. I woke up at 2:00 a.m. the morning after I got Serra's invitation and scrolled through her online wedding registry. I could have bought her up to twelve hemp napkins. A pour-over coffee system. A portion of a water buffalo in her name, which would help support a family in Nepal.

I couldn't decide, so I clicked over to Artattack.net and started browsing. I hadn't seen her in more than a year, but I could still know her taste. I looked at block prints, ceramic vases, shadow boxes. All under $200 and compact enough to pack in a carry-on. Nothing seemed like her style.

I almost gave up and went for the hemp napkins.

Until bleary-eyed, ready to go back to sleep, I remembered an article I'd read at work that week about a woman in Boston who found the heirloom Steiff teddy bear she'd had as a child by posting a picture of it on a specialized collector site. The article featured a cute picture of her and her two-year-old daughter clutching the one-eyed bear, nuzzling its nearly bald head. *A heartwarming reunion!*

I couldn't get that over-loved bear out of my head.

*If only I could find a gift like that. A lost piece of Serra's past.*

Curious, I began poking around online and discovered a whole new world of helpful specialty web pages, searchable by artist and title, image and year and show.

A few hours in, and I was more excited about hunting down the triptych than I'd been about any project that's come across my desk in years. Size and price considerations went out the window.

When I found two sections of Serra's piece—the left and middle panels, inseparable now because the hinges connecting them have rusted—I knew that I had to locate the last third. We'll pick it up in Fort Bragg on Saturday morning and then head to the hotel for the out-of-towner wedding weekend activities: a crabbing expedition, a wine tasting.

A phone rings. A hippie wind chime, the ringer set loud enough to be heard even over Green Day.

He leans forward and his left index finger hastily stabs the down-volume button on the dash.

*Tap-tap-tap-tap-tap-tap.*

He answers his phone with "Hey, Ann, you saw the numbers?" and disappears again.

I can't make out any more words through the strata of our gift wall—cardboard, Bubble Wrap, present, Bubble Wrap, cardboard. But he sounds smooth and confident. Putting a deal together or putting out a fire.

I'd love to ask if he picked the soothing chime for its irony factor. Once, I would have been sure that he'd noticed the humor in his ringtone, that he'd turn to me and laugh at how busy and important he is.

But he's so serious about his job now. And I don't know if he chose it as a joke or if his assistant programmed it for him.

I don't know who the *Ann* on the other end is.

I don't know if he considered backing out of this weekend.

Maybe he already wishes he had canceled. I wouldn't know, and I'm not sure I want to.

All I know is that the man beside me is a stranger.

I haven't seen him in ten years.

# 5

## Graduette

June 17, 1994

WHERE I WAS SUPPOSED TO BE | Lined up behind Tracy Rasmussen
WHERE I WAS | The Orange Park High Media Room

"Do you think they'll cancel graduation?" shouted a girl over the Green Day blasting from someone's boom box.

"No way. Parents would freak."

The ceremony was running late. We were supposed to proceed into the gym, resplendent in our rented green gowns, half an hour ago. Instead we were watching TV in the media room, a glorified closet lined with AV equipment, packed wall to wall with other almost graduates. O.J. was so close we could hear the *wop-wop* of news helicopters heading to the freeway.

In front of me, Serra was swimming in her gown. It was supposedly an extra small but it pooled around her ankles so much I worried she'd trip onstage. Her honors sash wasn't pinned on right so it looked like it was choking her neck. "This is so weird," she whispered.

"I know," I said.

Eric stood a few feet apart from us, behind Robin Engles, a sophomore the three of us couldn't stand. Her brother was graduating so she'd been lurking around all afternoon.

Eric put his hand on Robin's shoulder and said into her ear, loud enough for me and Serra to hear, "So many helicopters. It's like *M★A★S★H*."

Leave it to Eric to find the movie reference.

Eric hated Robin Engles. When she wasn't sluttifying a Halloween costume, Robin was daring frosh football players to drink Everclear until they had to get their stomachs pumped.

I knew exactly what he was doing.

Serra leaned her head back, whispering up at me so only I could hear, "Nice performance. Are you burning with jealousy yet?"

She'd warned me many times this year that Eric wanted more than friendship from me, and I'd laughed her off. But Eric had barely spoken to me since the barbecue.

"Shhh."

"Okay, I'll be good." She took off her mortarboard and ruffled a hand through her chin-length hair. It had been a month since she'd cut it and she couldn't stop running her fingers along the black strands, as if surprised every time by where they stopped. She'd had a long ponytail like mine ever since I'd met her in seventh grade chorus, when she'd sung soprano in the spot right in front of me. I'd stood inches from that ponytail for weeks, so close that I'd blown strands of it around with my breath during the loud parts of "Viva Tutte Le Vezzose."

The day Serra and I officially met, we were digging in the tub of moth-eaten, unisex green cardigans that served as our performance uniforms. I'd snagged a medium that wouldn't be too horribly big if my mom tailored it. Serra had rolled up the sleeves on the smallest one she could find, but it was still so huge on her I couldn't help laughing.

"My mom could take that in for you," I'd said. "She sews." Such a simple, casual offer, but it had decided so much in my life.

She never did remember to bring the sweater over, but we'd become best friends so fast, it was like all my other friends—perfectly nice, smart, pleasant girls—simply receded.

Mrs. Featherton, the assistant principal, discovered our hiding place. "You naughty children. You were supposed to line up twenty minutes ago! Come along, graduates and graduettes." She shooed us out, but not before peeking at the TV, too.

We pulled ourselves away and followed Mrs. Featherton down the hall to our places in line. Kids were sagging against walls, melting onto the floor in green nylon puddles. Finally, "Pomp and Circumstance" floated down the hall and we stood. First Serra went outside, with the I's, then Eric, with the L's. And finally my segment, the R's.

I passed Eric's mom in the front row, chatting with the woman next to her, casually running a hand through her long blond hair. Perfect Orange County–wife hair, the shimmering result of some mysterious and expensive chemistry. Eric's father sat one row behind her and one person to the left, as if to say they were still connected but no longer paired.

No sign of Donna's lover.

That was good of him, not to intrude on Eric's day. He was probably off on a sail to Catalina. I imagined him alone on his boat and wondered for the hundredth time what Eric had sprayed on the side.

I spotted my mom waving from the top gym bleacher, right hand holding her silver Olympus ready, the left wiping away tears.

She'd been trying not to cry all day. Her eyes had been glassy when she gave me my graduation gift—the perfect present, a refurbished Compaq laptop that she must've scrimped for all year—and though I'd said, *Mom, it'll be okay. I'm not going for twelve weeks*, the fact that I'd soon leave her now seemed unbearably sad.

She'd worked so hard to get us to this moment. Not once complaining. I felt her pride and excitement and eighteen years of sacrifice, shock waves of them, from across the overheated gym.

Fighting back tears myself, I smiled for the camera. *Thank you, Mom.*

★

Later, she said some parents were mad they didn't reschedule the ceremony. A few minor relatives couldn't make it down the freeway in time because of the chase.

We threw our caps in the air just as O.J. surrendered in his driveway.

Three days later

WHERE I WAS SUPPOSED TO BE | My Intro to MS Office Class at the community center
WHERE I WAS | Eric's room

Eric and I sat on his bedroom floor with a mountain of clothes between us.

I'd had to beg him to let me come over. Finally, he'd said, "Whatever," grudgingly accepting my offer to help him pack and treat him to a movie after.

I picked up his frayed black Joy Division T-shirt. "This is the softest thing in the world. If you don't bring it I'm going to steal it and make it my new woobie."

"Take it."

"Honestly?"

"It'll just get thrown out otherwise."

I smoothed the T-shirt over my knees, tracing the design on the front with my index finger. The lines looked like a series of seismograph readings or mountain ranges. I toyed with a thread in the ripped collar. "I'm going to miss you. You know that, right?"

Eric looked down at the hiking socks he was rolling together army-style. "I'll miss you, too."

I stared at him but he wouldn't look up. "I guess we'll have to go on our road trip to the Mystery Spot and that gas station made of petrified wood another time." We'd made grand plans for our summer, before he decided to bolt early.

"Let's do that."

"Where are all the polo shirts? And the crested blazers and deck shoes?"

He smiled at the floor. "Right, and you're packing head-to-toe tie-dye?"

"Of course, George. Berkeley has a compulsory tie-dye seminar for freshmen."

"You're never going to let go of the George Hamilton thing, are you?"

"Nope."

"Your ideas of the East Coast are about fifty years out-of-date, Becc."

"So I'll come visit you. See what it's really like."

"Sounds like a plan."

Progress, even if he said it to his socks.

Eric and I had watched *Where the Boys Are* on TCM in the closet over spring break, after he got his Brown acceptance. When George Hamilton's character said he was a Brown man, I'd shrieked in delight and Eric had buried his head under a pillow, knowing I'd never let him live it down. I knew perfectly well that Brown wasn't the soft, preppy world it used to be, but my private school/public school bit was too good to resist. I'd even invented a servant named Duckworth, who would leave mints on Eric's pillow during the dorm turndown service.

He held up a green cord button-down.

"That's nice on you. And warm. Bring."

Next came the black jeans he'd worn forever. He'd snagged the left knee on a ladder, helping my mother prune a jacaranda tree in the backyard, fall of sophomore year.

"You should mend those, but bring."

His baggy gray drawstring sweatpants. He'd had them since freshman year. Serra and I called them "The Whalers."

"Hmm."

"These are comfortable! They're the only warm pants I like besides my jeans."

"You need to think more fitted."

"I'm not wearing ass-hugger pants."

"Did I say ass-huggers? Just avoid the opposite of ass-huggers. Meaning any pants sewn out of enough fabric to make you two pairs of pants."

Eric's mom opened the door, singing, "Knock, knock." She always managed to appear right when we were saying things like "ass-huggers."

"Rebecca, stay for dinner?"

"Remember I said we're going to a movie?" Eric dug into the pile of clothes.

"Right, I forgot."

I stood up for a silent, stagy hug. She'd also hugged me downstairs when I'd arrived. But the stories that had leaked out of her household made her kindness seem like something I couldn't trust. She left without shutting the door all the way.

Eric waited a minute, got up, and shoved the door shut. He rolled his eyes.

"Come on, she's trying," I said, settling on the floor again.

"She used to be an actress, remember. It's still acting, never reality."

"So tell me about reality."

"I'm getting away in two days."

"That doesn't mean it wouldn't help to talk about her. Them. Have you seen your dad?"

Eric shook his head, dealing out six different baseball caps. Some were so crisp they'd clearly never touched his head. The few he did wear in constant rotation had yellow stains on the brim.

"I've always liked this one on you." I handed him his red Angels baseball cap. The logo was an A with a halo on top.

"They'll probably think it's some Christian thing," he said, but he shot it into a suitcase. "Nothing but net."

"You won't be like them," I said. "Your parents."

"Everyone believes that. It's our universal delusion. So what movie are we seeing?"

"Anything but *The Fly.*"

"Paper's on the hall table."

I crept downstairs, and luckily Eric's mom was on the phone in the kitchen, her back to me, talking about "mid-tier donors." She had a big event-planning business. I'd been spared another daughter-she-never-had hug.

Eric's mom was always so polite, asking me about school and my "mother's" job. She said *mother*, not *mom*. That was one thing. She was way less intimidating than Eric's father, but her formality and surface perfection had always made me nervous. Mrs. Logan's affair with her handsome neighbor up the street seemed so impulsive, so out of character. It made me almost like her, learning she wasn't as flawless as she pretended.

I grabbed the *Register* off the table and headed back to the staircase, pausing in the hallway outside the study. Just for a few seconds.

The door was open halfway so I could see the green water of the fish tank illuminated in the dark. But the room was silent.

When I got back to the bedroom Eric had a fresh pile of clothes out. Sweaters and a bunch of other warm items I'd never seen. I picked up a gray overcoat with a J. Press tag still attached. Cashmere, and $2,600.

"Wow." I petted the soft collar.

"The mother ordered it. A little too George-Hamilton-in-January, right?"

"No, it's beautiful. Of course you're bringing it. I don't want to think of you cold."

I studied the newspaper. Eric had circled two movies. He knew I was dying to see *Four Weddings and a Funeral* but I didn't recognize the other. "What's *Return of the Secaucus Seven*? Some Western?"

"Not a Western," said Eric. "Old John Sayles movie I've been wanting to see."

Of course, he'd already seen it, and what he really meant was "I've been wanting to secretly observe you while you react to all my favorite parts." Eric loved to bring people to his favorite movies and pretend he'd never seen them before.

*Secaucus Seven* was at the revival theater, where you had to pick your seat carefully because the springs had busted through most of the cushions.

"Hold up the paper and we'll let chance decide," I said.

He took the top corners of the paper from me and held it between us like a curtain while I pretended to close my eyes. But I peeked as I punched with my index finger.

"*Secaucus Seven* it is."

He lowered the page and smiled wryly. "You're a nice girl, Becc. Has anyone ever told you that?"

"Only about a thousand times. Can we make the seven?"

Eric leaned to read the showtimes, so close his hair tickled my ear. If I tilted my neck a tiny bit to the right we'd almost be kissing.

His breath hitched and I held mine.

I was curious. I was. But I didn't move.

He was leaving.

And something was missing. Some dark matter that existed in the study, and that, I was sure, waited for me in the uncharted land of college.

*More breakable than he seems.* I wouldn't break Eric into pieces for an experiment.

So instead of moving closer I pulled back. "E. We need to talk about this."

"Talk about what?"

"You know."

His eyes shifted from mine to the wall of movie posters behind me. "I think it's too late to make the seven."

"What? We have an hour."

He looked down at the tag on the fancy overcoat, yanked it carelessly. "I think we should skip the movie. I still have a ton of packing."

"E. Come on. It's our last day. Let's figure this out." I scratched his knee gently with my fingernail.

"What do you mean?"

"Don't do this. Don't leave like this. We can figure it out."

"Why don't you say *figure it out* one more time, Becc? *Figure it out.* Like a calculus problem?" He lobbed the coat into his suitcase, hard.

"No. Not like that. I'm not saying it right."

"I think you're making yourself pretty clear."

I waited for him to say anything, to meet me halfway, to at least try to reach across the awkwardness.

But he only crumpled up the newspaper and tossed it at the garbage. Missing, I noticed with cheap satisfaction.

"You're acting like a pouty kid." I stood. Waited thirty seconds. Nothing.

I left, and he didn't stop me.

# 6

## Busting Out

August 1, 1994

WHERE I WAS SUPPOSED TO BE | The *Orange Park Courier*
WHERE I WAS | The square

I settled into my "office" at the newspaper—a card table in the hall by the copier, violating fire codes.

I'd talked Les Corcoran, the owner/publisher/editor of the *Courier*, into giving me a job for the summer. He'd worked at the *LA Times* decades before and told me he'd bought the *Courier* only to keep busy between fishing trips.

I'd interviewed wearing my mom's blue skirt suit, safety pinned to hold the waist up, clutching a long, narrow notebook that made me feel like Rosalind Russell in *His Girl Friday*. (Eric had gone through a screwball comedy phase junior year.) Les took one look at my starry eyes and reporter's notebook and said, "This ain't journalism."

But he took me on.

Les produced the *Courier* on an ancient PageMaker layout system and he wasn't always big on journalistic integrity, gleefully bumping town council articles for paid advertorials from tree pruners. My only payment was a few bylined clips and the glory of saying I worked at a newspaper.

I loved it anyway.

I loved running around town digging up stories. Meeting strangers, triple-checking their quotes, reading their voices for tones that told me they were a little too eager to be in print, and I should be wary. Or that they were a little too defensive, and I should press harder. When I'd decided to be a reporter, back in grade school, I'd known only that it felt important, and it still did. It sounded so simple—setting facts down in black and white. But it rarely was, and I liked that.

I loved revising my articles until they were fair and balanced and clear, until the writing was *muscular*, as my newspaper faculty advisor in high school had always put it.

I even loved the lingo. *Slug* and *lede* and *drop-dead*. And I loved the frantic hour on Friday afternoons before closing the next week's issue, racing to make the printer's deadline. Les called these "fire drills"—like the time when an advertiser pulled out so I had ten minutes to cut an AP article on the new beach resort in Newport from eight hundred to two hundred words to fit the hole. The adrenaline rush was addictive. After every fire drill Les said that was it, he was going to "sell the old rag like I should've done a decade ago."

He pretended he didn't care about the newspaper anymore. Once, when I spent a weekend revising an article he'd already approved, Les said softly, "Ah, you poor kid, you've got the bug, don't you?" But his voice told me I'd joined a secret and important club.

As usual for a Monday, Les wasn't in. He didn't show up until at least Wednesday afternoon. But he had left me an advertorial to fix. Four hundred words on the new frozen yogurt shop, written by the franchise owner, who described "toppings" in breathless detail. I cleaned it up and played with headlines, settling on "Yo-Fresh Serves Up Cool Treats."

Then I turned to my pet project, a story on the Orange Park movie theater. I called the new owner of the long-shuttered building for the fourth time because I was trying to get a private tour. But once again I got shunted to her assistant.

"Okay, we'll just have to run the story without a quote from her, I guess," I said. "Thanks!"

Les hadn't agreed to run a thing.

"Wait, what story?"

"About the remodel. How people fear it's stripping out all of the historic features." *People* was one lady I'd interviewed at the Orange County Historical Society.

"That's not true, it's a beautiful restoration." Whispering, paper shuffling. "Wait, could you come Friday at ten?"

"That would be great!"

Then I had five more hours with nothing official left to do but explore yogurt puns, so I called Serra.

She answered in a swoopy customer service voice. "Baskin-Robbins, home of the original thirty-one flavors, hoooow may I help you?"

"It's me. Can you sneak away for a sec? I got some interesting mail this morning."

"Eric?"

"Nope. He clearly still hates me. I wish I hadn't said anything about the boat."

Every day when I left for work I searched the mailbox for a letter from Eric. He hadn't returned my emails or written since he'd left for Brown.

I wanted to make things right. I wanted to lie near him on a stack of pillows in his closet theater and breathe in his familiar smell. Coast soap and Soothing Aloe Barbasol and root beer. I wanted to force the old playful look back into his eyes. It had only been a month but it felt like time was running out, as we drifted away into our new lives.

"He'll come around, Becc. So, mail?"

"The roommate letter came." It was in my pocket: a pink envelope I'd identified immediately from the Maine return address and girlish printing. Serra and I had been assigned a triple room at Berkeley, in a high-rise a block from campus. We'd been waiting all summer for letters from our future roommate, speculating about what she'd be like and planning the hundred thoughtful ways we'd make sure not to leave her out.

"Holy fuck, I need to see it immediately."

★

Baskin-Robbins was a five-minute walk from the *Courier* office, across the town square.

When I opened the pink-trimmed glass door, setting off the little bell, Andrew Meade was wiping down tables and Serra was manning the counter.

I waited while she served outrageously big scoops of bubble-gum ice cream on sugar cones to two wide-eyed little girls, handing them over with a conspiratorial smile. Then she helped a mom dithering over ice cream cakes in the sample book. Finally, the lady ordered a Batman cake.

"We're going outside for a sec, do you mind covering the counter?" Serra said this to Andrew in the same un-Serra voice she'd used to answer the shop's phone.

"Not at all, take your time!" Andrew said.

Serra had had a crush on Andrew all year. She sat behind him in honors physics, and had become obsessed with the two triangles of hair on his neck, which changed from buzzed to softly curling between haircuts. She'd monitored their status like phases of the moon, giving me daily updates.

She'd asked him out a week ago, and it hadn't gone well. Apparently he'd turned all stiff and told her he was dating Erin O'Connor, this awful JV cheerleader from The Heights.

Erin O'Connor: if she worked at Baskin-Robbins, she'd serve stingy scoops.

We sat in the square, on the low brick bench-wall that surrounded the last of Orange Park's orange trees. The groves that had once blanketed our part of the county were long gone, so this bedraggled sole survivor had a plaque in front of it: *Planted in 1937.* Everyone just called it The Orange Tree.

"Things with Andrew still seem a little…frosty," I said.

"He and Erin are going to Big Bear with their parents this weekend. It's like now their families are united against me."

"Like the Mafia?"

She scrunched her face at me.

"He's an idiot," I said. "Erin O'Connor's the worst."

"You can say it. She's racist trash."

"I know." Erin was always complaining about *gardeners* eating lunch in the square. I touched Serra's hand. Her round brown eyes were still laughing, but I didn't know how she kept her spirits up dealing with daily crap like this. Erin O'Connor wasn't the only one I'd heard at school who used *gardener* as a catchall term for anyone who didn't need a punch card at Gold Coast Tanning.

"I'm sorry," I said. "Just think of the gorgeous, enlightened college boys waiting for you."

"Look." Serra nudged me.

Mrs. Logan was across the street in front of the theater, carrying her Dominico's grocery bag to her car. She'd probably been shopping for a dinner with him. Tonight they'd eat poolside, then ascend to the Logans' perfect beige master bedroom… Would they set the silk throw pillows aside? Or did they do it on top of the pillows, too frantic to wait, crying out like people did in movies?

There was something wrong with me, trying to picture these scenarios.

"Should we say hi?" Serra asked.

"God, no."

Smiling to herself, Mrs. Logan opened the door of her black BMW coupe and settled in the low driver's seat, her long, bare legs stretched to the asphalt, her shiny blond hair disappearing for a second as she dipped to set the bag on the passenger side. She popped up, pulled her legs into her car as gracefully as an Olympic diver doing a tuck, shut the door, and drove off.

"She looks happy," I said. "Don't you think?"

"Of course she's happy. She's off for a hookup with her boy toy."

"Gross. He's not…"

"What? Not a boy or not a toy?"

"I don't know, I just hate that expression. Let's read the letter." I read aloud—

*I'm Margaret Jane Estes and I'm going to major in chemistry. I have four sisters and a border collie named Stuey. I can't wait to meet you!! We're going to have so much fun!! I'm flying out August 19. My comforter is a pale rose color, in case you want to coordinate. And I'd love to go in on the rent for one of those tiny frig's.*

"Well…" I searched for a tactful way to address the obvious. That Margaret sounded like an insufferable priss. And she'd misspelled *fridges*.

Serra wasn't tactful. "Fuck. Could she be more wholesome?"

"She's going to be the early-riser type."

"Margaret from Maine. I picture her in, like, head-to-toe L.L. Bean," Serra said. "Plaid, turtlenecks. Duck shoes."

"It's okay, Serr. Because even if Margaret from Maine gets up at the crack of dawn, we'll be at college." I said the word reverently.

*College.*

We'd dreamed about it forever.

The crisp wind off the San Francisco Bay blowing away the stale, hot air of the OC. Forty thousand students from around the world. Freedom and brilliant professors and a real art studio for Serra, a real newspaper for me. Hordes of intriguing, intelligent college guys and certified, grown-up dates.

Serra shouted to sleepy Main Street, "You hear that, Orange Park? We're leaving you!"

The only pedestrian in sight—a dapper gray-haired man walking his terrier across the street where Donna Logan's car had been a moment ago—turned, startled.

I laughed so hard I had to press my thighs together so I wouldn't pee as Serra stood on the brick and called cheerfully to him, waving Margaret Estes's pink Hello Kitty stationery. "Nothing ever happens here so we're busting out!"

August 20
Move-in week

Serra and I walked home from the student union, loaded down with textbooks.

We were in love with the proud weirdness of Berkeley. Noisy Telegraph Avenue, where people sold jewelry and bongs on the sidewalk. (We'd bought matching leather cuff bracelets but not bongs.)

Chaotic Sproul Plaza, where you could add your name to a thousand petitions. The Naked Guy, who was famous because the university allowed him to attend classes without a stitch on. We hadn't spotted him yet, but we were desperate to, so we could act nonchalant.

Even the graffiti thrilled us.

Serra liked to evaluate its artistic merit, while to me the ugliest scrawl was beautiful. Proof that we'd escaped suburbia.

"How do you rate this one?" I pointed at the spray paint defacing the front of the Earth Science building: a haughty black cat with the cryptic tag The Cat Knows under it, the letters *Fe|Co* inside its tail.

"It's not bad. Sort of art deco."

"Fe is the symbol for iron, and Co is cobalt," I said. "They're next to each other on the periodic table. Maybe it's a chem department thing."

"Even the graffiti is smarter here," Serra said, giddy. "You're missing out, Margaret!"

Because Margaret from Maine still hadn't shown up. We'd waited for her to come through the door all day yesterday, as we unpacked in our tenth-floor room. We'd been considerate, making sure our stuff didn't take up more than two-thirds of the space.

Still, it got dark and Margaret hadn't arrived. Our moms hugged us goodbye, wiping their tears but smiling bravely, and still, she hadn't arrived. We had a dorm floor get-to-know-you ice cream social but no Margaret from Maine.

"Maybe she withdrew," I said.

"I'll bet she heard about The Naked Guy."

But when we got back to our room, there she was.

She did not wear a turtleneck under a plaid coat. She wore a Bikini Kill T-shirt and an eyebrow ring. She had black hair with blond roots.

"I freaked you out, didn't I?" she said, dumping an armload of clothes into her top dresser drawer. "So my parents think they're punishing me by banishing me to California, because they *hated* my last boyfriend, but what they don't know is I *wanted* to bail. Never date a bass player..."

She'd flown out from the East Coast alone, and her only contributions to our joint housekeeping were blackout curtains, an elephant-shaped bong she bought on Telegraph, and something she called a *sploof*—made out of a paper towel roll, stuffed with dryer sheets—that she breathed into to minimize the pot smell. (We called the sploof Laura Ingalls, because its towel cap, secured by a rubber band, looked like a bonnet.)

Maggie snored heavily and she drank heavily, she had no

verbal filter, and she grabbed whichever of our three shower caddies caught her eye, even using our razors.

We adored her.

She couldn't replace Eric. But our little dorm room began to feel like home.

# 7

Beat the Clock

June 23, 1995
Dear Mrs. Haggermaker,
I hope this letter finds you well.

My first year of college is over and I'm on the bus heading home to our beloved Orange Park.

I learned so much in my courses this year, and as you'll see from the attached transcript I earned a 3.9 GPA and made the dean's list.

I was thrilled to secure a spot as a junior reporter for the student newspaper, where the senior editors have gone out of their way to mentor me. I cover campus beautification, an extremely high-profile beat for a freshman.

I've met dozens of fascinating new people at school,

and especially enjoyed getting to know Margaret Estes, my roommate from Maine. She's as sweet in person as she was in her introduction letter. Margaret is an <u>excellent</u> student who was in several of my freshman lectures. The two of us made a habit of meeting weekly for study sessions at a quiet café on campus. We helped each other prepare for upcoming exams, memorizing the Laffer Curve for Economics 101 and the stages of a black hole for Astronomy 10 in a rapid-fire drill we devised called Beat the Clock.

But of course my Orange Park friendships will always hold a special place in my heart. We may have graduated and dispersed, but the hometown bonds are unbreakable.

I'm looking forward to another productive summer writing for the *Orange Park Courier*, helping my mother in her garden, and getting an early start on next semester's reading. As you can see from the attached syllabi, I will study the *Iliad, The Canterbury Tales*, and *Beowulf* next fall. I can't wait.

I am, as always, deeply grateful for your generosity.
Sincerely,
Rebecca Reardon

I scanned the letter and added an exclamation point:

I will study the *Iliad, The Canterbury Tales*, and *Beowulf* next fall. I can't wait!

I sealed the letter inside its matching blue-and-gold envelope and looked out the window as the Greyhound groaned into the station.

My mom was trotting beside the bus. Looking up anxiously,

hand visored over her eyes. She wasn't pleased that I'd skipped my last class to come home a day early, though I'd explained that it was only office hours, for kids who hadn't turned in their papers yet.

I'd told her three times that I'd catch a local bus home from the depot, but here she was, like a nervous pilot fish.

Three months of her hovering and hand-wringing. After my freedom in Berkeley, it wouldn't be easy.

But I'd escape at the *Courier*. I was determined to write something important this summer. My "campus beautification" assignment at school (aka the custodial beat) hadn't yielded much. Though I did have a grand time coasting around in a cart with the head maintenance guy, craggy-faced Albert Crenley. He played oldies radio and made me laugh, though he pretended to be surly. I helped him with his graffiti log, a clipboarded form on which we noted the hundreds of *Fuck Yous* and *Berkeley Sucks Asses* requiring erasure.

Unlike Serra and me, Albert wasn't a graffiti fan; it just meant more work. He was especially peeved by the elegant black cat Serra and I had noticed our first week. It had appeared frequently spring semester, not just on the science building but all over campus. Albert was sure "frat punks" from Kappa Alpha Tau were behind it, but I'd interviewed them and didn't think so. Someone was sending secret messages out into the void. I had to know what they were trying to say, what was so important—and seditious—they had to encode their words.

My section editor at the campus paper, a sophomore named Brent who wore ironic red bow ties, had grudgingly allowed me a single brief on the cat: Uptick in Campus Graffiti Concerns Maintenance Staff.

Everyone knew *uptick* and *concerns* meant Bullshit Story.

But one decent *Courier* clip this summer was my ticket out of the custodial beat. As long as I covered the basics—the July Fourth pet parade down Main and the newest Orange Julius franchise—Les had promised I could pursue any features I wanted.

I'd work hard and the summer would fly by.

★

The phone rang in our little U-shaped kitchen after dinner, while I was washing dishes and my mom, at my right elbow, was scooping ice cream.

"I'll let the machine pick it up," she said. "My girl's home."

This was a major rebellion for her; she always scurried obediently to the phone when it rang, though I'd bought her the Sony answering machine for Christmas with babysitting money four years ago.

A man's voice boomed from the counter to our left, where the machine sat in the corner by the chipped yellow teapot that served as a utensil holder. "Becc. Les here. Sorry to break it to you so late but I'm stopping the presses. For good. Got an offer I couldn't refuse, as they say. Well, you don't need this piddly rag anyway..."

*Fuck.*

The ice cream scoop clattered to the counter and my mom sucked in her breath. "Oh, no... What will you... Shouldn't you pick up? Honey?"

"Give me a buzz and let me know where to send your rec letter, doll. Real sorry."

I stared out the window at the dark backyard. This wasn't ideal.

My mom silently resumed dishing Häagen-Dazs Vanilla Swiss Almond into our bowls.

"Don't worry," I said, turning to smile at her. "I'll get something else."

"I'm not worried! Of course you will!" Scooping like a champ. And biting her upper lip so hard it whitened.

"I knew this might happen," I lied. "He's been struggling to get advertisers. I'll drop off résumés tomorrow."

"And you'll have a job by noon, I'll bet!" Now she sounded like a game show host. She secured the ice cream lid, bustled to the fridge. "I'm sure Mrs. Haggermaker will understand."

A pause. "There's nothing in my scholarship about working every summer," I said evenly, picking up my bowl and spoon. "Not one word."

"Of course not! You'll just write her a little note about your change in plans, and I'm sure she'll completely understand. I saw her in the elevator last week at the hospital, and she was so gracious, asking when you were coming home. I was flattered she even remembered me."

"She's not Queen Elizabeth."

She stared at the fridge door, hurt.

*Be kind.* I repeated it in my head whenever she got on my nerves. Then I always thought of the Blockbuster Video slogan— Be Kind. Rewind.

My mom had been so relieved when I won the scholarship. Early in senior year of high school, I'd seen the notebook in her desk drawer, tallying my college expenses. We both knew her $37,000 insurance coder level I salary from the hospital wouldn't stretch far, and the numbers had practically vibrated with worry.

"I'm sorry, Mom. Just...don't stress, okay?"

She turned and nodded.

"It'll be fine." I forced myself to eat a spoonful of ice cream.

"Well, I'm just tickled that you're back," she said. "Even though the job didn't work out. I know I'm a poor substitute for Serra. You said she's nannying in Berkeley?"

"Tahoe, for her art professor's family. But they're flying her down for Fourth of July week." I'd met Yvonne Copeland in Serra's studio. A tall, broad-shouldered woman with a child's haircut—bright red hair cut into a pixie with unforgiving half-inch bangs. She always wore flowing black dresses and had a seemingly endless collection of pop art earrings. Serra called Yvonne's style choices witchy-kitsch.

"How generous. And I want to hear all about Margaret. Your... What do they call it? Your study buddy."

I nearly choked on a Swiss almond.

Maggie was on academic probation; Serra and I had never seen her go to class before noon.

Maggie and I did meet for Beat the Clock, though. As in the promotion at the Bear's Lair, where pitchers of beer were $4 at four o'clock, $5 at five, and $6 at six. Brilliant marketing.

"Maggie's a chemistry major. She's taking summer session because she's... To get a jump on next year's courseload."

"She sounds extremely conscientious."

"She is. You'll meet her sometime."

"I'd love to. I'm sorry she couldn't visit. Well, at least Eric will be home soon, so that'll be nice for you. But of course, you and Eric must call each other all the time."

"All the time."

★

After she went to bed I wandered rooms like a nosy houseguest, examining the framed botanical prints in the sunken family room, finger-combing the fringe on the fuzzy red sofa afghan, turning the knobs on our decades-old intercom panel. Serra and Eric and I used to play that we were DJs on it.

The books on my bedroom shelf and the clothes in my closet seemed like someone else's, like riches, and I couldn't remember why they hadn't made the cut when I'd packed last summer.

I picked up the framed picture of Eric and Serra and me after the Senior Awards ceremony. We were grinning into the sun with our arms flung around each other, clutching our prizes— me the Haggermaker, Serra her Artists' Network certificate, Eric the Rotary Club's bright medal.

*You must call each other all the time.*

Eric and I hadn't spoken once. We'd emailed. But for every five hundred words I sent I got five back:

E—

When you stand at the top of the Campanile (that's our gorgeous clock tower, the third tallest in the world) at noon, you can feel the bell concert sort of shimmering through your bones, like the tower's going to crumble down. But it's wonderful, and on a clear day, you can see all the way to the point of the Transamerica building in the City. (That's San Francisco, by the way. They just call it the City here.) On a Clear Day, You Can See Tomorrow—isn't that a movie we saw together once? About a clairvoyant?

I miss seeing movies with you. I miss you. I'd love to visit Rhode Island and check out all the theaters you've surely discovered. (Hello—tell me about them please!!) I'll buy the popcorn. And the Milk Duds to melt in. K? I'll scrounge $ for the flight somehow.

I hope you are happy and learning and having fun, and all those good things.

Eric's answer:

We have a clock tower, too. Brick. Has design of fruit at the base.

As fall wore on and he didn't warm, my messages cooled, too. I described my favorite late-night study spots—but not the pangs of loneliness that sometimes hit when I looked at the hundreds of strangers at other desks, hiding inside their headphones and squeaking away with their highlighters.

Eric mentioned movies he'd seen, but didn't tell me if he'd gone alone or with a pack of friends or some girl.

I'd planned to work on him in person, over Thanksgiving. For weeks I'd rehearsed what to say when we saw each other in November, different ways to go back to how things used to be. Except Eric didn't come home for Thanksgiving. And though

Serra and I watched the Martha Stewart Thanksgiving Special twice, howling at her elaborate turkey centerpieces and stuck-up enunciation, underneath I'd been sad knowing I wouldn't see Eric until Christmas.

But Eric didn't come back to Orange Park for winter, either. He went to some friend's house in Boston. And he ignored my offer to meet somewhere cheap for spring break.

See you this summer, I'd emailed in May. I'm the tall girl with glasses and shoulder-length brown hair. An Eric move, hiding my feelings in a joke.

★

At midnight I lay in my bed, wide-awake. It was too quiet; I was used to the constant hallway action in my dorm. I muffled my squawking modem under a pillow so I could email Serra and Maggie to bemoan my job loss. It had only been a day, but I already missed them.

I had this waiting for me:

From: ericlogan98@brownuniversity.edu
Not coming home this summer after all. Internship with
Tribeca film fest. P/T, but couldn't pass up.
Eric

# 8

## Focus

Late June 1995

Every day my first week back, I sat at my bedroom desk under the street-side window, trying to adhere to the schedules I printed neatly in the squares of my blotter calendar:

> *8:00 to 9:30:* Beowulf *reading*
> *9:30 to 10:00:* Beowulf *paper brainstorming (min. one page!)*
> *1:00 to 2:00:* Beowulf *paper outlines (rough)*

It looked so reasonable, so achievable, contained in the blotter squares.

I sat in the chair during my prescribed times but made little progress. Maybe it was the footnotes or the impenetrable names that all sounded like someone hocking phlegm loogies: *Wiglaf* and *Hrothgar* and *Hygelac.* I couldn't keep the horses straight from the humans.

Maybe it was me.

I'd always been so good at tuning everything out and focusing on the task at hand.

*Time is passing. Will you? Focus!*

But these days I stalled. I doodled. I drew a creature with the face of Scott Baio and the body of a wolf, my eyes drifting from my desk out my window. I hadn't seen the blue vintage convertible or the little black BMW since I'd come home, and imagined their owners on vacation together, in Catalina or Mexico or some other fabulous place.

I began staying up until two and sleeping until noon, adjusting my blotter schedules accordingly. I spread tasks out, trying to give my days structure. I watered my mom's plants or took the bus to the beach or watched TCM, lying on my side on the living room shag carpet, next to the air-conditioning vent.

I prepared elaborate dinners, taking the bus thirty-five miles to Shun Fat Supermarket in Garden Grove for pho noodles, or twenty-five miles to El Super in Santa Ana for *queso fresco*. My mom always dug into her meal appreciatively, no matter how burned or oversalted.

But the Thursday I wrote out trivia cards so we could learn about Italy while we ate manicotti with all-day, old-world tomato gravy, her voice quavered and the telltale vertical line above the bridge of her nose appeared.

"These…theme nights are lovely, Becc. But…" She shook her head, dabbing marinara from her lips with the cloth napkin I'd ironed and starched into a mini Leaning Tower of Pisa. "Never mind. I know you tried to find a job. Forget I said anything."

The next day I stared at the cellophane-wrapped package of index cards on which I was going to write France factoids to accompany our coq au vin. It was already 102 degrees at 11:00 a.m., and hot, winey stew was the last thing my mom would want after dragging herself across the broiling driveway. *I* didn't even want coq au vin. Anyone sane would prefer a salad, or a Popsicle.

*You've lost it, Becc.*

I threw the chicken in the fridge, slammed the door, and went to the one movie playing in town.

★

I got one of the last seats, in the back row. The audience was mostly teenage boys, heckling each other across rows and chomping popcorn. They sounded like a bunch of grasshoppers destroying a wheat crop.

*Batman Forever* could have been a brilliant, subtle piece of filmmaking, but I wouldn't know. The sound effects gave me too much of a headache to figure out the story, and I regretted heaping praise on the cutting-edge speaker system in my article.

I got up, whispering, "Excuse me," to the boys between me and the aisle. They didn't make it easy, didn't angle their legs or jackknife their seats and dangle their butts down into the crevasse to give me room as adults would have.

I wandered across the street to the square, blinking at the bright sunlight. I'd wasted $4.75 to feel more restless than before the matinee. Next summer I'd start applying for jobs in January. I'd walk dogs or clean pools or—

"Rebecca!"

He was sitting on the rectangular brick bench that surrounded The Orange Tree, right in front of the plaque.

Him. Flip phone in his hand, sleeves rolled up, coffee cup at his hip.

"Were you on assignment?" He snapped his phone shut and slipped it in his shirt pocket.

"Assignment?"

He pointed behind me, at the theater. "I read your article last summer. I liked it, how you described the old lamps, the drinking fountains. I'd never noticed them."

"Thank you."

"So are you working on part two?"

"I wish. The *Courier* shut down."

"Right, I heard. I forgot."

"I was just killing time at the matinee. But the sound effects gave me a headache."

"Sit." He hopped up, sweeping leaves off the bench.

"No, I should get home."

"Please sit. I'll run to Fenton's for Advil and a drink." Fenton's was our old soda fountain/druggist on Main, a block away. They still sold splits and patty melts at the counter. "What's your poison? Coke, iced tea, juice?"

"You don't—"

"If you don't tell me, I'm going to make it an egg cream."

I smiled. "I like egg creams. But I'll have a Coke. Thanks."

Five minutes later, he returned with another iced coffee for himself, my Coke, and a foil travel packet of ibuprofen. I popped them and we sipped in companionable silence, people-watching.

Our sleepy downtown had had a cutesy revival. People drove in from all over to stroll our main street, take pictures of The Orange Tree, eat chicken Caesars under misters at one of the fancy new cafés, and shop. Dusty old Bernadine's Closet had been bought and renamed Casual Friday by some woman with a Range Rover who always had a Chihuahua with pink-painted nails dangling from the crook of her arm. She sold $200 khakis and $50 baseball caps with rhinestone crosses emblazoned on them.

I'd asked if she had openings but she'd said, *I'm turning girls away left and right, honey,* in this impatient but fake-nice voice that made me wish I'd never come in.

"Feeling better?" Cal said.

I nodded. "Eric used to call it reentry. How you feel going back to the real world after a movie."

"That sounds about right." He paused. "So he's majoring in film now, did you hear?"

I shook my head and toyed with my straw, taking measurements of my hurt. Eric hadn't bothered to share. "That's great, though."

"He didn't tell his mother, either," he said gently. "It showed up on some forms."

"I'm sorry, by the way. You asked me to watch out for him. But he doesn't tell me much anymore."

"It wasn't fair, expecting you to check up on him."

"I wanted to. I've emailed him a ton, but his answers have been..."

"What?"

"I don't know. Brief."

"Sounds like a euphemism."

"I should probably stop emailing him. It's getting pathetic."

"*Pathetic* is not a word I'd associate with you."

I ran a finger through the beads of moisture on the sides of my clear plastic cup, merging the drops. Wondered which words he did associate with me. "Well, I lost my internship. I'm wasting the summer. And I'm starting to realize my prospects aren't so great for a real journalism job, either. After graduation." I smiled faintly.

"So the newspaper folding left you hanging?"

"It didn't fold, exactly. The owner sold it to the *County Chronicle*. But yeah."

"And now you go to movies in the middle of the day. Not that I'm one to judge. I regularly take three-coffee lunches." He shook his iced coffee. "It's the new three-martini."

"I could use the caffeine."

"You do seem a little tired. You look lovely, of course. Just a little... Are you sleeping?" He crinkled his eyes in concern, looking at me.

I cradled my cup in my lap and tucked my hair behind my ears, sure I looked like hell. I'd rushed to the matinee in rumpled shorts and a tank top, without brushing my hair or even scrabbling it into a ponytail, without a dot of makeup. "I sleep ten hours a night. Sometimes more. I..."

"What?"

"It's been a strange summer."

He nodded thoughtfully. Then, abruptly, he said, "Work for me," bouncing his cup on his knee. "Not *technically* me. I'm not running the place. But I just staked this fun incubator in LA, and you can tell me if they're spending my money wisely. CommPlanet, it's called. There are some clever little hatchlings in the mix.

"You could research, write. Hell, I don't know what, exactly, but they'd slot you in for the rest of the summer. Most of the concepts are media related in one way or another."

"I wasn't hinting for a job."

"I know."

"You're serious?"

"Sure. Work whatever hours you like, word it however you like. You can be…an analyst. Isn't everyone an analyst these days?"

"It's tempting but—"

"That way you'll have something to put on your résumé for the summer. You can say you…let's see…verified facts and generated time-sensitive content. Now, doesn't that sound related to your chosen field?"

His eyes flashed mischief at the absurdity of it all, the ruse of the professional world. He nudged my knee with his. At the casual brush of sun-warmed fabric on my bare skin, I glanced down. His pants were navy linen, decadently wrinkled and expensive looking. One soft blue fold tickled the side of my leg, just above the knee.

*Something to put on my résumé.*

I'd heard the phrase so many times it had started to make me crazy. We weren't even sophomores, but I knew a dozen kids whose parents had friends manufacture internships for them. Then they could say they spent the summer at a lab in Boston or an anthropological dig in Bolivia. It was one big, nepotistic racket and we all knew it.

His phone rang and he pulled it from his pocket, flipped it open to see who it was. He pressed a button, silencing it. "Think about it. I'm rarely there but I have a little pull."

"Don't they have a thousand real applicants who'd kill for an internship?"

"Probably. What'd they pay you at the *Courier*?"

"Nothing."

"I'll double it." He grinned. "No, seriously, we'll figure out something fair. What do you say?"

"I'm more of a print person."

"How's that working out for you?" He pointed his phone at the newspaper kiosk on the corner of the square. It was empty, streaked with icicles of white bird poop, topped with an array of theater soda cups.

"I'll think about it."

It would be wrong for a hundred reasons. I didn't like the sound of someone "slotting me in" as a favor. Or "generating content," whatever that meant.

If Eric found out, he'd sever any wispy thread of friendship still dangling between us.

But mostly, it would be wrong because I knew, with the part of me that was as secret and cool and selfish as a movie theater full of people on a weekday, that the excited flutter in my belly had little to do with putting something on my résumé.

# *9*

## Civilized

2008
Thursday, 11:35 a.m.
Outside Santa Barbara

I keep expecting him to act like the person I remember, the still-boyish man who ducked out of the office every chance he got. My coconspirator, urging me to set my own hours. Not this man welded to his phone, ignoring the beauty around us.

True, the prettiest view is on my side of the highway. At fifty-five miles per hour the public beach we're passing is a rainbow-sprinkled blur. A streak of yellow confetti'd with bright blankets, coolers, bathing suits.

Beyond this bright human chaos is the endless Pacific, only one color—soothing blue.

Maybe he'll relax at lunch.

Maybe he's as ready to stop as I am.

I'm thirsty and stiff and tired. Hoarse from shouting over the wedding present. I want the world's biggest Arnold Palmer, a spiked one, and a conversation without a barricade of cardboard and Bubble Wrap involved. A civilized conversation.

That's the note the two of us are trying to strike: *civilized*.

I chose the most civilized restaurant I could find, read dozens of Yelp and Califorkia.com reviews before picking the Harborside. Classy decor, impeccable food. It's a popular spot for business lunches—the kind of place where a crumb scraper scoots a silver squeegee around the tablecloth between courses.

I thought it was far enough from the big conference hotels. We're miles away, and I haven't been up here since I worked at CommPlanet.

But as I pull off the freeway and loop toward the beach, the midday light so bright even through my sunglasses that it's transformed the ocean into flashing silver, I'm back in those dark conference rooms.

My leather seat is warm from the sun, but I can feel the hotel air-conditioning blowing behind my knees.

More than a decade ago, and I can still see the damn slides. Those cocky marketing slogans.

"Cool. Comm. Connected."

"Visionary brand alignment."

And the hyperbolic finale—"Tomorrow starts now!"

Was that last one prophetic?

Was that the day it started? The day curiosity tipped into desire?

Or maybe it had started the first morning I watched him from my room. And everything after was inevitable.

# 10

## Good Influence

July 4, 1995
Dusk
Crystal Cove Beach

"*Someone* in Tahoe must need a nanny." I patted clumps of damp sand on my sunburned feet to cool them. "I'd be a great nanny. I'd be Mary Poppins. Maria."

"That bad?" Serra swigged her raspberry Snapple.

We sat on the sandy ridge above the beach shacks, watching the bustling mass of high school kids down the slope below us.

There were at least thirty of them, and their anticipation of the fireworks and everything else that the night might bring was palpable. An energy that floated up to where we sat observing from our dry towel. They were splashing each other, shouting, play-dueling with sparklers. Pumping their pony keg. Whooping at the sporadic, echoing booms of the first fireworks, previews of the elaborate show to come.

The more industrious among them had stacked logs into a

teepee for the bonfire, but they hadn't lit it yet. There was still a peachy glow of sunset tinting the world.

"What'd you do all day?" Serra asked.

"Let's just say I'm never letting you leave. Why do you keep looking at the parking lot?"

"Thought I saw someone trying to break into the Stay Wag. Can't you work somewhere for free? At the *Times* or the *County Chronicle* or wherever?"

"I offered. I guess the custodial beat didn't impress them."

I'd applied to every publication from San Diego to Fresno, including my most gripping work on the switch to eco-friendly vomit-dissolving powder and graffiti solvent, but I had nothing. I'd tried non-journalism jobs, but it was so late even Baskin-Robbins didn't want me.

Here was where I should have told Serra I did have a job offer. In *my chosen field*, even. If you didn't look too closely.

But I couldn't tell her, not until I'd decided.

"I'm sorry," she said. "I'd love to have you up in Tahoe with me, making fluffernut sandwiches and blowing up water wings. But can't you at least enjoy your freedom?"

"I'm trying."

"Hey, guys!"

It was Robin Engles, who'd been a sophomore when we were seniors. She wore a pink triangle bikini top, pink velour sweats, and a rhinestoned trucker cap.

"Nice hat," Serra said under her breath. "Hey, Robin."

"It's so weird to see you guys without Eric! Is he home?"

"He's in New York for the summer," Serra said.

"Wow. Cool." Robin's friend tugged her down the sandy trail toward the bonfire, where she was immediately offered a cup, flanked by two shirtless boys.

Someone lit the woodpile and Serra and I watched silently as it caught, first only a charcoal plume, a thin dark line against the orange sunset. Slowly the image reversed, the fire orange against the gray sky. Until it was a roaring, snapping pyre.

This was where we'd met Eric, the July before high school. He was lying on his back in the shade of one of the abandoned beach shacks. I'd never seen him without his gang of friends from The Heights. The older ones drove ridiculous cars—BMWs and Lexuses—and that was enough to make me dismiss the whole crew.

When I'd walked past him to buy an Icee at the snack bar, I'd seen the cover of the book tented over his face. *The Pigman.* It surprised me, Eric Logan reading alone. He was still *Eric Logan* then.

"That's a great book," I'd said. It wasn't like me to talk like that to a boy from The Heights, but I was in a good mood. Summer stretched ahead, and Serra was right down the sand, and the sun made everything seem easy.

He'd lowered the book and gazed up at me. "You've read this?"

"Twice."

"I'm only twenty pages in. Are they going to kill this old guy?"

"You'll see. Stick with it."

I don't remember Eric pulling his towel over to ours, but he must have. Because the three of us sat together until the sun melted into a red glow across the water. Other kids had paired off and spread out, their giggles and murmurs shutting off, couple by couple, as they generated their own heat, but Eric and Serra and I sat cross-legged on our damp towels, talking near the fire until near midnight.

So that was it. By October of freshman year, Eric had stopped hanging out with the boys from his neighborhood. Me and Serra became me and Serra and Eric.

"Miss him?" Serra asked.

I nodded.

"Me, too."

So Serra saw Eric-shaped holes everywhere, too.

By the bonfire. Her bedroom floor, where I'd slept over for the last two nights. In her pool, on Space Mountain at Disneyland, and the Giant Dipper in San Diego. And in the gently lapping ocean, where a gangly boy was skimboarding in the fast-disappearing light.

We'd had a blast, driving to all our favorite places in the shuddering Stay Wag, but ever since Serra had flown in I'd felt his absence more. The missing third Mouseketeer.

"Has he emailed you lately?" I asked.

"Not much."

"You don't have to lie. I know you get longer emails than I do."

"He'll come around."

"Maybe I could've handled it better, but he doesn't have to be so…extreme."

"Don't take it personally. He's sorting stuff out. Stuff that has nothing to do with you, like his parents splitting up. Mr. California banging his mom. Hey, my dad saw Mr. California at the office the other day, some meeting for investors… What?"

"I hate the word *banging*. Whatever, forget the Logans. Let's talk about you. Are you getting enough time to paint?"

"I'm militant about bedtimes." Serra capped her Snapple and raised an eyebrow, attempting to look like a sinister babysitter and failing utterly. Her cherubic face wouldn't allow it. "But I'm not *painting*. Yvonne has this fantastic loft studio she lets me use whenever, with bins of all this great material just sitting there for the taking. I'm pretty obsessed with my latest experiment. Yvonne thinks I should stick with it, at least. It's a triptych."

"What's that?"

"A piece with three parts. Beginning, middle, and end. I got the idea from one of Patti's old toys." Patti was Yvonne's seven-year-old, Serra's charge for the summer.

"Sounds cool. I want to see it."

"It's either brilliant or complete garbage, but that's all I can say for now." Serra spied something behind me and grinned, waved. "This might cheer you up. And you're allowed to take it personally."

I turned.

Maggie stood near the beach volleyball court: black hair, black shirt, black bag. Morticia Addams among Malibu Barbies. She spotted us, ran over, and collapsed onto me. "Surprise!"

I clung to her. "Are you seriously here?"

"Serra said you were desperate. So I told my parents you were a good influence and it would be okay if I missed one tutoring session Friday as long as I studied on the plane, blah blah, and they bought it. And the ticket."

Serra laughed. "We *are* a good influence."

"I need to test this ocean of yours," Maggie said, unlacing her Docs and rolling up her jeans. "Come on!"

The three of us ran downhill, past the tilting, abandoned beach shacks, with their peeling turquoise and pink and lavender paint, and the bonfire, which was just starting to crackle. We sloshed into the knee-deep water.

"So three days is enough to teach me to surf, right?" Maggie said.

★

We never found time to get Maggie surfing lessons, but it was a glorious weekend.

The Orange County that Serra and I took for granted, Maggie saw as exotic. The birds of paradise in my backyard, The Orange Tree in the square, the baseball fans swinging stuffed "rally monkey" mascots at Angel Stadium to get some mojo going in the ninth. We were her tour guides. My mom was charmed by Maggie's earnest questions about her garden, and for the three days she stayed with us, my mom spoiled us with lemon-blueberry pancakes and fresh juice before leaving for work.

But when Serra and Maggie left, my world felt more cold than before. Like the moment a smile vanishes from a face.

I took the job.

# 11

## GDI

July 18, 1995
4:00 p.m.

"How's Rebecca?" Cal peered down at me over my cubicle wall, a lock of blond hair hanging over his eyebrows, tanned arms in rolled-up sleeves hooked over the edge.

"Hi!" I clicked Hotmail, whisking my personal email account into a tiny flame at the bottom of my screen.

"Am I interrupting some important analysis?"

"I can take a break."

I was the summer media content analyst at NoozeButton.com. The only thing I'd analyzed so far was the menu at the Coffee Bean and Tea Leaf.

Cal surveyed the unused orange work spaces surrounding mine like an empty honeycomb. "Sorry I haven't checked in on you until now. How about a quick bite tomorrow? If they can spare you..." He flashed a smile at me and the shallow laugh lines flaring from his eyes deepened, reminding me that we were in on the joke about the incubator.

"I'd love that."

He drummed with his hands, a casual rat-a-tat on my orange cubicle wall. "Let's say one?"

★

"You look happy. Was it an exciting day at the News Planet?" my mom asked cheerfully on the way home from the bus stop.

My commute to LA was ridiculously long, so most nights the bus didn't pull into Orange Park until well after six. But she was a good sport about it, picking me up in her AC-less white Civic.

She was just glad I was spending my summer productively. In other words, in a manner that would prove to Francine Haggermaker that she'd backed the right horse.

"NoozeButton," I corrected her for the hundredth time, not addressing the dorky *the* she always added before each bungled attempt at the name. "CommPlanet is the incubator, the bigger company, and NoozeButton is one of its babies. The littlest one."

"Of course. I'll get it eventually. When can I read some of your writing?"

"Oh. Soon. Things are still, you know. Gearing up."

So far my "writing" was a single, three-inch-square article for the mock-up of a NoozeButton Southern California website: "LA's Top Five Pet Spas!" It was going to appear on a marketing slide. I'd gotten this hard-hitting assignment only because I'd begged Stephen Liu, the fresh USC MBA who was vaguely in charge of me, to let me help.

I'd told my mom and Serra that Les, my old boss at the *Courier*, had arranged the job for me, and that I'd only found out later that a certain neighbor up the street was an investor.

I'd also told them that I'd never see Cal, and I hadn't.

Until today.

That night after my mom went to sleep I ironed my dark

purple linen dress. Someone told me once that my eyes looked extra green when I wore purple.

I set my alarm to buzz half an hour earlier than usual so I'd have time to blow-dry my hair. I arranged equipment out on my small bathroom counter—fresh contacts, my lipstick brush, the tiny wire eyelash comb I'd used only for grad pictures. A perfume oil I'd found in Berkeley called Rain.

I hadn't done any of this for Les at the *Courier*.

The next day

WHERE I WAS SUPPOSED TO BE | My well-appointed cubicle
WHERE I WAS | Feeding a lion

I started checking the time on my computer monitor at ten. To make the hours pass faster I opened the *Wall Street Journal* as I did every day, trying to figure out exactly what NoozeButton was. My coworkers seemed nonplussed by the fact that if you extended the alarm-clock metaphor, it implied that their "content," which nobody seemed to care about, was a big old snooze-fest.

Nooze would never be news; I wasn't that naive. I knew it was going to somehow customize ads, and a sprinkling of real articles, based on people's search histories. I pretended I was an embedded journalist, there on assignment to observe the inner workings and report back. Not a real part of the company.

But though I'd tried to get more answers from Stephen on how NoozeButton would work, he only tossed back words like *secret sauce* and *scaffolded back-end data*.

Someday I would find the elusive article that would explain secret-sauce scaffolding, but not today; I was too jumpy.

At eleven I visited the ladies' room to check my hair, my eye makeup.

At noon I scattered papers from the recycling bin on my desk so I'd look busy when Cal came.

At 12:30 I started listening for the *whoosh-thunk* of the elevator doors.

And at 1:04 he appeared, hanging over my cubicle wall right where he'd issued the invitation.

"Oh, hi." I looked up from my fake work.

"Still a good time?" he asked, as if I was the busy one.

"Perfect."

In the elevator, both of us were quiet, smiling into the middle distance. Until he pressed P instead of L.

"We're driving?" I'd assumed we were grabbing lunch nearby.

"There's a great café on Spring Street."

In the cool underground parking lot he opened his passenger door for me, and there I was, in the blue convertible I'd watched from my room so often. I clipped on an old-fashioned seat belt, like on an airplane, and ran my hand on the burnished wood dashboard.

"I like this font," I said about the svelte, tilting numbers on the clock. A random conversational opener, though it was true. I noticed fonts.

"Me, too. They should have it in Microsoft Word and call it '63 Roadster."

"This is a '63?"

"Year I was born." He grinned, turning the ignition. "Vain, right? Who does that?"

"No. I wasn't thinking that." *I was thinking that you're thirty-two.*

We drove through downtown. The streets were still cool, shaded by skyscrapers, but they'd be baking soon enough.

He clearly enjoyed his old car, with its dials in glass globes, its long chrome gearshift jutting from the steering wheel. It required all kinds of special ministrations and adjustments, and his forearm tensed and softened as it moved back and forth between the steering wheel and gearshift.

When we stopped at a light I said, looking not at him but at the funhouse version of my face reflected in the chrome glove compartment handle—"Thank you again for finding me the job."

"It's working out?"

"Yes. It's been great."

"Great."

★

The restaurant was called Poppy. We faced each other across a small wooden table in the courtyard, next to a trickling wall fountain of a lion's head.

"I do like this place," I said, my neck bent, elbows pulled close to my body. My shy bird pose, Serra once called it. "It feels kind of hidden and European."

I looked around at the ivy on the walls, the water bubbling from the lion's mouth into a pond, the gold-trimmed votive candleholder on our table. Anything but his face. The ease that had come over me unexpectedly in the study, by The Orange Tree, was long gone.

I felt sure he knew I'd spent hours thinking about what for him was only a casual, courtesy *bite*.

"I had a feeling you'd appreciate it. So, *NoozeButton*," he said. He pronounced it mockingly, giving *ton* a French twang. "People treating you well?"

"Everyone's been great. Really great, thank you."

I reached for other adjectives, came up empty. *The fountain's great. This is great iced coffee.* My English major was really paying off.

"Do you need to get back soon?" I blurted. We'd been seated all of ten minutes. Our salads hadn't come, our drinks had only dipped an inch.

He shook his head and smiled.

But instead of laughing at my distress he found a project for us. He reached into his pocket and set a dime and a nickel on the table. "Gotta do it," he said, sliding the dime to me, flicking his eyes at the lion's head fountain on the wall. "House rules, must feed the lion."

I clutched the dime for a second and wished the only thing I ever did. Not *let me stop making an ass of myself.* My standard fountain wish was simple. One word that encompassed these thoughts, and the unnamed ones on the fringes. *Happiness.* I held the word in my mind for a second and tossed the coin in.

He threw his into the rings from mine, and we listened to the second, neat *plunk.*

"I heard once you should only make a wish in calm water, while looking at your reflection," he said.

"Really? That invalidates every wish I've ever made."

"Sorry."

"I read that the Trevi Fountain in Rome gets more than a million dollars in coins a year. Or whatever that is in lira. They give it to charity."

"How much do you think this one gets a year? Should we do an audit?"

We leaned over to inspect the fountain.

"About a dollar?" he said.

"There's a lot of silver in the back. So I guess…a dollar sixty-three."

"Can't you be more specific?" he asked, tilting his head, his blue eyes flashing amusement.

The waiter came with our blackened-salmon Caesars. "Here you go, doll," he said as he set mine down. The guy was fifty-something, probably one of the many waiter-slash-actors that staffed LA restaurants, and he said it sweetly. But I must have flinched. *Doll* made me feel like a little girl. Or like a toy, like I should have two perfect circles of rouge on my cheeks.

"Remind me never to call you doll," Cal said when he left.

"You can tell that bugged me? It's just…we don't call men… train set. Or football. Here's your salad, football."

He laughed. "I'll call you…human."

I smiled. And muscle by muscle, I eased out of shy bird pose into alert bird pose.

Cal seemed oblivious to the fact that in addition to our waiter, two other customers in the courtyard—a girl my age and a man slightly older—were checking him out. He leaned close. "So how's college?"

I told him about my roommates and my favorite classes, how I audited courses in the journalism grad school. About being relegated to the custodial beat on the paper, and how I feared I was facing another year of riding around with Albert Crenley, noting graffiti on a clipboard.

"I like Albert, though, he's a character," I said.

"In what way?"

"Oh…like there's this one spray paint tag, this cat with a slogan under it. *The cat knows.* It's from T. S. Eliot: *the cat himself knows and will never confess.* From 'The Naming of Cats'?"

"Mysterious."

"Right? My editor thinks it's lame but I'm kind of obsessed. I keep a map over my bed where I mark my sightings, and a list on my computer. Location, date. I named the file Hiss."

He laughed appreciatively. "It's probably a guerilla marketing campaign for a pet food company."

"I hope it's more interesting than that. Anyway, the custodians have a theory that Kappa Alpha Tau fraternity's behind it. So whenever we see a new cat, Albert pretends he's going to drive the cart to their house up on the row and make them clean it up."

"Go Albert. He should."

"He calls them *frat punks*. Were you in one?"

"I was a GDI. Do they still say that?"

I nodded. GDI meant Goddamned Independent.

He asked where I wanted to live after college (anywhere a newspaper would hire me), whether I'd been to Europe or got my fountain factoids from books (the latter, but I hoped to swing a semester abroad).

"You should do it," he said. "Do what makes you happy."

"How is your happy place?" I asked. "Have you sailed there a lot this summer?"

"Happy place?" he said, confused.

Silly to think he'd held on as tightly as I had to this scrap from our year-old conversation. I stared down at the fountain wall by my knee, the green fur on wet stone. "Catalina."

"Oh, of course. I go there too much. Way too much."

"Do you mean you're getting bored with it?"

"The opposite. I've let other things slide." He grinned, and leaned back, balancing his chair on two legs. "I'm afraid it's a problem."

Did he mean his investments, or his relationship, or his tri-athlons, or all of the above? It wasn't clear.

And though he said he was *afraid it was a problem*, he couldn't look less troubled, tipping his chair back in the sun next to the bubbling fountain, the hair on his forearms bright as the gold paint on the stone lion's mane.

He had floated over the adult problems waiting for me and found them amusing. I smiled back.

# 12

## Impressions

The next day, every time the elevator *whoosh-thunked*, I sat up straight, waiting for him to pay another visit over my cubicle wall. But he didn't.

He didn't appear the next day, or the next week. And though I knew it was unreasonable, I felt strangely hurt by his absence.

I didn't see his car pass through the gate, though I watched for it, and I didn't bump into Donna Logan in town, though I hoped to. I wanted to see if she still looked happy.

I wondered, more than once, if all was not well at 26 Jacaranda Heights.

I tried to keep busy, hanging out in the one lively corner of the office—the web cataloging room, where a bunch of recent college grads did nothing but record the addresses of new websites all day for $20 an hour. They'd nicknamed their office Sears and made an archway around their door from ripped-out pages from catalogs—guys posing in tighty-whities, pool decor, garden gnomes.

The catalogers found a lot of porn and competed to find the

weirdest sites, shouting, "We have a new front-runner!" across the room. No URL was off-limits. I wasn't approved to catalog, but I fetched coffee for them, and they were always welcoming.

When I wasn't lurking in Sears I read the *Journal* and the *FT*, cleaned my keyboard with a nifty can of compressed air. I persuaded Stephen to let me help him prepare for what he called a *boondoggle*, a big off-site marketing meeting coming up in San Diego.

Stephen grudgingly let me collate PowerPoints on the rosewood table in the conference room. The sheets about Nooze-Button, still warm and fragrant from the Xerox, all had violent words on them: *slice* and *grab* and *push*.

"These make me feel a little sorry for NoozeButton's future readers," I said.

Stephen didn't break a smile. "Not readers, Rebecca. *Impressions*. Once it gears up, it's going to be bigger than HotWired or Salon."

"But what *is* it?"

"A proprietary algorithm that mines search terms for demographic data, then scaffolds it," he said, dealing copies of a colorful bar graph facedown around the table.

"So scaffolding is like giving readers—"

"Impressions."

"Giving *impressions* more stories they'll like based on their age or gender or whatever?"

A tolerant, inward smile. "You're thinking way too front end. We're going to optimize utility on the back end. It's totally robust, totally scalable. Data scaffolding's only a conduit to ad partnership opportunities."

"Got it. Partnerships with...?"

"Netscape, ideally."

I was pretty sure he had no idea what he was talking about.

Stephen disappeared and I had nothing to do, so I checked my Hotmail account.

The week I'd started, I'd confessed to Eric that I was working for one of the companies Cal had invested in.

I'd said that the opportunity *just came up*, that I'd gone mad, drifting around Orange Park alone. That Cal was hardly involved.

I'd read over it obsessively, each time wincing a bit more. It was such a transparent plea for absolution—

> This is the strangest place, E. Empty and full of itself at the same time...
>
> I'm sort of helping my sort-of boss get ready for a marketing "boondoggle" in San Diego. (The word *boondoggle* reminds me of Moondoggie, that surfer in *Gidget*. Remember?)
>
> But mostly, I take coffee orders. I pocket free granola bars from the breakroom, ask people if they need me to copy anything (they rarely do), and wait like a good girl for five o'clock...
>
> Be honest, E. Am I paying my dues or selling out? I can't tell the difference.

He still hadn't answered.

But Serra and Maggie and I had a summer-long chain of messages going.

Today Maggie had emailed about a blowout *Midsummer Night's Dream*/Jell-O-shot party at Plato House, this ratty co-op where she was rooming for the summer. The cops shut the party down but nobody got in trouble.

Serra shared funny stories from babysitting in Tahoe and cryptic hints about her triptych project. I'm obsessed, she said. I'm lost in it. I'm only sleeping three hours a night, but I've never had more energy. The only frustrating part is figuring out how to connect the three pieces. There's this metal artist in Berkeley who might be able to make what I want, but do you think that would be cheating?

The triptych was apparently so big that Yvonne, Serra's teacher/ boss/idol, was renting Serra a truck to transport it back to campus before fall semester.

I told Serra it didn't sound like cheating and I couldn't wait to see it. I told them about my job, Sears, and my orange cubicle, avoiding any mention of my friendly lunch with Eric's enemy. I described the beater car I had my eye on, at the used lot in Santa Ana. $750, a 1971 silver Volvo diesel wagon.

I can call it Wag Dos, I wrote, and hit Send.

I was about to wander to the breakroom for another granola bar when it popped up:

New message from ericlogan98@brownuniversity.edu

Three and a half weeks after I sent my email to him. It would serve him right if I trashed it, unread.

My hand hesitated on my beige plastic mouse. But I clicked it open—

Congrats!

I gripped the mouse tight, swirling the cursor around the screen of my spanking-new Dell.

*Congrats!* I'd poured my heart out in 907 words. In return I got one, with a bullshit exclamation point.

*Congrats!* As if a stranger had hijacked his keyboard. *Congrats!* As if I was a stranger.

I caressed the mouse, dancing the cursor around and around Eric's reply.

And clicked Delete.

# 13

## Friends

2008
Thursday, 12:10 p.m.
Santa Barbara
Harborside Restaurant parking lot

I walk over to his side but he's lost in phone world, oblivious to the fact that we've stopped. Head down, *tap-tap-tap-tap-tap*, like whatever he's sending is as urgent as Morse code from the *Titanic*. He glances up and I get a polite smile, a lifted index finger.

I'm not a fan of that wait-a-sec finger.

At least a middle finger would say it directly: *Go fuck yourself... for a sec.*

When I picked him up this morning, it was still dark, so as he walked toward me down the long, curving stone walkway, between rows of flickering solar garden lights, he couldn't see my hands trembling.

We had projects to keep us occupied: checking out the car,

chuckling about the size of the gift, stowing his suitcase in the trunk. Aware of sleeping neighbors, we hushed our voices.

*Can I help?*

*I've got it, thanks.*

*The seat adjuster thingy is down there, on your right.*

*Found it…*

But now I'm standing in a bright parking lot, project-less. Painfully aware of the sun on my hands, my face, my wind-whipped hair.

I don't know what to do with my body, where to look. Now that I'm out of the car, there are too many choices.

I do some calf stretches, breathing in deep, pulling the briny air into my lungs like a hearty sailor. I survey the white-tipped waves, the long, dockside outdoor seating area of the restaurant.

Then look back toward the car, a vague, no-rush smile on my face.

He glances up at me, squinting. He's always eschewed sunglasses, and in the unforgiving noon sun, the lines fanning from his eyes are pronounced. Ten years will stamp themselves on your skin, no matter how careful you are with the sunblock.

But his hair hasn't thinned since we last saw each other; he's fared well in that department. And he works out, I can tell from the way his shoulders pull the seams of his white button-down shirt as he gestures on the phone.

He'll evaluate the changes in me, too. Compare the twenty-two-year-old he last saw with the thirty-two-year-old before him. Anyone would.

A gust of wind off the ocean shoots up my pale blue T-shirt dress and I hold the fluttering hem down on my thighs just in time.

At least it gives me something to do with my hands.

After trying on six possible outfits for this day, I'd decided on the T-shirt dress weeks ago. Simple and comfortable. But five minutes before I was supposed to leave my condo in Dana Point this morning, I caught my reflection in the hall mirror and decided the dress was a shapeless bag. I yanked it off and pulled on black shorts and a gray tank.

But then I decided I looked like I was trying too hard to prove I *wasn't* trying too hard, and went back to the light blue bag.

I should've worn the shorts.

I wander away from the car, stretch my arms over my head.

"Sorry about that!" he calls.

I whirl around. Here's where we could finally get serious. *Real.*

Like that irritating slogan from *The Real World*: here's what happens when people stop being polite and start getting real!

*Finally,* he could say. *Finally, we can catch up. I want to hear everything!*

He strolls toward me, slipping his phone in his shirt pocket.

"Sorry," he repeats. "You know how it is."

"I do. I get it, no problem."

He joins me in my casual stretches on the dockside walkway. He's doing back twists and I'm using the do-not-feed-gulls! sign for balance as I pull my ankles to my butt.

It's like we're warming up for a 10K.

"Nice place," he says politely as we walk down the dock to the outdoor host stand. "Have you eaten here before?"

"No, but they're supposed to have amazing scampi, and I requested a table by that side window there, so we can keep an eye on the gift." I give him a self-deprecating smile. "I know it probably sounds paranoid."

He returns my smile. "Not at all. It sounds organized. You can't neglect your third passenger."

"No." I laugh. A little too loud.

We walk in silence, looking anywhere but at each other, squinting into the sunlight dappling the water. As we approach the restaurant, he knocks dock posts with his left hand, as if he's from quality control and just here to test the wood.

"Well, I'm starving," he finally says.

"Me, too."

We're early, and our northside, two-top corner table with partial views of water and parking lot is not ready.

The hostess asks, "Would you like to wait at the bar?"

"Sure, that'd be—"

"I don't think—"

"What were you saying?"

He says, apologetically, half to me and half to the hostess, "Oh. I was just wondering if we could get it to go and eat there?" He points at the row of concrete benches by the parking lot.

They're for the food carts in the neighboring alley. Commander Shrimpy and Killer Korndogz.

"Of course," the hostess says.

To me, he asks, "Is that okay? We still have that stop and I'm kind of anxious to get up to the hotel so I can hook up my laptop."

"Sure!"

"Work's insane right now."

"I totally get it, let's not waste any time!"

So we eat in the parking lot. Batting away gulls, scarfing pan-seared grouper sandwiches from white sacks. On a bench shared with a cranky Sacramento family on their way to Disneyland. The Bevins clan.

Instead of jazz we listen to four-year-old Katy Bevins wailing that her Polly Pocket has taken a header into a storm drain. Instead of a tablescape swept free of every unsightly grain of flour, we eat over our laps. We might as well have gone through a McDonald's drive-through for Filets-O-Fish.

But we have an excellent view of the car. And he's polite, cheerful, taking an interest in my life.

"So how many are on your team?" he asks, referring to my job as West Coast content officer of newzly.com. *News You Can Choose!*

"Nineteen right now. It should be more but we're in a hiring freeze because of the downturn."

"I get it. That's impressive, though. Nineteen."

"Thanks. So how do you like your iPhone? Tech support's issuing them to us next week."

Everyone in the Newzly office was *aflutter* when we got this news. The BlackBerry stowed in my purse, coveted and cutting-edge only three years ago, is already out.

"I love it," he says. "It saves me so much time."

We both nod enthusiastically.

He sets his sandwich down on the to-go bag between us and takes his phone out of his pocket to show me how sleek it is, how thin and light. How you can drag and drop "apps" around the screen.

When I point at a bright weather icon, I accidentally brush my bare wrist against his. I twitch away and busy my hand, smoothing the bag on my lap. "I can't wait to get one. It'll make it so much easier for me to work when I travel."

"Why don't I drive the next shift so you can check in at the office?" he offers.

I'm tempted, but not because I want to check in. After a morning folded into clown-car position in the driver seat, the passenger side, with its precious extra inches of pedal-free leg room and opportunities to do spine twists, would feel like first class.

But this trip was my idea, and I've witnessed how slammed he is. I promised he could work on the road. "No, it's fine. The car's pretty fun to drive and I can see how busy you—"

His phone chimes. "Excuse me," he says and scoots away a foot, to the end of the bench. As he listens intently, he turns and we make eye contact. *I'm sorry*, he mouths.

I give him a dismissive, casual wave—*no problem, I get it!*

I wait for a little more from him. An eye roll, maybe. But he's already looking through me, picturing whomever he's talking to.

I smile at Katy Bevins in front of me. The mourning period

for the lost Polly Pocket is over and she's shyly showing me an impressive case of other Pollys, their plastic pets and accessories. "Which pet do you like best?" I ask her. She hands me a koala the size of a pencil eraser. "I think this is my favorite, too. But the raccoon is cute, what's its name...?"

Being with him again isn't what I imagined. He's so upbeat, fielding his work calls. So smooth, so in his element. Seeing me for the first time in a decade hasn't affected his productivity in the slightest.

I didn't expect a sappy reunion, but I didn't imagine this... casual efficiency, either.

I prepared for awkwardness, tension. Not loneliness.

I thought we'd hug this morning when I picked him up. Maybe not for long.

But I thought we'd find a way to acknowledge who we used to be to each other. Try to hold those past selves in our arms for a minute before letting them go.

I didn't know that our ghosts would get in the way.

★

I spend the rest of our lunch chatting with Mr. and Mrs. Bevins. She's a health-care consultant and he's in copper rain gutters. They're grateful for my Disneyland tips, but I'm distracted. Trying not to eavesdrop on his work call.

Trying not to be disappointed that we're dining in a parking lot.

"...I should be checked in by four, I'll pull it up right away..." He laughs. "Yeah, I'm with a friend..."

I draw on Mrs. Bevins's Disneyland map, showing her how they should boogie immediately to the rear of the park, Frontierland or Mickey's Toontown, the second they're through the gates, then work their way back toward Main Street, USA. in a reverse commute.

But my mind's on *friend*.

When coworkers have asked me if I'm taking a date to this

out-of-town wedding, their voices and eyebrows floating up, mischievous, I've quickly corrected them:

*No, I'm going with an old friend. The bride invited each of us, it's a long story.*

"Can you circle the ride you were talking about, the tree?" Mrs. Bevins asks.

I mark her map. "It's not really a ride. Swiss Family Robinson island. Sorry, Tarzan's Treehouse, they call it now. You have to take a boat over, but she'll love it. It's one of the oldest attractions."

"We really appreciate it," Mrs. Bevins says. "You know, we couldn't afford to stay inside the park so we want to make the most of..."

I smile at her, but I'm listening to him on his business call. "I know, the timeline's brutal, I get it..."

*I get it.*

We've said this to each other at least ten times, in our emails leading up to the trip and today.

Three syllables meant to convey pure empathy.

Do *you get it?* I want to ask.

The Bevins family leaves and I call, "Have fun!"

He waves to them. A distracted goodbye, but I store it up as another small, consoling sign. *At least he waved to the Bevinses. At least he called me a friend.*

But the second they're out of sight, he's back to talking stats and jump reports and quarterlies. I notice a big drop of red-pepper aioli oozing from his sandwich, clinging to his focaccia roll for a minute, shivering, attenuating.

My hand jerks out to catch it with my napkin, but I pull back.

I crumple my napkin and watch as the pink glob breaks free and lands just above his right knee, melts into his expensive linen pants. Spreads into a peach-colored, thumbprint-size stain.

"Sorry about that, ready to hit the road?" His call over, he's standing, stretching.

"Yep, all set."

I don't point out the stain.

# 14

## Boondoggle

August 7, 1995
9:55 a.m.
Hotel Del Coronado, San Diego

The boondoggle was at the Hotel Del, as everyone called it. A sprawling California castle in San Diego—white with red tile funnel roofs, right on the sand.

Attendance at the boondoggle was mandatory.

"Derrek Schwinn's coming to the breakfast meeting so we need bodies," Stephen told me.

Derrek Schwinn was the money behind The Sexiest Search Engine in the Valley. That was what *Forbes* had called his company in an article I'd read twice, trying to understand data scaffolding. He'd been on the cover of that issue, not looking especially sexy. A pale man with lashless mole eyes behind horn-rimmed glasses, thinning strands of black hair pasted to his skull.

The article hadn't deciphered data scaffolding for me, but it had given me an excellent primer on "data sorting," the technology that first earned Schwinn big money. Schwinn was apparently the sorting king of Silicon Valley.

I dressed carefully that morning, in a narrow black skirt, ivory blouse, and black blazer I'd bought full price at Macy's. It ate up a whole paycheck—my only splurge this summer besides Wag Dos—but I wanted to look mature, professional.

And yes, pretty, in case a certain other *body* showed up. A body that had vanished since our lunch.

I'd been scanning the conference room for an hour, helping Stephen set up, but though I recognized Derrek Schwinn, Cal wasn't there.

Stephen stationed me on the wall in front of a blasting air-conditioner vent, between the door and a table of Danish, then bustled off importantly to help with the projector. Two long, white-clothed tables were arranged like a giant equal sign in the red-carpeted room. Derrek Schwinn took the seat reserved for him. The best spot, a chair closest to the projector screen at the far table.

Inside the equal sign, the chief marketing officer paced, psyching herself up for what Stephen called her "preso."

"We're just about to get started, so load up on those pastries while you can," she deadpanned, and everyone laughed.

I forced a smile, feeling like part of the show because of my proximity to the Danish. He wasn't coming. I'd been so sure he would.

Someone dragged the curtains shut, the first slide appeared on the screen, and everyone turned to watch.

He sailed in a second before the lights went out.

Sailed—there was no other word for it.

Unhurried, smiling, smooth, gliding across the front of the room. Not ducking, though the projector beam covered his suit in logos: CommPlanet's little chomping globe, the fat red *N* for NoozeButton, a dozen other focus-grouped images that, with hard work and luck, would become *huge*.

He claimed the seat at Derrek Schwinn's left. Clapped Schwinn on the shoulder as he settled into his chair, reached to pour coffee from a thermos, shifted his body to the right to watch the screen.

*So this is how he acts in a meeting. This is how he sits in a gold hotel chair.*

I watched him. No boyish tilting back today, like during our courtyard *bite*. But the ease was the same.

He listened attentively, taking in CommPlanet's "global branding reach…its highly scalable, customizable utility…" And my old friend, "scaffolding."

No one would guess that he mocked such jargon in private. He seemed as comfortable with the billionaire beside him as he was with the gate attendant at The Heights. He seemed not to care what anyone thought of him.

Was that the secret, not caring so much?

There were thirty-one slides in the presentation; it was identical to the packets I'd compiled with Stephen around the conference room table. On the tenth slide, as my mock-up article on pet spas flashed on the screen, he poured more coffee. On the twentieth slide, Schwinn whispered to him. On the twenty-fourth, he knit his fingers, rotated his hands, and stretched his arms high above his head.

On the twenty-fifth, he looked my way.

I smiled at him.

He didn't return my smile, as people say. Because mine was a discreet greeting, one corner of my mouth barely curving up. *Yep, it's me. Manning the pastry table in a power suit.*

What he returned was a brilliant, surprised grin.

And then his face changed. Surprise fell away, and I caught the faintest of head shakes. *Look at these poor souls*, his expression said. As if he was telling me something that only I would understand, sending the private message over every other attentive-but-clueless head in the room.

I dared myself not to look away.

★

When the lights came on and everyone stood, I lost him.

"You should head back now, Rebecca," Stephen said, impressing the out-of-town partners standing nearby with the fact that he had an underling.

There were more activities planned—a bocce ball tournament on the lawn with mimosas, a luncheon in the four-star Hotel Del restaurant—but apparently they were for VIPs only. My *body* was no longer needed to impress Schwinn or anyone else.

Irritated, I followed the hotel's network of thin outdoor boardwalks and narrow, red-carpeted halls to the front lobby. I took my blazer off and slung it over my shoulder; the AC in Wag Dos was busted, and now that I didn't need to look professional I wanted only comfort.

In an alcove by the gift shop I spotted flickering grayish light and bodies packing in. Impulsive, curious, I ducked into the standing room–only space: it was a film about the hotel's history, played on a loop.

I'd missed the beginning, but I caught the section about how *Some Like It Hot* had been filmed at the Hotel Del, and how the ghost of a murdered woman supposedly haunted the halls. Much more entertaining than the *Global Branding Opportunities* show I'd just watched.

*Take that, Stephen. I'll make my own boondoggle.*

When the lights came on and we filed out, I found myself wedged in the middle of a pack of bodies. A German tour group, a family with two whiny toddlers.

And Derrek Schwinn. "Did you enjoy that?"

I assumed he'd recognized me from the presentation and answered with salesy brightness. "It was really interesting!"

"Have you seen the movie? *Some Like It Hot*?"

He pronounced the title too slowly, too academically, and if his eyes weren't roaming down the neckline of my blouse as he asked the question it might have been funny.

But instead I was acutely aware of how thin my blouse fabric was. It was called a "shell," not a real shirt. I'd never intended to wear it around work people without the jacket.

"Yes. A long time ago."

"They show it here every night, I read. In every room."

Perfectly harmless words, on their face. But he was married, I knew from the article. And his eyes were still inches too low. I felt pinned and only managed a quiet, "How cool."

We were at the door now, him a little in front of me, holding up the family behind us. But he seemed in no hurry to leave.

I wanted to be in my Wag Dos, miles up the freeway. Breathing in exhaust fumes in bumper-to-bumper traffic, my thighs sticking to the torn upholstery—it would be heaven, if it could get me away from this man and his roaming, shameless mole eyes.

But I couldn't cut in front of him. He'd been on the cover of *Forbes*.

"There you are!"

Cal. Behind me, beaming.

"So you've met? Rebecca, Derrek Schwinn. Derrek, this is Rebecca Reardon, one of our best summer analysts. On the media side. She goes to Berkeley."

I extended a hand and Derrek Schwinn shook it.

When he spoke again it was to my face, not my blouse, and his voice no longer hinted an invitation to watch *Some Like It Hot* in his suite.

The sorting king had moved me into another category. "Very nice to meet you, Rebecca. I'm a visiting lecturer at Berkeley, in the biz department. Beautiful campus."

"Yes."

"You've got to make an appearance at that bocce whatever-it-is, Derrek, or people will lose their jobs."

Schwinn laughed. "We can't have that."

Cal clapped an arm around him and led him toward the door. He threw me a quick glance over his shoulder, rolling his eyes.

# 15

## The Person Who Says Yes

August 25

WHERE I WAS SUPPOSED TO BE | My well-appointed cubicle
WHERE I WAS | The *Summer Hours*

After the boondoggle in San Diego, the success of my workday depended on if I saw him or not. If he came in more often
than he used to or not, if he talked to me more than necessary
or not, if it seemed his eyes lingered on mine, or on my lips or
legs, a second longer than the last time.

I tried to ignore the countdown of weeks until I had to return
to Berkeley. I stared at myself in my bedroom mirror, replay-
ing our conversations, trying to determine what he thought of
me. I tried to look pretty for him. I calculated and fantasized.

I knew my interest in this person was only a naughty game
I was playing in my head. Like the job, it was ridiculous. Only
a way to pass the time until fall.

But the last Friday before school, I returned from lunch to a blinking amber light on my phone. The beginning of the voice mail was broken up and crackly.

"…having a little thing on the boat and I forgot…marketing brochure I promised…the blue glossy one from the off-site, if the office can spare you, I'd love it if you could bring a few… convenient."

The end of his message was clear, as if he'd held the phone closer to his mouth and stopped walking around for that part. "…but, hell, it's a beautiful day out here, you can have a long lunch. Balboa Marina, slip 19. Call me on the cell if you have trouble finding it. This is Cal, by the way."

I imagined him sitting on the boat deck in rolled-up white pants. Whipping wind and seagulls.

I punched 1. "…having a little thing on the boat and I forgot… marketing brochure I promised…the blue glossy one from the off-site, if the office can spare you, I'd love it if you could bring a few…convenient. But, hell, it's a beautiful day out here, you can have a long lunch. Balboa Marina, slip 19. Call me on the cell if you have trouble finding it.

"This is Cal, by the way."

He had no reason to ask me to fetch brochures. The office spent a fortune on messengers.

I looked around the deserted office. Everyone was across the street at Little Green, filling plastic containers with overpriced arugula and cherry tomatoes, or else in San Francisco for some funding meeting.

I grabbed the brochures from the dark storeroom and drove to Balboa Marina, parking on PCH. I tilted the rearview mirror down but couldn't read the expression in my own eyes. Fear and excitement battling to form something I hadn't seen before.

★

My pumps had horrible kitten heels that felt like they'd been placed for maximum instability, even though the saleswoman at

Macy's had talked them up as a comfortable alternative to real heels. A total lie.

I had to mince down the bouncing network of wooden ramps, passing boats with witty names painted onto their expensive rears. *Aquaholic. Mark and Rita Ville. Good Moorning.*

Then, when I was about to turn back, the one I was looking for, way at the end. *Summer Hours.* I stepped carefully onto the deck, setting my shoes on the elegant towel provided, next to expensive-looking loafers and heels. Laughter and jazz floated from the other end, and a caterer in a black skirt and white button-down nodded to me as she ducked down into the cabin with a tray.

I'd been so sure he'd made up the "thing on the boat." That the slick blue brochures I clutched were only a pretext, and I'd be the only guest. But it was too late to leave. I'd been spotted.

It felt like the boat was packed, because everyone was so sharply dressed and confident and loud, although later I'd count only nine people. Cal held court in the center, in a blue dress shirt with rolled-up sleeves, as always.

"This is Rebecca Reardon," he said, accepting the brochures. "She's interning for that thing I was telling you about and they need her. So don't anybody be hiring her away."

He pressed my arm. "Please stay."

I ordered white wine from the makeshift bar and the bartender gave me more choices—*dry, sweet? Dry* sounded more sophisticated. The glass he handed me was shaped like a wineglass, but it was plastic. Real boat people were serious about keeping glass off the deck, Eric had told me once.

Eric. I pictured him in New York in a dark warehouse, sorting through dusty film canisters.

*Look at you, Becc, with your hair up and your glasses off and your straight skirt and your sale-bought heels sharing a towel with all that designer leather.*

*What did you do with my friend?*

Cal wouldn't have invited me in midday sunlight, in front of a bunch of professional contacts, male and female, if he was thinking anything close to the things I was thinking. My fantasy was the result of too much time alone and too little time with anyone my age. I'd gulp my wine and jump ship.

And next summer I'd finally get a journalism internship somewhere. Or even a nanny gig with Serra in Tahoe, or fly to Maine with Maggie and take phone orders at L.L. Bean.

A heavy guy in a pink shirt introduced himself, pumping my hand, but I immediately forgot his name. You were supposed to repeat names out loud immediately, then come up with a mnemonic device. Like, picture a person named Sam eating green eggs and ham.

The pink shirt man asked how "the kids" were watching movies these days. "Do you still go to video stores, Rebecca?"

"I do, but I may be the exception."

"So what are you going to do after graduation?"

"Work at a newspaper."

The word *newspaper* was so beneath consideration that it got magically transformed between my lips and his eardrums.

"Online news, brilliant. If I were your age, I'd move straight to Silicon Valley. Go north, young woman." He said this last bit in a shaking old-man voice, waggling a finger. "Pick the right startup, get a piece of it, then hold on like a dog with a bone until you're vested."

*Vested.* I'd heard it at the office. It didn't seem apparel related; I'd look it up.

Everyone on the boat made an effort with me, and because it was easier, and I feared my foolish daydreams about our host were obvious to them all, I let myself become their project.

There was a bald minor producer. "Know that famous Robert Evans line? Everywhere you go there are a hundred people who can say no and only one person who can say yes? So the idea is you're supposed to find that one person who can say yes? But he was wrong."

Dramatic pause as he ate a big piece of salmon sushi. He wiped wasabi off his lips with a napkin.

"The trick is to *become* the person who says yes. Right? Don't you want to become that person?"

"Yes."

But I didn't know if I wanted to become that person. Or join the internet gold rush, or hold on to my piece of the startup pie like a dog.

All the opportunity in the world. Scrimped-for ballet and clarinet lessons and three pairs of $80 running shoes a year, the Francine Haggermaker Scholar, and I was wasting it, resisting everyone's advice. Maybe I was just being stubborn, frittering away my brain with my dreams of working in a dying medium.

At least when I wasn't busy flirting with my thirty-two-year-old pretty-boy neighbor.

I slipped downstairs and opened a sliding door, looking for somewhere to hide out.

I found myself in a bedroom. The main one, from the looks of it. The bathroom tucked inside had a cunning little wood-paneled medicine cabinet above the sink.

I splashed my face and smoothed my hair. Patted my face dry and folded the towel back into thirds, threading it carefully into the wall holder.

Knowing the whole time that I would open the medicine cabinet.

Inch by inch I slid it down the groove.

He used Crest and Right Guard and Tylenol. Disappointing. But his shaving cream was a good find. Imported, retro English hard cream in an enamel mug, with a brush. It went with his car—no boring can of modern foam for him. It smelled, faintly, of vanilla. I replaced everything where it had been, re-splaying the hairs on the shaving brush, and slid the panel closed.

I touched the bed. There was something spongy and boat-specific about the mattress, and I sat on the edge to test it.

I leaned back against the pillows, and one minute turned to five. If he caught me, I'd say I had a headache. I closed my eyes. *Catch me.*

★

I woke to the sound of footsteps outside the door, and my first instinct was to pretend I was still sleeping, to stretch my limbs into some alluring, elegant grown-up pose. But at the sound of the door gliding open I couldn't do it, and when he came in I was scrambling up, hair pasted across my cheek. Far from elegant.

Cal laughed. "Were you napping?"

"Sorry. I had a... I should get back to work."

"Nonsense. It's what, 4:30? Join me on the deck for a drink. Everyone's gone."

★

"Sorry I can't offer you an egg cream," he said, pouring two club sodas, adding an inch of scotch to his.

"I'll have some of that, actually."

He hesitated, amused. But he uncapped the bottle and sloshed a bit into my cup, enough to tint it gold.

We sat on the stern, facing the open ocean, watching the boats coming and going. The breeze had picked up and there was a good-natured humming from the restaurant down the water. Once in a while a woman's voice separated itself, rising in a burst of merriment.

"Who were your guests?"

"Hmm. Two guys I did a deal with a couple of years ago, and the rest... Oh, I don't know. Former deals or future deals, former partners or future partners. Mostly former, I'm afraid."

"You're not as excited about your investments as you used to be?"

"Observant girl."

"They all had good advice for me."

"Such as?"

"I'm supposed to go to Silicon Valley and become the person who says yes and hold on like a dog with a bone." I sipped my drink. "Not necessarily in that order. Don't you think that's good advice?"

"Say it."

"What do you mean?"

"Tell me what you really thought. Of the advice. The party. I'm two drinks beyond being insulted."

"Doesn't it usually work the other way?"

"Not with me. I'm less touchy the more I drink. Shoot."

"Everyone was nice. Generous. Just so…sure of everything."

"I'll let you in on a state secret." He turned to me, his face grave. "Everyone's pretending."

"Even you?"

"Especially me. What a hideous sunset." He crinkled his eyes at me because it was, in fact, gorgeous on the harbor, the water tinged pink, the sky streaked orange and violet.

We watched the sun's accelerating fall to the horizon. Any minute it would touch water. White triangles, big and small, were heading out toward a low mass of land.

A speedboat swerved past one of the sailboats. Carelessly close, blasting music, seemingly oblivious to the near miss.

"Everyone goes a little crazy the last week of summer," he said, shaking his head. "I should call the Coast Guard on them."

"Are they all heading to Catalina?"

"Most are cocktail charters, they'll only do a two-hour loop. Listen. That's the *Sea Nymph II*. It plays the same damn song at the beginning of every cruise."

It was "Sailing."

"I like that song."

"Wait'll you hear it every sunset for two months. Next is

'Southern Cross'..." He froze with his drink aloft as the dreamy melody faded out and the emphatic guitar chords of the new song reverberated across the waves. "Another perfectly good tune ruined by Captain Gary of the *Sea Nymph*."

I leaned against the thin silver rail, straining to hear the lyrics. Something about survival, and being *vested*... "I keep hearing that word. *Vested*."

"It's *bested*," he said. "*Vested* relates to stock options."

"Oh—"

"Don't be embarrassed. Now listen. When they get to the line about *Avalon* they'll scream, because Avalon's the capital of Catalina," he said. "Wait for it..."

Sure enough, the drunken voices on the *Sea Nymph* rose up, ecstatic at this coincidence.

He smiled, raised his cup in a sarcastic toast to the receding charter boat.

"I think you're too hard on Captain Gary," I said. "It's not his fault if there aren't many decent sailing songs."

"Or that he's surrounded by men who suddenly find themselves without proper Southern California lodging, and have to sleep on a boat."

"I didn't... I hadn't heard. I'm sorry."

"It's okay. It's been almost two months now. We parted as friends, as they say." He drained his drink and set it on the seat. He hung his arms over the guardrail, resting his chin on the shining silver cord. "And boat living has grown on me."

A wake from the *Sea Nymph* reached us, heaving the boat up and down. "That's nice," I said. "Like a cradle."

"Are you implying that recently broken-up men like yours truly revert to babyhood when they come here? That we've got a little *regression* situation?"

"I didn't say that."

He laughed. "But there's probably a brilliant business in there somewhere."

"Do you see potential startups everywhere?"

"No." He shifted to face me, hooking his arm over the rail, his cheek on the top wire. His wide charmer's grin relaxed into a real one. "I'm talking nonsense. I think you make me a little nervous."

It wasn't too late to leave. To pretend he'd meant something else. I looked past him, at the small white triangle of the *Sea Nymph*. "I have a theory about why people carry lattes around. They're like sippy cups for grownups," I said. "Is that a business?"

I dared a glance, confirmed that his blue eyes were still watching me. I looked away, scanning the ocean, but I'd lost the *Sea Nymph*. "No? Well, I think it is. It's scalable, right? It's all about scalability, I've learned. Scalability and scaffolding and partnership synergy."

If I said goodbye and left right then, we could still act like he hadn't said it.

But I didn't say goodbye. And I didn't go.

I breathed deep. "You make me nervous, too."

Slowly, biting his lip in thought, he pulled his body from the guardrail. Took my cup and set it carefully next to his on the deck.

It was still light out. There were people on half the boats, starting their weekends.

But he slipped one warm hand under my knee and one under my jaw, tipping my chin up. He kissed me, a shallow kiss with the sweet, smoky kick of scotch, pulling back a degree until our lips were barely nuzzling, then pressing close again, his right hand venturing lower on my neck each time. His left hand circled the hollow behind my knee. The rocking of the boat, the undulating voices from the restaurant, the hard-then-soft rhythm of his hands and mouth, felt like part of one thing.

But when I opened my lips and crept my hand up to his shoulder, he pulled away. "Sorry."

Triple losses: warmth gone from my lips, behind my knee, my neck.

"Should we go downstairs?" I asked softly.

He shook his head. "That was a mistake. You're a nice girl, Rebecca. Did anyone ever tell you that?"

*Only about a thousand times.*

I made my voice light and teasing, brushed a hand on his knee. "I'm not that nice."

He removed my hand, squeezed it. "Don't."

"Don't what?"

"Pretend you're someone you're not."

I busied myself with my purse so he wouldn't see the tears gathering.

"Rebecca."

I stood. "I should get back. I have a ton of packing."

He grabbed my hand but I stared the other way, out toward Catalina.

"Rebecca, look at me. I lost my head for a minute and I'm sorry—"

"It's fine. Like you said. Everyone goes a little crazy the last week of summer."

# 16

## Hello, You

June 12, 1996
Dear Mrs. Haggermaker,
It's hard to believe it's been a year since my first letter
and half of my time as an undergraduate is over.
I remain incredibly grateful for the Haggermaker
Scholarship, and think of you daily.

While the last-minute closure of the *Courier* last
summer changed my plans, and I'm sure you miss
our dear old weekly as much as I do, I was able to
secure a job at a highly promising media incubator
in LA, and ~~was enriched by grateful for~~ learned a
lot from the experience.

~~The senior employees made an effort to mentor me.~~
~~Others on the team went out of their way to~~

By the end of the summer I'd

My roommates and I moved into Plato House, a well-respected community housing complex close to South campus.

Sophomore year flew by, and I maintained a 3.4 average. I wrote twenty-four articles for the student newspaper, including a prominent feature on

I bit my pen, staring vacantly out the porthole-style Victorian window of the narrow attic bedroom I shared with Serra and Maggie in Plato House. We kept the window cranked open all the time, even when it rained, to combat the funk inside our peeling Victorian co-op: curried lentils, pot, a top note of decades-old BO.

How to describe my journalism pursuits this year?

I was still stuck on the custodial beat. My punishment for refusing to give up on the cat graffiti, which hadn't abated.

"It's a small story, Rebecca," my editor, Brent of the ironic bow ties, had said. "Cute in a campus-color way, but small. When you have more experience you'll see. Bring me something *big*."

But when he was flattened by mono in November, I'd persuaded his fill-in to run what I thought was a decent article:

---

Cat Graffiti…or Rorschach Test?
*Theories about unofficial campus mascot abound*
By Rebecca Reardon

---

I'd not only written the piece—my longest yet, a whopping six column inches—I'd taken the photograph.

When Brent came back, he wasn't pleased. He assigned me three hundred words on the new hand dryers in the football stadium.

I'd made a copy of the graffiti story for Francine because at least it had run on the second page, but now it seemed too silly to include.

I settled on:

*I wrote twenty-four articles for the student newspaper, including a prominent feature on a popular campus artist.*

*I'm looking forward to a productive summer interning for the County Chronicle in Los Angeles. I'll be in the research department, though I hope to earn a byline before summer is over. I'm so grateful for the opportunity!*

*In my free time I plan to read John Donne, Emily Dickinson, and Emerson in preparation for next term. As you can see from the attached syllabi, it will be a busy year, and I wouldn't have it any other way.*

*I hope that you are well, and I am, as always, deeply grateful for your generosity.*
*Sincerely,*
*Rebecca Reardon*

"Becc! You up there?"

"Yeah!" I sealed the letter and stamped it.

*Thwack. Thwack-thwack-thwack.*

Hacky Sack Glenn was in the hall. He was like the human pet of Plato House. I found the constant, muffled whacks of his little sand-filled bag meeting flesh comforting. But he drove Serra nuts.

"It should be against house rules to hacky sack in only a towel," I heard Serra say, her usually sweet voice acid.

"Dude, I'm really sorry. I thought everyone was gone." Poor Glenn. Our room was tight for three, but at least we had a window. Glenn's $150-a-month converted closet, down the hall, was not only airless but so small he slept curled up, possum-style, on a crib mattress.

Serra bounded into the room, pink-faced and sweaty from loading the Stay Wag. She leaned against Maggie's tall, many-layered bed. (We had no bed frames, so all three of us slept on teetering stacks of futon pads and mattresses that had been abandoned in the co-op over the years, with our own new mattresses on the top. Our housemates called us the Princesses and the Peas.) "I made the *best* mix CD for the drive, wait'll you hear it. Are you ready?" She spotted the three balls of reject Francine letters on my desk and laughed. "I thought reporters were supposed to be good on deadline."

"It's hard to sum up a whole year."

"Last summer I had a boring internet internship… That's hard to say. In September I moved into the rattiest co-op on campus and, despite the CONSTANT hacky-sack noise outside my door…" this was shouted, for Glenn's benefit "…I passed all my classes. I survived on Blondie's pizza and Margaret's Chocolate Margs, a tasty beverage invented by my second-favorite roommate, made from one part tequila and one part General Foods International Suisse Mocha…"

"Ugh, don't remind me—"

"…the delightful concoction only made me throw up once. This summer my best friend and I will carpool to work in LA together. She's interning at LACMA and I'll be writing page-one scoops for the *County Chronicle*…"

"I'm an unpaid assistant to an assistant—"

"…and we're going to have a total blast. Thanks again for the dough, Rebecca Reardon."

★

This time my newspaper internship lasted nine days. Progress.

Nine days of carpooling to LA in the Stay Wag or Wag Dos with Serra, belting Indigo Girls. Nine days inside a real, big-city daily, the smell of newsprint and the vibration of the presses through the floor. Every morning, I passed the office of Harve Crane, a columnist who used to handcuff his leg to his desk until he filed his pieces, back in the 1950s. It was now a shrine, with a velvet rope across the doorjamb.

I got to see great rolls of newsprint, big as oil drums, in the docking bays by the parking lot. I eavesdropped on the reporters in the breakroom, covertly scribbling in my notepad when they used jargon I didn't understand, so I could look it up later.

I convinced an editor on the metro desk to read my clips, hoping she'd let me help her with research if she got to trust me.

She flipped through my stack of articles, laying them out silently, one by one, on her messy desk. They looked puny, pasted onto black eight-and-a-half-by-eleven pieces of construction paper.

"Eco-friendly vomit powder, huh," she said.

"I'm working my way up the masthead."

"This isn't bad, this graffiti thing."

"Thanks."

"Well, you're making the most of a shit beat. And I respect that, so I'll tell you what. Maybe at the end of summer you can shadow me to a council meeting."

"Thank you! I'd love that!"

"No promises."

But when I walked into the paper my second week I felt it in the air.

Closed doors, nervous phone whispers. The *Chronicle*'s classified ad revenue had tanked, and a bunch of veteran employees had taken buyouts. Including Gabe Hewitt, the fifty-nine-year-old editor in charge of me, the one who'd reluctantly agreed to my internship after I sent him a dozen emails.

"It's a pretty good deal," he said to the grim-faced colleagues clustered around his desk. "They've been wanting to get rid of my flabby butt for a decade."

To me he said, "I'm sorry, hon, ask HR what they can do," and gave me his dog-eared *AP Stylebook and Libel Manual* handbook.

The frazzled HR woman said, "I'm sorry, there's nothing I can do," and gave me a *Chronicle* windbreaker.

"But I'm working for free," I said. "There's a reporter in Metro I can help, Carla Dewey, she's already read my clips—"

"Carla accepted a job at Disney.com this morning. Maybe next summer."

So my internship floated away on Gabe Hewitt's golden parachute.

I couldn't break it to my mom. She'd bought me a second-hand Coach briefcase, $60, black leather. She'd subscribed to the *Chronicle* specially, reading it from cover to cover every night with her tea.

So even after the paper booted me, I continued leaving the house in my pantyhose and skirt and blazer and heels, a sleeveless shortie sundress and Keds in my Coach briefcase. I drove up to LA with Serra as if I was still expected somewhere.

I became an expert on the best public restrooms, changing from my reporter costume into my killing-time-downtown outfit at 8:50 a.m., then back again at 4:45 p.m. I could change in less than forty-five seconds; I was Clark Kent in the phone booth. I frequented libraries, parks, hotel lobbies. The Elephant Hotel, the Hyatt, the W.

I crisscrossed downtown LA—avoiding only a four-block radius around the CommPlanet office.

I memorized *AP Stylebook and Libel Manual* rules from my *Chronicle* parting gift (I was on *allege*. *"The word must be used with great care. Do not say 'he attended the alleged meeting' when what you mean is 'He allegedly attended the meeting...'"*).

I nursed iced coffees, I people-watched. At 12:30, I ate my bagged lunches with Serra on a shady bench in the museum sculpture garden.

"You're planning to keep up this ruse all summer?" she asked the third afternoon, scraping the last spoonful of her raspberry frozen yogurt. "Bumming around downtown all day? It's not your fault you got canned."

"She'll still worry."

"*I'm* worried."

"Don't be. And I'm not *bumming around.* I'm memorizing the whole *AP Stylebook.* I'm memorizing the streets of LA. By August I'm going to know them better than a cabdriver. It's actually a great opportunity. It'll come in handy when I'm a real reporter."

"Uh-huh."

The next morning I discovered a grand place for my studies: the Aquarius Hotel. A five-star, recently renovated. Sparkling restrooms, atrium lobby big enough that I didn't have to worry about being outed as a non-guest.

I'd been there for an hour when a businessman sat next to me, disturbing my peace. He was simultaneously talking on his phone, spreading a travel-size cream cheese on a toasted bagel from the coffee kiosk, and eyeing my legs. When he finished his bagel he strode off with his wheelie suitcase, leaving his plastic knife and napkin on the arm of his leather chair.

*Pig.*

But under the napkin, his gold keycard glinted at me.

I palmed it and rode the elevator up twenty floors. The bagel man's slob ways were my ticket to the rooftop pool: misters, music, padded chaises under shades big as sails, sweating glass urns of ice water in which lime rounds and mint fronds bobbed.

I claimed a lounger in a quiet corner by the glass safety wall, set the gold keycard on the table next to me so I'd look legit, and pulled out my *AP Stylebook* (I was now up to *damn it. "Use instead of dammit, but like other profanity it should be avoided unless there is a compelling reason."*)

And no one bothered me.

The card was deactivated the next day, but I snuck in behind a squabbling family of five.

I was proud of myself for finding the perfect hideout, for dealing with the problem of my mother so creatively. There were worse ways to spend the summer.

★

The next day I brought my swimsuit. It was ninety-eight degrees by one o'clock, according to the sleek digital thermometer by the exit door. One hundred degrees by two. I spent the afternoon submerged in the shallow end, the edges of my *AP Stylebook* ruffled from splashes.

At three, when the wall thermometer hit 102, I came out for a drink—lemon-basil today—and that was when I noticed it.

Three blocks west, in the hot, wavering air between me and the ocean.

CommPlanet, in chunky blue-green letters on the roofline of a silver high-rise. The *C* like the globe formed into a chomping Pacman mouth.

I left without toweling off.

★

"You're quiet," Serra said on the drive home.

"Am I?"

"What'd you do today?"

"Oh. Read in the main library again."

"Maybe you should go to the pier tomorrow. Get some fresh air?"

"I think I will."

But the next day I returned to the Aquarius, to a chaise directly facing the blue sign. I came back the next day, and the next.

After a fourth afternoon of staring at the bold blue-green letters so long they danced across my sunstroked eyelids when I shut them, I rode the elevator to a pay phone in the lobby and pulled a business card from my briefcase.

"McCallister here."

"Hi, it's…it's me."

If he didn't recognize my voice, I'd hang up.

A pause. "Hello, you. What a nice surprise."

"I was just calling to say I felt bad. For how I took off last summer."

"It wasn't your fault."

"I wasn't very mature."

"You were extraordinarily mature, considering what an idiot I was."

I felt the warming in his voice behind my knee, on my neck, my lips. Between my legs. I leaned my forehead against the cold glass door of the booth and closed my eyes. "You were right. It was crazy for us to… It wasn't a good idea."

"But it was highly enjoyable. And highly memorable."

"Well. That's all I wanted to say."

"Wait, how was your year? Are you up in Berkeley?"

"I'm… Oh, no. I'm in LA. I was working at the *County Chronicle* but they downsized. I seem to bring a curse to whoever hires me."

He laughed. "Not CommPlanet, at least, it's going gangbusters." A moment's hesitation, a husky lowering of his voice. "Hey, you know I would've called you. I didn't know where. Or if you wanted me to."

"I know."

"I thought about you this year." A pause. Wind, flapping; he was outside, on his boat. "If you're bored, I'll bet they could use your help at the incubator again. I was just in there last week. They're on their fourth round, hiring like mad. They've taken over three whole floors on Wilshire. Signage and everything."

"Really? I haven't seen it. But I've got my summer pretty mapped out."

"Sure, sure. I just thought… Hold on a sec."

I recognized the creak of the door to the cabin, stair *thumps*, the bounce in his breathing as he settled back on the bed. He'd carried me down into the bedroom, to speak in private.

"You still there?"

"Yeah."

"What I meant is, if you wanted to grab a coffee, or go for a little sail sometime, I'd like it very much."

"I'm not a sailor."

He laughed. "No certification required. You'd be my guest."

"Still. I wouldn't want to *pretend to be someone I'm not.*"

His voice grew more serious, confidential, as if we were in that dark study again, hiding away at a party. "I thought about that all year. About you. Maybe I was...hasty."

I'd told no one about my humiliation on the boat last August. I'd returned to school, determined to forget. I'd gone on three dates a week, sometimes more. Piling on memories of other smiles, voices, bodies.

I'd had dates to the chancellor's ball, Fondue Fred's restaurant. Study dates at Caffè Strada, group dates at football game bonfires. Dates to frat parties.

*Don't say* frat, *Rebecca,* red-faced Keith Furyg had scolded me, pumping a keg in the Kappa Ep courtyard during Pimps and Hos. *Say* fraternity. *Would you call your country a cunt?*

I'd had kisses. Rushed, wet, tasting of beer, right out in the open. I'd messed around with a funny sophomore in my anthro seminar and a shy journalism grad student, and while these nights were satisfying in their way, the pleasure didn't last past 2:00 a.m.

I missed patience, the sweet, smoky taste of scotch. And the gut thrum of the forbidden.

Instead of obscuring my memory of Cal, the hours I spent with boys at school slid to the edges and collected around it, like a frame.

Nearly a year since I'd spoken to him last, and he was still in the center. The picture varied but it was always shining, intact: him across a café table, tilting his chair back and laughing, hanging over the wall of my cubicle and drumming his hands. Leaning over the wire safety rim of his boat and smiling lazily, a moment before...

I gripped the phone tight. "Maybe I could think about the job."

# *17*

## She-Ra

July 11, 1996

Two weeks after I started working at CommPlanet again, Cal left me a message, asking me to go to San Diego Comix-Fest to take notes on a friend's presentation. "Sorry to ask because, I won't lie, it'll be a snooze." It sounded like he was outside.

I told Stephen and he said, "Whatever." Distracted, half-hidden behind the pink tent of the *Financial Times*. "Record your mileage."

The convention center was overflowing with people dressed as She-Ra and Batman and a bunch of characters I didn't recognize, and some boring people—the money people, I guess—who were dressed in suits or trim dresses like I was.

The presentation was called "Advertising Opportunities in Massive Multiplayer Game Platforms."

Cal's friend hadn't exactly packed them in. And we didn't have any of the costume wearers. I took a seat four rows back and diligently took notes.

Half an hour into the presentation, someone picked my jacket up from the seat next to me. I whispered a protest and then saw who it was. Not a stranger in a costume or a suit.

Him, in a white button-down with the sleeves rolled up and elegantly wrinkled navy linen shorts. Smiling at me.

I tried to concentrate on the presentation. And my breathing.

Ten minutes later, he passed me a note on the back of a Comix-Fest map.

*Guess I dragged you to the worst presentation in the building.*

I smiled, looked back at the podium. There was no earthly reason for him to be there.

I scribbled illegible notes on *lightweight plugins* and *player portability.*

When I wanted to write, *What are you doing here? What are you doing here? What are you doing here?*

Five minutes later, he handed me the paper again. He'd made a grid of dots in blue pen.

It was the beginning of a game. Dots and Boxes. You were supposed to take turns connecting two dots, and every time you completed a square, you put your name inside. The goal was to get the most squares.

I connected two dots and passed him the paper. He drew his line and passed it back to me. We looked at his friend droning on, and tried not to draw attention, like we were in school and we'd get in trouble.

I won the first game, and dutifully recorded my miniscule *Rebecca* inside the box, even though my hand was sweating so much my handwriting was wobbly, and even though my mind was on repeat (*what is he doing here what is this what is this well you know exactly what he's doing here. He's called your bluff now, Becc*).

He won the next game and recorded his *Cal* in tiny printing.

We'd won four squares each when he gently pulled my elbow. "Come on," he whispered.

As people started lining up behind the mics, full of burning questions about lightweight plugins, we slipped out the back.

"So I guess...you were able to come down after all," I said in the hallway.

"Yeah. Change of plans."

"Should you wait to say hi to your friend?"

"I should." He looked at me evenly. "What I shouldn't do is ask you to eat lunch on the beach with me. Play hooky for an hour."

★

We spread a windbreaker from his car on the sand near the amusement park in Mission Beach. Far enough from Belmont Park that the boardwalk and roller coaster noises didn't drown out the surf, but close enough that we could hear the people screaming on the PenduLator, a ride that swung back and forth like a giant metronome, and see the cars on the Giant Dipper coaster as they creaked up to the peak. I loved that pause right at the top, before the plummet.

The windbreaker we sat on said Ironman SuperFrog 1990 on the pocket.

"What's a SuperFrog?" I asked.

"A race I had no business entering. I did it on a dare, but I was completely unprepared. Nearly drowned and blew out my ACL on the run." He bent his right leg to show me his knee.

I toyed with the plastic wrap on my sandwich from the conference center, staring down at the four pale pink dots around his kneecap. Chopstick surgery, they called it.

I wondered if the scarred parts felt the same as the surrounding skin.

He unwrapped his sandwich and took a big bite, swallowing politely before speaking. "So CommPlanet... It's either turned you on to an internet career or soured you on it for good."

"Yes."

He laughed. "A wonderfully clever dodge. So, still stuck on the dead trees?"

"I wish I could've bought the *Courier*. Is that nuts?"

"I wouldn't have advised it from an investment standpoint."

"Not that I'm not grateful for the money. And it feels good to have people expecting me, someplace to go every day besides the movies or the beach."

"She says from the sand."

"It wasn't my idea."

He grinned, stared out at the water. "I *am* a degenerate. But here's a secret. Your tidy orange cubicle makes this…" he waved his sandwich at the supine bodies, the wet heads bobbing in the waves "…possible. One can't exist without the other."

"Are you saying work is only ever…a place we escape? It only exists so we can enjoy our free time?"

"Precisely. What? You don't agree."

"I hope it's not true. It can't be true. Not if you find work you love."

"Remarkably uncynical of you."

The Giant Dipper was near the top, under the flags, on its final clicking ascent, and we craned our necks to watch it. Riders would be holding their breath, closing their eyes. They screamed as it whooshed down the white track, pivoting, swooping out of view.

"That's one of the original wooden coasters," I said.

"How reassuring."

"They're solid. Better than those rusty carnival rides. Have you ever seen the crews fit one of those together? I think they leave parts behind in each town. And at the Orange County Fair the operators are always methed out."

"Stop." He pretended to shudder. "I have a slight coaster phobia."

"I thought you did those crazy triathlons for people who're bored with regular triathlons?"

"Ah, but then I'm in control," he said. "It's funny. You never struck me as the roller-coaster type. More…"

"The watching-them-from-a-distance type?"

"Hmm."

"I guess I am. I have been."

I set my sandwich aside, untouched, and ran my hands in the sand, sifting it through my fingers, forming a little hill. He reached down, too, his fingers occasionally brushing against mine as we dug and scooped, playing in the silky pile.

"People resist all our attempts to make them predictable," he said.

I looked up, but he was staring off at the roller coaster, smiling.

When he smiled, there was a little sadness in his eyes, a flicker I could only see up close. Without that I might have fled. But it felt like honesty and drew me closer.

★

As I headed home on PCH, I wrote a mental list:

*He's too old.*

*He smiles too much.*

*He'd lose interest the second you slept with him.*

And another reason, of course. The one that was so big, stretching in every direction, it was like the infinite surface on which all of the others were only scribbles:

*You can't do this to Eric.*

I studied my reflection in the rearview mirror. My eyes were lit from the side, strangely shadowed from the sunset. Today we hadn't done any more than touch hands under hot sand. We hadn't even kissed. But the thrill of the brief, hidden contact and what it promised had produced a look on my face that I'd never seen before. Equal parts excitement and disbelief.

*You should look surprised.*

*You shouldn't believe it.*

*Because it's wrong.*

But at the first stoplight I examined the girl in the rearview mirror again. And burst out laughing at our shared secret.

# 18

## Ships Passing in the Night

July 12, 1996
6:30 p.m.

"Honey, guess what? Where are you?"

"In here!"

My mom appeared in my bedroom doorway pink with excitement, holding her overstuffed paper grocery bag. Celery leaves poking over the top shook as she burst out, "I ran into Donna Logan in the Ralph's parking lot and she's having a pool party tonight and she invited both of us!"

Everything about this sentence was wrong.

1. Donna Logan didn't shop at Ralph's. She shopped at Dominico's Fine Gourmet or used caterers. 2. Her parties, though usually centered around the pool, had never involved actual *usage* of the pool. 3. My mother never got invited anywhere. 4. She never wanted to go anywhere.

She looked so eager. Flattered that Donna Logan had tossed an invitation down to her, a woman whose low brown house crouched below hers like a supplicant kneeling before the pope.

*You know it was a pity invite, right?*

"Mom. I really don't want to go up there. We won't know anybody."

"We'll know each other! Get your suit on, it'll be good for us! We can't mope around here every Friday night."

She meant me. I was the moper. Serra was in heaven at her gallery job and worked a lot of openings and benefits, so she couldn't hang out on weekends as much as I wanted to. I had spent my summer nights alone in my bedroom, staring out the window as headlights glided down from The Heights.

Lying on my bed imagining another kiss, his hands on the small of my back. I would not be wearing a Gap sundress this time, but something elegant and backless. And his hand wouldn't hover politely as it had in the study at the graduation party. Skin on skin, him tugging my dress down, me unbuttoning his shirt, his pants. These thoughts were so exciting I feared that they would seep through my closed bedroom door down the hall.

Evidence of my wrongness that could get me busted, like the pot smoke Maggie took great pains to conceal at school. But clearly I'd hidden my fantasies well enough; from the other side of the door, my excitement looked like depression.

My mom was in her room already, humming, opening drawers. "Wear that black one-piece bathing suit, it's so cute on you," she called.

"Nobody actually goes swimming at Mrs. Logan's parties."

"She said *specifically* that there would be swimming. I wouldn't be caught dead in a suit, of course, nobody wants to see that spectacle. But you should swim. It's so hot, it'll feel terrific!"

"She doesn't really want me there. I only got invited in high school because—"

"She does want you there! She adores you, she said so. *How's that gorgeous, brilliant daughter of yours?* I told her how great you're doing at school. And she said she'd invited Francine Haggermaker!"

*Ah. Way to bury the lede, Mom.*

"Don't just sit there, get dressed!" She'd already changed into her hot-pink paisley-print dress and white blazer, her gold earrings, necklace, and bracelet. It was her best outfit, the one she wore whenever a friend from work had a birthday or retirement dinner at Chili's.

The color of the dress did bring out the pretty bloom in her still-soft cheeks, but it was so '80s. Too bright, the shoulder pads in the linen blazer too bunchy. Too many pieces of too-delicate gold jewelry. White Naturalizer flats matching the jacket. She'd placed three pink hot rollers in her hair: one on her bangs, two at her temples. When she removed them they'd frame her face in three shiny brown hair cylinders, something she always did to fancy up her no-nonsense bob.

So much effort to look so wrong.

Mrs. Logan would host her party in a simple tennis dress, hair skinned into a chic low ponytail.

"Mom, please. I don't want to go."

Her face fell. "But you have to. You *have* to. I told her you would and she'll... They'll... Everyone will be so disappointed!"

The Logan house was haunted. In Eric's bedroom, faded versions of Eric and Serra and me sprawled on his floor, laughed, dug through the CDs and tapes in his music crate. Another Becc, a more innocent one, blushed in the study while her friends waited for her above.

Ghosts everywhere. Part of me wanted to burrow under my bedspread and hide from them.

"She said she's always wanted to have a girls lunch, get to know the two of us better, isn't that nice?"

So flattered that Mrs. Logan had confided to her in a parking lot, taking the BS lunch invite seriously.

"Please, Becc. It's her birthday and she told me she's a little sad about it. She said she's had a rough year, the divorce and that... fling with that younger man and all."

Was that what we were calling him? *That younger man.*

*Hey, guess what? I saw that younger man a few hours ago! He's not younger to me, of course. He has a constellation of four scars around one knee, did you know that? I think about touching them all the time. Connecting the dots. Dots and Boxes, that's a game we played. It sounds boring but with the right person, a child's game with pen and paper can be as exciting as a kiss…*

"That's why it'd be weird, with me working at her ex's—"

"Oh, that's silly, you said he's hardly involved."

She looked heartbroken, standing there in her freshly ironed, clearance-sale Royal Robbins linen jacket, holding her arms out to the side, scarecrow-style, so she wouldn't wrinkle it. She'd never asked me to go to a party with her.

*Be kind.*

*Be kind. Rewind.*

The *rewind*, in her case, was that she hadn't dated since my father died. Seventeen years. He got esophageal cancer when I was one, and though I'd stared for hours at pictures of him cradling a swaddled-up, infant me, fascinated each time that this stranger gave me my widow's peak and long legs, I'd never felt I had a right to miss him.

My mom said, *It was horribly sad but I'm perfectly content now.* Her other big motto was *I'm just fine on my own!* She'd supported me all alone; she'd tried so hard to give me everything. Working at her soul-draining job, never complaining.

But her life seemed so lonely, so safe. As small and stuck in the past as the house.

And though I knew it was wrong, a sliver of me wanted to observe Mrs. Logan, the woman who'd intoxicated Cal. See if she really didn't mind me working at her ex's company.

"I'll go for an hour."

★

I floated on one of Mrs. Logan's designer rafts in the deep end. The only other guests who'd gotten wet were two couples in the hot tub, their drinks raised high above the waterline.

My mom had found her own raft: the white-tableclothed hors d'oeuvres table in the shade, by the pool house. She clung to it, telling everyone loading up their plates that they should try the dates stuffed with goat cheese—*they're delicious!* In her white coat, she looked like a caterer.

Mrs. Haggermaker was a no-show, thank god.

Mrs. Logan had been surrounded when we'd arrived so she'd only smiled at us and called to my mom, distracted, "So glad you could make it. We'll have to have that girls lunch soon!"

The empty pleasantry thrilled my mom.

I observed Donna Logan from my raft, this woman Cal had desired enough to *keep a few things* at her house. She owned her own business. She was confident and undeniably beautiful. Her white halter-tank dress set off her tan tennis-toned shoulders, and blond ponytail.

Bits of her conversation floated to me over the water. She thanked people for coming, introduced them to each other, accepted compliments on her unusual sandals: wedge-heeled, indigo espadrilles with ballet straps that she'd "picked up on the street" on a recent girls trip to Capri.

"We'll go together next time," she said to someone. Like the promised girls lunch with my mother, I knew that this Italy trip would never happen. It was only an expedient thing to say in the moment.

Maybe this was what he'd admired—her deftness at parties.

And my awkwardness, my inexperience, were only his new kinks. He'd get bored with them, too. Probably in way less time than his *fling* with her.

A burly, new man lingered near Mrs. Logan, staking his claim. A dark mat of hair sprang from his forearms and the collar of his white Nike golf shirt, but he was bald inside his black visor, which ringed his shiny head like a monk's tonsure. Was she interested? Mrs. Logan touched his elbow a few times, so it seemed she was.

She'd rebounded with Cal's physical opposite and seemed happy. My mom had made it sound like she was devastated.

Speaker jazz, laughter, the *clinks* of forks on china. Except for my mom's social flails by the buffet table behind me, it wasn't so bad. I'd cruise around on my raft for another half hour, then slip out the side gate when nobody was watching.

The music stopped, the *clinks* of one fork rose above the others, purposeful, and everyone hushed. Mrs. Logan's voice carried, sure and smooth, across the yard, and her guests gathered close until I couldn't see her.

"I didn't want to jinx it, because I wasn't sure he'd actually make his flight, but…" A shuffling near her. Her voice dropped as she murmured to someone nearby, "Come over here." Louder: "Look who's here. My prodigal son. He only flew into John Wayne from Boston an hour ago, so he's a little shell-shocked by the OC. We need to let him acclimate."

Everyone laughed.

"Anyway, I couldn't ask for a better birthday present. He'll be mad if I get too mushy, but I'll say one more thing. He's only here for the night because he has a big job in Vancouver this summer, but I'm a happy girl. Yes, *girl*. We'll ignore the horrid number that shall not be named."

More laughter, *aws*. A few *hear, hears*.

I couldn't see him. He was hidden behind a wall of polo-shirted backs.

But I felt him. A warm knot behind my breastbone that uncoiled until it was a line, living and taut, pulling me.

"Becc!" My mom, gleeful. "Becc, can't I keep a secret? Look!"

I pretended not to hear. I let the raft spin me away from the patio and closed my eyes.

The conversations and music rose up again, just like before.

Except that warm line from me to him was still there, tugging me. I knew what Mrs. Logan would be doing now. She'd be hugging him too tight, ruffling his hair.

He'd be pulling away from her, scowling at the new, bald consort.

"Becc's here somewhere," Mrs. Logan would say, scanning her yard for her only other guest under thirty.

So. That was why she'd invited us. And my mom had known, assuming—why wouldn't she?—that I'd be thrilled to see him.

He hadn't emailed in months, not even to say he'd be in town. He'd offered me no reason to believe that he missed me. And now he was blowing through Orange Park on a one-night layover.

*One whole night! So nice of you to give me a heads-up. So generous of you to grace us with your presence, Eric. Your mom's birthday and all. You really went out of your way.*

"Becc!" My mom, louder now, positive that I simply hadn't heard the news or I'd be tearing across the patio, dripping wet. "Becc, get out, look who's here!"

I rolled off my raft, face-first into the silky water, kicking hard until I touched the slick white bottom of Mrs. Logan's pool. I waited in the beautiful empty room. For what?

For Eric to cannonball down to me.

I could see it.

It would be like the old him to splash into his mother's perfect party. One well-placed cannonball would soak the couples in the hot tub, dilute their cocktails.

If he plummeted down here, if he sensed where I was and came to me, maybe I'd forgive him. Maybe.

It was the only reunion I could handle.

Just us, hiding. A silent, shared joke.

My lungs were still strong from my years of high school track. They protested and burned, but I stayed under, waiting, watching the surface. It remained clear: an undulating, bright blue OC sky. I waited and waited, but no crash came.

Gulping air as I burst up, I found him out of the corner of my eye. A tall, dark shape, standing with my mom by the crowded food table.

"Look! Becc, look who it is!"

I side-stroked to the ladder and climbed out, sat on the edge.

He waved. A slow, exaggerated greeting, a full 180-degree sweep of his arm.

I returned the wave, degree for ironic degree, my dripping arm mirroring the arc of his.

His hair was a little shorter but still messy. His shoulders strained against his dark T-shirt. And though he was still thin, the taut, boyish lines of his body had changed, his divots and angles had smoothed out.

But the sun was behind him and I couldn't see his face.

My mom, wound up as a child, patted his arm. "Eric, can you come for ice cream? Spend the night? No, of course you'll want to spend time with your mother. But how nice of you to fly out for her birthday! Becc, isn't it wonderful? Get over here!"

I stood. Slowly. Pausing to wipe my nose and tug my suit down at the hips.

"Hey," he said when I walked over. "Been a while. Two years?"

*Twenty-three months and one week.*

I cleared my throat. "Yeah."

"Give him a hug!" my mom said.

I looped an arm over his shoulder from a good foot away, bowing awkwardly at the waist, stepping back with a nervous laugh before his hands could leave his sides.

"She doesn't want to get you wet. He's only here for one night, Becc, but wasn't it sweet of him to arrange a layover?"

"One night?" I said.

"You didn't hear my mom's big intro?"

"I must've been underwater," I lied.

"Got it. Yeah, I fly up to Vancouver to meet a good friend from school tomorrow, first thing. She got us work on a cable series in her hometown."

*Good* friend. I imagined her, the offspring of Pamela Anderson and Steven Spielberg. My replacement.

"Your mom told me all about the job this afternoon, Eric. She's so proud of you! Becc, isn't it wonderful? Look at you two, it's just like back in high school!"

*No. It most definitely isn't, Mom. And you know it isn't, or you wouldn't be working so hard to bury that fact in chatter.*

"They need us right away," he said. "A last-minute thing, you know how it is. You have another big media internship this summer?"

Subtle emphases on *media* and *internship.* Still disgusted about CommPlanet.

"She's working so hard, Eric. Going to conferences out of town and putting in late hours and everything."

"Oh, yeah? That's awesome." To my mother, nodding his approval.

"They offered me a good salary for the rest of the summer. I'm learning a lot."

"Well," Eric said. "Sounds like you're in demand. I wouldn't have expected anything different."

"Becc, tell him about the article in the *Times.*"

"You wrote something for the *Times?*" Eric said. "I'd like to read it, where—?"

"Mom, Eric doesn't want to hear my boring work stories."

"It's not boring! Eric, she didn't *write* the article, exactly—"

"I didn't write it at all."

"Well. Okay, but it was about the ten hottest new companies in LA, Eric, and one of them is where she's working. It made it sound *so* exciting... Becc can explain it better than me. It's really too bad you're only here for one night. You two are like... ships passing in the night. Or...you know what I mean."

"I do," he said to her, kindly.

"Next time you'll stay longer. Maybe at the end of the summer, before you go back to school? Wouldn't that be nice, Becc?

We'll dust off the pinball table in the garage. Becc hasn't played pinball *once* since high school."

"Serra will be sorry she missed you," I said, staring right at him. "She's working at the museum tonight. An opening."

"How cool. She emailed about the job, she said she couldn't believe they were paying her."

"She'd have blown it off if she knew you were in town. If you'd let us know." I couldn't hold back the needle of accusation.

His voice was tight but he kept his eyes on mine. "Like I said. It was a last-minute thing."

I looked down, nodding.

Words were messing everything up. I wanted to jump into the pool and hide out at the bottom, where we couldn't talk if we wanted to. Eric and I could stay down there until everyone else left and we could figure it out.

*Figure it out? Like a calculus problem? Why don't you say* figure it out *one more time, Becc?*

My mom, almost pleading now: "We're just glad to see you, even if it's not for as long as we'd like. Right, Becc?"

"Eric! Come say hi to the Garlands!" Mrs. Logan, summoning him to the patio.

"You should go say hi," I said. "The Garlands await."

A pause. "Right, I guess I should. Well, I'll find you later. And we'll catch up."

"Sounds good."

He waited for me to say more. To look up.

And I wanted to. The warm line was still between us.

I wanted to give in to it, to come close and search his eyes for something real, hurt or hope or confusion mirroring my own in their brown depths.

I felt him watching me. But I stared at his black Vans a second too long, and by the time I looked up, he was saluting me. An army gesture, flat hand knocking his eyebrow.

Once it would've been funny.

★

I sat on my bed with the door shut, trying to tune out the distressed cabinet bangs and whisks in the kitchen. My mom was preparing a special mint-chip freezer cake to cheer me up.

She'd been shocked when I tugged her wrinkled sleeve after Eric left us and said firmly, "We're leaving. Right now."

But she hadn't argued.

The whole, hot walk downhill to the gate, as the sounds of the party became fainter and fainter behind us, she hadn't spoken.

Not even a simple, "Did something happen with you and Eric?"

I loved her for that.

# 19

Joy

2008
Thursday, 3:30 p.m.
Outside Big Sur

The address I'm looking for is 12 Seakist, but we're hardly kissed by the sea. We're miles east from the waterside cliff mansions, down a series of dusty farm roads. We've passed three vineyards and an abandoned artichoke stand.

It's hotter and drier, well removed from the moist ocean wind I've been breathing since dawn. By the time I park on the dirt road next to the tilting 12 Seakist mailbox, my blue T-shirt dress is soaked under the arms.

I come around to the passenger side, stretching my legs, rolling my neck. Taking in the rambling, weedy property up the hill. Assorted outbuildings with corrugated iron roofs, two camper-vans, and an Airstream in the distance. Abstract, rusted-metal sculptures the size of whale ribs strewn everywhere.

He joins me by the mailbox. "Interesting place. The vibe

is…" He surveys the dozens of oxidized metal pieces, many of them bigger than us, scattered around the shaggy yellow fields flanking the driveway. "Artistic."

"I was thinking post-apocalyptic."

*Like Mad Max.* I still think in movie references sometimes, but I keep this one to myself. It feels wrong, like treading on sacred ground.

"That, too." We walk up the dusty gravel driveway side by side, careful to keep a good foot of separation between our shoulders. "It seems like a lot of trouble to go to for hinges. You couldn't find anything in Home Depot that would join the panels together, huh?"

"Serra obsessed over the hinges. She wanted them to blend perfectly."

"You're going all out."

"Oh, not really. It only took me one Google search to find this woman. Artist AND Joy AND Gold. But it took *her* forever to find the hinges. She only emailed Tuesday to say she still had them."

"It's a real quest. All that's missing are some trolls and a dragon."

We look around at the bleached-out fields scattered with tawny metal. And I know he's kidding, but it is a bit creepy, like a giant's boneyard.

"So which one do you think is the main house?" he asks.

"Not sure, she just said she'd be outside."

We continue our march up the driveway, drawn to the hiss of a blowtorch. But when we spy a corrugated metal shed a hundred yards away on our right, at the end of the curving driveway, we slow down. Inside, a hulking figure sprays a shower of amber sparks in the dark.

We look at each other and he says, low and serious, "The dragon?"

I laugh. "Maybe."

"Seriously, does anyone know we're here?"

"No, but she sounded pretty normal on the phone. I'm not too worried. Her name's Joy Gold—that's not the name of a blowtorch murderer."

"Famous last words."

I smile, grateful for this brief silliness. Too grateful, maybe. But he's come out to play again. The boy inside the man—he's still there. "I think we'll survive, her internet site's pretty normal—"

Wind chimes. Not the good kind.

"I'm sorry, I've got to take this one," he says, hurrying off down the driveway.

*This one?*

"Hey, thanks for calling me back..." His voice recedes, fades away.

I feel foolish, standing alone here seconds after joking around in our old way, just when I thought he was getting into this trip.

It's like being abandoned on a dance floor.

I head into the shed, surprised by the intensity of my hurt. If I'm blowtorched, it'll be his fault.

My eyes adjust to the darkness and I watch the strange creature inside. Not a dragon. A tall woman in denim coveralls and face mask, thick, curly gray-brown braid. From her heavy movements I guess she's in her late sixties, maybe older.

She's completely absorbed in her work, oblivious, and I don't want to break her concentration as she circles a long, slender curve of metal propped on two sawhorses. She prowls around it, evaluating, touching it up with her blowtorch.

Then she sees me, jumps.

She switches off the blowtorch and flips up her face mask. "Well, I don't need my afternoon coffee now."

"I'm so sorry I scared you. Joy?"

"The very. You made good time. I'd shake your hand but..." She holds up a grimy glove.

"I love the…" I consider the piece on the sawhorses. Little Bo-Peep sheep crook? Giant candy cane, pre-stripes? "I love this."

She cackles. "It's going to be a handle for that beauty over there."

Joy shows me another piece—a rusty half dome the size of a café table, formed of giant, overlapping leaves.

"A leaf umbrella." I kneel to touch it.

"Yes. They'll go over the outdoor tables at this tech campus in San Jose."

"How beautiful."

A snort. "I thought so, too. Six umbrellas ago. But I've got to crank out a dozen more in two weeks."

She leads me to the back of the shed, where six finished umbrellas are lined up.

They don't look like assembly-line pieces. They're like the fairy cups I used to craft up on the wild hill across the street, out of leaves and sap, before The Heights was built. Fairy cups and daisy chains. I spent hours sitting in the shade of a scrub oak, happily absorbed in fitting them together. But some things don't fit together forever.

I glance over my shoulder at the sunny driveway but he's nowhere in sight. He's probably down at the car, taking his call in peace. He couldn't possibly let one roll to voice mail.

I've been storing up energy for every smile, every laugh. Taking his cues, acting light, changing my lunch plans to suit him.

And he's only humoring me, passing the time until he can ditch me again for the next call.

It's pathetic.

Pathetic *is not a word I'd associate with you.*

Joy and I wander out, cross the driveway toward a silver Airstream trailer without tires.

"That's my overflow storage," she says. "The hinges are in there, all ready for you. Though it took me some digging."

"I really appreciate it."

"It was kind of fun. I found some stuff I haven't thought about in years. So are you staying up in San Francisco tonight?"

"No, near Big Sur. This inn on the cliffs I found online. I thought it would be nice to avoid afternoon rush hour. So we could relax a little, break up the drive."

"Smart plan. Traffic in the Bay Area's gotten…" She shakes her head. It's too grotesque to articulate, what's happened. "It's one reason I moved down here. Is it the Sandpiper Inn?"

"Yes, that's it."

"It's a gorgeous place, the views are unbelievable. Doesn't get more romantic. And they do a phenomenal apple Dutch baby for two, make sure you stay for breakfast."

She gazes down her driveway at the red convertible, curious about the *we* joining me at the Sandpiper Inn for relaxation and a romantic Dutch baby breakfast.

He's in the car now. He's reclined his seat so all we can see are his long legs splayed over the windshield.

"Sorry, he's working. He really wanted to introduce himself."

"Oh, sure. You're lucky you didn't have to drive up solo. I can't stand doing I-5 all alone. Around Bakersfield my ass goes numb and I start muttering to myself."

Sympathy is mine for the taking. Right inside this stranger's good-natured brown eyes.

*Actually, we took PCH, not I-5. I thought it would be prettier. But all it added was another hour to the drive.*

*I've driven every inch myself so not only is my butt numb, both cheeks, and I mean dead-asleep numb not tingly almost numb, but my right leg and arm are killing me.*

*And that man in the car? He's hardly good company. He's on his phone most of the time.*

*To be honest, Joy, at the moment I kind of want to whack him with an artfully rusty umbrella handle.*

"Yeah, the drive's fine with two people."

"I'll get the hinges, back in a sec."

She disappears into the Airstream, returns with the triptych hinges in a small plastic bag. "I threw in a couple extra. Will you say hi to Serra for me? And congratulations, of course."

"I will."

I slip the bag in my purse and pull out five twenties. "Thank you so much."

But she shakes her head. "I have no use for them these days, honey. No charge. Just take them."

"Please, let me pay you for your time."

After a moment's hesitation she accepts one twenty, stuffs it down a coverall pocket. "But I'll keep this only if you take something else. Your name's Becky, right?"

"Becc."

"And your friend down the hill lounging in the red Mercedes? What's his name?"

I tell her and she disappears into the trailer again.

She returns with two miniature sculptures the size of doorknobs. One red and one green.

Mine's the red one. My initial, a sleek *B* made out of flayed, flattened Coke cans. His is made out of 7 Up cans.

"I used to sell them in Berkeley. Had a blanket on Telegraph and asked three bucks each. Good beer money, back then. Now I'm doing the fat corporate commissions."

I wave goodbye and trudge down to the car. I have the hinges, and I should be cheered by their new silver-dollar shine, their reassuring weight in my shoulder bag. Serra will love them.

When I reach the car he's not on his phone anymore.

He's asleep.

So peaceful. His mouth relaxed, slightly open, the phone detached from his ear for once. Instead of his silver money-making machine, there's a tiny yellow leaf in the stubbly place where his sideburns would be, if he had sideburns.

He still looks so young, so vulnerable, when he sleeps.

I know the curves and shadows of his face, how he breathes

when he's dreaming. I've watched him sleeping next to me so many times.

I don't feel like hitting him with the artsy umbrella now.

I want to brush the leaf away.

*Hey, Sleeping Beauty.*

He opens his eyes, jerks his legs, and I'm embarrassed that he's caught me staring. "I guess I'm still a little jet-lagged," he says, blinking, looking around, trying to figure out where we are.

He fumbles for the seat adjuster. Raises his seat back up and smirks. "Guess you escaped the mad blowtorch lady."

"Barely."

"So did she have the things to connect the triptych panels?"

"Yep, and this."

"She made you do her recycling?"

"It's art."

He reads the 7 Up slogan. "'Crisp and clean and no caffeine.'"

He flips and rotates the green soda-can sculpture like he's working on a Rubik's Cube, puzzles it out.

Until he realizes it's his initial.

*E.*

## 20

### Long Lunch

July 19, 1996
One week after my picnic with Cal in San Diego

WHERE I WAS SUPPOSED TO BE | The empty honeycomb
WHERE I WAS | Catalina

"My favorite analyst." Cal's head appeared over my cubicle wall. "Are you the only one here?"

Not quite. There were distant hums and clicks from Stephen printing presentation booklets, but otherwise the office was dead. A bunch of other people had the week off, and the handful of the Sears gang who weren't away had bailed early for drinks at the Lux rooftop bar down the block, urging me to join them.

*Maybe I'll come at five*, I'd said.

This summer Stephen had me filling swag bags. Goody bags for the press, stuffed with stress balls and visors, golf tees, and eyeglass wipes. Some embellished with CommPlanet's logo—the globe with a wedge cut out so it looked like a swirly blue,

Pacman-like *C*—or NoozeButton's chunky, shadowed red *N*. The rest were stamped with the symbols of sibling brands that I knew little about, except that everyone was sure they were going to be *huge*.

Once again, we'd circled the gigantic oval table in the conference room. Not collating presentations this time but filling bags, double-checking their contents.

*Duck, duck, goose*, I'd said.

*You're funny*, Stephen had said, unsmiling.

So much was the same. Laps around the conference room table. Humorless Stephen. Cal grinning over my cubicle wall when he dropped in. The trickling fountain in the Poppy Café courtyard.

We'd had three coffees and one lunch.

But other things had changed. *I* had changed.

I was less afraid of what Cal thought of me this summer; there was power in not caring so much.

He drummed his fingers on my cubicle wall. "Care to take me up on that sail? Meet me at four? It's dead here, they won't miss you."

★

"Down here," he called when I stepped onto the deck of the *Summer Hours* an hour later.

I hesitated at the foot of the stairs, taking in the gleaming wood, the tidy bench seats and narrow oval table. And finally, his face. He looked amused. As he scanned my dove-gray pantsuit, he raised an eyebrow jokingly. "*Slightly* formal attire for a deckie."

"I didn't have time to change." *I didn't make time, because I didn't think we were actually sailing.* I took off my blazer, grateful that at least I wore a sleeveless blouse, and rolled my tailored pants up as high as they'd go. Not the slinky, backless getup I'd imagined wearing on our first…whatever this was.

"I thought we'd have a picnic on the island."

"How far is it?"

"A little more than twenty miles." It seemed so important to him to go through with the sail. Part of me wished I wasn't so resistible.

But maybe:

1. He wanted to give me another chance to change my mind. As if a few stops and starts, his insistence that I think things over, made what we were about to do less wrong. 2. He was worried some marina neighbor would stop by the slip, five o'clock Coronas in hand, and find us together. Or 3. He hoped that disconnecting from the mainland would relax me.

Maybe it was all three.

At first I helped him with little bits of work—winching and tying up the odd line—but when we were safely out of Balboa Marina, I settled near the bow, one arm and one leg hooked tight around metal safety cords, and let the wind flap under my blouse. Once in a while he'd yell, "Tacking—hold tight." Then the boat would tilt, dipping me so close to the waves I could almost have dunked the tip of my ponytail in seawater, or lifting me so I felt like a mermaid carved on the prow of a ship. Each time, he watched me until we leveled out.

Halfway to the island, dolphins started swimming with us. Four or five of them, impossibly close to the boat, just saying hello. I pointed, silently, and turned back to smile. He shouted over the wind, something I couldn't hear. It might have been "beautiful."

Catalina was like pictures I'd seen of Mediterranean fishing towns, with orange cliffs rising up from turquoise water. We anchored off a thin strip of empty beach and sat next to each other on the gently rocking boat, our bare feet dangling off the side, while he pointed out things on the island. "There are wild buffalo over there in a field, left here after a movie shoot."

"It's so peaceful," I said. "I thought Catalina had ferries."

"They dock in Avalon, in the big tourist harbor. The other side of the island has a totally different feel."

"I'd like to live here."

"Another bit of trivia. Marilyn Monroe lived here once."

"To hide out? It's perfect for that."

"Stars do hide here." He nodded toward the top of the island, where tiled roofs peeked out from clusters of trees. "But no. She lived here when she was Norma Jeane."

The sun was directly overhead, but we had a soft breeze. He pulled his baseball cap off, slipping the plastic band over his wrist and releasing a smell of fresh sweat. It made me remember why we were here. Not to watch dolphins. Not to talk Catalina history.

We rowed the dinghy to shore and hopped out by a thin crescent of beach, wet up to our knees. I cupped water in my hand and splashed the back of my neck while he dragged the dinghy and stowed it in the shade of the bushes.

He returned to the water and copied me, scooping up seawater to douse himself. Then he bent over and wet his hair, shaking it and sending cold drops my way. "Now. A little hike… Steep, but worth it."

I followed his hard-flexing calves up a narrow, sandy trail until he disappeared into a cluster of green.

And then I was with him, in a shady spot at the top of the cliff. Like a room made of wind-bent trees, cool and dark.

I touched the satiny leaves. "What are these?"

"Catalina mahogany. Unusual, aren't they?"

We spread the plaid picnic blanket out in the darkest corner of the tree room. I nibbled a wheat cracker, not tasting it, but polished off half the cold wine in my glass in one gulp.

He didn't eat much, either, I noticed.

"William Wrigley once owned Catalina," he said. "They call it 'the island that gum built.'"

I set my plastic wineglass down on my plate and sat closer. I touched his knee, my hand covering the four shiny, pale pink scars.

"He owned the Chicago Cubs so they used to have spring training here," he said. Mr. Trivia suddenly.

"That's interesting," I whispered, not moving my hand.

"And you know there are few cars allowed? Everyone has golf carts."

"You could be a tour guide."

He set his plate down with a laugh. Then he kissed me, slow and gentle. Still a question in it. I lay back on the wool picnic blanket and slid my fingers into his hair.

Time slipped, the way it does so rarely. I've read that time only slips when you're drugged, or doing something you're meant to do.

After five minutes, or an hour, he pulled away and whispered groggily, "We should get back, don't you think?"

I shook my head and unbuttoned his shirt, pulled him close again. "No. We should stay."

He lifted off my shirt, then his, bunching them under my head. He rolled my bra straps down, unhooked it in the back. A twig snapped and I tensed, pressing against him so he'd cover me, even though we hadn't seen a soul since we'd left the boat. But it was only a bird.

I lay back with my eyes closed, my bra tangled around one wrist and his mouth on my neck as he unzipped my pants. Then, as I held my breath, his mouth moved lower, and that was almost enough. His hand rested, warm, over my underwear, then slid the tight cotton to the side, and I nearly came from those clever, clever fingers, but he stopped, turning my breath ragged. He pulled my drenched underwear below my hips and kissed my belly button. And lower. For a second I worried about what I might look like, but then his tongue found a spot that made me entirely liquid and I didn't care about anything but the possibility that he would stop.

I balled up the bra in my hand, squeezing it over and over, digging my fingernails into the soft fabric.

And when I came I laughed, it was so good.

He settled close by my side, running his fingers in a lazy

triangle, from my left hip bone to my right, up to my belly button, back down to my hip.

"You're laughing?" he said. "I'm here all week."

"That was… No one's ever." My temples were wet with tears. I wiped them with the heels of my hands.

"Never?"

I shook my head.

"And have you also never?"

I could have lied. Instead I simply didn't answer.

"Then let's definitely wait for that," he said.

I kissed him, pulling at his shoulders until he was above me, propped on his elbows. I bent a leg so my thigh pressed up on him through his thin swimming trunks.

"We don't have to rush anything. We have time, you should make sure you…" But he hadn't moved, and I was below him, wearing only a bra around my wrist, and now his eyes were half-closed.

He shut them and let himself sink closer, whispering something unintelligible into my neck before rolling away to sit on the blanket.

A valiant effort. A moment's suspense. But I'd won. He was slipping off his bathing suit and rummaging in a pocket. I closed my eyes. A snapping, a soft kiss on my breast, and then he was above me again and it was happening for real. He moved carefully but it hurt. A deep, pinching pain.

When the edges of the pain softened to a dull ache, I opened my eyes and watched him.

Such hard work, such a strange thing, really. But kind of nice. I studied his face, memorizing how it looked the moment his expression changed from taut and closed off to completely unguarded, not too different from fear.

★

After, he kissed my neck and dozed, his arm draped over my stomach. I wasn't remotely sleepy. I could have run a marathon. Could have entered a tri, and won. That was what it felt like.

Victory.

Despite the soreness between my legs, despite how wrong everyone would think it was. I could say I felt guilty but I didn't. Not then. Not yet.

"Cal?"

"Hmm."

"You're thirty-three, right?"

"'Fraid so." He looked at me, biting his lip. He brushed the damp hair off my forehead and kissed it. "What are you thinking, you wide-awake person? That I'm ancient?"

"I was thinking about Knightley and Emma."

"What's Night Liunemma?"

"Mr. Knightley and Emma Woodhouse. From Jane Austen. Our age difference is less than theirs."

"Ah." He lay quietly for a minute, staring up at the ceiling of leaves. "You're working hard, trying to make this okay. You're worried about what people will think."

"No."

"Sure you are." He kissed my forehead again.

"Anyway. Why does anyone have to know?"

He laughed. "No, you're not worried in the slightest."

I lay on his chest and listened to the soft island sounds. Birds and waves, the beating fabric of an awning or sail in the marina far below.

★

On the way back, hours after sunset, I leaned over the bow guardrail, wind whipping my hair.

When I saw the glow on the beach from the kids' Crystal Cove bonfire, a bright amber dome, my mood flickered darker for only a second before brightening again, stronger than any memory.

# 21

## Time sheets

August 1996

WHERE I WAS SUPPOSED TO BE | My cubicle
WHERE I WAS | The boat. And the island. And the Cellar

The end of summer was hot and sticky. Long, sweaty afternoons in the rolling master berth of the *Summer Hours*, long nights when I twisted in my sheets, too keyed up to close my eyes.

We met as often as we could. I took long lunches, or slipped away at 4:30 or 4:00 or 3:45. My small work assignments had never felt mission critical, and now, though I needed the money, they seemed utterly pointless.

But one morning after I failed to unpack a shipment of swag (retractable dog leashes with the CommPlanet logo), I found a blue Post-it on my computer screen from Stephen:

*Rebeccca. Pls see me immed. Thx. S.*

I walked to his office with my heart in my throat. Sure he'd dropped by my cubicle the evening before and found the box untouched—and me MIA.

Stephen scowled at his computer screen, tapping furiously. "Sorry to tell you this…" he said, pausing and shuffling through some papers in his black wire In tray.

I knew it. Punishment would rain down on me, right through the five high-rise floors above my head. Punishment and disgrace and ruin.

"…but you'll have to redo your time sheet for the last five days." He tossed me the yellow triplicate form. "We have new department codes. You need to put 14, not 11."

★

At the annual boondoggle, this time at a Santa Barbara resort, I again watched Cal from across the conference room. Thinking about how he'd look later.

*Knowing* how he'd look later.

The two of us stole away after our agreed-upon seventy minutes (me) and eighty (him). We met at the boat, laughing, flushed from our separate escapes.

And no one noticed.

Sometimes we sailed to Catalina, to our shady spot on the hill.

Often, we didn't make it out of Balboa Marina, and had to stifle our cries, still our sticky limbs, when voices approached above.

This summer, he did not say, *Don't pretend you're someone you're not.*

He said, "You're so…" and trailed off. He said it and shook his head, marveling.

The Friday three weeks after our first time, we lay in the bedroom of the *Summer Hours*, late-afternoon sun seeping in behind the curtains over the high windows. On our stomachs, him over me. Positions altered only by inches from how we'd been rocking together moments before.

"You're so…"

"I'm so what?"

"You're the word person," he hummed into my shoulder blade.

"Aggressive."

"No."

"I think what you're trying to say is you've corrupted me."

He bit my shoulder blade. "Wrong again. Hot enough for you?" He lifted the hair from my neck, blew on my sweat-glazed skin.

"Let's sail somewhere private to swim. I have a little time."

"I have a better idea. The coldest place in Orange County. It's like a cave, you'll love it. Dark, air-conditioned, and utterly discreet, for those who worry about such things."

We hadn't met anywhere public since we'd started sleeping together. Only the boat and our hiding place on the island.

If it was light out when we sailed, I tucked my hair down my shirt as I navigated the swaying white ramps, walking briskly until I was safely on board. Even then I insisted on staying below, like a stowaway, until we were out of the marina.

We were careful, the few times we spoke in the office. Careful to keep our voices casual instead of intimate, careful not to chat too long over my cubicle wall.

But off land he was sometimes reckless and laughed at my elaborate efforts at concealment.

Once when I'd arrived to find four men on the neighboring boat drinking Coronas, I'd retreated and called from the Crab Shack up PCH, insisting I couldn't come until they'd left.

"Those clowns wouldn't say anything."

"You have a pact? All the men in the marina?" I meant it as a joke.

But there was a slight pause as he assessed this, and then tuned his voice to a lower, more serious tone. "All I meant is you worry too much."

*Maybe you don't worry enough.* I'd waited until they left.

★

"Get dressed! You'll love this place."

"I really shouldn't go," I called from the boat's bathroom as I splashed my face. I'd blown my mom off all summer, and the evidence of her lonely evenings—blue-and-yellow video cases from Blockbuster, dinner leftovers carefully Saran-wrapped in the fridge—plucked at my heart when I saw them in the morning.

And it didn't seem smart to go to a restaurant, no matter how *discreet*.

When I looked up from the sink, Cal stood behind me. Dressed in a fresh white shirt, hair brushed. I was naked, face dripping.

I watched his reflection lift my hair, kiss the nape of my neck. I closed my eyes as his mouth moved to my shoulder, his hands sliding down my back to my hips.

"We'll go another night," he murmured. "I'll just have to sit in the air-conditioning with my ice-cold drink all alone. Poor me." Hands between my legs now. One exploring from the front and one from behind. I wanted to step wider but the bathroom was too small.

"Poor you." I pressed my forehead against the mirror.

6:00 p.m.
The Cellar restaurant in Fullerton

We hid in double darkness. A curtained booth inside the candlelit underground dining room. It was stone walled like a wine cellar, with the same damp, chilly air. A place so clearly for new lovers that the velvet curtains might as well have surrounded beds instead of tables.

"Like it?" Cal asked.

"How have I never heard of this place?"

Someone cleared his throat tactfully outside our green velvet curtain.

"Come in?" I said, trying not to laugh.

The waiter slid the curtain open, revealing a silver trolley of steaks. We chose our filets, ordered sides of creamed spinach and potatoes au gratin, then he slid the curtain shut and rolled the cart away on silent casters.

"What did he think we were doing?" I said.

He laughed. "I'm sure he's seen it all."

"What *are* we doing?"

He reached for my hand. "Getting to know each other."

"I don't know you. Who are your friends? Not the boat people."

"No."

"That guy Schwinn from the boondoggle?"

"That clown? The Footsy King of Silicon Valley?"

"The what?" I sputtered.

"It's this stupid joke. First you have to know that there's a famous guy in London called the Footsy King. Big analyst on the FTSE index."

This was the *Financial Times* stock index. "Okay."

"Well, a couple years ago at CommDex in Vegas, Schwinn became notorious for playing footsy with his female dinner companions. He slips his shoes off under the table and…explores the territory under the tablecloth. Sees if any feet want to reciprocate. He's a weird guy, but basically harmless. A useful lightweight."

"That *is* weird. And gross. Did he ever end up investing in CommPlanet?"

"Alas, I couldn't get him to bite. It's too bad, because I'd really like to sell him my stake."

"But I thought CommPlanet was going to be *huge*."

"I'm not so sure now. Anyway, it doesn't matter because I'm stuck with it. I think I'm losing my touch."

But I knew this wasn't true. He took great pride in his ability to connect ideas with investors, though he downplayed it. He said he wasn't a real VC, just a matchmaker who paired startups with investor friends for fun. That there wasn't much skill in it these days, it was so easy. Millions of dollars being thrown around at the Woodside Deli over chicken sandwiches.

*Not so much rainmaking as turning on a tap,* he'd said. *I'm a glorified washroom attendant.* Everything was diminutive. Like it was play money.

"Okay, so you're not best friends with the Footsy King. Who *do* you hang out with?"

"I have some guys I play tennis with, do races with. My college roommate and I talk on the phone once a week."

"That's cute. I don't know one thing about your childhood. Tell me where you grew up." I withdrew my hand and settled back.

"Wisconsin."

I couldn't keep the surprise from my voice. "Really?"

"Why's that so shocking?"

"Because you're so...California. *Wisconsin?*"

"Tiny little Craftsman house in Deer Lick Valley. An hour outside Madison. Snow. Tuna casserole on Friday nights, basset hound, public school with twenty kids to a grade." He shrugged. "My dad worked at the post office."

I tried to picture this. A blond boy in a red hat and mittens making a snowman, getting called to dinner. But I couldn't connect the innocent boy in my head with the man in the booth across from me drinking his scotch on the rocks. He'd landed in my life fully formed. The ultimate successful California male, amused and assured. Complete with boat and convertible.

I'd never even seen him in a sweater.

"Didn't you go to USC?"

"For biz school and half of undergrad. I started at U of Wisconsin, in Madison, then transferred out here junior year."

"Are your parents still alive?"

He nodded.

"Are they happy?"

"They think they are."

"Do you visit them?"

"Twice a year. Any other questions from the press pool?"

"Sorry, I'm just trying to get my head around it."

"It's a sweet little town, but California always had a hold on me. From TV, I guess. *Three's Company* and *CHiPs*." He laughed. "Anyway. I wanted to move here and I did."

He caressed my wrist with a hand still cool from his drink, his fingers brushing the tender spot perfume articles in magazines called a pulse point. "What? You're thinking something serious, I can tell."

"I was thinking that you didn't just *move to* California. You became it. Your name."

"Well...yeah." He smiled at this, tilted his head as he considered. "Clever human. And now you. What do we know about you?"

"You tell me."

"Rebecca is twenty going on thirty. Like me, she knows she's bound for bigger places than her hometown—"

"You make me sound awful, that's not—"

"Hey, my turn. She *is* bound for bigger places than her hometown. She loves roller coasters but not crowds. Books but not *Beowulf.* Sun but not heat. Rebecca is tenacious, *especially* when you tell her she can't have something."

"Like...?"

"Oh. Scotch." He tossed back the rest of his. "Answers. Such as what is data scaffolding..."

"You explained it well."

"...which promotion outfit is spray-painting cat graffiti around Berkeley."

I laughed. This had become a running inside joke, one of a handful, and I enjoyed it when he teased me about my lingering obsession: *my cats,* as I called it. I was no closer to an answer than I'd been freshman year, despite a notebook scrawled with interviews of marketing firms, fraternities, security guards, paint stores. One night I'd even staked out a spot in East Campus, by the health center, where there'd been a cluster of recent appearances. All I got was a hand cramp from gripping my pepper spray too tight.

But I liked our moments of good-natured teasing because it proved that our hours together, though often short on conversation, were not as shallow as the outside world would think.

"Please stop with your boring theory about my cats," I said. "I'll be so disappointed if it's all some lame commercial. How else am I stubborn when people say I can't have things?"

"I said tenacious, not stubborn. You were tenacious about me."

"Nobody told me I couldn't have you."

"No?" When I didn't answer, he said, "Well. I did."

"Briefly. I'm starving, aren't you?"

"See. It's hard to be in the hot seat. You prefer doing the reporting."

★

We were heading for the stairs when I saw them. On the landing above us: blue espadrilles with ballet straps crisscrossed chicly around shapely calves.

I pushed him against the dark wall.

"Well, now." He grinned, thinking I had other intentions.

I clapped my hand over his lips and pointed up at the staircase landing.

I held my breath, waiting. It would serve me right if the blue espadrilles were followed by my mom's white Naturalizer flats, if the promised lunch had become dinner. I'd treated her shabbily all summer; the answering machine tape on the kitchen counter was full of my lies. The latest, left only a few hours ago: *Hey, I'll be home pretty late. I'm invited to the company box at the baseball game.*

*I have to make an appearance*, I'd said.

If my mom found out about me and Cal, she'd be horrified and blame him, raise a fuss. Mrs. Haggermaker would yank my scholarship. And Eric would find out.

In that moment, holding my breath in the darkest corner of the cold basement restaurant, each of the three seemed inevitable and equally catastrophic.

But the shoes that appeared behind Donna's were men's leather loafers.

Cal and I watched the two of them descend the stairs.

Her smooth calves, white tennis skirt and tank, a red sweater knotted around her shoulders, her hair down. His sharp blue suit on this hot day. I knew from the fit of the jacket that it was the husky, attentive man from her pool party.

*Please don't come this way.*

If she decided to visit the ladies' room before being seated, there would be no place to hide. What would we say?

*Hey, Donna! Great place. Try the flourless chocolate cake!*

We froze, silent, until they were seated.

★

The next morning at the sunny white breakfast table, my mom turned the pages in her Gardening section without her usual cheerful commentary.

"Are you okay?" I asked.

"Of course! How was the game?"

"We won, 5–4." I'd checked the score in the paper while she was getting juice. "We all went to sushi after. Did I wake you up, I..." I spotted the tickets propped against the pepper grinder.

The Pageant of the Masters. It was our annual tradition—a living-portrait art benefit in Laguna, in an outdoor theater. Actors dressed up like *Girl with a Pearl Earring* or *The Last Supper*, replicating the outfits and backgrounds, painting their faces. It was pretty cool. And it had been on my blotter calendar all summer.

"Mom. The pageant."

"Oh, it's all right."

"I can't believe I forgot."

She took her Cheerios dish to the sink and rinsed it. "Would you like the last bit of OJ? There's a splash left."

"I'll pay you back for the tickets."

She spoke over her shoulder. "It's okay, honey! I'm glad you could blow off steam with your coworkers. You've been working so hard."

## 22

### Reservations

2008
Friday, 9:00 a.m.
Big Sur
The Sandpiper Inn

"Would you like more coffee?" Eric asks.

"I'd love it. Thanks."

We sit side by side at a windy courtyard table overlooking the ocean, taking in the tree-covered bluffs below us, the strip of dark blue morning sea, the wall of fog that's receding by the minute.

Eric is on my right again, just like in the car. The host had asked if we wanted our chairs moved to face each other or left like this, *So you can both enjoy the view?*

We'd jumped at the side-by-side option. A duet: *This is fine!*

The view is unbelievable, just like Joy said.

The bluffs below us are not the brown, vertical cliffs we passed on the drive yesterday. The inn is perched over a section of coastline with gentler angles. A fluffy blanket of green stretching down to the water.

"The trees make it look so soft, like a bunny slope." I sip my coffee, gazing out. "Like you could roll on your side all the way down and not hurt yourself."

"It's a beautiful spot. Thanks for picking it." Eric butters his toast.

"Sure."

I stir berries into my oatmeal. (No Dutch baby for two, though the honeymooners next to us are *ooh*ing and *aah*ing over their shared, puffy pancake, feeding each other bites. *Sorry to disappoint, Joy.*)

"How's your oatmeal?"

"Delicious. How about your eggs?"

"They're perfect..."

We go on like this. Discussing the food, the view. The wedding, our gift. How we both worked in our rooms and *crashed early.*

I don't tell him about the long walk I took last night, down a green-canopied, zigzagging trail to the beach.

How I sat on the sand alone and pictured him up in his room, his laptop and room-service tray in front of him on his hotel bed.

At least he's been more helpful since we checked in, more of a participant in our quest. Yesterday he talked the inn's owner into letting us park the convertible in her personal garage, to avoid the hassle of moving the gift into the hotel for the night.

I'm trying not to associate this gesture with how relieved he looked when the desk clerk handed us keys to two separate rooms.

I want to ask him, *Were you seriously worried there'd be some kind of reservation snafu and we'd be stuck in one room?*

But I bite the words back.

"So were the panels in the car really at a preschool?" Eric asks.

"Yeah, in Tarzana. I'm thinking we don't tell her that part."

"Agreed." He nods.

*Cute 3-D wildlife scene with fun detail, great condition!!!* the listing said about the left and middle panels of Serra's triptych. The seller didn't know that she'd only had two-thirds of it. The minimum bid was $200 but the second I saw the photo I clicked Buy It Now! and offered $350. It will buy a lot of paste and construction paper for the kids.

"How long did it take to find the section we're picking up tomorrow?" he asks.

"Weeks longer than the ones in the car. It's in a real collector's house."

"Do you think we'll need a dolly?"

"No, with two of us I think it'll be fine. The panels aren't super heavy, just big. I really appreciate you helping..."

This is how it started in June, with me politely asking for his *help*.

I've never seen him during one of his rare visits to the West Coast. Never reached out before, though I'd thought about it hundreds of times. But that night I emailed that I'd heard he'd be in San Diego for his mother's fiftieth, six days before the wedding. That I'd tracked down two sections of Serra's triptych, and could he possibly drive up to Oregon with me, help out?

> I'm hoping to find the last third. We could make it a joint present. But I totally understand if you can't do it...
> I know it's a lot to ask.

I sent the email late one night, giddy after finding the first two panels.

It had seemed like a perfectly logical plan at 1:00 a.m. He was still close to Serra, and the present would mean everything to her. What else was he going to do with those six days between celebrations?

Another minor factor—I didn't want Serra to worry about

me and Eric on her big day. But if she knew we were driving up together, if we could deal with the awkward reunion privately, it would make things easier on everybody.

I could see it. Eric flying out for his mom's fiftieth. Us driving up the coast together, on speaking terms again. Bearing Serra's piece north to Oregon. All three sections of it, beginning, middle, and end, as gleaming as on the day of her first exhibit. The perfect gift.

One that would make all of us remember how we were.

After I clicked Send I couldn't sleep all night. I pictured a network of zapping internet cables delivering my email from California to New York, imagined locating the crucial wire, sawing it.

But I knew it was too late, that my message was already waiting for him in his New York office and I couldn't pull it back.

What had I been thinking? I hadn't been. I'd been buzzed and sentimental from my internet find—drunk dialing without the fallback excuse of alcohol.

He answered the next morning:

> That's really thoughtful & I'm sure she'd love it. I'd have to
> work on the road but I could probably swing it...

He pours more half-and-half into his coffee, stirs vigorously. The clinks ringing from the inside of the white ceramic cup sound so merry.

"You went all out," he says yet again.

I try to accept *you went all out* at face value, as a compliment.

But it seems to be a euphemism for something unspoken, and I didn't like it when he said it yesterday, either. He talks to Serra more than I do, and I can't help but read a little dig in *you went all out*. As if he really means, *you went too far, considering I'm better friends with her than you are.*

I'm beginning to wonder if maybe I have gone too far. The

gift might have survived shipping. I could have given up on the hinges. We could have scheduled a one-on-one dinner up in Oregon before the wedding, to keep everyone from worrying.

We could have had a coffee.

"She'll be so surprised," he says.

There's a softness in his voice now, and I glance at him; he's staring out at the ocean.

We gaze out at the blue, shimmering water. Clinging to conversation about the gift.

It's our life raft; it's safe.

When Eric agreed to drive with me, I'd let myself hope.

I hadn't realized how much, how carried away I'd gotten, until last night when I was sitting on wet sand in the dark, alone, listening to the waves crash on the shore.

Trying to remember why I'd thought this trip was a good idea.

# 23

## Picnic

2008
Friday, 3:00 p.m.
Berkeley

Serra's triptych placard is waiting for me at the front desk of
the museum, right where the woman on the phone promised it
would be. I buy a chocolate-chip scone at the museum café to
celebrate—and get me through the last hour of driving today.

I'm tired, but soon we'll be in San Francisco. And the placard
in my hand has given me a lift; it's going to make Serra smile.
It still hurts a little that I'm not in her bridal party.

**I hope you understand,** she'd emailed.

I do. But weddings are brutal that way. They put the friendship caste system into perfect focus. You can't avoid it: there are a
hundred reminders of how you rank. Maid of honor down to an
insignificant soul marooned at the table at the tip of the dining
room archipelago, farthest from the head table. Where the guests

merit only a distracted, "Hey, so glad you could come," as the couple takes their courtesy lap around the room.

If you're at one of those distant tables, you say something like, "I love your dress." You weren't there when she chose it. And she didn't send a picture.

But if you know the right gift is waiting? The one that will obliterate all the others, and make the bride smile, remember the Three Mouseketeers? That might help you bear it.

I look down at the placard, intact after so long, a little two-by-three-inch miracle:

Triptych: Grownups/Suspended Animation. Serra Indrijo. Urethane, plastics, and paper. $800

I leave the museum and head down Bancroft, debating between affixing the placard to the triptych or slipping it inside Serra's card. I'll ask Eric which he thinks would be more fun for Serra.

But when I spot him in the convertible I stop short.

He's shifted to his left to face the box, cupped his hand over his right ear to drown out the chatter and laughter on the sidewalk. People are lining up for the matinee of *Picnic* outside the museum's attached movie theater.

Not realizing that they're disturbing Mr. Eric T. Logan's *important business call.*

Eric works for a consulting company that test screens movies and trailers. He's good at his job, from what I've read, good at predicting which movies will have "big" opening weekends, and which are too "quiet" to get attention. He's part of a vast number-crunching, hand-wringing, second-guessing enterprise that decides which films the studios will promote and which they'll leave to flail. And drown.

I can't take my eyes off him.

Eric and I watched *Picnic* in his closet once, and I can still see his face that afternoon: rapt, lit by the flickering screen. But today the pivot of his body says how annoyed he is with the high spirits of the matinee crowd interfering with his work call.

As I get closer, he shouts into his phone, "We have to take the 30,000-foot view here, Ted."

And it's too much. I can't take the 30,000-foot view of Eric saying *30,000-foot view.*

A woman in my office says it in meetings all the time. Quinn Hartly, a Vitaminwater-guzzling client exec who has, despite middling numbers, survived two rounds of layoffs since last March.

*Let's take the 30,000-foot view here, people.* Every time she says it, I want to shove her veggie-cream-cheese-schmeared bagel in her face.

*Just breathe, Becc. He said he had to work.*

*What did you expect? It's not like you're the same person you were ten years ago.*

*Just get in the car and drive.*

I hurl the scone at Eric's back and hurry down the street.

★

I sit on a bench in the front garden of the Berkeley Arms apartments, a block from the car. A cheap, U-shaped brick building, laughter and radio drifting down from upstairs windows holding Obama 2008 posters: *Hope*, with a rising sun in the O.

Students are blasting KFOG and KITS as they pre-party. I remember so well that feeling of anticipation before a big Friday night out.

I am feeling decidedly post-party. Deflated. All of my hope for what the weekend might bring has drained away.

I wind the weeds growing through the bench slats around my fingers, trying to process the fact that I just threw a baked good at Eric.

What comes next? He won't stay, not now.

And I'm not sure I want him to. I'll drive him to the Oakland

Airport so he can fly up while I continue in the car alone. Pay strangers to help lift the gift or guard it when I stop at restrooms along the way.

He doesn't want to be here. I'd hoped part of him did, that there was a little of the Eric I knew still left. Serra insists that there is. So does his mom.

I pull my BlackBerry from my purse and fire it up. Fifteen voice mails. Fifty-eight new emails. I open one with the subject line Format Tweak. A proposal to embed advertising links within content.

Newzly uses a search-engine-optimization algorithm to deliver "articles" based on what people type into search fields. We pay writers $7 a pop to write "How to Make a Chihuahua Darth Vader Costume" or "How to Find a Katy Perry Fan Club in Duluth, Minnesota." It's a journalism sweatshop, but advertisers love us. We're shoveling the monetized 1s and 0s out there as fast as we can.

For a long time, I bounced around at dailies and alt-weekly papers, but two years ago, Newzly recruited me to head their West Coast content team. I was flattered and broke and weary from never-ending rounds of newsroom layoffs. Seeing good people sniffling outside the HR office, constantly bracing for my turn. It was a way to take control. I needed the money and hoped Newzly would be a somewhat sheltered port in the storm. I'm not sure any company is safe now.

But I know I'm absurdly lucky. My salary is $104,000 and my strike price is $7. We're down to $12, as of yesterday's closing market bell, but I'm forty percent vested, which is pretty good. If Newzly survives I'll be one hundred percent vested in four years.

Four years isn't long; undergrad is four years and it flies by. As I remember.

I told myself I'd write on the side.

That it would only be for a year.

I've tried not to look back.

But if Eric saw me leading last week's all-team meeting, reminding my staff that all pieces have to meet our under-four-hundred-words rule, he might feel the same wave of disappointment at who I've become.

*So who are you really mad at, Becc?*

★

He's found me, this stranger. Thick black hair tamed by an expensive haircut, pressed button-down shirt, linen shorts today.

He approaches, wrapping up his call. "We'll be checked in soon. I'll catch you then. Yeah, Monday."

He detaches the phone from his face and greets me. "I gave the ticket guy at the theater twenty bucks to keep an eye on the gift."

"Thanks."

He looks up at the apartment windows behind me. "Are we meeting someone here? I thought the last part of the gift was up north."

"I just wanted to give you privacy. For your calls."

"Thanks. We bought CineTek for a song because it's struggling, so now we're officially the volume leader. In terms of cumulative box office."

"Wow. Congratulations. The highest cumulative box office volume service in the industry."

Once he would have known this was sarcasm. Once he'd have gone management-speak on me only to make me laugh.

He brushes crumbs off his shoulder. "Can you believe one of those kids in the movie line threw a muffin at me?"

*Really? That's awful. They were probably high. You know, Berkeley.*

I'm off the hook. I could continue up to the wedding with a pasted-on smile. Just get through Sunday, for Serra's sake. Pretend I'm fine with this man and his *you really went all out* and his nonstop phone calls.

"Scone."

"Excuse me?"

"It was a chocolate-chip scone."

His eyes widen for a second, then he nods. Sits. Rubs his hands through his hair.

He smells of the same orange-clove body wash I used in my hotel shower this morning. He's real, warm, breathing. Sitting next to me, after ten years of existing only as a name in an internet article, a face on a company home page, a word my mom and Serra try to avoid saying in my presence: *Eric.*

He's right here, but I miss him more than I have in ten years.

"It wasn't my most mature moment," I say quietly. "This is harder than I thought it'd be. I thought..."

"What?"

"I guess I thought it'd be kind of hard for you, too. Seeing me."

He sits still for a minute, then pulls his iPhone from his pocket, taps it to life.

And I'm astonished by his cruelty.

He's going back to his stupid calls, his CineTek deal or whatever. He's not even going to acknowledge my confession.

Then he holds the phone up for me.

I expect to see a string of numbers with power area codes— 212, 650, 415, 408.

But it's an application called Date Insurance. The icon is a cartoon of a blond woman with red lips in a worried O, bugged-out blue eyes. I read about the beta software on Fortune.com; it lets you program times you want to be interrupted so you can cut a bad date short.

"You've been pretending."

"Yes. And I'm exhausted." He smiles, embarrassed. "Hell. You have no idea how tiring it is to make up fake phone conversations all day."

"Why?"

"You know why, Becc."

The first time he's said my name. "You were horrified by

the prospect of talking to me for three days. Sitting in the same car with me."

"Not horrified."

"So you just wanted to make me feel like an idiot…?"

"That's not why I did it," he says. "It was…the only way I could let myself come. Pride. Or…insurance, I guess. Protection."

"Protection from me, Eric?"

His phone rings, one of the scheduled interruptions he programmed to shield himself from our time together. He taps the screen, powers it down. "Becc. What did you expect? This isn't easy for me, either."

It's a crumb, a welcome one.

## 24

### Marilyn

August 1996
Nine days before junior year

WHERE I WAS SUPPOSED TO BE | Serra's
WHERE I WAS | Marilyn's

To celebrate the end of summer, Cal booked us a house on Catalina for the weekend.

"It's gorgeous, totally private," he said. "You'll love it."

I called Serra to secure my alibi, asking her to pretend I was
spending the weekend with her if my mom called.

"I knew you were seeing someone!" she cried. "You've blown
me off all summer. But if it's for love I forgive you. So spill."

*It's not love, Serr. I'm not sure what it is.*

I wanted to say this to her. I wanted to say, *You won't believe
who it is. Promise you won't hate me?*

But if I told her who I was seeing, her voice would change.
And even if she didn't say, *How could you do that to E?* she'd
think it.

"It's this guy in the office. Stephen. Just graduated from USC Business School." *Who never smiles at my jokes and has had a serious boyfriend for three years.*

"So has the momentous occasion already happened or is it this weekend?"

"This weekend."

"Becc! I'm so happy for you."

Serra had told me everything about her first time at seventeen. She'd done it with Tim Alton—a stocky, one-year-younger, vegetarian, theater guy—in the back of her car after dinner at the Infinite Salad. She'd told me everything, down to the CD they'd played. *Sarah McMaudlin*, she'd said. The second half of "Adia" and the first half of "Angel," so we calculated that the entire act took, maximum, three minutes. Also, Tim had gone overboard on the Tuscan herb salad dressing. Serra had lost her virginity in a haze of oregano.

We'd made a pact: I'd promised to report every detail, as she had.

"He's cute?" she said.

"Extremely."

"How old is he?"

"Um, I think twenty-two or twenty-three. Around there."

"Older man."

"Hmm." I squeezed the receiver.

"Are you nervous? Are you sure you're ready? Because—"

"I'll tell you everything, Serr, I promise. Soon. Thanks for covering."

★

I drove a golf cart up to the Catalina house. He was to follow on foot from the boat half an hour later, to be safe. My idea, but since the sandal incident he'd gone along with my rules.

*Drive uphill until you can't go any higher*, the map he sketched for me should have said. I felt like I was on a movie lot, driving the golf cart around. I took a wrong turn, confusing Vieullesaint Place for Vieullesaint Terrace, and hoped Cal wouldn't get lost.

The front entrance, through a tunnel of trees, was private, a nest like our first trysting spot. I punched in the security code and shoved the heavy front door open—it was one expensive nest. Spanish Revival, views of the Pacific along two sides. Wrought-iron balconies inside and out. A design of the Hollywood "more is more" school.

I dropped my backpack on the red tile and trailed a hand against the cool stucco wall. I crossed the living room, opening French doors to the patio. A huge rectangular pool in the sun, and one almost as big that I discovered, after kicking off my sandals and dipping a toe, was hot. A grotto, and one of those slender pools that pummel you with artificial currents for exercise, and a pool that was half outdoors and half indoors, divided by a glass wall on tracks.

All of it intricately tiled and fountained: a high-class water park.

Back inside, I walked from room to room. Gym, screening room. Upstairs, a vast bedroom with a balcony facing the mainland.

"Rebecca?"

"Up here," I yelled. "Master bedroom. I think.

"This place is unreal," I said over my shoulder at the sound of his footsteps. "How'd you find it?" I looked back at the ocean. There was a ferry leaving, and a dive boat off Avalon Harbor, froggy shapes bobbing nearby.

He'd peeled off his shirt and tucked it into the side of his shorts during his uphill run. His chest was slick, leaving damp marks on the front of my blue sundress when he drew me close.

"You're boiling, I thought you were going right for the pool," I said. "Your Nestea plunge commercial."

"Wanted to find you more, warm person. Undoll. Thinking, living, soft—"

"Shh."

★

We nicknamed it the Marilyn house, because it would have been a perfect hideaway for her, post-stardom. It was like her, showy and trying too hard. But irresistible.

We didn't leave the house all weekend. We didn't need to.

I remember lying back in the grotto, dizzy and weak. And laughing, because sex in a pool is overrated on a number of levels. We finally gave up and moved to the lawn. Me on top, moving slowly, the way I'd just discovered felt incredible.

I'd been self-conscious the first time, doing it like that, but now I pinned his hands over his head, bending down to tease him with my hair or my breasts, then bending back. It felt impossibly deep, just this side of painful. He wanted to move harder, faster. He ran his hands up and down my waist, frantic, and I knew from his breathing, his tight clasp on my hips, that it was all he could do not to flip me over. I liked watching him when he shut his eyes.

Sunday afternoon, we sat on the balcony in the cool, humid air blowing up from the Pacific. He was reading the *Wall Street Journal* and I was typing my fall semester reading assignments into a WordPerfect document on the poky refurbished Compaq laptop my mom had given me for graduation. Trying to make up for the fact that I hadn't cracked a book since my abandoned *AP Stylebook*.

In a little over a week I'd be back at school; it was hard to believe.

When I shut down, the computer shuddered and whirred and groaned as always. I liked its quirks, and even though it was slow, it was reliable. A girl down the hall had lost three term papers to her fancy new laptop.

"Technical difficulties?" Cal said. "Want me to take a look?" He'd been an EECS major at USC and was still proud that he knew his way around a computer.

"It's just doing its thing. See? It's done now." I closed the laptop and set it on the balcony.

"I'll get you a new computer. Or at least a new memory card, so you don't have to rely on that dinosaur for your papers this year. What is that thing, on a 286 chip? How much RAM do you have?"

"I'll get through the year just fine," I said. "You don't have to worry."

A pause. "I find that I don't want summer to end," he said. Laughing, as if surprised. His voice was light, and he flashed me his widest grin, the one I secretly called his "beach volleyball" smile.

"You're sweet," I said.

But he didn't turn the pages of his *Journal* after that.

It had been a perfect, exhausting long weekend of playing house, every moment brighter because it was stolen.

And because it couldn't last. I knew it couldn't. I'd tried to imagine what would happen to us after Labor Day, but the screen just went black.

"Look at that color," he said. "It's the magic hour. The Impressionists thought they could only find that light on the Riviera, but it's not true."

But the light was already changing. The pinkish-gold darkening to red, his shadow elongating behind his lawn chair, distorting his body into an alien form.

"Someday we'll go there together so you can see," he said. "And before you say *you're sweet* again, which I know perfectly well means *you're full of it*, open this."

He handed me a small white box. "I had some time to kill after my meeting in San Francisco last week. Found it at a little vintage jewelry place in Sausalito. You ever been there?"

I shook my head.

It was a necklace. Heavy, 1920s looking, a sleek arrangement of stepped copper and turquoise triangles on an aged, beaded copper chain. I held my hair up and he fastened it, then kissed me on the nape, lips brushing up and down my neck. "You have this downy line right here, it drives me crazy."

I stood to catch my reflection in the sliding glass door, caressing the cold puzzle of metal on my chest. It wasn't something I'd have ever picked out, but it was undeniably stunning. "It's the prettiest thing I've ever owned. Thank you."

"It's not the real gift." He tugged my elbow until I tumbled onto his lap, then shook the necklace box so I could hear it rattle.

I lifted the square of cotton batting: a key.

"I found us a little place for this year, in Sausalito. Up the hill from the jewelry store, hidden in the trees. All the privacy you require, human."

I took the key out, set the box on the table.

"I'll be up next weekend, is it a date?" His smile gave way to a flicker of disappointment when I didn't answer. "It's a quick ferry ride from Berkeley."

I examined the key in my hand: silver, unmarked, with an unexpected heft.

He was trying so hard to sound casual I felt a surge of tenderness for him, but my response surprised even me. "All our dates require a boat."

"Aaah." A mock-crestfallen look. "Maybe you like the boats better than me. This was just thrill seeking, wasn't it? Like your roller coaster in San Diego? The Big Dipper."

"The Giant Dipper."

"I knew it." He sighed heavily, lying back on his chaise and closing his eyes. "I'll soon be replaced by an amusement park ride. I'm...incidental."

"Of course you're not." I reached for his hand but he kept his fist clenched. I poked at it with the key until he relented, opening his hand so I could lace our fingers together, the key inside them. "You surprised me, that's all."

His eyes still closed, he said, "So you're happy about the apartment? Swear?"

"I swear." I leaned to kiss him, but he kept his lips pressed tight. I tickled them with my tongue, trying to tease them apart. "Cal. I swear I'm happy."

"Solemnly swear?" One eye open.

"I solemnly swear," I said. "We can call it...Marilyn Two."

He opened the other eye.

"Marilyn North?" I said. "Winter Marilyn."

He grinned and pulled me to his chest. Everything was still playful, as rosy gold as the late-summer light that had slanted onto the balcony just moments before.

The key was sweet.

The plan was thoughtful.

And the necklace *was* the prettiest thing I'd ever owned. But as I admired it, I was already plotting how to hide it from my mom, my roommates. It was expensive enough to require explanations.

As he murmured about Sausalito, its trees and hills, its charming shops and foghorns, I caught my mind wandering to how I would steal away to get there. I'd need to invent another boyfriend, or pretend I was crashing at the newspaper. It wouldn't be hard, with a little planning. I'd found I had a knack for it.

He had surprised me. Shocked me, even. I'd been so sure that he and I would be over once I tore the August page from my blotter calendar. I had prepared for it; I knew who he was. What *this* was.

But I never considered handing back the key.

And he didn't feel incidental. Not that night, after I dropped it back into the box to kiss him again, seriously this time. We lazed under the stars, entangled on the chaise, until it was dark.

His finger traced the triangles of my necklace as we talked about how we would extend our stolen summer into fall, winter, spring.

A different boat, a different latitude, a different hideaway.

But everything else the same.

# 25

R-squared

September 3, 1996

"You're so organized." My mom came into my bedroom as I was zipping my duffel. "We should leave for the depot in five minutes. You have some junk mail." She set the stack on the corner of my neatly made bed and bustled out. "I can only imagine the pile you're going to have waiting for you by Thanksgiving!"

She was trying hard to be cheerful, though I knew she was sad that I was leaving. And that I'd spent so much time away from her this summer. *Working.*

I was taking the noon bus. By eight tonight I'd be up in my third-floor room unpacking with Maggie and Serra, joking around and catching up, lighting green-apple candles to combat the Plato House smells, singing along to KFOG.

Imagining the secret pied-à-terre that awaited me across the water.

I flipped through the mail. Two credit card offers addressed to Ms. Rebecca Reardon, both proclaiming that I was *prequalified!*

And a yellow-and-black card with the slanted letters VFF and the slogan Membership Has Perks! Since my mom had cosigned for my prepaid $500 credit card, I was a popular girl.

Except VFF wasn't another company trying to get me hooked on plastic; it was an ad for the Vancouver Film Festival. I could become a Back Lot Sponsor or Red Carpet Sponsor or Balcony Sponsor.

On the back was a collage of black-and-white movie stills, and one was from *His Girl Friday*. Rosalind Russell, the wise-cracking, uncompromising newspaper reporter in her gigantic shoulder pads, writing in her notebook.

Eric and I had closet-screened it at least three times.

The first time we watched it together, freshman year of high school, I'd said I wasn't in the mood for a classic. But it won me over.

*We have the same initials*, I'd said. *We're both R-squareds.*

*I think that's a sign from the movie gods you're on the right career path*, Eric had said happily. It always thrilled him to convert someone to his favorite films.

He hadn't signed the postcard, not even with an *E*.

But he'd sketched glasses on Rosalind Russell, in black ball-point. The frames were delicate and slightly cat-eyed, like the ones I'd worn in high school.

*What are you saying, Eric?*

I'd sent him an email from my CommPlanet account the Monday after his mother's party, back in late July. Not a rambling message desperate for forgiveness this time. A defiant one:

Great to see you in the OC. Say congrats!

He hadn't answered. But maybe this was his response at last, to remind me how far I'd strayed from Rosalind.

Or was it an apology, an innocent bit of nostalgia? A reminder of all those hours in his closet on our mountain of pillows, jok-

ing around, bathed in flickering movie light? Not a nasty, judg-
mental reminder, but a sweet one.

Sweet hurt more.

# 26

Perfect Time

2341D Telegraph Avenue #3
Berkeley, CA 94450

Mrs. Francine Haggermaker
7 Old Grove Drive
Orange Park, CA 90667

June 13, 1997
Dear Mrs. Haggermaker,
Junior year was incredibly productive, and I finished with a ~~3.24 nearly 3.3~~ solid GPA. I even earned one A+ ~~in badminton~~.

I had more opportunities to explore Northern California this year. I made a <u>wonderful</u> new friend from a small town across the Bay, and I often

*accompanied her on weekends when she took the
ferry home to visit her parents.*

*Her name is*

I stared out the round window of my Plato House bedroom
at the green Berkeley hills. Biting my pen, I considered possible
names for this dutiful daughter.

Calista? Callie?

It would be there in black Bic, a secret signed confession right
under Mrs. Haggermaker's aristocratic Roman nose.

All year, I'd walked out the door of shabby, noisy Plato
House, grabbed a bus to the port, stepped onto the *SF Bay
Freedom*, and after sixty-four minutes of staring at the heaving
horizon behind its white railings, entered another world. Adult,
refined, expensive.

*It's incredible*, I'd said the first day I saw the apartment, admir-
ing the floor-to-ceiling Bay views.

*Isn't it? Water, water everywhere, just like Catalina.*

But inside it was not like Catalina. That was ochre and gold
and excessive. This was white and cream and minimalist. Calculated blankness, punctuated by a handful of red accessories: a
red line drawing, a stack of red antique books.

The kitchen was white marble, and on the wall, there was
a vintage IBM office clock. Black hour and minute hands, red
second hand, just like the ones at Orange Park High.

TIME IS PASSING. WILL YOU?
FOCUS!

*How funny*, I'd said, back in September, touching the glass
dome. *We had these clocks in high school.*

*They're worth a fortune, or so the decorator persuaded me when I got
the bill*, he'd said, laughing.

Him overpaying for the clock became another of our jokes.

But it kept perfect time; I checked it before running down the hill to the *Bay Freedom*, the ferry that connected my two lives.

By the end of September I knew the *Bay Freedom*'s schedule by heart.

By October the snack bar man had stopped asking for my order.

In the fall, we'd met once a week, sometimes more. Cal would call or email from the airport and a few hours later I'd slip out of a lecture early, my sturdy green JanSport backpack stuffed with books so I wouldn't fall behind. Everything else was in Sausalito. I didn't even have to pack a toothbrush.

To cover for our trysts I made up late study sessions, evenings crashing on the sofa at the newspaper after researching the graffiti story. But I hardly needed to. Serra worked at her studio late into the night. Maggie was dating the woman who lived in the room below us at Plato House, and slept there most of the time.

In Sausalito, Cal and I made love, we talked, we cooked. We walked along the quay at midnight, holding hands, when no one could see. He said someday, when I wasn't worried about hiding, he'd take me to the little apartment he owned in San Francisco. Close to the Fairmont Hotel in Nob Hill, with a Juliet balcony and a sliver of a Bay view. "Just an investment property, these days. But I think you'd like it."

"Sausalito suits me fine," I said. Secrecy suited me fine, too.

★

For months I'd expected him to pull away, bored. If he had, I might have clung tighter. I was as perverse as any human.

But by February, while he was as attentive as ever, part of me missed my college life. My clean twenty-year-old's life: blue books and flash cards, oversize sweatshirts and overstewed student union coffee. Walking to pizza with Serra and Maggie. Goodnight kisses that didn't lead to anything else.

Like temperature readings, my ferry return times revealed the cooling pattern of our affair:

February, 7:06

March, 6:07

April, 5:03

May, 4:06

But I didn't suggest ending it. I was still holding on to our golden beginning. And there were times, in the dark with him, when he still made me feel happy, like the only person in the world. His effect on my body was the same. It was the before and after that had changed, and I couldn't figure out why.

I began to lie to him. I made up study sessions, overdue papers, head colds.

I said that I had to enroll in the summer class at Berkeley, when I could've easily taken it down south. I pretended I was sad that we wouldn't have another summer on Catalina, that my classes and my job up here would make it harder to meet.

I canceled a whole weekend in May, emailing at the last minute:

> My English class is seeing *A Midsummer Night's Dream* at
> the Shakespeare Fest. I have to go!! I'm so sorry. Xoxoxo.

I spent that weekend in the stacks, catching up on my reading. Now I had two sets of lies to keep track of, one on each shore.

The last time I'd met him in Sausalito, ten days ago, I'd worn the necklace he'd given me, to prove things hadn't changed. I tugged him into the bedroom within minutes of arriving—"Well, now," he said, pleased—and it was as good as ever.

But while he slept soundly on my chest afterward, his lips parted like a child's, I couldn't sleep at all. I lay awake for hours, looking at him in the moonlight. The bright triangular pieces of my necklace entwined with his hair, like a broken crown.

I watched him sleeping, trying to figure out what to say, how to explain. Maybe we only made sense in the summer and had stretched our affair too thin, trying to extend it into other seasons.

The next morning I sat on the top deck of the ferry, where the lashing wind made it too cold to think.

★

In my shared room at Plato House, I stared at the letter to Mrs. Haggermaker.

> I made a <u>wonderful</u> new friend from a small town across the Bay, and I often accompanied her on weekends when she took the ferry home to visit her parents.
>
> Her name is

Callie was too much; I wasn't that far gone.

When it came to me I wrote it slowly, with a flourish: a round *M*, a *y* flowing long as a mermaid's tail:

> Marilyn.
>
> It was absolutely lovely to have a "home away from home" with Marilyn's family. We spent most of our time studying but took occasional breaks to picnic or hike.
>
> On every ferry crossing, as I returned from Marilyn's, I thought of the <u>inspiring</u> Latin inscription on the plaque you gave me three years ago:
>
> "To truly learn is to sail, anchorless yet unafraid, the vast oceans of the unknown, looking always at the horizon."
>
> They are wise words that perfectly capture my college experiences so far.
>
> This summer I am staying in Berkeley for the first

time, as are my roommates. Two mornings a week I'll be taking a three-credit rhetoric course to free up my schedule for an honors seminar next fall.

I'll also be editing the in-house publication at a respected San Francisco ~~real estate~~ firm; it's a wonderful opportunity.

I'm enclosing four articles I wrote for the campus paper this year: a feature on a karaoke fund-raiser for our sister school in Japan and three on student union elections.

How _thrilling_ to think that when I mail my next letter, I will be a college graduate, ready to voyage into the adult world. I can't wait.

I am already looking at the horizon, unafraid.

With my deepest gratitude,

Rebecca Reardon

# 27

## Surprise

June 15, 1997

The Sunday evening before my first day as newsletter editorial intern at Elliot & Healey, Industrial Realty, Serra and Maggie and I were hanging out in our bedroom. Apple candle flickering on our thrift-store dresser, cool evening wind puffing in from the round window by Maggie's bed.

Serra paced our brown carpet, organizing pieces of an art project that involved her latest mania—a series of office-marker self-portraits drawn on overhead projector transparencies. She had the clear rectangles laid out in rows; we'd been jumping between them for weeks. It was like playing negative Twister.

"Are those for the invitational, Serr?" I asked. "Part of your triptych?" Yvonne Copeland, her mentor/professor/boss at the museum, was putting on a student show this summer.

"No, that's too big to work on here," she said. "This is to get my mind off my showpiece because I'm convinced it blows.

Maybe I should bind these into a sort of flip book. You know? Like those early animations? But disturbing."

"That sounds cool," I said.

"I like it, make your public work a little." Maggie aimed a gray plume of smoke out the window. She'd set her bed stack up there expressly for this purpose. With one leg dangling off the layers, she looked like she was melting down the side; Serra called it her Dali *Floppy Watches* look.

"What'd'you think, glue or three-hole punch? Never mind, I'll test both." Serra plugged in her hot glue gun.

"You're not going down to Bonnie's tonight, Mags?" I asked.

"It's the third time this week she's bailed on me. And even when we do hang out, all she talks about is her hobo markings." Maggie gazed wistfully at the floor. Bonnie was writing her dissertation on the codes homeless men chalked onto buildings as warnings and advice during the Depression, things like Work Here and Dangerous Man. "Wanna hear how desperate I've become? I suggested we trace hobo signs on each other in bed. You know, sort of incorporate her thesis into our sex life."

"That's weirdly hot," Serra said.

"Well, she didn't think so," Maggie said. "I'm out of ideas. Draw me a sign for Frustrated Woman, Serra."

"You're a thesis widow, Mags," I said.

"Yep." She blew a smoke ring at me. "But this is nice. The three of us haven't hung out in ages."

"It is nice," I said. "I've missed you guys."

"We should—" The phone cut Serra off.

"I'll get it," I said, sliding off my bed. We kept our phone, a beige '70s Trimline from Goodwill, on top of a cluttered bookcase by the door.

Cal. "Guess where I am, human."

"Hey, Jess! Sure, let me check." I grabbed my backpack off

my bed, fished out a notebook, pretended to hunt through it. "Found them."

"Give my regards to your roommates," he said, laughing. "I'm on campus, changed my flight from SFO to Oakland. Thought I'd surprise you. I'm at some place on Bancroft Avenue, Caffè Strada. White awning out front, you know it?"

"No problem."

"I've got a couple hours before I have to leave for the airport. Thought we could have a bite."

"I hope you can read my handwriting!"

"I've got us a booth in back so you don't need to worry. Unless you want to check into a hotel in Berkeley. You can stay after I go, take one of your baths. I can picture you as I sit through that endless due-diligence meeting tomorrow morning. All soapy and slippery, your hair wet..."

This wasn't just dirty talk; baths were another of our inside jokes. At Plato House I didn't have a tub, only shared access to a tepid, mildewy shower.

Cal had urged me to use the Sausalito place whenever I wanted, to make it my pied-à-terre. But I'd never gone alone, not even to take advantage of the pristine, jetted tub. I didn't want to think of myself as a kept woman.

"Rebecca?" he said. "What do you think?"

"Let's meet at the café."

"See you in twenty?"

"Sounds good. Bye, Jess."

I zipped my backpack, brushed my hair. The sounds were the same as before: the zither-y music of Serra rearranging her plastic pages, Maggie's languid exhales. The *thwack, thwack* of Glenn, hacky sacking in the hall.

But now the silence seemed assertive.

"That was just this girl who wants to borrow my American lit notes for summer session," I said. "Jess."

Maggie coughed, but was it her usual lazy pot cough? And was Serra concentrating too hard on her transparencies? I was being paranoid. Secondhand effects of Maggie's weed.

"I'm going to run meet her at Café Diavolo." Everyone hated Diavolo. It was overpriced and served burned espresso; there was no chance they'd want to come. "What were you saying before, Serr?"

"Oh. I was going to suggest Chocolate Margs."

"Excellent idea," Maggie said.

When I stepped onto the porch, they were in the kitchen, laughing over the blender's roar.

It hit me with awful clarity as their happy sounds faded behind me: I didn't want to go.

★

It was a ten-minute walk across campus from Plato House to the café. I could do it in half that if I rushed.

But I dawdled. I waved at a boy from my Shakespeare section and chatted. When I passed the econ building, I spotted new cat graffiti on a door and took out my notebook, carefully logging the details of the sighting as I always did—date, location—so I could note it on my map and enter it in the Hiss file on my laptop later.

I didn't get a charge out of the Fe|Co symbol tonight, and I wasn't eager to get to the café to tell Cal so we could joke about it. "Co" probably did just stand for company like he'd said; it was a depressing marketing scheme.

Serra still asked me the occasional polite question about what she called *your multiplying kitties*, but everyone else thought I was wasting my time. Maybe I was.

I glanced up at the hands on the clock tower. 7:30. I should have been at the café half an hour ago.

In Sproul Plaza, a woman was playing the marimba, a sweet,

echoing tune. I dropped a dollar in her bucket and lingered on a sunny patch of grass to listen.

Five minutes, ten.

He'd be checking his watch, wondering where I was.

I was supposed to be happy, eager for a few stolen minutes. My lover hadn't *bailed on me* like Maggie's. He'd changed his plans to see me. But instead of anticipation I felt only resentment.

*It's over,* I whispered, testing the words.

I couldn't hear them over the marimba. Island music, a sound that belonged to beaches, sailboats. The thought made me so sad, picturing last summer, that I almost went home. If only I could tell my roommates, cry with them and let them console me, ply me with drinks, like everyone else going through a breakup.

But I'd reached for him in secret, and this was my punishment; I had to let him go in secret, too.

I would do it tonight. I would be *direct*, like the magazines advised. I would be *mature, direct.* We would *part as friends.*

★

I spotted him in the café before he noticed me. At a shadowy, indoor table like he'd promised. Shirtsleeves rolled up, tie loosened. Working on his laptop, his navy suit jacket folded crisply over his briefcase on the table. He was surrounded by summer-session kids. No one I knew, thank god. They were hunched over their textbooks, tinny music escaping from their headphones, shabby backpacks thrown on the dirty floor.

Compared with them, he looked so…complete.

A pretty redhead at the next table was eyeing him, had no doubt been neglecting her textbooks for the last hour, distracted by this beautiful, older, completely out-of-place man. But he wasn't looking at her.

I wished he was. If I caught him flirting back, it would make it easier.

He saw me and beamed.

"Trouble getting away?" he asked when I sat down.

"Yeah, sorry. My roommates were on me."

"Are you glad I switched my flight?"

"Of course!"

"So. Big first day tomorrow," he said. "I still wish you'd let me—"

"Don't, please, I—"

"Okay, okay."

He'd offered to find me a better summer job. But much as I dreaded the real estate newsletter gig, at least I'd gotten it myself. "They're letting me work my schedule around my Tuesday-Thursday class, it's perfect."

"Got it. Everything good?" he asked, a flicker of worry in his eyes. "You seem..."

"Just nervous about my first day of work tomorrow, I guess." I made my voice light. "Should I buy you my favorite drink from here? Coconut Italian soda."

He made a face and I laughed, trying to dredge up our old playfulness.

"I wish I could stay," he said.

"Me, too." We held hands under the table. Talked. Joked about my upcoming job, his. He pulled my foot onto his lap, slipped off my shoe, massaged my instep.

But surely he had to feel that things between us were not the same. That he didn't belong here on campus.

When it was time for him to call a cab, he said, "See you Friday, human." He stood, brushed his lips on my bare shoulder, hiding the kiss behind his briefcase.

"Wait."

He turned. "Ah, now she wants me to stay."

I couldn't do it. Not yet, not here.

Whoever said *just be direct* hadn't looked into blue eyes as bright as this, eyes that went from serious to laughing so quickly you wanted to watch them, try to pinpoint exactly when they changed. "Just. Have a safe flight."

I'd do it next week when we were alone. So I could plan exactly what to say.

Later that night

Serra and Maggie were out when I came back, so I booted up my laptop to note the graffiti marking I'd seen on the econ department door.

I had to keep busy.

Waiting for my computer to groan to life, I stared down at Serra's transparencies. She'd drawn a fake hobo marking for Frustrated Woman, as requested. A cartoon version of Maggie, shaggy hair and smoking blunt in her hand. Normally it would make me smile, but I was too sad tonight. I stared down at the picture and it started to blur.

I don't know how long I cried. But when I stopped, I felt better. I'd decided. I felt emptied out, clear. Calmer than I'd felt in months.

I wiped my eyes and surveyed the transparencies on the floor. Serra was so talented. She wasn't frittering away her time in indecision; she was making something that mattered. She worked late into the night on her project for the invitational—at her studio, conferring with Yvonne at the museum. Returning to Plato energized and purposeful. The way I'd once felt about reporting, about fitting pages together at the Orange Park High *Squeeze.*

I stared at the clear pages on the floor for a long time.

I hopped down, grabbed some blank sheets from the box,

scrambled back onto my bed. Slowly at first, I held them over
the campus map on the wall and marked them, dividing the
sheets into groups based on the month and year they'd appeared
on campus. Then, one by one, oldest sightings first, I placed the
marked-up sheets over the map to see if my hunch was right.

After the second clear page I could see them. Circles around
at least five buildings on campus. Not random. Not a joke.

When Serra and Maggie came in I spoke in a rush. "I think
the graffiti marks specific people. Surrounds them. Targets them,
or says something about them, like hobo markings."

"What makes you think that?" Serra asked. But she had the
funniest expression on her face. Like a kid who's been caught
being bad and is proud of it.

"What?" I asked.

"Hypothetically, what would you do if I knew something
about it?"

"You do know who's—?"

"Answer the question."

"I don't know. I just want the truth."

"Attached to your byline on the front page."

"That would be nice," I said.

"Could someone please fill me in?" Maggie said.

"Swear not to write about it," Serra said to me, stern. "Not
unless we say it's okay."

"I swear," I said fast. "Who's we?"

"I swear, too. What'm I swearing to?" Maggie flipped through
my scribbled-on transparencies, baffled.

*Thwack, thwack, thwack.* Glenn was hacky sacking outside our
half-open door. Serra slammed it shut. "That boy is going to
drive me to the counseling center."

But when she turned she was smiling. She laid her right
arm out across my mattress, palm up. Unsnapped the faded tan
leather cuff bracelet she'd bought on Telegraph freshman year,

the one that matched mine. She wore it night and day, even in the shower.

On her wrist was a tattoo: black cat's whiskers like the ones in the graffiti. Two delicate arrows with the tips touching:

# 28

## Upgrade

2008
Friday, 3:40 p.m.
Oakland

I rise up in my seat to help Eric with directions. "We can get in the left lane of the bridge, it might be less jammed. The hotel's way out on the west side of the city, by the Presidio."

For the first time, he's driving. He insisted. *Please let me help a little*, he said.

We're approaching the Bay Bridge but stuck in gridlock on the east side. It's rush hour on a Friday, and traffic's as hideous as Joy Gold warned. The trip isn't going exactly as I'd imagined. But since he showed me his Date Insurance program in Berkeley, the edges of my anger toward him have softened.

He's trying. At the gas station in Berkeley, when the guy at the next pump asked him *what the heck* was in the box, Eric answered, without missing a beat, "Dining table from IKEA. The Shwizzlefloozen?"

"Good luck putting it together," the man called. "Looks like a real beast!"

When the man drove away, Eric stood by my window wringing out the dripping blue ARCO station chamois he was using to clean our windshield. His smile had fallen away. "Hey, Becc?"

My breath caught as I asked, in the most neutral voice I could manage, "What is it?"

"Oh, nothing." He shook his head, lobbed the windshield rag into the tub.

*Hey, Becc?*

I want to know what he was about to say. But those two sweet, short words will do for now.

He didn't have to come. It's not easy for him, but he's here.

I glance down at my map and go on with my directions. "Once we get across the bridge we can cut west on Fell or Geary to avoid some of the Embarcadero mess. Then Park Presidio's probably going to be the fastest way up to the hotel. If we ever start moving!"

No answer.

"Eric?"

He clenches his jaw, turns to me without a smile.

It's strange, because we've been so much more relaxed with each other since our joint confessions in Berkeley. It broke the tension a little. But now he looks uneasy, like he's bracing himself.

"What?" My quads and arms are getting tired from the awkward little chin-up maneuver I'm doing to keep my head above the box. "Is traffic getting to you? It's awful, isn't it? You probably don't drive much in New York—"

"About the hotel. I sort of...upgraded our lodgings last week."

"Upgraded?"

He hands me a computer printout over the wall.

I sink back down into my seat to read.

And close my eyes.

"I've been trying to get us something else since yesterday," he says, an apologetic strain in his voice. "That's why I was late to breakfast this morning. But I haven't been able to book anything so last-minute yet. High season."

All I can focus on is the hum of the idling motors around us, the wind whooshing overhead.

*He didn't.*

"Becc?"

Except the words in my hand prove he did.

"I booked that one on impulse when I got your itinerary. I did it late at night when I wasn't thinking straight and I've been trying like crazy to undo it."

I don't answer him.

"I didn't realize at the time… I mean, can't we…make the best of it? Let's stop at a restaurant and make some calls. There'll be more cancellations by now, maybe we'll find something else."

There are many reasonable responses to the pages he's handed me.

*You know, I put a lot of thought into where we were staying tonight.*

*This might make bringing the box inside a little tricky. I didn't want to deal with elevators.*

*You could have let me know earlier, at least.*

*Yes, let's go to a restaurant and call triple-A until we find a different place.*

But what he's done is awful. And even if he says he tried to undo it, the *impulse* is so unbelievably twisted.

I open my eyes. "For the record, I reserved two cottages." My voice is ice.

He lifts himself above the box and stares at me. "What?"

"Tonight's reservation. I know it showed up as only one address on the itinerary, but it was for two separate cottages. They're converted officers' quarters. I wasn't going to climb into your bed while you were sleeping."

"I wasn't—"

"That's obviously what you were afraid of, booking this place instead. It's okay. It was my oversight. I should have made it more clear. That I wasn't going to bother you."

He shakes his head. Huffs through his nose, a rapid yeah-right snort.

"What?" I ask.

"Nothing."

"What, you obviously thought I'd booked one room, and you did this because you were afraid I was going to—"

"Believe me, I wasn't thinking anything close to that, Miss Let's Erect an Actual Fucking Wall in the Car!"

He's looming over the box, stretching his seat belt to the limit.

My voice is small, shocked. "What? It was the only way the present would fit, the two pieces are stuck together and I—"

"Are you kidding me?"

"I told you, it only came this week because the preschool lady was on vacation, and I spent all Wednesday night trying to find a better way—"

"Sure. You keep telling yourself that. But this…" he slaps the box "…is some repressed Freudian-level shit, Becc. You could've rented another car. A van, whatever. You wanted it here, your little *barricade*. Admit it!"

It's horrible to see Eric's sweet brown eyes flash, to hear the anguished tremor in his voice. To feel his anger, hot waves coming off his body in the cool San Francisco air.

"You want everything on your terms, Becc. Same as always. You say you want my help, but you plan every goddamned mile. You figured out the whole four-day trip before I had a chance to weigh in on one fucking *minute* of it."

Someone's honking behind us but he ignores them. "You decided where we should stay. Stop. Eat. Admit it!"

I'm the one who should be furious after what he's done.

But all I feel is stunned.

We'd been doing okay. I thought we were over the hard part

after Berkeley. No more Date Insurance, no more scone pelting. *Shwizzlefloozen.*

*Admit it!*

He doesn't mean *admit you dominated the planning for the trip.* Or *admit you're still a control freak.*

I know exactly what he means. And I know he's not mad because I worked on the itinerary without consulting him.

We stare at each other for a minute.

"I admit it," I say quietly. "I screwed up."

He's breathing hard. Waiting for me to surrender in this awful game of chicken we're playing while the disgusted drivers around us honk and edge past.

"Let's just stay there," I say. "We'll go with your plans tonight."

He hesitates a minute.

*Please say no.*

I shrug. "It's fine. It's just a building, and we're grownups. It's no big deal."

*Please, please don't make us go there. Stay in this lane.*

"Perfect," he finally says.

He disappears.

Flicks on the turn signal. *Tick, tick, tick, tick...*

And at the first gap, he lurches into the right lane. The one that will take us to the last place on earth I want to go.

# 29

## Scoop

June 15, 1997

Fe|Co was not a dull marketing initiative for a cat food company.

It stood for Feline Collective. It had started in the '80s, when a lit professor, one of the top five living experts on T. S. Eliot, had an affair with an art grad student. He'd been married with three kids and a nice wife in another department.

"Some people say the wife was in history and some say poli sci, but that part doesn't really matter," Serra explained.

"Go on," I said. "The student started it."

"Yes. She broke it off with the professor. Fell in love with someone else."

"And the professor murdered her? And your feline gang is out to get justice…"

"Sorry to disappoint you, Becc, but nobody killed anybody. She dumped him. But…" She paused for effect.

"Come on, what?" I asked.

"Stop milking it," Maggie said, laughing.

"But then she lost a fellowship, and a teaching job she was supposed to get after graduation. He went around smearing her, quietly making her life hell. While *his* career was totally unscathed."

"Was her art any good?" I asked.

"Yes. I've seen it." Serra waited for me to catch up.

"Yvonne."

She nodded. "After she got her life back together, she got the tattoo. To remember, she says. To remind herself... Oh. It's like that Eliot line you wouldn't stop quoting sophomore year, Becc. When you made the T. S. Eliot connection so you were *positive* some disgruntled theater geek was behind it? Because they didn't get a part in *Cats*?"

I recited: "My ineffable, effable name."

I'd repeated the line in my head, pounding the clay stadium track, trying to puzzle out why the graffiti had such a hold on me. *Ineffable, effable. Effinaneffable.* It perfectly matched my running stride.

Serra went on. "Yes. *The cat knows* its real name, it knows itself, the good, the bad. And nobody else's words can take it away. That's the general idea.

"Anyway, the asshole professor had died by then, but she started this group, with a couple friends, to go after men who were abusing their power on campus. We send an anonymous letter, then, if they don't resign, the graffiti. To put them on notice."

"Why not just go to the media?" I asked.

"Useless, it's been tried. Sorry, Becc. They wouldn't cover the OB in the health center who 'forgets' his gloves, either, because the girls' parents had second thoughts and decided to keep it quiet. Plenty of other delightful stories like that. Our method is...surprisingly effective. Two profs have resigned so far. We're going after this repulsive lecturer in the econ department now, a real piece of work, this tech gajillionaire who plays at teaching."

I knew it before I asked. Those wanton, lashless eyes on my blouse. "Derrek Schwinn?"

"Yeah, how'd—?"

"I'll tell you later. What's he done?"

"He offers letters of rec and jobs if students blow him. But pretends it's a joke.

"He's tricky because he sits on the museum board with Yvonne and he's loaded," Serra said. "We have to be careful."

"Does everyone have the tattoo?" Maggie asked.

"Whiskers optional."

"Where do you meet?" I asked.

"The museum basement. It's a perfect cover. And..."

"What?" Maggie and I said in unison.

"Okay. You won't like this part. Yvonne dips into the museum fund to help women who've been screwed over. Calls them grants or fellowships. You should see some of the wack projects she funds."

I said, "You could just warn other—"

"We're on it, someone's working on a private chat board. Like...virtual graffiti warnings."

"Like the hobo marking for Dangerous Man," Maggie said.

The three of us sat in silence for a minute.

"Why didn't you tell us before?" I asked.

"I wanted to. I almost did. But Mags is on academic probation—"

"I don't care," Maggie said.

"I know *you* don't, but Disciplinary Comm might feel differently. Vandalism? Yvonne dipping into donor money for her pet cause? Also..." Serra crossed the room to our bookshelf, crammed with paperbacks and textbooks, candles and CDs. "Guess who's one of the museum's biggest donors, who sits on the board with Yvonne and is tight with the gentlemanly Derrek Schwinn, and who would *definitely* close her checkbook if she knew?"

Serra grabbed something from my top bookshelf. She spun around holding it, smiling like Vanna White.

My Haggermaker Scholarship plaque.

★

How badly I wanted to tell my editor, right to his ironic bow tie, that the story he thought was *small* had legs. Big, muscular legs.

Late that night I wrote the article I'd always dreamed of writing. But not for the paper.

It was Serra's idea. "I know you, you have to get it out of your system," she said. "Write it and then erase it."

So, sipping a Chocolate Marg, I wrote a juicy, detailed, thousand-word story about the Feline Collective and scummy Derrek Schwinn, with real quotes from Serra and imaginary quotes from Yvonne Copeland and everything.

By the time we got to headlines we were feeling no pain. Maggie was big on *litter box*.

"CLEAN SCHWINN'S LITTER BOX!" she yelled from her bed.

"No, write something with Yvonne's name," Serra suggested from the floor, where she was lying on her back, a transparency portrait over her face. "Cope. Land. A NEW LAND! LAND OF OPPORTUNITY!"

"I love you guys, but these are not good headlines." Finally, spent, I typed in The Cat is Known! Recognizing even in my Chocolate Marg euphoria that my imaginary newspaper wasn't the *Enquirer*, I took out the !

"There. Okay, come verify this tragic moment." I changed the file name on my computer from Hiss to Memory, my little nod to *Cats*. Dragged the file into the gray trash can icon on my screen.

"It's not really gone," Maggie said. "Hit Empty, Trash."

"I know." I emptied the trash. "Buh-bye, front-page scoop."

# 30

## Viking

June 20, 1997

That week I threw myself into my new job, dull as it was. Anything to get my mind off what I planned to do Friday.

Because I was certain now. It was over. The Derrek Schwinn thing only confirmed it; I didn't feel good about Cal anymore.

At Elliot & Healey, Industrial Realty, I helped with the "real estate trend" newsletter, a thrilling document called the *Pulse & ForeCastr.* I worked hard while the brokers paced around like tigers behind glass walls, hunting commissions over their speakerphones.

I worked too hard, because the week passed quickly.

But when Friday came, and I finally stepped onto the boat to tell Cal it was over, I felt brave.

My backpack held an empty duffel bag for my Sausalito things. I wore my work outfit: black pants and a soft white blouse, the necklace he'd given me tucked against my chest like armor.

It was a cold, foggy day and I stood near the bow, a Viking in a purple North Face parka. Ready for battle.

I would say, *It's over.*

Simple, clear, irrevocable.

He wouldn't arrive in Sausalito for three hours, until after meetings in the city, but when he came I'd be in the living room waiting, my Sausalito things gathered and packed in front of me. He'd see the bag, and he'd know.

But when I opened the door he was already there, his back to me, looking out the window. And the room was gold.

Gold helium balloons clung to the ceiling, ribbons spiraling down. The gas fire glowed on low, cake and champagne on the dining table. Something smelling of brine warming on the stove.

He turned, proud. Shoulders decked in gold ribbons. Holding a white box with a gold ribbon. "Surprise. I blew off my meetings."

"It's too much," I said. "My birthday's not for eight days."

"Twenty-one's a big deal, human. This way I get to be first to toast you."

In the box was a wide, wavy gold cuff bracelet from the vintage shop.

"You wear it above the elbow, the girl said. Flapper-style." He rolled up the left sleeve of my blouse, guided my hand into the cold circlet and gently worked it up my arm to near my shoulder, shaping the metal so it stayed.

I looked down at the armband, touching the small zigzag window of my flesh framed in gold. "You didn't need to do this."

"Of course I didn't *need* to. I wanted to. You'll get your big present in the morning. I just have a little bit of prep before it's ready."

After dinner, he kissed me. He tasted of chocolate frosting, sweet as he had been all night.

It would be brutal to do it now.

"Don't you want to?" he asked in bed when I caught the hand caressing my thigh, squeezed it gently, and pulled it from my skin.

"Too much champagne." I kissed him on the cheek and turned my back to him.

★

I didn't drift off until three, but then I slept heavily. I woke at nine, groggy from champagne, and found him grinning at me across the bed, excited to show me my "big" present. A brand-new, fancy laptop, festooned with more curly gold ribbon.

"All the latest software's on there, a TX9 Graphics Booster and 32 megabytes of memory, and I mirrored you over, you only need to start it up, it's got SmartBackup and—"

"It's too much," I whispered, trying to make sense of the jargon.

"Stop. It's for me, really. I can't stand watching while you wait for that clunker to boot up, and you'll get used to it, I swear, once... Hey. Hey, birthday girl, what's this?" He touched my wet cheek.

I shook my head. "It's all too much."

The only sound was the whisper of the ribbon from my present as I raked it through my fingers, pulling the curls, wrapping them around my hand. "It's gotten too complicated."

"You mean us?"

I nodded.

"I told you we don't have to hide like criminals. That's your thing."

"It's not that."

"Is there someone else? Is that why you're staying in Berkeley this summer?"

I shook my head.

*Then why?*

I had prepared for him to ask why, and had decided on this answer: "I care about you, but it doesn't feel right anymore."

But he didn't ask me why. He looked so surprised that I weakened again.

I hedged. "I need some time to think. A break, to figure things out." I slid the fancy new laptop across the sheet to him.

"Keep the damn computer, Rebecca." He ventured a smile, half of a beach-volleyball smile. "You can use it for emailing me when you change your mind."

I shook my head, only half of a Viking. Not accepting the computer, but not admitting the truth, either. "Let's just see how the summer goes."

On the ferry ride home, I clutched my key to the Sausalito house, willing myself to drop it into the water. But I couldn't get my hand to open.

# 31

## Hold On

June 26, 1997

The week after Cal's surprise birthday party was rough. I had trouble falling asleep, and made zero progress on the *Pulse & ForeCastr*.

But each day I was more sure I'd done the right thing, trusting my instincts. Like with the graffiti—my gut would always tell me when to hold on and when to let go.

I wouldn't go back to Sausalito.

And life would get simpler, more honest.

I felt it.

★

I slept until 9:50 Thursday morning, almost missing my rhetoric lecture. But if I sprinted, I'd only be a minute or two late.

I speed-walked across the squeaking front porch, digging in my backpack for quarters. I'd treat myself to a chocolate-chip scone and a coffee after class. Something massive, topped with whipped cream.

"Watch out, lady," someone said, holding me by the shoulders so we wouldn't crash.

Gentle hands on my bare shoulders. Warm ones.

Hands that had met mine in high fives over the pinball table in the garage, hands I'd dueled with at the bottom of a popcorn tub, hands I'd watched flying over piano keys, rooting in cassette crates.

He hadn't emailed for more than a year. The last proof of life he'd sent was a pair of eyeglasses doodled onto a film festival postcard.

And now he stood ten inches away, his J. Press coat thrown over one shoulder, his duffel bag hanging from the other. So close I could see the way the inner edge of his left eyebrow fanned the wrong direction, like a silky brown paintbrush tip.

Eric.

# 32

## Bridge

2008
Friday, 4:30 p.m.

Eric and I are suspended over the water, halfway between Oakland and San Francisco.

A romantic way of saying we're stuck in traffic on the Bay Bridge.

I have nothing to do but stare out my window at the scenery.

Lush, graceful Angel Island.

Barren, lumpen Alcatraz.

The hills of Sausalito in the distance, beyond the fog.

Ferries whisking tourists and commuters across the water.

Does the *Bay Freedom* still run, carrying lovers back and forth?

I can't look away.

On the front bench of the top deck I see a Becc who's becoming restless. She's always been so clever with words, but she can't seem to say, *It's over.*

And she doesn't know why.

I want to tell her that sometimes the words just won't come. Especially when you're twenty, and you've never been with anyone else. And you're clinging to the sweet start, holding on a little longer than you should.

Another Becc is standing at the bow of the rocking ferry, holding her key. Trying so hard to release it into the cold waves.

I see Cal across the bed. Looking confused, surprised that even his charm has limits.

I picture the bottom of San Francisco Bay littered with the discards of other affairs. Other keys. Some are still floating down. Some are settling into the silty ocean floor, and some are rusty and buried, crumbling into nothing.

I thought I'd forgiven myself for the choices I made ten years ago. The decisions that I knew were wrong at the time, and the ones I thought were right.

## 33

### Alcatraz

June 26, 1997
Morning

WHERE I WAS SUPPOSED TO BE | Rhetoric 103
WHERE I WAS | Giving a tour

We stood on the porch. Eric smiled and released my shoulders, as if it was no big deal that he'd dropped back into my life.

It had drizzled overnight. Summer came late to Berkeley. But now the puddles on the porch steps reflected blue sky, and we listened to the last of the rainwater dripping down the gutter. The drops were slowing, but just when I thought we'd heard the last one, another *plink* would ring out from the metal chute.

We listened to nine *plink*s before he spoke again.

"Hey," he said finally. "Long time no see."

I didn't say a word.

"How was junior year?"

I shrugged.

He dropped his duffel and tossed his coat on top of it carelessly, so a sleeve landed on the dirty porch boards. He strolled around, stretching his arms high above his head.

He knocked the barbecue lid with his fist. "Nice barbecue."

It was a terrible barbecue. The lid was covered in more rust than red paint. It was a brand nobody had ever heard of called Viper, with the font designed to trick people into thinking it was a Weber.

Eric walked back to me, so close I thought he was going for a hug. Instead he held my hands and raised my arms, like London Bridges. "You look good. Except for the toothpaste on your lip." He released my hands and tried to brush my lips with his thumb.

I dodged his hand, wiping my mouth. "What are you doing here?"

"I was in the neighborhood. I thought I might as well make sure you and Serra hadn't joined the Moonies."

I wanted to grab the barbecue lid and crash it on the base like a cymbal. Throw his too-formal coat in the mud.

Anything so he'd stop pretending everything was the same.

"Actually, I'm here for the summer," he said. "I got an internship in San Francisco, with this TV show. It's pretty lame, but it's a good opportunity."

"Congrats."

He nodded, looking down at his shoes.

I concentrated on breathing. Three breaths in, five breaths out, like it said on the relaxation tape Maggie bought at the gas station.

"I deserved that," he said. "You have every right to be mad."

"I'm not mad. Just surprised to see you."

"Becc." He dared a glance at me. "You're mad. Shaking mad. Sweating mad."

"I'm sweating because I was running to class."

"You're madder than that day in ninth grade when Beth Tiernan giggled during your Marie Curie speech. Madder than when I was playing keep-away with your Knott's Berry Farm sweatshirt on the pier in Santa Monica and your wallet flew into the ocean. Tell me why."

I made myself meet his eyes.

"Say it," he said. "I can handle it."

"Why would I be mad? After your many letters, your long emails."

"Keep going."

"The way you were so sweet when I offered to fly out, or meet you somewhere. What...five times? Six?" The bitterness in my voice was so strong I could feel it, a sludgy thickness in the back of my throat.

I was trying to maintain control, to speak like the sophisticated Becc I thought I'd become, but the anger and hurt and confusion I'd tamped down for three years had broken free: "The way you told me in advance that you were coming home to Orange Park for a whole day last summer. A whole, entire day!"

"I know," he said quietly.

"So after all that, why the hell would I be even the *slightest* bit mad, Eric?"

We stared at each other. I was breathing hard. My sarcasm hung in the air between us.

Slowly, he nodded. Smiled a sad, resigned little smile.

"You should be mad. I would've been." He picked up his bag and coat, walked toward the porch steps. "I'll get a room at the Fairmont."

"It's across the Bay."

"I'll swim. If I need a break I'll stop on Alcatraz."

"Good idea."

He looked over his shoulder. "I'll lock myself in the coldest cell. For the crime of? What? Insufficient emails?"

"Desertion."

"Excellent. I'll go, then." Attempting to make a rakish exit, he jumped off the porch, clearing all five steps like Evel Knievel but landing with a skid on the soggy grass. He tried to use his duffel as a counterweight but he slid and fell on his ass, his fancy coat flying into the dirt.

I couldn't help it. A corner of my mouth crept up.

Because I wasn't sure, anymore, who had deserted who first. I wasn't sure that it mattered. I had chosen Cal over him three years ago, and even if Eric didn't know that, maybe it made us even.

"Come back," I said, my voice an exaggerated sigh.

He gathered his things, brushed off his butt, and walked up the steps. "You wanted me to fall, didn't you?"

"Yes." I smiled. "Are you okay?"

"I'll survive."

"So where are you staying this summer? The city?"

He pointed at the door behind me. "I got a great deal on this guy Glenn's room. He said it's pretty small, but the price is right. You going to poison me in my sleep?"

"I should."

We smiled at each other for a minute. The breeze had picked up and we listened to the lazy *tings* of the wind chimes over the porch stairs. My breathing had relaxed and the bitterness was gone, replaced by simple relief that his eyes were still kind, still such a soft shade of brown.

*I'm sorry*, he mouthed, his eyes fixed on mine. Beautiful eyes: wide set, dark lashed, large as a fawn's. I'd missed them. I'd missed him, more than I'd have thought possible.

He was holding his breath. Waiting for me to decide if I'd take him back.

"I guess the dimensions of your room are punishment enough."

★

Eric surveyed the front room of the co-op. Plywood covered broken stained glass, purple paint flaked off the high ceilings, and the moldings were battered. The living room furniture consisted of a brown vinyl beanbag chair, its gashes repaired by a network of silver duct tape, and multiple futons that had been left behind over the years. On one futon, a guy I didn't recognize slept on his back, a half-eaten plate of nachos riding up and down his chest.

"Can I reconsider the Alcatraz cell?" Eric asked.

"Be nice. You're still on probation."

I led him up two sets of creaking stairs and we stashed his duffel in his closet-size room. Eric shuddered at the crib mattress but said gamely, "Maybe I can sleep with my legs in the hall. Show me your room? Or do you still need to run to your class?"

"I can skip."

He raised an eyebrow. "What happened to Miss Perfect Attendance?"

"She's long gone. I'd win the Imperfect Attendance award now, easy."

Eric paused by the mural on the bathroom door. It was supposed to be Abbie Hoffman in his American flag shirt. Serra and Maggie and I had gotten excited the day we moved in, touching the thirty-year-old paint. It was an awful mural, and something about the way the artist had exaggerated his cleft chin and botched his hair made Abbie look more like John Travolta. But still, it was so perfectly Berkeley in the '60s. Someone should have unhinged the door long before and put it in a museum.

"Did Serra paint that?"

"No, but wait'll you see her new stuff. She's gotten really good. We're down here."

I showed him our little bedroom, tucked under the eaves at the other end of the hall from his. Eric looked around, appraising, so I did, too, as if I didn't know every split in the plaster walls by heart. Serra's Miró and Klimt prints, Maggie's Sleater-Kinney and Breeders posters, and my marked-up campus map and newspaper clippings covered the biggest cracks.

Eric touched the slanting ceiling, traced the round frame of our window. It was so small that the room was dark except for one precious hour a day.

We sat on my bed in a warm oval of sunlight, a few feet apart. I looked down at Eric's black jeans, the ones he'd snagged helping my mom trim the jacaranda tree in our backyard six years ago. When we'd packed them after graduation, the damaged part had been a fuzzy rectangle the width of a postage stamp, barely noticeable. Now his skin was starting to show through.

I pointed at the loose webbing of threads over his left knee. "You've been fidgeting with that. You need a patch like Raggedy Andy."

"I'm bringing back the '80s look. Distressed denim." Eric picked up my pillow and studied it as if the plain white cotton was the most interesting thing he'd ever seen. Then he placed it back carefully at the head of my bed and nodded at my Haggermaker plaque on the bookcase. "How's the Franster?"

"I write to her but she doesn't write to me. And please don't call her that."

He toyed with his jeans, running his index finger around the perimeter of the damaged part and plucking at the loosening threads. His nervous energy, in high school a whole-body thing, had apparently been transferred to that small patch of denim.

"Hey," he said. I was close enough to hear the small hitch in his breathing that made the word two syllables.

"Hey."

"It's extremely good to see you," he said.

"You, too."

"Sorry things have been so weird."

"Me, too. I'm sorry about how I was at your mom's. It was… childish."

"Interesting," he said. "Someone called me that once. A pouty child."

"Who would be that mean?"

"She was right. I was being a pouty child about a lot of things.

Including my parents. I just came from there. A real visit, six days."

"How are they?"

"My dad's the same. I thought maybe he'd take me to a Dodgers game and Disneyland and buy me a sundae. You know, like divorced dads in movies? But we went to Roy's Steakhouse and it wasn't too weird."

"That's great."

*What about your mom?* It was the natural next question. But I didn't trust my voice.

"My mom and I had a real talk, though. I told her how much I'd hated her, for being with Cal. And I told her it wasn't exactly fair of me. After being with my dad, she had a right to someone different. Someone... I don't know. Lighter."

I willed myself not to react. No blushing, no change in my breathing.

I was better at that now. How strange that back when I had nothing to blush about, I couldn't stop it, but now it was easy. The trick was to force yourself to think about something else. Avoidance coping, a term Maggie had introduced to our conversation after Psych 1.

I made a mental list of places to show Eric this summer.

The room where they kept dinosaur fossils in the clock tower.

Blondie's pizza.

The Greek Theatre.

"You probably got to know him," he said. "When you were working at SnoozeNews or whatever it's called."

"Not really."

"She says he's a compulsive flirt who never grew up," he said. "That I was right, that she needed someone fun and easygoing to break from my dad, but in the end *there wasn't a lot of there there.* Her exact words."

We could go to San Francisco, brave the tourists at Pier 39. Do Chinatown. Ride cable cars.

"Notice how I use his real name now?" Eric continued. "No nicknames? Impressive, huh? Cal. Cal. Cal, my pal. Wait, scratch that last part, it's a hard habit to break. I'll use his full name. Mr. Devin McCallister."

I stood and crossed the room, pretended to root through the clothes in my closet. Avoidance coping had its limits. "So is your mom dating that short man from her pool party?" I yanked a sweatshirt from the bottom of a neat pile, tossed it on top.

"No, that's over, too. She said she's okay being alone for now. But she says it's going to be hard to trust anyone ever again. She thought Cal really liked her, but I guess he was sleeping with other women on his boat the whole time they were together."

I wondered if this was true about him, or just a mean rumor, someone trying to make Donna feel bad. I wished I could shut the door, burrow into the soft piles of clothing and let myself process this information. For a month. I didn't want to imagine him seeing other women when he saw me. Though it would make me feel less guilty about breaking up with him, it would hurt.

And I wasn't sure I believed it.

"That's awful."

"You know what I spray-painted on that boat back in high school?"

I cleared my throat. "What?"

He laughed. "*Fraud*. Not one of my finer moments, but pretty accurate, it turns out. At least as far as my mom's concerned. Did you ever see him hitting on women at the office?"

One more deep breath. I came out of the closet, tying my biggest blue Berkeley sweatshirt around my waist. "He was hardly there. He was just a... What do they call it? Paper investor."

Eric tilted his head, scanning me with familiar, worried eyes. His chin, off center like that, said, *I don't buy it.*

"I was pretty mad at you for working there," he said.

"I know."

"Did you do it to get back at me? For not emailing. Leaving how I did?"

"I'm not sure. Maybe. Why did you leave the way you did?"

"I needed time away from everything. My parents. The whole scene in Orange County, the gates and the cars and having three plastic surgeons on my block. You know."

"Yes."

"And..."

"What?"

"I was sure I'd ruined the only part that was real. The one thing in that town worth anything to me. I guess I needed time to deal with that, too."

"You didn't ruin it," I said softly.

He looked down at the hole in his jeans, then flashed me a slight, relieved smile. "Any way we can call it even? Be *surprisingly mature* and start fresh?"

*Oh, E.*

Because he was still E, with his good smell, root beer, and aloe shaving cream. His long pianist's fingers plucking at his torn jeans. His broad, honest forehead under his black, every-which-way hair. His wrong-way eyebrow that I always wanted to brush back.

His jokes that tugged at my heart, because they came from caring too much instead of not enough. A kind of purity I hadn't recognized before.

We still had our own unspoken language, a river of shared memories running under our words.

I could tell him, right now.

But he sat next to me with such hope in his eyes, such certainty that he still knew me.

"I'd like that," I said.

We didn't talk about me working for CommPlanet again. I knew what Eric thought. That I sensed or even witnessed something ugly there. Cal and some attractive partner in a supply closet, maybe.

I let him think this.

And, over time, because part of me wished it were true, it became the version of events I almost believed.

★

We wandered from North Gate toward Sproul Plaza to meet Serra after her class. I pointed out the distant stadium and the Greek Theatre. I saw a Fe|Co and sloppy elongated cat painted on a retaining wall (a poor rendering, not my favorite) and didn't say anything, but Eric noticed it.

"Whatever happened to that story you emailed me about, freshman year?"

"Oh… I'm still working on it." Serra could decide whether or not to tell him. "So you did read my long emails, huh?"

"Every word. I decided the graffiti was probably by someone named Felicia Colpepper. That or Fergus Cogswaddle."

"Intriguing theory."

"Someone at Brown writes E. E. Cummings poems in restroom stalls. No animal drawings, but maybe Fergus Cogswaddle is bicoastal."

"You can be my East Coast correspondent."

"Sign me up. So this is protest central, huh?"

The Sproul Plaza clipboard patrol was out in force.

"Some are protesters. Some are selling phone plans and credit cards."

I'd perfected the decisive head shake that meant, "No, thanks, not gonna sign up for anything right now so leave me the hell alone," but Eric kept getting embroiled in apologetic conversations.

I pulled him by the elbow. "This is Dwinelle Hall. Allen Ginsberg and a bunch of beat writers had a poetry-in here in '64. Serra should be out any minute."

"How is she?"

"Loving her art classes."

"Dating anyone?"

"She had a few dates with this pre-law guy who worshipped her, but she ended it. She said she wanted to focus on her art, but he was a good guy. Everybody liked him."

"What about you?"

"I liked him, too."

"That's not what I meant."

"Dating, you mean?"

"Yeah."

"Oh…nothing serious. You?" I tried to sound casual, sure he was going to mention that he and his Vancouver lady were going strong. I deserved it. I deserved worse.

"Same."

A warm wave of relief, so intense it surprised me.

But if he'd said his girlfriend was flying out for a visit, I'd have worked overtime showing I was thrilled for him. Offered to trade rooms so they could have a bigger bed.

★

"No. Way!" Serra spotted Eric and ran to us, a blur of denim and shiny black hair. She nearly knocked him down throwing her arms around him. Then she took a step back so she could shove him. "Asshole. We thought we'd lost you to the preppy New Englanders forever."

"Ow! Becc's forgiven me so you have to, too. That's how it works."

"Is it, Becc?"

"He seems repentant."

Serra pulled him in for another hug. "Don't abandon us again."

We showed Eric everything. Bowles Hall, the Gothic, ivy-covered male-only residence on the hill. The Greek Theatre. The steps above Sproul Plaza, where Abbie Hoffman changed the world with his megaphone in the '60s. Serra's studio, where she pointed to the canvas sheet covering the triptych but wouldn't give us a peek.

As we walked home the clock tower began the noon carillon concert, and we stopped under the wide, green-patina'd arch of Sather Gate to listen.

I loved how one person, hidden up high, could cast a spell over the sprawling, chaotic campus. The protesters and credit card marketing minions with their clipboards, the pigeon scavenging in the pizza box on the ground, the pear-shaped, greasy-haired guy hurrying to class in front of us, his frayed purple JanSport backpack strap repaired with safety pins.

I closed my eyes. Even if I was late for a lecture, I always stopped and focused on the tunes falling magically from the sky.

After the last golden note had sifted down, I opened my eyes to find Eric watching me. He was unsmiling, his eyes intent and serious. But when I grinned at him, he grinned back.

My E.

# 34

## A Little Crazy

When the three of us returned to the co-op after Eric's campus tour, Maggie was lolling on a futon in the front room, her head on Bonnie's lap. They were back on now that Bonnie had turned in her thesis, and Maggie hadn't slept in her own bed for weeks.

Maggie looked him up and down. "So this is the famous Eric. You know, you really hurt their feelings."

"I know," he said.

"How long are you here?"

"Two months. I sublet Glenn Fisher's room."

"How tall are you?"

"Six-two."

"Are you flexible?"

"I've seen the room. I'll deal."

"You planning to bolt again?"

"No." He looked at me and Serra, a promise in his eyes, a private smile. "No."

Maggie stretched the silence out, making him wait. Then

she grinned. "Okay, I guess I approve. You can have my bed tonight."

The three of us stayed up talking until four. I told Eric about my favorite classes in the English department, and the ones I audited at the journalism grad school. I described my ups and downs at the paper, my condescending bow-tied editor. My dear, seventy-three-year-old English adviser who knew Harper Lee and Truman Capote. Serra filled Eric in on her museum volunteer job, her terror over the invitational.

She told him about Yvonne Copeland and how generous and encouraging she was, but didn't mention Yvonne's after-hours "hobby," or how it intersected with mine via lines of spray paint.

In the dark, her too-casual tone warned me not to, either.

Yawning on Maggie's mattress stack under the open, round window, Eric described friends in New York and Boston, how he'd started therapy and swimming laps an hour every morning. Then dropped the therapy and doubled the swimming.

"Why'd you drop it?" I asked.

"The guy kept offering these over-the-top pet theories. Like, remember how my dad froze my driver's license?"

How could we not? It summed up Mr. Logan so perfectly. Absent and disinterested for months, then swooping in for some bizarre attempt at "strong" parenting.

Eric had passed his first driving test with thirty-six out of forty on the written exam. But that wasn't good enough for Mr. Logan. So he'd put Eric's license in a Ziploc, submerged it in a Tupperware of water, and stored it in the freezer. He got the idea from some article on credit card debt—you were supposed to freeze your credit cards so they wouldn't tempt you. Mr. Logan wouldn't let Eric defrost the card until he took another test at home, with Mr. Logan proctoring, and got a perfect score. It took five tries.

"I remember that," I said softly. I'd only got a thirty-five on my driver's test, and my mom had made me a special mocha ice-cream cake that night, decorated with a car made out of licorice whips she'd cut up.

"Okay, so the therapist was *positive* that my dad froze the license because on some level he really wanted to keep me a little boy. That *that's* why I was so desperate to get away. When, really, my dad's just a dickish control freak. And an unhappy drunk. So I started going to Al-Anon meetings. They help way more than the therapist ever did."

I was glad to hear that his voice didn't veer from bitterness to false levity anymore when he described his family's problems. It stayed even and direct. Almost accepting.

We talked about his major, his roommates. The differences between the coasts.

Serra quizzed him on his love life at Brown and he admitted that he'd lost his virginity to a girl in his freshman film survey class, then slept with another girl in another film class two weeks later. Then "others."

He didn't elaborate but it sounded like a lot.

I felt Serra looking at me across the dark room. But after what I'd done, Eric could sleep with half of Rhode Island. He was back, and that was enough.

★

On weekends and evenings, Eric and I ate dim sum in Chinatown, leaving the restaurants with stuffed bellies and cheeks moist from steam. We went to the de Young Museum, the Exploratorium, Golden Gate Park, Haight-Ashbury.

One Saturday I won buy-one-get-one-free tickets to the wax museum from the Whirling Win Wheel, a promotional gimmick on Pier 39, and we screamed and laughed through the series of dark rooms with the other tourists.

I daydreamed about our excursions, past and future, while I worked at the real estate company. I'd taken the job because the pay wasn't bad, the office was in San Francisco, near the Embarcadero BART station, and at least it was vaguely related to journalism (as I reminded myself ten times a day).

It was as dull as I'd feared. Some days were so tedious I felt my gray, tweedy cubicle walls closing in on me. One broker named Stan Case kept a bowl of blue jelly beans on his desk labeled Viagra and offered me some daily, winking, or else tried to sell me Amway shampoo. But most of the guys—and they were all guys—were okay.

I was allowed to listen to headphones, Seal singing over and over about how we'd never survive unless we got a little crazy.

It helped.

Eric and I rode the train together, and that helped, too.

He wasn't faring much better in his internship, at a cable series called *Golden State.* The listing called it an "experimental documentary series." But Eric said it was fake—trumped-up story lines about the telegenic daughter of a computer baron and the telegenic boys she wasn't really dating. Eric hated perpetuating a lie that was so successful the show sometimes beat MTV in its time slot.

Mostly, he hated himself for not quitting.

We commiserated about our jobs as the shimmying BART car whisked us into the dark tunnel under the Bay, lights flicking on and off.

"Are we paying our dues or selling out?" he asked. "Remember when you wrote me that?"

"Yes. And I remember you didn't answer."

"I didn't know the answer. I still don't."

July 21, 1997

> From: ericlogan@goldproductions.com
> Meet me for *L.A. Confidential* at the Roxie at 1? I'm
> dying here.

From: rebeccareardon@ehindustrial.com
Go back to work, brat. We're lucky to have gainful employment.

From: ericlogan@goldproductions.com
Gainful=painful. Please. My treat? They'll never miss you. C'mon… I know you want to.

From: rebeccareardon@ehindustrial.com
You're going to get fired. You're going to get me fired. Email is for work correspondence only; please stop trying to negatively impact my career performance.

From: ericlogan@goldproductions.com
It's just a movie. What, are you trying to earn one of those nifty mustard-yellow blazers with the patches?

From: rebeccareardon@ehindustrial.com
Wearing it now, snob. Kindly cease the personal emailing during work hours, as E & H policy forbids it.

Eric didn't cease.

All through July, I said no.

When I turned my calendar to August, I continued to say no.

On August 5, the afternoon I heard Stan Case hollering to another broker across the office, describing his date's breasts as "like tennis balls in tube socks," I said yes.

And I continued to say yes, as the days got hotter and the air-conditioned theaters—and Eric—got their hooks into me.

August 14

From: ericlogan@goldproductions.com
Chron/E3. TL. AL1205. OM, S.

That was all.

We'd worked out a code. Today's message meant Eric wanted me to look in the *San Francisco Chronicle*, page E3. The Entertainment section, main movie review at the top left of the page. Today, it was *Grosse Pointe Blank*. In Eric-ese, the email was an invitation to meet him at the 12:05 matinee at the Fillmore. OM, S meant lunch and candy would be on him, a surprise.

Sometimes the message ended OM, WUW? (Lunch on me, What do you want?) or OM, B/P/G/H (Lunch on me, Do you want a burrito or pizza or gyro or hamburger?).

Because just calling me up would be too simple. And not nearly as much fun.

If anyone ever read our messages, they'd suspect us of something far more nefarious than slipping away from our sucky jobs to go to matinees and eat junk food.

I emailed back:

100

One hundred percent chance I'd be there. It was our fourth workday movie of the summer.

I left my coat on my chair and scattered reports by my keyboard. My signature moves. I grabbed a blank CD and waved it at the receptionist as I passed the front desk. She was on the phone, whispering urgently to somebody.

"I'm going to lunch and the printer," I said. "Need anything?"

She shook her head.

Sweet freedom. The Fillmore was only a couple of blocks away. Eric sat inside already, four rows from the screen. He chose his seats with geometric precision, factoring in the screen size, the type of film, and the placement of the speakers.

"Aren't you that guy I saw in *Teen People*?" I said. "With, like, Krista Gold from *Golden State*? Can I have your autograph?"

Eric flipped me off. A blink-and-you'd-miss-it, one-handed flip-off.

"Are you ever going to let that joke die?" he asked.

"Nope, it's still working for me."

"It was weeks ago, and you could barely see me. And I wasn't *with* her. I was in the background. Doing my job."

"Come on, you're famous. You should be milking it."

"Keep it up and I'm not feeding you."

"What's on the menu today?"

Eric pulled two fat foil tubes out of a white bag and handed me the one with NG scrawled on it in marker. *"No guacamole para usted."*

"From the good place?"

*"Sí."*

"Yum. Thanks."

"And for dessert…" He rummaged under his seat and pulled up a bag of toffee. He'd already rolled down the top of the bag so it wouldn't rattle during the movie.

"Such a balanced meal," I said. "So how's it going this week? How often do you think about quitting?"

"Only every half hour. I might as well be a paparazzo. Take pictures of celebrities sneezing and say they're crying."

"It's an internship. It's supposed to suck."

"Want to trade?"

"I don't think I can handle more glamour than the Elliott & Healey, Industrial Realty newsletter."

The previews started. "Hey, Eric," I whispered.

"Yeah?"

"We've got to stop doing this."

"You say that every time."

★

Serra called us brats. We agreed, and agreed we had to stop.

But the glorious dark theaters drew us back. We munched our smuggled-in food, keeping the wrappers low when the kid came in with his flashlight to do his check. We never got caught bringing in our outside food or drink to save money, and our bosses never caught us skipping out, either.

"What did you think?" asked Eric after *Grosse Pointe Blank*, as we stood on the sidewalk blinking ourselves back to reality.

"A nine," I said.

"I say eight and a half."

Eric would happily sit in a café and deconstruct *Grosse Pointe Blank* with me for another two hours, but I resisted. "I'd better get back."

"Yeah, me, too."

We went opposite ways on the sidewalk, Eric to help record manufactured crises for his taut *Golden State* blondes, me back to my humming Dell monitor at Elliott & Healey.

The first time I'd ditched work to meet Eric at the movies, I'd felt guilty the whole time and actually looked over my shoulder when I walked into the theater. Not anymore.

Of course, everyone in the office fudged their schedules. They got their teeth whitened and called it a meeting. They lingered at the park an extra hour after they finished the last bite of their turkey cheddar on whole wheat. But there was something about going to the movies during work hours that felt like crossing a line of decency.

Eric and I reminded ourselves all the time that we were lucky. I could parlay my dry newsletter into something better. Eric was learning the business.

"We have to stop," we said as summer waned.

August 19

WHERE I WAS SUPPOSED TO BE | Sitting in my gray pneumatic chair, my upper arms hanging vertically and elbows bent at ninety degrees, the top of my monitor no more than ten inches below my line of sight, as recommended in the office-wide carpal tunnel syndrome prevention presentation meeting we'd had the day before

WHERE I WAS | The 12:55 matinee at the Vogue

August 21

> From: ericlogan@goldproductions.com
> Chron. E3. BR. P1225. OM, H/P/C

> From: rebeccareardon@ehindustrial.com
> Reply—99/C

I'd been craving a calzone. We saw *The Full Monty*. Eric gave it a 7.0 and I gave it a 7.4.

August 22

> From: ericlogan@goldproductions.com
> E1. TR. R1255. OM.

> From: rebeccareardon@ehindustrial.com
> Reply—50

I really believed there was only a fifty-fifty chance I'd make it to the revival of *Harvey*. But by eleven, I'd finished all my work for the day, even made the rounds, asking the guys if they needed help.

I refreshed my inbox robotically for ten minutes, put my head on my desk.

I grabbed my purse, jammed out the door, and jogged the four blocks to the Balboa. I slipped into the seat next to Eric as the opening credits rolled. He handed me a root beer.

"I knew you'd come."

# 35

## Grownups

August 23, 1997

WHERE I WAS SUPPOSED TO BE | Welcoming new English majors
WHERE I WAS | Staring at myself

More than two months after the last time we'd seen each other, I got an email from Cal.

> How's your summer gone? I blame that prehistoric laptop for losing the many emails you've written to me since June. (?) The Rebecca-lessness of my inbox couldn't possibly be due to the fact that you never sent them.
>
> Life is dull, dull, dull. All VC types, all the time. Big, boring parties. No you. I have daily thoughts of divesting from everything so I can sail around the San Juans.
>
> I miss our parties for two. I miss you, human. But I understand, and want only good things for you.
> Take care,
> C
> xx

A good-natured, restrained message, considering how I'd left things.

I almost typed, I miss you, too.

But it wasn't true. I'd been too busy to miss him. Taking my class and working and sneaking out to movies during the day, playing with Eric and Maggie and Serra at night, making up for lost time.

I'd had a few guilt pangs, sudden images from my good moments with Cal, and the vague, immature way I'd left things, that intruded into the present.

Once, after a movie, Eric and I went to an old soda fountain on Cole Street for chocolate shakes, and there was a black-and-white sign on the door: Summer Hours. I'd been laughing when I swung the door open, and I had to force myself to keep the laugh going as we sat down at the counter.

But by the time our order came and Eric automatically dropped his cherry into my glass—I loved maraschino cherries and he hated them—I felt okay again. They were just two small words.

And the next time I saw one of those signs it barely registered.

My summer had been full, fun, easy. With Eric, I didn't feel that thrilling-but-draining temptation to act more detached and cynical than I felt, like I had with Cal. We fell back into our high school friendship effortlessly, both of us appreciating it more now, knowing how unusual it was. How easy it was to misplace.

I turned off my laptop without replying to Cal, and it shuddered and clicked as it powered down.

I'd compose a reply in my head, during the English department reception. The reception would be *dull, dull, dull,* like Cal's events with the VC types. These department mixers were always sparsely attended, sweating-cheese-cube affairs on the lawn by the clock tower. Nervous freshmen and a few TAs, rarely any faculty. But since this was my last one I'd decided to make an appearance before running across campus to Serra's art show.

I pulled on my new green shift dress, swiped on lipstick, got my purse together. Keys, cash, my congratulations card for Serra, the Artek gift certificate I'd bought her.

The phone rang and I answered hastily. "Whoever this is, I'm late for the English department mixer."

"It's not going to sell. Fuck. I was an idiot to say I'd do it."

Serra, calling from a pay phone in the gallery, though the invitational wasn't for two hours.

"It'll sell, Serr."

"Yvonne talked me into pricing it at $800," Serra said. "She's insane. I was thinking more like $8."

"It's going to be worth $8,000 when you're famous."

"You should see the other work. I look like the kiddy corner."

"I'll come early."

"Don't skip your English thing, Becc. I'll be fine."

"I'll get there as fast as I can."

★

I crossed the sculpture lawn in front of the gallery, a low-slung concrete building on Bancroft. Serra was pacing inside, behind the glass front wall. She spied me and acted out a silent scream— wide mouth, rattling head.

I pantomimed my calm-down response—yoga thumb-on-index-finger gestures. (Maggie and Serra and I had taken yoga together sophomore year. The teacher had to split us up because she said we were *disruptive*. Maggie made us laugh too much, gyrating in goddess pose.)

"I'm a wreck," Serra said, opening the door.

"I got that."

The only people there besides the two of us were the caterers arranging glasses at the bar.

"I can't even look at it," she said, pulling me toward a pedestal in the Emerging Artists room.

From the way Serra had tried to downplay the event, I'd expected her piece to be shoved into some dark corner of the gallery. But Yvonne had given the new artists primo real estate near the front.

*Triptych: Grownups/Suspended Animation*, the placard on Serra's piece said. *Serra Indrijo. Urethane, plastics, and paper. $800.*

I circled it, not speaking for a long time.

When she'd explained what a triptych was, I envisioned three separate paintings. Nothing like this.

She had created an entire aquatic world inside three thick, clear panels of plastic, held together with blue metallic hinges. She'd made it sound childish, like a grade school diorama, but it wasn't. It was dreamlike, intricate as a Brueghel painting.

At first glance the animals in the aquamarine waves all looked alike. But when I leaned close to the third panel I saw it was us. All of us.

We were a herd of tiny furry creatures with gills. A different scene in each panel. In the first one we were sleeping, in the second swimming, and in the third...it was hard to say exactly. Maybe floating.

I examined the middle panel and found Serra—the round creature with the dark hair and paintbrush. Me—holding a notebook, one long mousy leg tangled in seaweed, beneath a stern white-furred animal with a ribbon on its gray head. Maggie— a whirling platinum-spiked critter with gray eyes. Eric, with a cowlicky pelt. And dozens of others, all paddling, some looking over their shoulders in fear, some closing their eyes, some gazing up at the luminous surface.

Scraps of paper and objects surrounded us in all three pieces of the triptych—textbooks, a miniature Rancilio espresso maker, a corner of Serra's Perkins loan statement, a Barbie-size suit, a laptop, a TV, a bundle of cash. In the upper-right corner of the middle piece, a gold graduation cap, like the mouth of a tuba, pulled in the sea, but we fought against it, swimming away and tugging each other.

"What do you think? Tell the truth. It's garbage, right?"

"It's incredible," I said. "I've never seen anything like it."

"Honest? It's not too literal?" Serra furrowed her brow.

"It's brilliant," I said.

"Last night I had a nightmare that a critic said it had 'all the subtlety of a Kuddli Kreaturz Treehouse toy set.'"

"The fake childish thing is what makes it good. Because it's not childish. It's…semi-frightening. Hopeful, though, with the sun shining through the water here." I started to tap on the top of the first panel but stopped myself. It wasn't good form to touch art—of course I knew that—but that wasn't what stopped me. I stopped because for a second I worried my tapping would disturb the animals inside the glass. That was how real the piece felt.

"How do you get everything in there?" I asked.

"I do it in layers, it takes forever. It's a bitch to get it clear enough, and attached right. I'm still not one hundred percent happy with the technique. I wanted it to look seamless. And I didn't make the hinges, I didn't have the tools."

"Where'd you get them?" I asked.

"Yvonne hooked me up with this awesome metalwork artist, Joy Gold, and she made them. Great name, huh? Like, the perfect artist name."

"I think Serra Indrijo is a perfect artist name," I said.

She smiled. "Anyway, she did just what I asked, but I feel kind of guilty that I didn't make them."

"It's a world," I said. "You created a world, Serra. What else matters?"

People started trickling in. The young artists were the first to arrive. They did excited laps around the gallery, trying not to stare at their own pieces too much.

Eight minutes before showtime, Yvonne walked over and hugged Serra. "Aren't you proud of this girl?"

I had to resist the temptation to roll up Yvonne's long sleeves to hunt for a whisker tattoo. I'd promised Serra I'd be patient.

"Yes," I said. "Proud but not surprised."

"She's going to be huge," Yvonne said, blowing her garnet bangs out of her eyes. Today she wore earrings that looked like Lichtenstein comics. She leaned in close. "We shouldn't crowd it. Give potential buyers alone time with your work. Lesson number 125 from Mother Yvonne. Come on, let's find you champagne."

I stayed in the Emerging Artists room, pretending to look at the other stuff but secretly babysitting Serra's piece from ten feet away. A man with round glasses and spiky white hair paced around it for a long time, and I had to resist the temptation to say, "Isn't it fantastic? What a bargain!"

He left, and then an older woman in a wrap dress and pashmina, who looked like she had a healthy art budget, examined it. I was pretending to admire some waxy masks on the wall, trying to resist peeking at pashmina lady, when someone draped an arm around my neck.

"Got anything with puce in it?" he asked. "I've got a lot of waaaall space." His nasal Daniel-Stern-as-Dusty-the-rock-star imitation from *Hannah and Her Sisters*. He smiled at me. "How's she holding up?"

"She's calming down. You look nice."

He had made a serious effort: unripped black jeans, black shoes that weren't Vans, a thin sweater in a heathery gray that made his deep brown eyes and hair look even darker against his olive skin. He'd pasted his hair down with water and smelled of Rainbath. Eric had been stealing pumps of it in the shower all summer, thinking we wouldn't notice. But the vaguely spicy scent was appealing on him.

"You look nice, too," he said.

And then something amazing happened. The next time I saw Serra's plaque, there was a small red dot on it.

It sold.

I searched frantically for Serra, tugged her over by the elbow to show her.

She stared at it in shock. She went to the gallery manager to double-check, and when she came back she was surrounded by a colorful scrum of beaming women in organic black cotton and statement jewelry. Yvonne's turpentine mafia, high-fiving Serra and toasting her first sale.

I scanned the women clustered around Serra, wondering how many were in Yvonne's collective. Hoping to glimpse a secret handshake or the cylindrical outline of a spray paint canister behind flowy trousers. Nothing.

"They look so benign," I said under my breath to Maggie.

"Is it killing you not to tell anyone?"

"A little."

"So what's up with your Eric?" Maggie flicked her kohl-rimmed eyes across the room to where Eric stood.

"He's not my Eric."

"Does he know that?"

"We're just friends."

"Oh, right, I know." She nodded, sipped her beer.

"Maggie, don't."

When the show finally wound down, we went to a café down the street. A shabby, tiny, overwarm Greek diner—me and Eric on one side of the booth, me in the window seat, Maggie and Serra across from us. Exhausted, Serra leaned against the glass, a red sale dot on her left earlobe over her two piercings. She glowed, ornamented and triumphant.

There was a poster of a Greek island above Maggie and Serra. No people. Only simple white buildings tumbling down hillsides, the water around it an impossible blue. Eric said, "Maggie, what island is that?"

She turned and read the bottom of the poster. "Nisyros. Dodecanese island chain."

"It's the bluest water I've ever seen," Eric said. "It's like what everyone thinks California's like before they get there and notice the smog and the cars."

"And the McMansions," Serra said.

"Let's all go sometime," Eric said. "Deal?"

"Deal," we said.

Out the window, kids were hurrying up and down Bancroft. We'd join them in a little while; we were part of that fast-moving current. But for now our ripped red vinyl booth was an island of stillness within it.

French fries and friends my age in a booth on a Saturday night, a Fleetwood Mac guitar solo on the speakers.

I'd been a fool to think it wasn't enough.

# 36

## Souvenir

2008
Friday, 6:30 p.m.

Our hotel suite is on the top floor. It's done up in pale yellow silk. Thick cream carpet, a sitting area with tufted club chairs and ottomans, acres of space between two separate bedrooms and baths. We have our own fern.

Except for the line of luggage trolleys bisecting the sitting area, marring the elegant decor, it's beautiful.

I shudder at the expense. Though Eric clearly doesn't worry about money anymore, I still do. And he's wasting a fortune to make his point. To rub my nose in my mess.

"Can we keep these up here tonight or will you run out?" I ask our name-tagged porter, Bryce W., about the two luggage trolleys holding the gift. "I hate to hog them, but it's breakable. And that way we'll be all ready to go tomorrow morning. We're leaving early."

"Of course, ma'am. Keep your souvenir on the carts overnight. Good plan."

Bryce is on my side. He's a planner, like me. The rest of the trip may have slipped out of my control, but at least I can get Serra's wedding present up to Oregon in one piece.

"And where would you and the other party like these?" Bryce asks, indicating our bags.

Bryce is a pro. He doesn't stumble over *your partner…your friend…your husband*. He says *the other party* without missing a beat. What a tactful, useful phrase. It gracefully sidesteps any potentially offensive assumptions about our sex life, or lack thereof.

Bryce has seen it all. Not just whatever mysterious, oversize *souvenirs* he's had to transport. All kinds of sleeping arrangements. Platonic friends. Honeymooners. Couples who are perfectly content, but haven't slept in the same bed for decades because she snores and she's got restless leg syndrome. People who only picked this most romantic of hotels because it's in a Joni Mitchell song.

Couples who only pretend they're sleeping together to keep up appearances, but retreat into opposing corners, shutting the two sets of French doors between them, before Bryce's white-gloved finger is on the elevator down button.

And whatever we are.

The *other party* gives me no help. He's sitting in a pale yellow club chair in the left bedroom, flipping channels on the TV. He's picked his corner.

"Just leave everything on the trolleys. Thanks."

Bryce shows me how the Jacuzzi settings work. Thermostat, room-service menus.

He says we shouldn't miss the famous roof garden. Recommends that we order the champagne and fresh seafood platter for two. It's his favorite. There's a seasonal special right now, the oysters and crab are local. "Caught this morning." He smiles, nodding west, toward the hall. His way of indicating the ocean.

Our windows face east; we have an incredible view of the city from the sitting room. The point of the Transamerica building and the firehose-tip shape of gray Coit Tower, the Bay beyond, covered in an evening layer of fog as dense and white as cotton batting.

"One of the best views we have," Bryce says.

At least someone's happy we're staying at the Fairmont.

7:00 p.m.

Eric's been in his bedroom with the door shut for half an hour.

When I came out to our shared sitting area after splashing water on my face, his suitcase and hanging bag were gone from the trolley train, and the door was closed.

I wouldn't be surprised if he's locked it.

Just so I don't get any ideas about sexy seafood platters for two, or long, heartfelt talks about him and me, or anything else he feared, making this reservation.

I press my ear to his bedroom door.

He's still got sports coverage on, louder than before. It's not something predictable, like baseball or soccer. It's dressage, some pre-Olympics event. Eric doesn't like horses; he got thrown at a Chaco Canyon summer camp when he was little and broke his collarbone. The horse's name was Mr. Salty, and Eric told me once he could still remember the feeling of flying through the air, how he hadn't been scared so much as *hurt* that Mr. Salty, up until then a placid, plodding animal, had turned on him.

But Eric would rather watch anything than be with me.

I'm mad about the dressage on the TV. I'm mad that we're stuck here for the night, that he accepted my bluff in the car when I claimed it was *no big deal* for us to stay here.

I wanted him to say, *Of course it is, it's a huge deal. No way are we going near there, Becc. It's too much.*

I set my ear to the door again, hold my breath so I can hear. Someone on Eric's TV is describing the different braids the horses get in their manes for a major event. There's the rosette braid and the continental style and the hunter plait.

I kick the door. A quick, quiet knock a few inches from the floor.

A kick just for myself, because Eric won't hear it over his horse hairstyle report. He's stretched out on the bed, or lounging in his stylish club chair in front of his TV.

The feelings between me and Eric that have loomed so large for ten years have been reduced to these small, petty gestures—scone throwing, Date Insurance, a changed reservation, a toddler's tantrummy kick.

But the kick feels so good I do it again, a little harder this time. Jamming my big toe, leaving a black scuff on the glossy eggshell paint.

*Shit.* I crouch to rub at it, but it doesn't come off. I've officially defaced the Fairmont.

There's a scrabbling from the other side of the door and he yanks it open so fast I don't have time to bolt.

"What's going on?" Eric's voice is accusatory.

He's taken off his button-down so now he's only in a white T-shirt and shorts. Barefoot. He could use a shave, his eyes are bloodshot, and he has a cowlick sticking up at the crown of his head. Even his fancy stylist in New York can't tame his hair. Not completely.

"Oh. I was..."

*I was just thinking of ordering room service and wondered if you wanted anything?*

*I was just thinking we should decide what time to leave tomorrow morning?*

"I was just kicking your door."

He narrows his eyes.

"And I left a mark." I point at the black scuff.

He bends to inspect it. When he rises he nods slowly, as if everything makes perfect sense now. "Oh."

"I'll pay for the damage," I go on. "I'm sorry I disturbed you, I didn't think you'd hear me over the TV."

He looks over his shoulder—sailing is on now—and runs a hand through his hair. He puffs air out his nostrils in a humorless half laugh as he sinks down onto the carpet, rests his forehead on his knees.

I sit down across from him. I want to reach through the doorframe. Touch the crown of his head, run my fingers through his hair.

We're quiet, listening to the reporting from Beijing. It's about the opening ceremonies now. It's going to be *spectacular... jaw-dropping...epic. Tickets have been sold out for weeks...*

He looks up at me, shaking his head ever so slightly. "Why the *fuck* are we here, Becc?"

I smile. "Because we're both stubborn."

"Yes. We're children."

"The creatures inside Serra's art are more mature."

"I did try to get us a different hotel reservation, I hope you believe me," he says. "I tried to fix things. But it was too late."

"I know."

## 37

### Kind of Blue

The second-to-last workday before Eric had to fly back to school, we met for a 1:00 p.m. showing of a noir, *The Lady from Shanghai* at the Balboa. The theater was halfway between our offices, and matinees were $3, so it was our favorite.

I settled next to Eric in the fourth row, content, laughing.

"So this is set in China?" I asked as we dug into our tub of popcorn with Milk Duds melted in. Instead of sneaking in bootleg candy I'd bought it at the concession stand as a splurge, a goodbye treat for him.

"No, you'll see. You're hogging all the Milk Duds!"

"Why would they want *Dud* in their product name?"

"It hasn't stopped you from hogging them."

Our hands battled for an extra gooey clump at the bottom of the tub. I won.

"Seal-on-repeat kind of morning?" Eric asked.

"Yes. But *surviving*."

Eric was the only one I could be honest with about my job, the despair I felt after hundreds of hours keying in sales figures and vacancy rates. Trying to pretend my real estate newsletter was anything close to my dreams. He didn't tell me to suck it up, or insist that it was just a stepping-stone. He simply asked what I was playing on my Discman and understood. Our private code.

We licked our fingers as the lights went down, and a man described Rita Hayworth, how she'd shattered him even though he knew getting involved with her would bring nothing but trouble:

*"And from that moment I did not use my head, except to think about her."*

It was a good story, tense and moody. I watched for twenty minutes before I realized that my right arm and Eric's left, sharing an armrest, were touching.

I concentrated on breathing normally. Half an hour into the movie his pinky touched mine. Ever so slightly, brushing my curled, still hand.

I stared straight ahead, just as he was. I didn't breathe.

Maybe it could happen. I could open my sticky hand, take his. Only that, for now, in the safety of the dark theater. And we'd see what came next.

In high school I'd been curious. Now that Eric had returned, older and wiser, more up-front, curiosity was tinged with an appreciation for how rare it was—the connection between us. How good it felt just to be in his company.

I leaned forward, startled. On the screen was a familiar dock, steep hills, a white frame house in the trees that I knew well. Unmistakable.

Eric tilted his head close to whisper in my ear. "Filmed near here, isn't it cool? In San Francisco or Sausalito. I forget which."

*Sausalito, Eric. See that dock there? I've walked on it dozens of times with your favorite person, late at night. It wasn't that long ago.*

*Although I like to pretend it is, try to put the memories in black and white.*

Thank you, Orson Welles, for reminding me this was impossible. I'd almost lost my head.

I shifted my hand away from his.

★

WHERE I WAS SUPPOSED TO BE | A party
WHERE I WAS | A party

We threw Eric an epic going-away bash. Serra strung fairy lights on the Plato House roof, I picked the music, and Maggie made the cocktails—not just her famous Chocolate Margs but martinis and Jell-O shots, and something she'd invented in Eric's honor called a Logan. It was tasty, perfect for the hot night because she'd blended it with crushed ice. Sweet but with a sparkly aftertaste I couldn't identify.

"What's in me?" Eric shouted to her, examining the mint-green slush in his cup. Word had gotten out that Plato House was having a party, and I couldn't recognize half the people bouncing on the roof to Moby.

"Vodka, limeade concentrate, ginger ale, and a splash of Scope."

"Eric doesn't drink," I told Maggie, downing mine and taking his.

"Logan, you should've told me." Maggie and I went downstairs to concoct a virgin drink for him.

When I came back to the roof with it, he was talking to a girl. Some delicate blonde in a yellow floral shortie sundress and high-tops. The sunset behind them had shot her wispy pale hair through with orange, like a spotlight. Like it had chosen her. She was a foot shorter than Eric so he had to lean down to talk to her, his temple grazing the crown of her waify little head, and even from across the room I could see that she was a giggler, and I knew they were going to spend the night together, and probably the rest of their lives, too, and I hated her with every cell in my body.

I had another drink, danced two songs. Had two more drinks. I lost Eric in the crowd. Hot and queasy, I pushed my way through the sweating bodies downstairs, across the front room to the porch for fresh air. My desire for cool and quiet took over.

It carried me to the bus, the ferry terminal, my favorite outdoor bench.

I was only dimly aware of what I wanted—the cool of the ferry wind and the quiet of the Sausalito house. Cal wouldn't be there on a Saturday night, and I still had a key.

Maybe I'd even sleep over. Blow off taking Eric to the airport tomorrow. Let his roof waif see him off. They were probably having sex right now, in the tiny room Eric hadn't slept in all summer thanks to Maggie's vacant mattress stack. Using the proximity of the walls to brace themselves, to contort into all kinds of sexy, acrobatic positions.

By the time the fuzzy male voice on the speaker told me it was time to *please disembark*, I was almost sober and irritated at the Logan-guzzling Becc for taking me here.

I heard the jazz first. *Kind of Blue*; he loved it.

Polite laughter. Not the wild whoops I'd just run from, but gentle titters and chuckles. Manufactured amusement, not joy.

There was another party going on, this side of the Bay. No dancing. Older crowd. Miles Davis instead of Moby, drinks mixed with gourmet bitters instead of mint mouthwash.

Cal was having *those VC types we hate* over for cocktails.

I spotted him right away: gorgeous, smiling, deeply tanned, his sleeves rolled up. *Ready to be amused.*

He could still command a room. His hair was longer, a little lighter after a summer in the sun, sailing around the Pacific. But the rakish, attractive swoop over his forehead was the same.

He stood inside, by the sliding glass balcony door, talking to someone I couldn't see. Laughing and gesturing with his glass. He was so intent on their conversation that he didn't notice me, even when I weaved through the elegant crowd to the middle of the room and stood ten feet away. I anticipated his surprise, the mischievous smile he'd send my way when he glanced over.

He was talking to someone shorter than him, just like Eric when I'd left him on the packed roof. Bending his neck to talk, just like Eric.

But this wasn't a stranger. And it was a man. Mole eyes, glasses, comb-over: Derrek Schwinn, the Footsy King.

*He's basically harmless.*

I left before they noticed me.

Hurried down the staircase, down the hill to the quay.

So fast that the ferry I'd just disembarked from still had its ramp down.

"Didn't I just see you?" the ticket taker said, winking. "Forget something? I can ask them to wait a couple of minutes while you look."

"I didn't forget anything."

But this was a lie, another lie added to the pile, because for a few minutes on the outgoing leg of my ferry ride I'd forgotten why I'd broken it off with Cal.

I'd believed he was sad about it. But he was fine, laughing with that vile man, so *useful*, everything *lightweight*. Did he know what Schwinn had done? It didn't matter. He wouldn't care. Once, I'd admired how he held himself apart from the world, how he didn't take anything too seriously.

But I knew now that his lightness was merely a bright curtain drawn over cynicism.

I wouldn't be like that.

I threw my key over the side and imagined it diving into the water in a perfect 10.0, splashless entry. *So dramatic, Becc. Such vanity. He's probably given out dozens of keys by now.*

I sat on my upstairs bench, leaning into the wind.

Furious at myself for what I'd given up to be with him.

★

I was back at Plato by midnight, and the party was still going strong. The first thing I saw when I walked in was Eric's waif on a front-room futon, making out with another guy.

Eric and Serra and Maggie were on the roof. "Where'd you disappear to?" Eric asked. "I've been looking for you for hours."

"We ran out of ice."

★

That night I couldn't sleep.

Serra and Maggie were dead to the world and I thought Eric was, too. He was silent, curled up on the extra mattress we'd thrown on the floor for him when Maggie and Bonnie broke up last week.

I went downstairs for a bowl of Corn Flakes at two, hoping it would make me sleepy. I crept back into the room and tried not to make a sound as I shifted under my comforter. But Eric reached up and fumbled in the dark to tap my hand.

"Hey, thanks for my going-away present," he whispered.

I'd given him an autographed copy of my final Elliot & Healey *Pulse & Forecastr*, formed into a scroll and tied with red ribbon.

"Something to read on the plane," I whispered back.

"Why did you really leave the party?"

"I went to get ice and got lost."

A silence. "I'm really glad I spent the summer here, Becc."

"Me, too." I shifted onto my side to face him, my arm reaching down. His white teeth and T-shirt were bright in the patch of moonlight coming through the round window.

I held my breath, bracing for him to touch my cheek with his free hand, to tug on my arm so I'd tumble down.

I hooked my foot on the opposite side of mattress so I'd be ready to resist.

Instead he gave my hand a friendly squeeze, released it, and rolled onto his side, his back to me. My arm hung out in space alone.

How many nights had Eric slept over at my house when we were in high school? Twenty? Thirty? Serra in the bed with me, Eric on my pulled-out trundle below us. He still sleeps on his left side.

I lay awake for a long time, watching him sink back into sleep. Studying the familiar whorl of his ear, unique as a fingerprint.

## 38

### Electric

1997
Sunday morning before Labor Day

After Serra and Maggie and I dropped Eric at SFO for his dawn flight to Boston, we returned to Plato hungover and a little blue. We'd made grand plans to go to the campus bookstore right when it opened, to get our fall textbooks before the crowds. But nobody made a move.

We lifted Eric's mattress back up onto Maggie's stack, I inserted the mix CD he'd handed me at the gate into Serra's boom box, and the three of us flopped on our beds.

"You two really never got together?" Maggie said. "Not even a tiny bit?"

I shook my head. I was reading Eric's handmade CD liner (he'd clearly burned the disc at work, using *Golden State* equipment). His handwriting was so sloppy, I couldn't make out half the song titles, but he'd named the mix after the Seal song I liked—"Crazy."

He'd remembered my description of my Elliott & Healey anthem, how it made the days bearable.

Eric had promised not to go dark on me again, that we'd call each other at least once a week and email a ton, but I still felt like crying.

Maggie went on. "Because there's this…electric thing between you."

"They've always been like that," Serra said. "Ever since ninth grade."

"A psychic link," Maggie said.

"He's still gone over her," Serra said. "It's so obvious."

"I know," Maggie said. "I watched him when we were at dim sum and she burned herself with the tea. The way he was dabbing her arm with his napkin was completely—"

"Stop talking about me like I'm not here!" This came out with a violence that shocked all three of us.

Serra and Maggie looked at each other.

"Becc?" Serra said, hopping down, rushing over. "Hey, why are you… Are you crying?"

I threw the CD jewel case to the floor, faced the wall. I wiped my face on my pillow, furious at myself, at everything. I'd been fine. This summer had been a gift. An unexpected, undeserved gift. And I was spoiling it.

Hands touched my back. The heavy, occasionally sharp shoulder rub of Maggie's, adorned with silver rings on eight fingers. Serra's gentle, child-weight pats.

"Hey, I'm sorry, babe," Maggie said.

Serra's voice—"Becc? It's a good feeling, being around you two. A contagious good feeling. It's, like…what people are supposed to be like together. That's all we meant."

"Sorry. I'm not mad at you guys."

Serra came around to face me at the head of my bed, smoothing the hair from my forehead. "Did you two finally give it a try this summer and it didn't work out?"

I shook my head.

"He didn't scam with anyone at the party, if that's what you think," Maggie said. "He could've. I saw that little rat Lily Brewer from International House try to mack on him but he blew her off."

"It's not Lily Brewer." I wiped my nose on my sleeve.

"Then what?" Serra asked. "You two spent every second together this summer, why can't you both just admit—?"

"We'll never be a couple."

"Why not?" Maggie asked. "He's hot and you're into him, I know it."

*Because I've lied to him. Every second I spent with him that I didn't tell him about Cal was a lie.*

I wanted to tell them about Derrek Schwinn and Cal's coziness, and the churn in my stomach that night that had nothing to do with Maggie's mouthwash cocktail.

How anytime I pictured the two men laughing across that impeccable white room in Sausalito, I felt faintly sick again, remembering how Cal had described Schwinn.

*Basically harmless.*

Was my time with Cal harmless? Even if he was a good guy to me, even though I'd chosen him, it didn't feel that way now. I wanted to tell Serra and Maggie, to have them say that it would be okay.

Even if that, too, was a lie.

"Why can't you ever be a couple, Becc?" Serra prodded gently. "Becc, talk to us."

"Oh…I'm just being…" I sniffed hard to clear my nose, rubbed the sticky skin under my eyes with my knuckles. "We've been friends way too long, it'd be too weird. I don't know what's wrong with me. I think the party did me in."

"There's nothing wrong with admitting you're sad that Eric left," Serra said. "Right? I mean, we all are."

Serra and Maggie shared a not-so-secret smile above me. Mischievous, as if it was only a matter of time before Eric and I got our romantic ending.

"Yes," I said. "I'm sad that Eric left."

# 39

## Liberty

Summer after senior year
Letter No. 4

~~June 20, 1998~~
~~Dear Mrs. Haggermaker,~~
~~I know I usually write earlier, but~~

*

~~July 21, 1998~~
~~Dear Mrs. Haggermaker,~~
~~I'm sorry this letter is so late, but~~

*

~~August 20, 1998~~
~~Dear Mrs. Haggermaker,~~
~~The months since my graduation from Berkeley have~~

~~been so hectic that I'm afraid this letter is a little tardy, but I'm sure you'll understand.~~

~~It feels so scary to be out of school. Like there's nothing to hold on to. No books. No class schedules to tell me where to go when. Like I'm floating and there's nothing to grab onto. Anchorless.~~

~~Do you remember that feeling? Do you, Mrs. Haggermaker? Doyoudoyoudoyou? Were you ever afraid of anything?~~

June 1998

From: ericlogan98@brownuniversity.edu
How's the job search going? You find anything near the OPP?

It sounds like your grad ceremony was amazing. The Greek Theatre, huh? Can't wait to see the pictures your mom took. Tell her to get the pinball machine ready.

Wish you could fly out to Providence for my ceremony. I can offer you a bed (I'll sleep on the floor, naturally, as is our custom) and all the dorm-smuggled tater tots you can eat.

From: rebeccareardon98@berkeley.edu
Do you know what OPP stands for, E?

I do. Look it up.

Despite being totally offended by your casual use of such a misogynistic acronym, I'd still visit you if I could. I'd love to see you graduate.

But cash is ridiculously tight for me, too. I could barely afford to pay Serra for my share of gas to go home to OP (note the one *P*) and buy the good paper for résumés. I've sent out forty-one but so far I've got nothing. I just applied to *Cat Fancy*.

I wrote in my cover letter that I had three cats at home and my hobby is frequenting cat shows "and other local feline events." But, not to fear, my "versatile writing and research background" is also suited to the publisher's other "respected media properties."

The same company also puts out a quarterly newsletter about reptiles and a publication called *Rat Rodder.* I thought it was about rats until I did some digging and learned it was for hobbyists who make cars out of scavenged parts. Good thing I didn't tell them I owned a rat.

Anyway, I'll update you on my dazzling journalism prospects in the next email. Any interview would feel like a lifeline at this point.

~~I miss you.~~ Enjoy the tater tots.

Becc

From: ericlogan98@brownuniversity.edu

*Cat Fancy* would be crazy not to hire you.

I got into UCLA film school off the wait-list. But my mom can't help me out anymore. She can barely pay for her new apartment in San Diego. Is it nuts to go into debt?

My other option is an actual PAID job as a production assistant on *Gold Coast.* Spin-off of *Golden State* starring Krista Gold's cousin, filmed around Newport. Sounds life affirming, huh?

I miss you.

From: rebeccareardon98@berkeley.edu

I'm in the same dilemma about journalism school. It sounds like heaven but everyone says years in a newsroom count for more, and it's so expensive. Though it killed me to give up on the idea of Columbia. Maybe I'll go next year.

Maybe this will cheer you up:

Fwd: from catfancyinc.com

Thank you very much for your application.

Unfortunately, you're not right for our hiring needs at this time.

We wish you the very best in your career search...

June 17, 1998

Deborah Buckley, managing editor of the *OC Liberty*, tossed a section of the newspaper at me.

"What do you think of this?" She tapped a blunt-cut fingernail on a column called Paula's Potpourri.

Recipes featuring dried-onion soup, cleaning tips, photos readers mailed in of their grandchildren and doxies, knitting fair dates. In short, the Women's Section. The *Liberty* didn't call it that anymore, but everyone knew that's what it was. Above the column, *Paula* was rendered in line drawing as a smug, bow-lipped blonde with a French twist and heart locket.

I'd never subscribed to the *Liberty*, which was owned by some filthy-rich Libertarian family in Santa Ana, and hadn't read Paula's Potpourri. The job listing had said only:

Assistant editor. 1–2 years of print or internet journalism experience preferred. Some writing opportunities for self-starter.

Nothing about the goddamned Potpourri.

But I said diplomatically, "I think Paula probably has loyal readers."

Deborah rolled her wide-set brown eyes. "You have no idea. Paula's Potpourri has run since 1937. We tried killing it two years ago and you would not believe the backlash. Every blue hair in the county wrote to complain." She ran her hands through her short, gray-black curls. "If you got the job, you'd be Paula. You'd have to run one pet photo and one kid photo a week, minimum. And test every recipe you run. Can you cook?"

"Absolutely." I'd attempted those multicultural meals that summer after high school. So I'd wrecked most of them. I could fake my way through some recipes. I had to get this job.

"So I'll level with you, the position itself is a bit of a potpourri. We need someone to monitor the comments on the internet version of the paper, as well. Personally I think it's a waste of resources but management is actually taking this online subscriber thing seriously. So you'd delete anything that's against policy, that kind of stuff. The reporters take it in stride but a couple of our older columnists can get…sensitive about what people post. You're comfortable with HTML?"

*Comfortable signing up for a night class in it.*

I nodded, smiling, radiating what I hoped was the natural tech-savvy of youth.

She scanned my résumé and flipped through my college newspaper clips.

Uptick in Campus Graffiti. I read the headline from my sophomore article silently, upside down. Then came my respectable though short clips from the last two years, the ones I'd focused on after I stopped reporting on Serra and Yvonne's group: Student Committee Protests Textbook Prices; Self-Defense Classes Draw Record Numbers. I'd never made the front page, but I hoped my modest articles would be enough.

*Ohplease, ohplease let me get this job.*

"You know we can only pay $13 an hour. You must be making more at the temp agency."

I was, but barely, and my last job had involved ten-key data entry for a mortgage firm. Eight hours of typing numbers into spreadsheets.

"I'm fine with that."

"And any reporting will have to be on your own time. The other tasks come first."

"I understand."

She stood and offered her hand. "Start in two weeks."

I emailed ericlogan@goldproductions.com only three words:

I got it!

He didn't email back, so I figured he was at the movies; he hated *Gold Coast* even more than *Golden State*. It never occurred to me that Eric could actually be out, you know, working.

But the next day there was a package propped against my apartment door. A white box with a red ribbon on it. The card said:

*B,*
*Sad to lose my matinee buddy. But you deserve this. I figure these'll be useful. Congratulations.*
*E*

Inside were a dozen slim reporter's notebooks.

# 40

## More Than Fine

July 1998

WHERE ERIC WAS SUPPOSED TO BE | *Gold Coast*
WHERE I WAS SUPPOSED TO BE | Typing up a recipe for igloo meat loaf
WHERE WE WERE | A small greenhouse

My incoming-call light flashed at 11:30, as I was finishing next week's Potpourri, sorting through pictures of cats, trying to find the least attractive one to feature. (I always picked the scrawniest cats, the rattiest dogs, the homeliest grandchildren. My silent rebellion.)

Eric. "Meet me at the beach for lunch? The bonfire place?"

Eric hadn't once asked me to play hooky from the newspaper. He didn't try to lure me to the movies for extended lunches because he knew I actually liked my job.

Deb had told me she was worried about the extra hours I logged, how I worked on Saturdays and even Sundays. She said I should take a personal day, but work felt personal finally. I spent almost no time in my tiny, $700-a-month, orange-shag-carpeted Costa Mesa one-bedroom. Because if this wasn't my dream job, at least I was inching closer.

One of the paper's columnists, Skip Theobald, was always on my case, blaming me for the comments people posted about him online. But I'd had three small stories in the print paper, and I was working on a long feature that I was really proud of—a profile of a seventy-year-old widow in Pasadena who'd started a kids' music charity with a West Hollywood ska band.

I didn't want to leave my desk today.

But there was something small and lost in Eric's voice. "Please, Becc. Just for a couple hours?"

"Sure, E. I'll meet you."

I left a Post-it on my monitor saying I was at a "Dr. appt.," just in case Skip came by to lodge another grievance about his internet "bullies," grabbed my lunch bag, and drove to the beach.

★

A group of struggling artists had built the Crystal Cove beach shacks out of scrap lumber and driftwood in the 1930s. The parks department had been waffling over the buildings for ages, not sure if it should demolish them or make them into a tourist attraction or sell them to a condo developer or what. So they sat, pastel relics of more free-spirited days. Some were sinking into the dunes but a remarkable number of them were still upright, as if their owners had just gone for a stroll down the beach.

Eric was close to the water, skimboarding with the loose-jointed ease of a high school boy.

I sat on my yellow-striped beach towel with my work pants rolled up to my ankles and watched him until he noticed me and waved, running up with wet hair.

I tried not to look at the comma-shaped ridges of muscle that curved into the waistband of his trunks, and the thin trail of dark hair in the middle.

"I'm starving," he said, dropping onto my towel. "I guess I forgot the food part of my lunch invitation."

I fished in my bag. "Try this delicacy, courtesy of Betty Ren-freau of Fountain Valley. One of my regulars. She calls it Fudgy Lovin'. I'm trying to decide if that'll sound too much like some kind of exotic sex act to Paula's readership, or if I'm the only one with a dirty mind."

Betty had mailed the recipe in on a flower-trimmed recipe card. It was basically brownie mix and melted Crisco spread on graham crackers. When I handed one to Eric, he sniffed at it before biting.

"Tell Betty it's not bad," he said. "How are your fascists?"

"Libertarians. They're in rare form. Actually, it's only the Opinion section that's Libertarian. The reporters aren't."

"Doesn't it kill you to help that bulgy-vein guy? And do that techy stuff you hate?"

"It's a foot in the door."

"And that crazy retro housewife column. Three Beccs for the price of one."

"God, you're being mean." I stood and gathered my things. "Your SOS call was a ruse. I thought something was up, that you really needed me."

Eric reached up and squeezed my wrist. "I'm sorry. I do need you."

"What's going on? You called because you're worried about me? Because I'm fine, more than fine—"

"I was trying to ask you a question and it came out wrong. How can you stand your job?"

"You think I'll be typing recipes for Oreo-Cool-Whip-Wonder Cake and sale dates for the Yarn Barn forever?" I said. "And placating morons like Skip Theobald?"

"I hit a nerve. I'm sorry. It's just that nothing's turning out the way I expected. I'm turning into one of them."

The despair in his voice broke my heart, and I sat back down.

I didn't need to ask who *them* was. He meant his parents, the guys at the brokerage office, the Gold cousins. Anyone who, according to him, had sold out.

I spoke gently. "We have to pay the bills. We're lucky to. And it's not selling out if you haven't given up the dream, E. Why don't you go to film school part-time next term? Suck it up like Serra and take loans, or get a night job?" I tried to smooth his hair but it was so stiff from salt water it barely budged.

"You're right."

"I've got to get back. And you should go to work, too. At least until you decide what to do."

"Yeah, I'm tired." Eric regularly ducked out of the *Gold Coast* production office to nap in his truck, in the cool underground parking lot. Serra and I had a theory that he wanted to get caught grabbing REM cycles on *Gold Coast*'s dime so they'd fire him.

"Brat. I mean go to your desk. Not go back and sleep in the cab of your truck."

Eric walked me to my car. Before I got in I reached over and pulled his hoodie up over his head, tightening the drawstrings until the fabric cinched around his face. I tied the strings in a neat bow below his lips.

"Do you need tough love?" I asked. "Tough life coaching?" We'd once searched for the certification requirements for life coaches online.

"Coach away," he said. He could barely move his lips because of the tight knot under them.

"My mom has worked as an insurance coder for twenty years, but she never complains. There are people who have to walk miles for clean water every day and we sit in air-conditioned offices for regular paychecks and sleep in warm beds."

"Or cold truck floors." He smiled but he looked so lost I untied his drawstring, pulled his hood down, and gave him a long hug.

"Your dreams aren't dead," I whispered into his ear.

He held me there, and his hand began making slow circles on the small of my back. Even through three layers of fabric—camisole, button-down shirt, chenille sweater—it felt good.

So good I closed my eyes for a second before shifting away.

"You have affluenza," I said. "The Desperation of the First Cubicle. Disillusionment of Youth. The *Liberty* did an article on it. It'll get better, E."

I didn't tell Eric that a regular commenter, AlGore-Rhythm2000, had posted that "generational disillusionment" was "just another way of saying 'brats kicked on their asses.'"

"Don't go yet, life coach," he said. "I'll buy you sourdough pancakes at Dani's to pay you for your services." He tilted his head toward the restaurant up the hill.

We could sit on the deck at Dani's and watch the surfers. The pull, from the hopeful shine in Eric's eyes and the vision of us sitting close to each other, was strong. We could eat our sourdough pancakes with maple syrup. I could call Deb and say I needed the rest of the day off.

"C'mon, you know you want to stay. I can scrape together enough pennies for one stack."

But just as clearly as I could see us laughing together on the Dani's balcony, I could see myself laughing with Cal on another balcony.

The Catalina house. *Look at that color. It's the magic hour.*

I had smiled, nestled close.

Only the pain of what I'd done to Eric could summon such a cinematic visual.

I hadn't spoken to Cal in over a year. He hadn't emailed me in months. He'd become a phantom behind my back that I was careful not to turn and look at, an uncomfortable feeling that I outran by staying busy.

"I can't, E. I really have to go back to work."

"More pancakes for me."

"Pick a movie for Sunday?" I called as I left. "Something early."

Eric and I saw matinees, never evening showings. I said it was because matinees were cheaper. But the truth was going out with him alone at night would have felt too much like a date.

At our bargain matinees, I always stayed within the boundary of my armrest. I kept things light.

I could have cut off all contact with Eric. Maybe I should have.

# 41

## Cracked

2008
Friday, 8:30 p.m.

We devour room-service burgers and steak fries and house salads in the "executive" armchairs of our suite's sitting room, in front of a big TV tuned to *Law & Order.*

"Maggie was on a *Law & Order,*" I say. "I forget which one."

"I saw that! I was at a hotel in Orlando, and there she was, in the credits and everything. Bailiff, Margaret J. Estes. Her hair was red but I recognized her right away." There's pride in his voice.

"Our shower tiles are still stained pink from when she dyed her hair for that audition. She works so hard. You should tell her." Maggie and I have been roommates for four years. Technically I'm her landlord, since I own our shared condo in Dana Point. But she doesn't treat me like one, which suits me fine.

She still keeps insane hours, she still smokes, and she never cleans the litter box, even though she's the one who brought in our stray cat, Eliot. She never judges me for my work choices, or the fact that I haven't had a proper date in two years. She's been seeing another actor, this older woman who started as a comic, for more than a year.

"So you're flying back with her Monday morning after the wedding?"

"Yeah. She has a callback Monday afternoon. She's trying out for a soap, this psychic character named Daphne. I've been running lines with her so long I've memorized her love interest's part."

"Oh, you have to do it for me."

"Picture a six-five guitarist-slash-firefighter named Jagger. Her script says he's 'hardened by life, but with a soft side.' *Daphne! I see us together! Like we were in Santa Fe!*"

"Brava. Maybe you missed your calling."

"Please. Anyway, it's brutal, all that rejection, but Maggie's really happy."

"She's doing what she loves. Serra, too, teaching her art classes." He nods at the triptych in the middle of the suite. "So have you looked at it?"

"Just the pictures, and I peeked at one side. The seller wrapped it up so carefully, I was worried I wouldn't get it back in. But now that you mention it…" I lick salt from my fingers, cross the room, and kneel in front of the triptych. Pick at some duct tape.

"What are you doing?"

"I just want to check that it didn't get damaged today."

I unfold the side flap of the box, peel at a little Bubble Wrap. The edge of the triptych looks exactly the same as when I checked it at my condo two nights ago. I pull the panels out a few inches, just to make sure.

"Is it okay?" Eric asks, shaking ketchup on his plate.

"Yeah, it's fine."

I should fold the Bubble Wrap back into place. Shove the panels all the way into their long cardboard sleeve and retape it.

Buy some paint or white shoe polish to cover my scuff mark on the door. Say good-night to Eric, shower, and go to sleep. Restore myself to fight another day. The last thing I should do is slide the box off the panels.

I slide the box off the panels.

Eric sets the ketchup down and comes over, stands behind me. I feel heat on my spine where his legs would brush if he were just a few inches closer and freeze.

"Becc, are you sure we'll be able to get it back in, maybe we should wait... Wow." He crouches on the floor next to me.

I undo more Bubble Wrap so we can see it clearly.

Some of the creatures are a little worse for wear. There's been a breach in panel two. A little crack running up from the right bottom corner. The small, furred figure Serra used to represent Glenn is orange and balding, and his hacky sack is gone. Poor Glenn: it's not something I can fix. But the piece looks better than I expected, considering that it's ten years old.

I pull it out a little more. Tear at more Bubble Wrap. Enough to see the small replica of Serra.

Then Maggie. Our other housemates.

Eric.

And me. Serra's sweet little critter version of me, clutching my skinny reporter's notebook so eagerly, a pen behind my bitty pink ear. Miraculous that I'm still intact, down to the pages in my dollhouse-size notebook and the shine in my eyes.

Here we all are, trapped in time. Little, fearful animals swimming against the current.

The piece is as unsettling now as it was when I was twenty-one. Whatever we'd been swimming away from, whatever we sensed lurking inside that gold nylon graduation cap above us, maybe we'd been right to fear it.

We say we'll never be like them, but it happens.

It happens gradually. We give in a little here, put off the hard decision there, say we're paying our dues. We forget to swim against the current.

"I forgot how detailed it was," Eric says, running his long fingers along the front. "The tiny espresso machine, the cash." His voice softens. "Look at you in there, with your notebook."

I rest the side of my head on top of the middle panel, and it's cold and smooth against my cheek. "Remember when you gave me those notebooks? After I got the newspaper job?"

His hand pauses for a second, but he doesn't look at me.

"Yeah, Becc." He says it sweetly. Not doubting, just remembering.

Those empty notebook pages had been so full of hope. Passion.

Searching for the triptych and retrieving its scattered parts has given me a taste of something I haven't had in a long time. The thrill of the chase. Entering other people's worlds, so different from your own. One fact leading to another, feeling your way through the dark, sometimes crawling and sometimes backing up and sometimes running. The certainty that the story is important, that you have to keep going because no one else will. Until you're out of the maze, holding a fragment of the truth up to the light.

It's been a long time, my shoe leather's thicker. But the feeling had rushed back as if no time at all had passed. And I still loved it.

"You okay?" Eric touches my hand, the one spread out on top of the triptych's second panel.

I shake my head.

"Maybe we should get some fresh air. Check out that roof garden Bryce was telling you about?"

I look up at him. "I didn't think you were listening."

"I was, and he said we shouldn't miss it. Come on."

# 42

## Bender

July 1998

WHERE I WAS SUPPOSED TO BE | The paper
WHERE I WAS | Crystal Cove

Eric never called about the Sunday matinee we'd planned to see together. He blew me off.

After eighty hours of unreturned messages, I told myself— *Good. Let him move on. It was just like after high school, and maybe that was how it had to be.*

He was the one thing I couldn't have, simple as that. I would be a grownup and accept it. Let him fall in love with someone else. Some lovely but previously underestimated fellow *Gold Coaster* who'd roll her eyes at him conspiratorially in a meeting about Suzi Gold's "internship" at the fashion designer.

Or he'd click with a random film buffette in a theater. They'd meet-cute. She'd fall into his lap trying to reach her seat, spilling popcorn, and he'd forget me, and we'd all be better off.

But after four days of not hearing from him, I couldn't take it anymore.

I drove to his apartment on my lunch hour, and his roommate Simon answered the door in a purple flower-print robe. Eric told me that Simon and his girlfriend had screeching sex all night, then slept until noon. Simon's parents were funding him. He took a smattering of classes at CalArts but was in no hurry to finish. I'd assumed Eric had been exaggerating, but here was Simon looking like a young Hugh Hefner.

"Jessica's," he explained, cinching the floral robe tighter.

"Ah. It's gorgeous." It was. "Is Eric home?"

"He moved out last week. Jess moved in... He said it was good timing, that he already had something lined up. He didn't tell you?"

*Oh, Eric.*

"No. Did he say where he was moving?"

Simon shook his head. "Shit, now I feel bad. I thought it was weird when he didn't take his stuff. He said he'd come back for it in a week or two. Come in for a coffee?" He opened the creaking screen door wider just as, behind him, Jessica leapt across the hall in a towel.

"Thanks, I've got to go. And don't feel bad... I'm sure he's fine."

But the second Simon shut the door I speed-dialed Eric from my black Nokia. "What's going on? You've moved out? Call me."

I dialed Serra. She was renting a garage apartment in Silver Lake, juggling three jobs (nannying, working at the museum again, helping a caterer). So I wasn't surprised when nobody picked up.

I called everywhere else I could think of. No Eric.

When I eventually got through to Serra, I asked her to try Eric's mom at her new apartment in San Diego, but not to let on that we didn't have a clue where Eric was.

"Why don't you call her?" Serra asked.

"It would be awkward. I don't want her to think I'm...acting like a crazy girlfriend or something."

"You are acting like a crazy girlfriend. But I know for a fact he's not dating anyone. In case you're interested. In case you're worried he's moved in with some lovely—"

"Serr. Don't. Just…can you call her? I'm worried."

"Fine."

I'd neglected Eric's offers to join him and Donna for lunch. She'd actually softened a lot since we were in high school, he said. I could tell it puzzled him that I was avoiding her. But the idea of being in the same room with her, even trying to make small talk with her on the phone, was not appealing.

*You know, we have more in common than you might think, Donna!*
No, thanks.

Serra called back in ten minutes.

"Okay, he's definitely not living at his mom's. But I'm sure he's fine, Becc. He's probably on one of his benders."

Serra and I had learned about Eric's benders during winter break junior year of high school, when things got so bad at home he disappeared for three days.

Eric told his parents he was going skiing at Big Bear with a bunch of friends from school. I called his house and that was what his mom told me, so I'd tried to sound casual—"Oh, right, he said something about going."

Serra was dating a guy on the ski team at the time so we knew within an hour that Eric wasn't in Big Bear. We'd spent forty-eight hours debating a missing-persons report before he turned up on my doorstep, acting blasé.

I was so relieved I'd only hugged him and rearranged his cowlicks. But Serra punched him in the chest.

"So where were you?" she asked. "Drug-muling in Mexico? Having a secret affair with Uma Thurman?"

"We didn't bust you," I said. "But skiing with the cashmere turtleneck posse? Please. I can't believe they bought it."

"Tell." Serra tilted her Mr. Pibb can above his head until he 'fessed up.

"The Red Lion in San Diego. The big one near the theaters. I go there sometimes. It's peaceful. And I wanted to rewatch all the Oscar movies."

Serra and I had stared at him.

"Except *The Player*. I've already seen it three times."

"We were worried sick, asshole," said Serra.

"What she means is tell us next time, so we can help," I said.

★

"I already tried that Red Lion in San Diego," I said to Serra. "So if it's a movie bender, he's found a new hotel."

"He's fine. Let's try not to stress."

I stressed.

On the seventh day of no Eric, when I dialed his *Gold Coast* number planning to leave my umpteenth "Are you okay?" voice mail, my call went straight to reception. A silky voice informed me that Eric "was no longer with the company."

I called Serra and she answered the way she always did, lately, when she saw it was me on the line: "I haven't heard from him."

"I'm picturing him on the street. Turning tricks, like River Phoenix and Keanu Reeves in *My Own Private Idaho*."

"He's probably sitting in a movie theater watching *My Own Private Idaho*. He's a big boy. You have to stop rescuing him."

"I know."

"Don't worry."

I tried not to. If *Gold Coast* had fired him, well, he'd been expecting it for weeks. He'd known all those five-hour lunches sleeping or watching classic double features at the Wiltern Theatre would catch up with him. Or maybe he'd quit. Gone out with a bang, telling them they could get another flunky to scout tanning salons and schedule Suzi Gold's "internships."

Serra was right. He'd surface when he was ready. Any day I'd get a postcard. Greetings from the world's largest ball of twine or the gas station made of petrified wood we'd always wanted to visit.

I threw myself into work.

At 10:00 a.m., Skip Theobald came over to lodge his daily grievance about the reader comments on the website. When Skip visited my cubicle waving printouts, I usually got an instant headache. But today I didn't mind the distraction.

"Can't you do anything about this?" he asked, eyes and veins bulging.

Skip's Sunday tirade against the firefighter union had all his anonymous enemies posting on the newspaper's website into the wee hours. I didn't have to look at the sheet he was shaking at me because I'd memorized the comments. My favorite was from reliable AlGoreRhythm2000. "Libertarianism is a cult, and Skip Theobald is the sect's nastier, less intelligent L. Ron Hubbard."

Mild stuff, really. No death threats.

I swiveled my ergonomic chair toward Skip and nodded at his monologue. My mind drifted as he went off on me, waving his stack of copied-and-pasted comments. Had he trained his Microsoft Word spellcheck not to autocorrect *Theobald* to *toehold* like I had? The winding vein on his temple resembled a switchbacking section of the River Thames in London. The part they showed during the credits of *EastEnders*.

Skip ran on. "So these idiots can post whatever they want and I'm supposed to take it... Isn't it your job to delete this crap?" An arc of saliva punctuated the end of his speech.

When Skip finally finished his rant, I kept my voice satiny and reasonable. "Skip, I can't delete posts unless they violate the newspaper's comment policy. That's no threats, profanity, harassment, or intimidation."

He humphed, but I continued. The expert mom at the playground, soothing a tantrummy child. "And I do delete that stuff. Every day. But people are allowed to say they disagree."

The vein in Skip's forehead throbbed at me, but he huffed away.

Alice, the sixty-year-old copy editor in the cubicle next to mine, peered over the gray wall we shared and nodded at my small victory.

I spent the rest of the day putting the Potpourri to bed. When my mind wandered to Eric, I yanked it back to Darla Talbert's mock beef Stroganoff and a wildly popular new feature I'd launched—Grandchild Quote Corner.

If I was stuck being Paula, nothing less than global syndication would do.

I was typing up a funny quote about dentures from some four-year-old boy in Garden Grove when the phone rang.

"Becc."

It was Eric. Thank God.

"What the hell? I did a Navigator search this morning on how to file a missing-persons report. I think I was serious."

"Can you meet me?"

"Half an hour."

It was four. I left my monitor on, draped my jacket on the back of my chair so it would look like I was still in the building if Skip came by in another snit, and drove to Newport.

When I got to Crystal Cove Eric wasn't at our usual spot near the shacks. A deeply tanned couple slept on towels down the beach, but otherwise it was pretty deserted.

I took off my shoes and put them in my shoulder bag, rolled up my pants, and walked from the hot sand to the cold, packed surface close to the water. I dragged my toes in the foam, turning around every once in a while to look for Eric. After fifteen minutes sweat trickled down my back and I was starting to worry again.

I walked up to a tilting old shack with green trim. It was slightly apart from the other houses. A keep-out sign had been revised, via black spray paint, to read Fuck Off. The green cabin was boarded up like all the others, but one side window had most of its planks missing.

I crept closer and peeked in. Something hairy moved inside and

I jumped, scraping the inside of my arm on the rough wood. An animal. A shaggy homeless dude, furious that I'd disturbed him? No.

Eric. Unshaven, hair wild even for him. But he came to the window like it was a McDonald's drive-up and in his goofy voice said, "Can I help you, ma'am?"

"Are you trying to kill me?" I leaned over, bracing my hands on my knees to slow my heart.

"Oh, sorry! You cut yourself?" Blood oozed down my forearm. "Grab my hand."

My heart still racing, I scrambled through the window frame into the cottage. Sun slashed in through broken boards. Almost everything had been ransacked over the years. There were broken cupboards in the kitchen, but no sink. An oval mark on the hardwood floors, but no tub.

It must have been adorable once. Whoever had built it, some artist in the 1930s, had wanted to hear the beach from her bed. She hadn't wanted to sell out, working at a job she hated to afford beachfront property. So she'd built this place illegally. Somebody had been happy here.

Now there were layers and layers of graffiti on the walls. Initials inside hearts and foul scrawls. Love and hate messages, nothing in between.

A stack of items was neatly arranged in one corner. A red sleeping bag, some water bottles, a roll of toilet paper, and a box of saltines.

"What is this, some documentary project? People are living in these shacks?"

Then I recognized the sleeping bag. It was Eric's red mummy North Face.

"No," I said.

A mound of trash filled another corner. Empty potato chip bags, beer bottles, some items best left unidentified. All courtesy of previous tenants. And next to the trash was a tree branch that Eric had apparently used as a broom. He'd swept up.

Eric grabbed the roll of toilet paper and unwound it, fashioning a compress for my bleeding arm. "Here... Sorry."

"You haven't been sleeping here."

"If you say so."

"You're telling me you spent the night here last night?"

"And the night before that. Well, the first night doesn't count 'cause I slept in my truck for most of it."

"No."

"Yes. I couldn't stand it at Simon's."

"So you've been playing homeless because your roommate has rowdy sex?"

"Nah. Well, the rowdy-sex part was the beginning. So I started looking for a new apartment, stayed with a guy from work for a couple nights."

"Get to the part where you end up here." I shivered and Eric took off his dirty sweatshirt, draped it over my shoulders. "Why didn't you just crash at your mom's?"

"I wanted to be alone for a little while."

"So what have you been doing all day?"

"I walk on the beach. Read. There's a Qwik-Mart up the highway. Good jerky."

"Eric." Pity overtook anger and I hugged him, trying not to get blood on the back of his Hitchcock T-shirt, even though it was so grimy the blood probably wouldn't show. He smelled bad, like a week of camping mixed with stale sea salt. "What's going on?"

"What's going on is I'm ridiculous. The only homeless person I know with a $100 sleeping bag."

"You're not homeless. Come with me. Surf on my couch for a while."

"I'm okay here. Just wanted to see you."

We sat on the buckling floor together, back to back. He leaned up against me and I closed my eyes, tried to imagine sleeping there for even one night. Maybe the white noise of the crashing waves made it relaxing. Maybe Eric no longer smelled the years of baked-in urine.

I didn't say anything. I'd let him talk when he was ready. I pressed on my cut until the bleeding wasn't too bad.

Finally, he said, "I stopped going to *Gold Coast*."

"I know, they told me you don't work there anymore."

"Really? I wasn't sure they'd notice."

"Sorry. Guess they noticed."

"I was such a hard worker. How will the show go on without me?"

I laughed.

"Do you think I'm a lazy brat, Becc? Tell the truth."

I thought for a minute. Eric wasn't lazy, and he wasn't a brat. He just cared more than he was supposed to. He didn't want to wake up at fifty and realize he'd become his dad, stuck doing work that made him miserable. The misery trickling down to his family. "No. I've never thought that. For someone who's supposedly good with words I was careless with that one."

"Thank you."

Resting our backs against each other, we listened to the waves.

"Can we stay here for a few minutes?" Eric said. "Before I go back to the world of résumés and paying my dues?"

"Sure, E."

He handed me a stack of saltines over his shoulder, reached back to awkwardly drape his sleeping bag over my legs. It was getting cold. The regular pounding of the waves got louder. High tide. And there was no more weak golden light piercing the boards. Voices came near the shack, and Eric's back tightened against mine as we both held our breath. It was probably only teenagers, debating on coming in to tryst, add their initials to the walls.

The voices receded.

When it was almost too dark to see, Eric said, "I'm ready to go now."

★

An hour later, in my warm, locked, orange-shag-carpeted apartment, we lay on my $90 Goodwill sofa with greasy fingers, surrounded by empty In-N-Out Burger bags.

"I'll try not to stink up your couch," said Eric. "I'm too tired to shower."

"And I'll try not to wake you up when I leave in the morning, but you'd better be here when I get back. Promise you won't disappear on me again?"

"Promise."

I tucked him in so everything but his head was covered in red nylon. He looked like a swaddled newborn. "I'm sorry I called you a brat."

"It wasn't because of that," he said. "Well, so much for my three-day career as a beach bum."

"You had housing. Real beach bums don't."

"That guy in *Gidget* did. Moondoggie."

"Not Moondoggie. You're thinking of the other one. Kahuna."

"That's right, the Big Kahuna." Eric smiled. "Who else but you would remember that? We should rent it this weekend. That and another movie with a beach theme, a good one."

"*Gidget*'s good. *Gidget* rules. But it's a plan."

"I won't stay past the weekend." He touched my arm.

I bent down to kiss the top of his head. Quickly, but long enough to breathe in his Eric smell. Seawater and sweat couldn't hide it.

"You can stay as long as you want." I went in my bedroom and shut the door.

# 43

## Curriculum Vitae

July 1998

WHERE I WAS SUPPOSED TO BE | The newspaper
WHERE I WAS | On the couch with Eric

I cut out of work at 4:35. I'd worked through lunch, but I still took the long way around the office to the elevator so Skip Theobald wouldn't see me leaving early and fume.

The shower was running when I got home. I curled up on the couch, my head on Eric's rolled sleeping bag, and waited for him.

"Caught me." He came down the hall, toweling his hair. "I only woke up an hour ago. And I used your razor. And borrowed your clothes. A little tight, but clean." He looked better, his cheeks smooth, his eyes brighter. His shoulders strained at my women's medium T-shirt from the Orange County MS Walkathon/10K. My blue Nike sweats were so tight on him he looked like he was wearing riding jodhpurs. But the length wasn't bad. There were only four inches of leg below the hem.

"Borrow whatever. I'm just glad you're here."

"There's pizza coming. Crispy bacon and anchovy."

I pretended to gag.

"C'mon, bacon and anchovy is like a warm Caesar salad," he said.

"That's not selling it."

"Kidding," he said. "I got your nasty Hawaiian for you. My new landlord."

We toasted with glasses of root beer (Eric) and Two-Buck Chuck cabernet from Trader Joe's (me), devouring the pizza on the sofa. Eric peeled the pineapple rings off his slices and set them on mine.

After dinner, I scooched to the other side of the couch to face him, pressing the soles of my feet against the soles of his so we could do a push-me, pull-you bicycle motion with our legs.

"I'll get my stuff together tomorrow while you're at work," he said. "And then I'll move into my mom's."

"Stay here while you look for a new job. As long as you want."

"I'm qualified to do nothing."

"That's outrageously untrue. Print your résumé tomorrow and we'll look at it when I get home."

Eric slept on the couch again that night. At 3:00 a.m., I tiptoed out to use the bathroom. He lay on the sofa, his rustle-y, red sleeping bag fallen to the floor. One long leg dangled onto the carpet and his mouth was wide-open. I pulled the sleeping bag up to his chin.

When I woke at seven he wasn't there.

A panicked five minutes, then he clomped up the stairs with two coffees and a white bag in hand.

"Sweet or savory?" he asked in a British accent.

"Sweet."

He handed me a chocolate croissant and took the ham and cheese for himself. We munched quietly and drank our coffees.

★

I ducked out early again. 4:41. Deb and the other bigwigs were in a meeting in the large conference room behind closed blinds, which was weird. Deb always held meetings in the morning, way before deadline. With open blinds.

Eric wasn't there when I got home, but his sleeping bag was still on the sofa, rolled up neatly in its mummy case.

He'd printed his résumé and left it for me on the kitchen table. At the top he'd written, *"Went to get dinner. 'Yet another in a long series of diversions in an attempt to avoid responsibility.'"*

The résumé wasn't bad. He had the Brown University degree, 3.5 GPA, junior production assistant for an "innovative, unscripted cable series."

*Unscripted*—what a sham. Eric said the show regularly paid people to appear as love interests. But the *Gold Coast* people were hardly likely to give him glowing recs. He'd have to say he had creative differences or something.

I turned the paper over to jot down possible wording. But the back wasn't blank. Eric had printed another version of his résumé there.

<u>*Curriculum Vitae Secretus*</u>, it said at the top. His secret CV.

*-Analyzed structure of* All About Eve *with apprentice film critic during ad hoc intensive media industry event.*

A movie afternoon with me in San Francisco.

*-Managed outdoor survival session as mental preparation for* Gold Coast *two-episode finale event.*

A camping trip Eric and Serra and I had taken to Pinecrest last summer. He hadn't told us he was supposed to be working that weekend.

*-Presided over floating pool chair, with headrest and cup holder, within tight window of* TV Guide *conference hours.*

That one I didn't know.

There were a dozen more bullet points like that. I'd thought my occasional sneaky work exits were bad, but Eric had made a whole career out of fudging his *Gold Coast* schedule.

"Honey, I'm home." He walked in with two crumpled brown bags and pulled out white boxes and chopsticks.

"What is it?" I asked.

"Thai." He dealt out napkins and we ate straight from the boxes.

"Daily takeout is not in your budget. We'll shop tomorrow."

"I'll bring the coupons."

"Yes, you will," I said. "So. I like this." I held up his résumé and set it near the edge of the round table, away from the drippy pad thai noodles and chicken curry.

"The real one or the fake one?"

"Both. But I meant the fake one. Your anti-résumé, or whatever it is."

"Know something scary? I could have made it five pages longer. I had more to print about the secret stuff than the not-secret stuff."

"We all have that."

"I have a theory."

"You always have a theory."

"You and I were extreme rule abiders in high school, right?"

I finished my mouthful of noodles. "After Serra and I got our responsible hooks in you. We established that a long time ago," I said.

"That's why we take extra pleasure in ditching our responsibilities now."

"Recovering goody-goodies. I like it."

"But I'm going to get my act together. Find a job I don't want to skip out on, like you."

"That's the trick."

That night we brushed our teeth at the same time. Eric had gone to the laundromat so he was wearing his own clothes again. Clean gray shorts and his Hitchcock shirt. I had on my ratty Beck T-shirt, the one Maggie had given me for my twenty-first, and the Nike sweats he'd washed for me.

He spat out white foam, then met my eyes in the mirror.

"Hey, roomie," he said.

"Hey."

I lay in bed thinking for a long time. About how right it felt with Eric.

And not just because of our shared history.

But because Eric thought he would find something new in a movie he'd already watched ten times. He was so sure there was still much to discover in the world, and I loved that about him.

For all the heat between us in bed, Cal had been passionless.

And now here were both kinds of passion on my beat-up sofa, ten feet away. Waiting for me, right there.

I don't know how many hours of sleep Eric got that night, out on his couch.

But even though I had the AC on and the alley below my window was quieter than usual, I only got about three.

## 44

### Coping Mechanisms

2008
Friday, 9:20 p.m.

We lie on the dewy grass in the lamp-lit roof garden, our heads near a big circular fountain. Everything on the square patio is laid out symmetrically—the benches, the curving hedges around the fountain, the potted flowers, and the ones in neat, low rows. It's relaxing.

We listen to the wind in the palm trees, the trickle of the fountain's spout, the occasional cable car *trings* from far below, on Powell Street. It's too foggy to see stars, but there are blinking red taillights from planes, taking off from SFO airport.

"This is nice," I say. "I should've brought my comforter up so I could sleep here. Though maybe the Fairmont wouldn't be so keen on that. I'd probably get grass stains on it, and I've already done enough damage to their property."

"It's been a day, huh?"

"It's been a day." *A day and ten years.*

"So Serra's little plastic Wild Kingdom put you over the edge?"

"Yeah."

"A compliment to the artist. And we don't even have the third section yet."

"I know. It just hit me. How different things have turned out compared with what I expected. Work, everything. You know?" I roll onto my right side to face him.

He's got his hands clasped together under his head, and the stretch has pulled his white T-shirt up a few inches, revealing his hip bones, a strip of midriff, the silky line of brown hair in the center. The treasure trail, it's called.

I roll onto my back again, searching for the next plane.

"So you're not that into your job right now?" he asks.

"Mild understatement. Do you know what I do all day?"

"You're a content officer. You...officiate content."

I confess to the night sky: "I monetize demographically sorted, SEO-keyword-generated paid media programming on vertical web content partner sites."

Eric doesn't answer, possibly stunned into silence by the force of my sarcasm. I'm just as surprised by the edge in my voice, the angry tremor. Though I shouldn't be. It's been building for a long time.

I've started my own graffiti club at work. It has a membership of one, and we meet in my corner office, under my polished rosewood desk.

I started the club one Monday a year ago. I'd just scored a huge victory for Newzly. A $300,000 ad-partnership deal. My email inbox was spilling over with congratulations.

Instead of celebrating with my colleagues, I locked my door, crawled under my desk, and drew a replica of the Feline Collective cat in red Sharpie. I remembered the tag exactly, down to the span of its raised tail and the curve of its haughty neck. *The cat knows.* Serra had said it was supposed to mean that nobody else could take away our name—our *ineffable* name. That only we knew who we were.

Yes, the act was entitled, self-indulgent, theatrical. Hunching under my desk in Armani silk-wool-blend tights to secretly tattoo the underbelly of my executive office furniture was all of these things.

But after I did it, I felt better. I crawled up to my chair and got right back to work.

For a while, it was the only mark down there. I pictured it, scowling in disapproval as I went about my workday. *Have you forgotten your name, Rebecca Reardon?*

Sometimes I'd touch it. I'd drawn it in a convenient spot, below the shift key on my keyboard, and it felt good to rub the underside of my desk where I'd hidden it. A quick, furtive stroke was all it took to calm me. My coworkers had all kinds of tchotchkes on their desks—Day-Glo Koosh balls to fondle, mini zen gardens to rake, silver Newton's cradle balls to clack together; this seemed no different.

I had a bad day a few months later and drew again. A question mark this time. My tribute to *A Room with a View*, a book I'd loved in college.

I began writing something weekly. A sum-up or epigraph.

Then it became the only thing that got me through the day.

A few months ago I started running out of space. I made my marks smaller and smaller, overlapping, fitting messages inside an *O* or a *B*. I decided that when I ran out of room I would quit my job.

That was a month ago.

"I hate it," I tell Eric, gazing up at a red plane light. It winks, rising, then disappears into the fog. "I hate what I do. I hate myself for doing it."

I've never said this out loud. I haven't even written it under my desk. I've scribbled *pig* and *go to hell* and once, after an especially tedious meeting, *That's 108 minutes we'll never get back, people. Nice job!!!!*

But now that I've said it, something cracks open. "The highlight of my day is writing secret messages on the underside of my desk. I spend all day luring people *away* from news, Eric. Away from what they set out to find. We're flooding the internet with junk."

It feels good to let it all out, without anyone trying to convince me otherwise.

I sit up, ruffle my palm along the damp grass in front of me. "I create little side routes, little…phony painted footbridges and gardens and rivers, all brilliantly designed to distract people from what's important. They type in a search about the Olympics and before they know it, they're reading an airline ad without realizing it.

"Our slogan is The News You Choose. But nobody's choosing anything. They're being manipulated."

I tug at a blade of grass. Another. Then a clump. *Rip. Rip, rip.*

"They want to find out what happened in Washington today and end up doing some cutesy poll. So some think tank…" *rip, rip, rip* "…can extract data on them. And they have no fucking idea what's real and what's not." I'm pulling hard at the grass now, indiscriminately. The Fairmont will have to reseed, but it feels incredible, better than tending any desktop zen garden. "And pretty soon nobody will remember. Or care. Maybe not even me."

I yank up a fistful of roots. Throw it at the trunk of a palm tree, where it hits with a sloppy *thwack*, leaving mud on the pale bark. "Add it to the damage fee."

I glance over at him, afraid he's going to be staring in horror at the bald patches in the Fairmont's grass.

But he's looking at me intently.

"Did that feel good?" he asks.

"Spectacular."

He sits up, tears a grass clump, and throws it at the tree, making a splat just under mine.

I do another, and then he aims for that mark, nailing it.

"Nice one!"

"And now, the curveball..." He stands, bends over. Pulls out a giant clump, winds up. Exaggerating, tilting back on one long leg, windmilling his right arm. It's a terrible pitch; the ball of grass lands on the trunk, inches from the ground. "I guess I'm a little rusty." He brushes grass from his hands. "So these secret messages under your desk. What do they say?"

"Oh. You know. *Shove your weekday click-through rate up your ass.* Stuff like that."

He laughs. "Your basic professional communication. I love it. Will you take a picture of your masterpiece and send it to me?"

"Sure. But don't show anyone. I'll never get another job."

"I won't show anyone. You know..."

"What?"

"Just that we're lucky. To have *any* job right now."

"I know. *Beyond* lucky. I am aware of that fact every single day. But..."

"Yes. *But.*"

He checks out a topiary in a pot in front of us. Three perfect spheres stacked on top of each other. *Edward Scissorhands.*

I will him to say it.

He doesn't, but staring out at the lights of the city, he says something almost as comforting: "I don't love what I do, either. Not all day, every day. Maybe it's foolish to think that's possible."

"Maybe," I say. "It's like...we pick this industry we're passionate about, and then if we're *really, really* good at it and *really, really* lucky, we get to watch the job become a total perversion of what we once loved. Maybe we'd be better off keeping the passions to the side. Separate from the paycheck."

"Maybe."

"But the way you felt about movies, Eric. That doesn't just die."

He's still looking out at the city, taking in the lights. The scattered bright squares of high-rise office windows, the draped Christmas lights of the Bay Bridge, and the white flares on the tip of Coit Tower.

"Maybe it can," he says. So softly I almost miss it. "If you want it to."

"Eric."

*Your dreams aren't dead,* I whispered to the twenty-two-year-old at Crystal Cove.

*Eric, you don't want it to,* I want to say now, a decade later.

But just then he turns to face me, leans against the stone wall. "Okay. I can tell you something that might cheer you up. But you can't tell anyone." He points at me, mock-serious.

"I won't tell anyone."

"And there's a chance it'll make you even more depressed."

"I'll risk it."

"I have my own secret work habit. My coping mechanism, whatever you want to call it."

"You crawl under your desk at the office and watch movies on a portable DVD player?"

He laughs. "You're close. There's this theater out on Staten Island, the Virago, that plays classics and second runs. Once a quarter, I blow off a big meeting and take in a matinee instead. Something so old that I can't analyze it to death. I sit there in my custom-made suit and put my overpriced shoes up on the seat in front of me and for a couple of hours I try to forget everything else."

*Once he didn't have to* try. But it does make me feel better. I smile, picturing him in some dark theater, getting popcorn butter streaks on his power suit. Making his quarterly escape from the day-to-day. Both an attempt to forget and an attempt to remember.

"Do you *schedule* these quarterly matinee outings?"

"Not in my calendar app. I track them mentally."

"But once every three months is enough for you? At least your habit's under control. You haven't accelerated, like I have lately."

"Maybe..." He hesitates, the lights of the city behind him.

"What?"

"Do you think you've had an extra rough time lately because... My mom told me. I was really sorry to hear about it."

His voice is kind, concerned. But this is a gut punch.

"Thank you," I say, rising, checking the dew on my back and the seat of my pants. "Well. We should probably go down."

He touches my wrist and the warmth sends tingles up my arm.

"Becc, sorry if it's hard to talk about, I didn't—"

"It's totally fine! It's just that I'm exhausted, and we have a long drive in the morning."

# 45

## Trifecta

August 1998

WHERE I WAS SUPPOSED TO BE | The newspaper
WHERE I WAS | Santiago Oaks Park

A long lunch hour.

I waited in the shade, near the park entrance. The groomed
and toned specimens on the sidewalk jogged past in neon sneak-
ers and glided by on Rollerblades and whizzed by on bikes.

"Penny for your thoughts, m'lady?" a voice growled in my
ear. Eric.

"I was thinking it must be hard to get old in Southern California," I said. "Look how perfect everyone seems."

"*Seems* being the operative word."

"True."

We walked deep into the park, near the lake, lay down beside
each other. The tree I'd picked made an island of shade just big
enough for the two of us.

"So how's the job search?" I asked.

"I have an interview to be a busboy at tumtum. That new restaurant way up in Silver Lake? Modern tapas."

"Topless?"

"You're hilarious."

"No, I'm proud of you."

"As far as jobs *in my field*, as they say, not so successful. Thirty letters out to the field last night. This is a nice napping spot."

"Don't let me fall asleep, you bad influence." I stretched my arms above my head.

Eric rolled onto his side and touched the inside of my bent elbow. I lay still, not breathing. "Your skin is so pale here," he said.

Behind Eric's shoulder, the dry leaves shivered. The sky, blue daubed with smog-gold, quivered, too, from the heat. If I smiled, he'd stop. But in the second it took me to move my eyes to his, I decided.

I didn't smile. I looked at his brown eyes as he slowly ran his finger inside the crook of my elbow, and as he leaned down and kissed me.

He pulled away to read my expression, his own face a beautiful mix of pleasure and surprise. I dug my hands into his soft hair and pulled him close for another kiss.

I got back to work only thirty minutes late.

So much can change in thirty minutes, if you let it.

★

"You're so smiley," my cubicle neighbor, Alice, said when I returned to the paper.

"Am I?"

I settled in and worked hard all afternoon. I made Paula's Potpourri as snappy and reassuring as I could. I turned in my final revision on the punk band charity story, and Deborah said she was considering it for the spotlight feature.

"This has a lot of heart," she said. Her highest praise.

Even when Skip Theobald made a fuming visit to my cubicle

to harangue me about online comments at three, I was professional and calm. My hatred of Skip had melted into generous
amusement.

Because I was happy. Eric and I felt inevitable, lucky, somehow unscathed by our years of near misses.

And the other thing.

My luck had held.

I knew I loved Eric. I hadn't told him, but I did.

And I hoped that would be enough to carry us.

★

They say you can have a good job, a good apartment, or a good
relationship, but never all three at the same time. But it wasn't true.

For one afternoon, I had all three. The twentysomething's trifecta.

4:08 p.m.

> From: hr@ocliberty.com
> To: allstaff@ocliberty.com
> We are pleased to announce that the OC Liberty is, effective
> this morning, a wholly owned subsidiary of CommPlanet,
> Inc…
> …You are invited to a company-wide meeting on Aug. 29
> to review new Team Wellness enrollment options…
> We will continue our time-honored tradition of quality
> journalism…

The office hushed.

People in cubicles whispered into phones. People in offices
shut doors. They were worried about their jobs, or the *tradition
of quality journalism*. Both.

But I couldn't focus on anything beyond the word *Comm-
Planet*. HR might as well have put it in double-underlined one-
hundred-point type, bold Gothic font.

"Did you see it?" Alice whispered into the gap in the corner where our cubicle walls joined.

"Yes," I whispered back.

It would be okay. The *Liberty* wasn't the only local newspaper that CommPlanet had bought; the press release listed eight others. The incubator had gone on quite the shopping spree. So it was fine.

Unnerving. But fine.

I took a deep yoga breath, like back in that college class with Serra and Maggie. Ten counts in, twenty counts out.

CommPlanet. If you heard it, you might think it was *Calm Planet*. A good name for a yoga studio or flotation tank place or herbal tea shop.

How could such an innocuous-sounding company be so menacing?

*Think, Becc. Don't panic like a child.*

But I felt queasy, motion sick without leaving my chair. One word had scooped me up and hurled me back to a time and place I wanted to forget.

*Breathe.* It would be nothing more than a company name on my paycheck. Maybe Cal didn't even know about it; he was barely involved with CommPlanet day-to-day. He was probably busy sunbathing in Catalina with his latest conquest or sailing in the San Juans, oblivious. It was fine.

It would be fine.

I clicked the CommPlanet website link in the HR email and scoured the Who We Are page for his name. And my stomach felt calmer because there was no McCallister listed. He'd sold off his stake, just like he'd said he wanted to.

I scanned the names again to confirm he was absent, relief spreading through my midsection.

And then another name jumped out, twisting my insides so I felt sicker than before, the churning feeling of too many of

Maggie's Chocolate Margs, a chalky sharp taste in my mouth: *Derrek L. Schwinn III. CommPlanet Board Member.*

"Do you think they're going to fire people?" Alice whispered.

"It'll be fine."

★

That night I told Eric we should take things slow, that he should still sleep on the couch. He looked worried for a second, but nodded. "I think that's a good idea. I was thinking exactly the same thing." He tried to suppress a grin. "Well, not exactly. But I can wait."

He hummed when he brushed his teeth that night.

I tried to match his gleeful mood.

"You okay?" he asked.

"Just tired. Weird day at work." I couldn't say that I was back in the CommPlanet fold. Because that would remind him of Cal, and he'd say something. If not *my darling papa*, then something just as excruciating. So I said only, "There are rumors we're getting bought by some big company. I don't know the details yet."

He looked concerned, touched my shoulder. "Sorry, Becc. I know how much you love it. They'll keep you on no matter what, you've got to be their best reporter."

"You're sweet."

And even those words stung. I'd stung myself, because I'd spoken them to Cal. *Don't say* you're sweet *again*, he'd said to me in Catalina. A million years ago.

Or two.

I kissed Eric and went to bed.

Cal must have finally succeeded at selling his shares to Schwinn. I couldn't stop thinking of how chummy Cal and Schwinn had seemed that night of the parties.

Maybe CommPlanet *was* going to downsize us, which was awful and depressing, but that had nothing to do with me and Cal.

Or me and Eric.

# 46

## Calm Planet

The next morning

WHERE I WAS SUPPOSED TO BE | My desk
WHERE I WAS | The *Liberty* ladies' room, farthest non-wheelchair-accessible stall.

Before I'd finally drifted off around 4:00 a.m. I decided, *no sudden movements*. That would be my approach. It would all be okay if I didn't make any sudden movements.

Yet I felt the *C* from the CommPlanet logo, that hateful little Pacman, chasing after me. It wouldn't stop; it would swallow everything important in my life.

So at ten, when the mail cart delivered an envelope to my desk and I saw that it was embossed with the initials *FAH*, I knew I was right even before I read the contents.

I could say *Calm Planet* like a mantra a million times, but it couldn't protect me.

*Dear Ms. Reardon,*

*Your mother mentioned where you are working so I hope you do not mind my reaching out to you. I had hoped to receive your senior-year letter by now. Perhaps you misaddressed it, dear?*

*But that is not why I'm writing.*

*I would like to speak with you at your earliest convenience. A museum board member/mutual acquaintance sent me a distressing article (attached) and shared some related information involving you, your roommate Serra Indrijo, your research for the Berkeley paper, and another mutual acquaintance who lives across the Bay.*

*As a museum donor for sixteen years, I have some serious concerns. Do call me at 310-555-0176.*

*Sincerely,*

*Francine Haggermaker*

She'd included six articles, neatly cut from the Berkeley student newspaper and held together with a paperclip. I took in the familiar headline font, the datelines. My first sensation was an irrational burst of nostalgia. I'd let myself become so cut off from campus news.

And then dread crept in, leaving no room for anything else.

The first article had run four days ago. It was about Yvonne Copeland, and it distorted everything. Yvonne had been fired for financial "inconsistencies" with the grants she'd administered from the museum fund. It said she'd used students to exact petty revenge schemes, including threatening letters and acts of vandalism, on "multiple university professors who had secured tenure ahead of her."

I speed-read the next few paragraphs—*anonymous tip from within the art department...improper...students unaware of scope—*

trying to make sense of the long, curvy column of words, a black-and-white snake in my hand.

Who would have ratted Yvonne out? Not someone *within the art department*. No way. The collective had been operating under the surface for years without interruption. What would have changed now?

But then I saw it. Two inches from the bottom. As if it was barely relevant: a quote from Derrek Schwinn III, who had dramatically increased his regular donations to the museum fund to "shore it up" after Yvonne's improprieties. Schwinn had, the article noted incidentally, also donated ten million to the business department and would return as a visiting lecturer the following spring.

It couldn't have been a coincidence. Schwinn clearly had found out he was a target and paid off the school.

I read the article again, not just *distressed*. Horrified.

Change some adjectives, leave out some facts. And the villain becomes the hero.

And it was right there in print so what was anyone going to do about it?

In one of my journalism classes, the professor had written on the chalkboard: *Ask Yourself...*

*Who wrote the story?*

*Who benefits from the story?*

*Who's missing from the story?*

The story painting Yvonne as a disgruntled, unethical wack job wasn't bylined, but it might as well have been written by Schwinn.

Who benefited.

But how had Schwinn found out?

The next clippings in the tidy stack were my pieces about the Fe|Co graffiti. All my "small" articles.

Mrs. Haggermaker had seen them all these years and saved them. She was an alumna and a big donor. Berkeley must mail her the campus paper as a courtesy.

*I would like to speak with you at your earliest convenience. A museum board member/mutual acquaintance sent me a distressing article (attached) and shared some related information involving you, your roommate Serra Indrijo, your research for the Berkeley paper, and another mutual acquaintance who lives across the Bay.*

Schwinn was Mrs. Haggermaker's fellow board member and mutual acquaintance, that much was clear. He'd found out about the collective, contacted Mrs. Haggermaker to establish his version of the story. Told her my roommate and I were mixed up with Yvonne's "petty revenge scheme" and, for good measure, that I'd had a sleazy affair with Cal, *another mutual acquaintance who lives across the Bay.*

If Mrs. Haggermaker knew I'd covered for Yvonne and Serra's "little club," which had not just been liberal with spray paint but with her donation dollars, and if she knew about me and Cal, she'd ask for her $100,000 back. Maybe get my degree yanked, and Serra's. She would tell Eric's mom, who'd tell him.

And he'd never speak to me again.

★

I went to email Serra, but I already had a message waiting for me:

> Fuck. I just found out that Yvonne's been fired from Berkeley in disgrace. She was protecting all of us and didn't say a word until it all went down. I guess that creep Schwinn found out about you-know-what. He knew EVERYTHING.
>
> I KNOW you didn't tell anyone. (Right?! You deleted your article?) Mags hasn't gotten back to me. It doesn't sound like something she'd do.
>
> I guess it was someone else who blabbed?
>
> Anyway. Call me tonight, 'k?

My article.

The one we had written the night Serra told us about the collective. We had deleted it. Serra and Maggie *watched* me delete it.

Unless.

I did an internet search and confirmed it; there was a way to copy over files, even trash, to a new system. Then I searched, Is there a way to recover computer files that have been emptied from trash?

There were multiple ways.

*I mirrored you over.* He'd said something like that when he tried to give me the new computer for my birthday.

Cal.

He'd told me to my face: *replicated* or *mirrored*. I couldn't remember the exact words he'd used that last morning in Sausalito. I'd been focused only on the words I was rehearsing in my head: *It's over.*

Cal had tried to be so sweet with his surprise birthday party and in return I'd ditched him. Then, that summer, whiling away time in Sausalito. Stung and surprised that I was ignoring his emails, distancing myself. Probably the first woman to do that to him. Curious, or even a little hurt…wondering if I was seeing someone else. He and Schwinn standing together across the room…

That stupid, stupid article I'd written out of vanity. Cal had pulled it from the nethers of the laptop I'd rejected last summer. Brought it back to life and given it to Schwinn. To get on Schwinn's good side, finally close the deal. Pay me back for ignoring him. The *useful, basically harmless* Schwinn had bought Cal's shares in CommPlanet as a quid pro quo for getting out in front of this story. And Cal didn't give a damn what kind of man he was helping, or how much it would hurt me. Or anyone else.

I pictured the two of them chuckling together. And why

shouldn't they laugh? It must be the ultimate high, knowing there'd never be consequences for anything you did.

Everything was a joke to him, I'd thought.

But now I revised to this:

Everything was a joke, *unless it was currency.*

★

I reread the letter and articles in my cubicle at 10:35, and again at 11:41, and on a park bench, not eating my peach frozen yogurt with slivered almonds, at 12:37.

At 1:03 I hid in the restroom for half an hour and read them over and over.

I typed out and deleted replies to Serra all afternoon. They all included the same concluding plea:

> I'm so sorry. I didn't tell anyone, not on purpose. Not directly. Please don't tell Eric and please don't hate me but...

> Remember that guy I'd been seeing at work when I was at CommPlanet? Please don't tell Eric and please don't hate me but...

> I have something to tell you. I think I'm the reason Schwinn found out... Please don't tell Eric and please don't hate me but...

I sent her this:

> How awful! I'm so sorry. You know I didn't say anything. I'm positive Mags wouldn't. Talk tonight xx.

I shredded Francine's letter and the articles in the copy room. *Childish, Becc.*

*Pointless, Becc.*

But I watched the machine's silver jaws gnaw every last page into illegible little accordion-folded strips. As if that could change anything written on them.

Alice, my cubicle neighbor, came in to use the Xerox while I was shredding and I jumped.

"Makin' coleslaw?" This was a joke she repeated often. Even if it had been remotely funny, the pride with which she delivered her witticism would have killed any laughs.

"Yep," I said, forcing a smile.

She lowered her voice. "I heard there might be layoffs. But I was thinking a buyout wouldn't be too bad for me. Maybe they'll be generous, right? Give me a good package, after forty-one years here?"

"I hope so, Alice. You deserve a good package."

After she left I reached into the bin and stirred the thin strips of Francine's letter and my articles around to mix them with other, less dangerous documents.

# 47

## Over It

I didn't call Francine.

I didn't call Cal.

I decided to tell Eric everything.

Driving home every night I rehearsed, imagining that if I could explain how it happened, how lost I'd felt that first summer alone in Orange Park, we might have a chance.

But he was so happy. Every night he came home from the restaurant buoyant, humming. Flush with tips.

We kissed, we held hands, we tangled limbs on the couch for hours. We were going to be patient, not mess it up, though it was hard for both of us to resist tumbling into bed.

What a sweet surprise, to find that our bodies fit together so well, that his skin tasted good to me and mine to him, that perfect pleasure was ours for the taking. Every familiar Eric muscle and shadow seemed as newly mysterious as the ones I hadn't seen or touched before, the places that had been hidden when we were just friends.

Anytime we came close I said, "I don't think we should sleep together yet."

He felt my body responding and balking, responding and balking. But he said he understood, that we should take it slow.

"And I don't think we should tell Serra or anyone yet, either."

"Why not?" he asked, puzzled.

"Let's just keep this between us for now."

We dined on tumtum leftovers. Mango-cod fritters and fried Manchego with avocado foam. Or what had been avocado foam a few hours earlier, and had turned into avocado dribbles.

One worknight Eric scored a big container of an experimental "blue" virgin sangria that hadn't made the cut. The mixologist had declared it unacceptable, even for tumtum's out-there menus, but it was pretty tasty.

We were sipping blue sangria and watching *Dawson's Creek* when he said, "My mom called. She told me she met up with Devin McCallister a few weeks ago."

Casual. Only the tiniest bite of sarcasm. Because these adult appointments and reconciliations were so distant from our happy, cluttered little apartment. His tone said, *This news means nothing to us, of course. Just thought you'd find it amusing.*

"They had a lunch, apparently. Sushi."

"Really?" *Dawson's Creek*–worthy acting skills, as I pretended this news flash didn't chill me.

"Yeah. She said it was, quote, *cathartic.* She wanted to let him know how much he hurt her or whatever. He apologized. Anyway, I guess they were pretty civilized. She said it was good to catch up. He was living in San Francisco for a while, I guess he had an apartment there? But he sold it. He's back down here now, just sailing and enjoying his millions. Did you know he cashed out of all his investments?"

"No."

*Did she tell him you're living with me? And how did he take that tidbit of news? And did he happen to mention if when he cashed out of CommPlanet, he sold his stake to a certain Derrek Schwinn, sweetening the deal with some useful dirt so Schwinn could keep his own dirt hidden?*

"Are they getting back together?"

"Who knows? We won't be like them." Eric smiled, ran his hand up my leg.

"Never."

I could see it, like a custom-scripted horror movie:

Cal: *"How's Eric doing?"*

Donna: *"He's living with that Rebecca Reardon. His good friend from high school, remember that tall, studious girl? It's awfully sweet, really, the way he talks about her. I think something might be happening there. I think they've liked each other for years."* She would laugh, running a perfectly manicured hand through her shimmering mane.

And how would Cal's face look when he learned this?

He would maintain his poise. He would say something dry and cavalier: *"Ah, young love."*

But he'd be angry, after how I left him and pretended there wasn't anyone else.

Because maybe there had been all along.

Maybe gifting Schwinn with my article on the collective was only a first warning. Soon he'd tell Eric. Why wouldn't he, after how I'd skulked away from him like a coward?

I wanted to throw up my blue sangria.

"I'm over it." Eric sat up and took my glass. "Over it and into you."

He set my glass on the coffee table, pulled me up, and danced me across the living room, whirling me around our orange shag carpet. I burrowed into his warm shoulder, holding him tight until his joy was all I could feel. We spun together, our own planet.

Eric was festive, happy, productive. Smiling. Always smiling.

I wouldn't be the one to make that smile go away.

★

The week after our kiss, a new plan emerged.

I came up with it the Friday Alice returned to her cubicle

sniffling and whispered to me that the *Liberty*'s HR director had given her her *package*. A week of severance for every year of service. It wouldn't last her long.

And then I got summoned into the small conference room, where the blinds were closed. No package for me. The HR officer informed me that my job would end in six weeks. I could extend my health insurance through COBRA for an extra two months. I'd get $500 severance.

"I'm so sorry," she said. "You've been doing good work."

So a new plan emerged: not honesty. Escape.

Eric and I would backpack in Greece for a while, where it was cheap. We'd check out Athens, Crete. That island from the poster in the Berkeley café. Nisyros, in the remote Dodecanese chain. Surrounded with the impossibly blue water.

The island with no people.

We'd joked about it often, but maybe it could be our happy place.

My lease was going month-to-month soon, and we calculated that we'd have enough for three months, maybe more, if we could get work here and there. We monitored CheapTicketz fares, bargain flights with horrid layovers.

I had $1,106 saved, plus the $500 severance. Eric had $980 and counting. He was the only person on tumtum's staff who wasn't a waiter-slash-actor, so our getaway fund benefited from his coworkers' callbacks and late shoots.

His tips went into a mason jar, marked with a sign that said Greece or Bust.

# *48*

## Road Trip

August 1998
A week after I got the letter from Francine Haggermaker

WHERE I WAS SUPPOSED TO BE | Writing a Paula's Potpourri caption about a shih tzu beauty pageant in Laguna Niguel
WHERE ERIC WAS SUPPOSED TO BE | tumtum restaurant
WHERE WE WERE | Heaven-Of-The-Sea

I got another letter from Francine. This time it was waiting in my apartment mailbox.

> *Rebecca, please do call me as soon as possible. It's quite important.*

No reading material attached.
I stared at it, tore it, and sent it down the disposal.
"Are you okay?" Eric asked that night, as we were watching *Friends*.
"I realized I forgot to write to Francine Haggermaker. I feel awful."

"How is the Franster?"

"I write to her. She doesn't write to me. But I'm sure she's fine."

"I have a theory about why you're so hostile toward her, why you're so intimidated. Want to hear it?"

"I'm not intimidated. But you'll tell me your theory anyway, so go ahead."

"You've seen *The Great Gatsby*. Mia Farrow, Robert Redford, not—"

"They recently made it into a book, too."

"She's your billboard."

"My what?"

"Your what's-his-name. The guy on the billboard over the road. Looking down on you as you travel through life, seeing all."

"The eyes of Dr. T. J. Eckleburg."

"Yeah."

"It's an interesting theory, E."

"But you're the most upright person I know. So what do you have to feel guilty about?"

★

I woke Eric at five. "I'm kidnapping you. Get someone to cover your shifts."

"Whuddabowgreesfun," he mumbled into his pillow.

"The Greece fund can spare a hundred. We're going on a road trip."

We sped up Pacific Coast Highway, pushing Wag Dos to its limit. Eric slept curled up against the window and I drove, feeling better with each mile.

I'd been drawn to the ocean with the vague idea that proximity to it would wash away my worries. A bright sweep of blue to my left, putting everything in perspective.

As the miles passed I imagined the shreds of paper floating up from the blue *Liberty* recycling bin. Slow-motion, like the halting, self-conscious special effects in an old Disney movie. I pictured them gliding out the window, west into the Pacific.

The words from Francine's letter and the damning articles were drifting far from each other. So that they could never be matched up again, not by the FBI or Eric or anyone.

Francine Haggermaker

earliest convenience

lecturer Derrek Schwinn III

Yvonne Copeland

Iron and Cobalt

deeply concerned.

mutual acquaintance

Popular theories

cryptic signature.

do call

THE CAT KNOWS.

quite important.

By Rebecca Reardon

★

By Santa Barbara I could picture the pieces floating on the water behind me, words swelling into nothing as the ink blurred and spread.

By Monterey the scraps were pulp, disintegrating into fragments. Fish food. Not even fish food.

Eric woke, yawned. "Where are we going?" His voice was husky from sleep.

"Do you care?"

"Not particularly." He smiled slowly. "You and me and the open road."

★

I drove us five hours to an unpretentious notch of beach south of San Francisco. Alice had told me about this place where you could get a room for $56 if you didn't mind sharing a bathroom. Right across the highway from the beach, at an old wood-shingled YWCA camp that had been turned into a hotel. Cielo-del-mar, it was called. A made-up word meaning Heaven-Of-The-Sea.

It was too early to check in, so we walked along the dunes, holding hands. We picnicked on peanut butter and cheese cracker packets and root beers from 7-Eleven that I'd picked up on the way.

"Gourmet," said Eric, brushing neon orange crumbs off his hands. "Wish I could treat you to one of those restaurants right on the water, and order only stuff that says Market Price on the menu. Lobster, Market Price. Sole, Market Price."

"I don't care about that. Anyway, 7-Eleven is a market."

"Market Price, seventy-nine cents," he said. "You have crumbs here." He wiped the corner of my mouth, then kissed me, his hand tucked into the right leg of my shorts. He was impatient for the hotel room, probably thinking this might be the night. "Think we can check in yet?"

"We should give it another half hour, I think."

We watched the surfers, four shining brown torsos bobbing way out in the water. The waves were poor. Instead of good, rolling sets they had to wait forever for the occasional decent wave. But they looked content out there, straddling their boards and scanning the horizon for something epic.

I lay back on the beach, not caring that it would take days to wash the sand out of my hair. In my rush to get on the freeway I'd forgotten beach towels. Eric reclined next to me, held a windbreaker over our faces for shade.

"I wish we were going to Greece tomorrow," I said.

"Soon," he said into my neck. He tickled me with his vibrating lips, trying to make me laugh.

We twined our bodies together in the sand under my windbreaker, listening to the surf. He ran his hand up and down the side of my waist under my T-shirt, from the top of my shorts to my underarm. I clasped his hand, then ran a finger up and down along the valleys between his fingers.

"I'm crazy about you," he said.

"I'm crazy about you."

"Why did it take us so long?"

"I really don't know."

★

Eric napped in the room while I wandered the hotel grounds, jumpy.

We'd kissed, peeled our sandy clothes off down to our underwear, locked together on the creaking bed. It felt so good I wanted to let it happen, let it obliterate everything.

I was touching him down the elastic waistband of his shorts, my hand around him for the first time. Then I'd looked at his face, dearer to me than anything, and I couldn't do it.

"Wait. Eric, let's not yet. I'm not ready yet."

He'd rolled off me, stared at the ceiling.

"Soon, okay?" I said.

He nodded, breathing hard, trying to make sense of why

I'd ripped us away from bliss. I watched him, my body pressed against his from shoulder to toe on the narrow bed. Nuzzling his arm until he relaxed and fell asleep.

I'd tiptoed out to the lobby, flipped through the little local newspaper, the *Breeze*. But I was on almost no sleep and the words blurred. I wandered to the vending machine, thinking I'd get a Coke.

There was a woman working the ice hopper, filling a clinical-looking rubber pouch. I picked up a stray piece of ice that had skated across the red tile floor, tossing it into the bin.

"Thank you, sweetheart. Are you and your husband having a good trip?"

She and her husband had checked in right behind us. I wondered if I'd get a *sweetheart* if she knew Eric wasn't my husband.

If she knew anything about me.

"Yes, it's beautiful here."

She was halfway out the humming vestibule when she turned, pulling a parchment-colored envelope from her purse. "Can you use this by any chance, sweetheart? It's a gift certificate to some fancy-pants Chinese restaurant. We won it at Pier 39 yesterday on some gizmo, this wheel like Vanna White."

"The Whirling Win Wheel."

"Yes, that's it. It was so exciting! But we've decided to stay in tonight. My husband's knee is acting up and I never cared much for egg rolls and such anyway."

"Are you sure? You could use it another time."

"We won't be back for years. You take it and go with that cute husband of yours."

I was tempted to let this slide; I really wanted the gift certificate.

"Actually, he's not my husband."

"Fiancé?"

"A good friend. Boyfriend, I guess. I'm not quite sure."

As I overshared, she tightened the lid on her ice bag and looked confused, and I thought Eric and I had lost the free dinner.

But the soft, pink-powdered flesh around her right eye contracted in a wink. "Well, then. You and your friend go and see what the night holds."

★

"Hey, Sleeping Beauty, wake up. I scored us some free food."

I sat on the edge of the bed next to Eric and tugged the paper from the envelope. It was stamped with grimacing tiki statues. Dinner buffet for two, plus two premium drinks, at the Tonga Room. Polynesian, not Chinese.

"Sweet, I've always wanted to check it out," he said, sitting up and pulling me onto his chest.

Everyone had heard of the Tonga Room.

It was inside the Fairmont Hotel.

# 49

### Storm

August 23, 1998

We drove up to the Fairmont, but my excitement had drained away, replaced by sadness, because even this little surprise had Cal's shadow over it. Or my heart did; it couldn't seem to outrun him.

The Fairmont was in the Nob Hill neighborhood, where he'd once wanted to take me to show me his little place with the Juliet balcony, his *investment property*. But where I'd refused to go for fear of being seen.

He'd sold his apartment, but I didn't want to go anywhere near *Snob Hill*. Derrek Schwinn's gargoyles were there, too.

"Maybe we should bail, traffic'll be awful," I said. "Let's have more cheese crackers on the beach. My treat."

"Are you kidding? I need to see a synthetic thunderstorm. You think people put newspapers over their heads, like at *Rocky Horror*?"

"It'll be valet. That'll probably cost as much as we save on food. And we'll have to wait forever to get the car after, I hate that."

"So we'll park on the street. In half an hour we'll be drinking lime from coconuts. Like the song." He glanced at me. "What gives? You're the one who scored the free meal. Always sweet-talking senior citizens in ice rooms. Why aren't you into it anymore?"

"I am into it. It's just I didn't realize how far the restaurant was and we have to wake up so early to drive back, that's all."

I couldn't shake the feeling that going to Nob Hill with Eric was trespassing. That the scowly tiki faces on the gift certificate were trying to warn me away.

Eric smiled at me. "We'll sleep when we're dead. Don't go getting practical on me now."

Our trip had been nearly perfect until now. Reckless, sandy, tiring, but just what we needed. It would be foolish to let the wispiest of threads connected to my time with Cal spoil it.

It wasn't like we were driving to Sausalito for dinner. So the Tonga happened to be inside the Fairmont. Tons of restaurants happened to be inside hotels. Cal and I had never even gone there. He was in LA, hundreds of miles away.

I reached for Eric's hand. "Do you think we'll get to keep the coconuts?"

## 50

### Night Life

2008
Saturday, a little before 1:00 a.m.

For months I'd told myself this was about Serra.

I could finally make things up to her, keep her from worrying about me and Eric.

With his mom's fiftieth birthday party on the fourteenth and Serra's wedding on the twentieth, and the stops spread up the coast like points on a line graph, ending at the wedding, it had seemed completely logical.

But it wasn't. Of course it wasn't.

And Eric had known all along.

From the very first email he'd seen what I hadn't—that this was not about Serra at all, but about me. Going through a midlife crisis, wanting an excuse to be with him again. To try to undo the past. To go back to a better time.

But he'd gone along anyway, saying what a nice gift it was, how much Serra would love it.

Because he felt sorry for me.

It's 1:00 a.m., and I've been lying on my bed for hours, staring at the ceiling. Against the blank white canvas, all I can picture is Eric's concerned brown eyes.

I need a new view, so I take the elevator down to the lobby, buttoning my warm navy peacoat over my leggings and T-shirt.

As I exit the hotel I see that the night doorman is the same.

Unbelievable, that he's the same from ten years ago, but I'm sure of it. That wide smile, wide brown eyes, that reassuring air of seen-it-all unflappability. He was certainly unflappable that night a decade ago.

"Do you need a cab, ma'am?" the kind doorman asks.

I'm sure I look like hell. Hair unbrushed, eye makeup smeared, wandering onto Nob Hill in the middle of the night.

"No, thanks," I say. "I'm just going for a walk."

I walk aimlessly. Past the spire of Grace Cathedral, the elegant homes and shopfronts of Pacific Heights, across bright, still-bustling Japantown. Through the Tenderloin, Gough, Divisadero, downtown.

San Francisco is forty-nine square miles, and I'd walk every one of them if it meant I could outrun the memory of that night.

And of tonight. Of Eric indulging me.

*I was really sorry to hear about it…*

*My mom told me you've been having a rough time since…*

Every time I picture Eric saying this on the roof garden, his kind face glowing gold from the lights of the city, another hot wave of embarrassment hits.

He said it so gently. The way you talk to someone mid-breakdown.

The whole time we were repacking the gift after returning from the roof—as he asked what time I thought we should get up tomorrow, how I'd found the collector who has the last panel—I was aware of his pity.

A third, unwelcome guest in the room.

It was in the warmth of his voice and the way his thick-lashed brown eyes sought out mine from the other side of the luggage trolleys. The care with which his long fingers smoothed out the duct tape on the edge of the box.

So Donna had urged Eric to come with me. Of course she did.

I walk fast, pulling my coat close against the fog. On Eddy Street I pass a rowdy group of twentysomethings piling into a cab after last call, then a man sleeping over a subway grate. I give him $20. The people out at this hour are the young and lucky and the old and forgotten. There's no in-between at 2:00 a.m.

I know I'm one of the lucky. My calendar is full—I have brunch with my mom on Sundays. I work, I let friends set me up on dates, I run every morning before my commute, I attend panel discussions at the First Amendment Association. I keep busy, trying to fill my time, to schedule over the longing.

I'm thirty-two, and yet I feel so locked into my life.

And I'm scared I'm running out of time to change it.

I walk past a flower mart, the sweet perfume so strong I stop to breathe it in, head to the Embarcadero, the ferry building, the misty piers.

*We won't be like them,* Eric and I promised each other.

There's no gate around my home. But I feel trapped all the same.

I sit on a damp concrete pier and watch people fish until the fog turns violet, and then orange. I only stand when light spills over the Berkeley hills, melting like butterscotch across the Bay.

# 51

## Enchanting

August 23, 1998

We left Wag Dos at the base of Mason Street and shivered in the fog that had crept in off the Bay.

"San Francisco in the summer." Eric laughed, pulling me close for warmth as we trudged up the steep hill.

The Fairmont emerged from the fog all at once.

We stood across the street with the rest of the photo-snapping tourists and took it in: bisque-colored and balconied, like a building in Paris. A large, curvy black awning over the entry. Flags from dozens of countries flapping across the front. It took up the whole block.

"It's a castle," I said, stepping into the road, my eyes on the flags.

Eric grabbed my elbow at the same time I heard the *tring, tring*: a cable car's jolly warning. I retreated to the curb to let it pass, a slow, boxy boat of gleaming wood and brass, the passengers half delighted, half self-conscious to be on display. The knot of tourists surrounding us went nuts with their cameras, trying to frame the perfect shot of the cable car with the Fairmont behind it.

"We're in a Rice-A-Roni commercial," Eric said.

"Stop it, it's beautiful."

"It is beautiful. But speaking of rice, dinner's waiting."

A bellman in a navy-and-gold uniform swung the hotel door open. I'd decided that dark could approximate dressy, so I was in navy sweats, black flip-flops, and my black Beck T-shirt, turned inside out and backward. With earrings and extra lipstick, I didn't feel too scruffy. Eric, with fewer options, had fared worse: ripped khaki shorts and frayed green Vans.

But the doorman smiled and tipped his cap. "Enjoy your stay!"

"He has to know we're not staying here," I whispered.

"But we will someday," Eric said. "Fanciest suite in the place."

"I'll take the Cielo. The rooms here are probably nothing special."

"Sure, I'll bet they're total dumps."

The Tonga Room

We were slightly disappointed in the mechanical thunderstorms. There was no rain over the tables. Only a faint mist.

"Now that I think about it, I guess people don't want soggy food," Eric said when we were seated.

"And rain would extinguish the flaming drinks."

But the cracks of thunder made us jump, and the lagoon next to our table had real water. Inside a thatched hut in the center, a woman plucked a ukulele.

"Aren't you going to say it's *South Pacific*? Or...some other movie set on an island that no one else but you has watched in fifty years?"

"Not everything is a movie reference, Rebecca Reardon," Eric said. "I will say only that this place is undeniably cool."

"'Undeniably cool.' I'd like to be undeniably cool."

"You are. To me, you are. Except when you wear those giant sunglasses from the thrift store, and you look undeniably like a fly."

"How gallant. And you are...what? We need a slogan for you. Eric Logan is..."

"Irresistibly hot? Magically delicious?"

"You are most definitely both of those. But how do you like Eric Logan: *beautifully himself.*" I leaned close to the centerpiece, a candle surrounded by a low ring of tropical flowers. Orchids or gardenias. "These are real. Smell."

He inhaled. "Glad we came?"

"Yes."

I ordered a Cobra's Fang, something sweet and deadly in a pineapple husk. Eric got a mai tai with passion fruit juice subbing for the rum, served in his longed-for coconut shell.

I relaxed. It was physically impossible not to.

If Eric and I ever moved to San Francisco, no matter how soul-crushing our jobs, we would drop by the Tonga after work every night. Smell sweet flowers, watch lightning bounce off water, listen to ukuleles and steel guitar. And every worry would disappear into the man-made mist.

We held hands, our knees touching under the table. We made two trips each to the buffet, loading our plates with crab rangoon and poi fritters and shrimp-and-scallion egg rolls. My ice-room lady had been a fool, passing up this feast.

"To my ice-machine lady," I said. "May the swelling in her husband's knee go down promptly."

"To ice lady and knee man. May they be having kinky sex right now."

"With the ice?"

"Oh, it has to involve the ice."

By drink two I was floating. "Maybe we shouldn't go back tomorrow. Maybe we can live here."

"Hell, yes. On that island where the singer is."

"It's not an island. It's an issmus. Ithmus. Issmus. E, why can't I say it?" My tongue had gone numb, temporarily paralyzed by Cobra's Fang venom; but with great effort, wiping tears from my eyes, I got the word out: "Isthmus."

"Just because you beat me in geography bee freshman year, you don't have to rub it in."

"Wait! It's not an isthmus, it's a peninsula." And that seemed funniest of all. "Let's toast to our peninsula. Our future home."

After drink three we constructed a boat. A miniature boat, made from a paper *Tonga Room, Enchanting Lovers since 1945* coaster and a drink umbrella. We both worked on the miniature craft, bending the coaster just so, poking holes for the toothpick keel with the skewer that had held our kalua pig. I reached between the faux-sugarcane bars, set it on the water, and launched it. It sailed a foot then circled back, clinging to the shore next to our table.

Eric pushed it with his fork. "Sail away, little thing."

"Be free."

We watched it float off, rooting for it to cross the small, man-made ocean.

"I lost it, did it sink?" Eric scanned the water.

"No, it's over there. By the bachelorettes." I pointed across the water toward a group of girls in matching purple T-shirts and feather boas. The bride-to-be's tiara sparkled as she danced.

A flaming drink passed our table.

The candle in our gardenia centerpiece flickered.

Light bounced off the singer's silver necklace.

His blond hair shone.

He stood near the bar, twenty feet behind Eric, a drink in his hand.

I didn't feel surprised. I didn't panic.

I only thought—*of course*. Of course he's here. That shadow over my heart.

He tilted his head, bit his lip, fluttered his fingers at me—a discreet, graceful little wave—and left.

I could have stayed at the table, faked my way through the rest of the night, pretending everything was as loopy and sweet as it had been moments before. I could have waited to confront him.

So why did I murmur, "Ladies' room," and stand?

Impatience, I guess. The simple need to know, even if the truth would hurt. I couldn't wait for my punishment any longer. It had chased me halfway up the state of California despite my best efforts, and I needed to know why he was there, and what other unwelcome surprises waited for me. In my mailbox, at work, at Francine Haggermaker's gracious old home on Orchard Hill.

"I'll be right back."

"Whoa," Eric said, as I bumped the table so hard my drink tipped. I blotted up the small spill. "You okay, lightweight?"

"Right back." My feet felt distant, stubbornly disobedient as I navigated the dark, red-carpeted hall, the too-bright lobby.

He almost got away.

If he hadn't paused at the door, he would have disappeared into the fog. I might have written him off as a ghost conjured by guilt and alcohol. But he stopped for a few seconds to say something friendly to the doorman.

Cal was always courteous.

We were outside when I caught up with him and reached for his shoulder. I was rushing and off balance; my grasp became a shove, though that wasn't what I intended. "Did you do it?"

He turned. Looked past me, at the front of the hotel. He still had his drink in his hand and I'd made him slosh it. He set the glass on a planter, scissored his fingers rapidly to dry them, flicking lamp-lit gold drops on the ground. "It's good to—"

"Did you do it? Snoop in my computer files somehow and tell Schwinn about Serra's group and my pretend graffiti article, to get back at me?"

I was inches from him. So close I could smell his English shaving cream, the scotch on his breath.

"Are you okay, miss?" The doorman approached, abandoning his post at the door.

I nodded and he left us alone, but I felt him watching just in case.

"You did. You dug it up and gave it to him to hurt me."

"To hurt—"

"The pretend article on my computer. About the graffiti thing, Serra's Berkeley graffiti thing. You gave it to Schwinn to get back at me."

"Pretend article?"

"Yes. It was never supposed to get out. But since Schwinn got his hands on it he was able to twist everything around. Wasn't that what you two cooked up?"

He sighed. "Shit. No, I didn't know it was pretend... What's a pretend article? I thought... Okay, yes, I was poking around in your files one night, a few weeks ago. The file was on your ghost drive and it was called Memory so I thought..."

"You thought it was about us."

"Yes. I thought maybe it was about us. Silly me."

I didn't want to, but I believed him. I'd laughed when I changed the file name from Hiss to Memory. Not knowing that this small alteration, a joke meant only for myself, would someday haunt me.

"But then I read it. And I figured it was a draft of an article you'd been working on that would come out anyway. You always made fun of the graffiti, and I didn't think it was a big deal. Swear to god."

"You didn't ask me."

"You haven't answered my emails in ages, Rebecca."

"But you told that...that *sleaze* who was behind the graffiti as a favor."

He hesitated. "Yes."

"So he'd do you a favor. What'd you get in return? He bought you out of the incubator?"

"Yes, but at the time I didn't think it was such a big deal—"

"Stop saying that! I know you didn't, because you don't think anything's a big deal. Schwinn was just useful to you, *basically harmless*—"

"I can see now that I hurt you, and I—"

"Not just me. You *have* to see it's bigger than that. And now... what, you're following me?"

"No. I was here signing some papers with the guy who bought my apartment. I just sold the boat to him, too. He's going to keep it at the Olympic Club." He pointed downhill toward the Bay.

As if it mattered whether the *Summer Hours* was moored east or west of the city, as if either of us cared.

"And you're with... It is him, isn't it? You're with him?" he asked.

"I don't know. Sort of. Yes."

"Ah." He nodded. "I guess it was my good luck to see you two."

"It was the Whirling Win Wheel."

"The—"

"Whirling Win Wheel. On Pier 39. We won a free dinner."

"Ah."

I felt sick. Too many Cobra's Fangs and too much of this conversation. Confirmation of what I'd guessed, fleeing LA: that Cal was the reason Schwinn's lies had overwritten the collective's honesty. The terrible fact that I'd helped.

Eric sitting inside, clueless, happy, trusting me. Everyone trusting me.

"Everything's messed up," I said.

"I'm sorry." He touched my shoulder. "I would never have done anything to hurt you on purpose, please—"

His expression changed, and I knew before I turned.

I'd been gone, at most, five minutes.

I wasn't sure how long Eric had been watching, how much he'd heard.

But the details hardly mattered. When two people have a conversation like the one Cal and I were having, there's a kind of circle around them that's visible to anyone with an emotional IQ above 70.

Eric's focus jumped from point to point in this circle, not venturing inside it to where I stood with Cal, whose hand was still resting gently on my shoulder.

"Eric," I said. And if Cal's hand on my shoulder didn't tell Eric everything, the anguished note in my voice did.

"I was worried." He stared at a point a foot above my head. "You looked like you needed help. Guess you found it."

"Eric," Cal said.

But Eric didn't look at him, either. He looked at the red carpet below his feet, the doorman, the fleet of gold luggage trolleys.

Then he walked past us, darting across the busy street before I remembered to run.

★

For blocks I was unaware of anyone following me.

San Francisco was only forty-nine square miles, and I was still fast, but they were steep, foggy miles, with a hundred opportunities to hide or double back and confuse a pursuer. Dark alleyways, souvenir shops with T-shirt racks out front, switchbacks and tunnels. Maybe I was too influenced by Eric's beloved old movies, imagining he needed any of these to elude me. Maybe he simply hopped in a cab.

For blocks after I'd lost sight of him, I still ran.

When I finally gave up I found myself at the bottom of the hill, near the eastern edge of the city. No coat, no purse, no cash, surrounded by the gray boxes of the Embarcadero Center parking complex—not the place for strolling in the dark.

Cal was there, right behind me. Panting, forehead slick with sweat.

"Just go," I said, sitting on asphalt, leaning against a cold granite wall.

He sat. Took my hand and caressed the skin on my wrist with one slow finger. It was hypnotic. It always was. But I yanked my hand away.

We sat in silence. His body next to mine was still, undemanding.

When he did speak, his voice was gentle. "I'm so sorry, Rebecca. Please, let me walk you back to the hotel."

We trudged back through spitting fog without another word.

But at my car he said, "Let's go somewhere and talk until you're okay to drive. Only talk."

Here he was. Wrong, broken, boatless. But here.

"Or we can sit in some coffee shop and I won't say a word. Just until your hair's dry."

I touched my hair and it was, in fact, nearly soaked through from the fog. *San Francisco in the summer.*

"Just until you warm up," he said softly.

I knew he would stick to his word in this one small way. If I asked, he would sit quietly across from me in a café as I warmed up.

I'd been wrong about him at every turn. I'd thought he was different from the drones in The Heights.

The truth was worse.

He hadn't done this to hurt me. But he hadn't cared about what kind of man he'd protected. Which meant he was no better.

What did that say about me, that I hadn't *seen* him? Had I been willing to overlook what he was in exchange for something he gave me?

I stared at the sidewalk, balling my fists so I wouldn't reach for him. Then I let him go. "Goodbye, Cal."

# *52*

## Where I'm Supposed to Be

2008
Saturday, 6:00 a.m.

I climb Nob Hill as the sun rises. The gray, dank world I've marched through all night is now a riot of color. The thinning fog is shot through with iridescent light, and it's bright enough for me to make out paint on the Victorians. Purple and lime green. Robin's egg blue and custard yellow.

The last time I was here, I didn't wait for sunrise. I got in my car to chase after Eric, but it was too late.

During that first raw, miserable month after he left, his mom invited me to coffee. A chic outdoor café in Laguna, against the seawall. I almost didn't go but then arrived first, bracing for her to sit in perfectly coiffed judgment across the zinc table. I expected coldness and accusation, words chosen to infect my wounds.

But when she appeared she was windblown, a good inch of dark roots showing. She threw her Gucci sunglasses down carelessly and clasped my hands. "I could kill him."

And I knew she did not mean her son.

Neither of us had seen Cal.

Someone heard he lost all of his money in the market last year and moved to Huatulco, where he lived cheaply, working around boats. Someone else heard he made a killing, and that was why he left.

But we weren't sure what's true.

Donna felt responsible for my time with Cal, though I told her of course she wasn't. She's still bitter about the wreckage he left in his wake, which is helpful. It means I haven't had to be.

Though the affair has shadowed me since. Apparently, Cal and I weren't as discreet as we thought.

I ran into Stephen Liu from CommPlanet at an LA coffee cart years ago, before a magazine job interview. A position I really wanted. He asked if I was still with *the blond bombshell*. Startled, I feigned ignorance, and he smiled to himself, sipped his espresso as I changed the subject. But I'd blown the interview that day, wondering who else knew. How it colored their view of me.

Even though I was only twenty, even though it was less than twelve months, my time with Cal will always be an unwritten part of my résumé. I will never be able to erase it.

While he sailed away.

I've dealt with it; I've accepted it. I've been okay.

Until now.

The sadness over losing Eric, the guilt over how I'd hurt him—I thought I'd confronted it years ago. But now I see all I'd done was simply tuck it away.

★

Back at the Fairmont I smile at the night concierge, the cleaning crew polishing picture frames and mirrors.

"Good morning, ma'am."

"Good morning."

If I'm going to drive today, I desperately need a coffee, but the Diplomat restaurant won't open for another two hours, the sign on the door says.

So I walk down a different hall.

I know, as I head slowly toward the sound of a vacuum cleaner, remembering the soft trickle of fountains and the hypnotic, harp-like *plunk*s of steel guitar, that this is where I wanted to go all along.

The door to the Tonga is open.

"Ma'am?" says the petite, graying woman on the cleaning staff.

"Sorry. I don't want to interrupt you. I just… Do you mind if I look around for a sec? I'm a hotel guest, I—"

"Sure! They're testing the storm system. But you really should come back later and see it right."

I step into the room slowly.

The caned chairs are different and the tables have been rearranged. They seem bigger. I remember that ours was so small we didn't need to lean forward to hold hands.

The Tonga looks crude in daytime, too exposed in the bright overhead light. It needs darkness for its magic to work; its secrets are laid bare right now. I can see the sprinkler heads that deliver fake rain, the seams on the bottom of the lagoon.

I choose a table by the shallow water, as close as I can get to where Eric and I sat ten years ago. Where we were last happy together, plotting our next escape.

I stare at the dark, vacant thatched hut, where no band is playing.

*Our future home*, I called the hut, laughing. Seconds before my past showed up and made any future with Eric impossible.

When a thunderstorm starts, flashing and drizzling across the lagoon, I wait for a deluge of tears.

But the only drops come from the ceiling. I could make a coaster boat, name it something maudlin like *True Love*, after the sailboat in *The Philadelphia Story*. Eric and I watched that in his closet in tenth grade, lying back on a mound of pillows.

Maybe that would bring on the fresh burst of grief I expected.

But I feel only an immense fondness for the person I used to be, how she needed to decide who she was on her own time, in places like this. Not where she was supposed to be.

She was stubborn and brave and childish enough to say—*no. That over there? That's not going to be my life.*

Eric guessed right; I feel the same way now.

And maybe he's just along for the ride this time. Maybe he's only here because he feels sorry for me.

We'll give Serra her gift, toast her. Get through Sunday with a minimum of embarrassment. Then say our goodbyes.

But that's okay.

That younger Becc was no one to pity. Gratitude washes over me, to know that that person still exists. That she's right here, right now.

# 53

## Ents

Lila Boone, the four-star-rated eBay seller who has the third panel, lives in a low brown prefab house near the water. The fancier properties are on the bluffs, but Lila is close enough to the ocean that salt has eaten into her paint job, speckling the brown siding with white so it resembles a cheetah print.

Her weedy driveway is narrow, a chute between two overgrown juniper hedges, but I back the car up without scratching it.

She opens the door in a baby blue sweat suit, a chocolate Yoplait in her hand.

"I'm sorry we're a little late," I say.

"Glad to finally unload the thing." She sets her yogurt on her porch swing and leads Eric and me around the side of the house. "It's out back, in the rathole."

*Rathole?* Eric mouths, raising his eyebrows in mock alarm.

"She just means the garage is messy," I say under my breath, stifling another yawn. I'm on zero sleep.

We follow her across the weedy yard, past a rusted-out Camaro, an empty aboveground pool.

"Are you okay?" Eric asks, touching my shoulder.

"Sure, why?"

"You're limping a little."

"Oh, these shoes aren't the best."

I'm wearing my most broken-in running shoes, so it's not their fault. My all-night march in sandals last night gave me a silver-dollar-size blister on my right heel.

Lila leads us to a peeling woodshed against a chain-link fence. A handwritten sign on the door says The Dave Cave.

She unlocks the door. "My ex. David Ratskeller. Also known as Ratbastard."

"Oh." I follow her inside.

When my sleepy eyes adjust I take in a jumble of objects— a shaggy Nerf basketball net, a dartboard, a Maxwell House can full of golf balls on a dusty workbench, a white-and-green nylon lawn chair. On every wall, stuffed animals. Not the cuddly child's kind. The killed-and-mounted kind—a stag head, a fish, a snake. What might be a possum; I don't want to look too closely.

I've lured Eric to a house of horrors.

"It's the storage shed from *Silence of the Lambs*," he mutters.

Tired and sore and blistered as I am, I can't stop smiling to myself.

"So was your ex the...art collector?" he asks Lila. Trying to sound chirpy.

"Collector. Ha!" Lila snorts. "He used to sit out here in that chair and stare at your friend's taxidermy doohickey for hours while he smoked out. He named the damn things. Frigging pets."

Serra's *taxidermy doohickey* is against the back wall. Panel three is the one in which we're just floating. Not swimming, and not drowning, either.

One side of the panel is concealed by junk, but what I can see is worse than I feared. The top filmed in yellow grime, much of the front vandalized by white *Hi, My Name Is* stickers. Glenn has been renamed *Geek Boy #3*. I'm *The Secretary*, I guess because of the notebook in my paw.

I work on a sticker corner with my fingernail, but a fuzzy white scar remains.

Maybe Serra would be better off not knowing what happened to her beautiful work. How this piece of her heart was bought by a man who only wanted to laugh at it.

Eric appears by my side and says of the white mark, "We'll buy some Goo Gone. That stuff'll clean anything. So what's the plan here?"

We don't have much clearance; the bottom corner closest to me is wedged against the wall behind a heavy wooden bench and the other end is half-buried under a jumble of camping gear.

I wish I'd packed work gloves. I wish Lila was offering to clear junk from our path instead of standing in the doorway, silently counting her cash.

"Can you lift it over that stuff?"

He checks it out. "I think so, yeah."

"Okay, you grab that end and when we've got it up, come toward me. I'll pivot toward the door. Then we'll set it down there and...regroup. So you can pick it up from the base and get a better grip." I point with my leg to show Eric how we'll rest the panel on the ground, perpendicular to its current position, then prep for the trip out the door.

"Regrouping station noted. We'll regroup and regrip. Roger."

"Lift on three?" I say. "One, two, three."

We work together. I'm monitoring Eric's strained face and he's focused on mine.

The panel is two feet off the ground and our spines haven't

snapped, then it's up to three feet. Four. We're killing it; we could get jobs as professional movers.

We only have to raise it a few more inches so I can swing my end over the bench. No problem. All is well.

Our eyes are locked together, our smallest muscles connected. We couldn't look away if we wanted to. And for a second, as we study each other, his expression says exactly what I'm thinking—*this isn't so hard*.

Our bodies are in sync. We will deliver the gift. Have a good time with Serra. *Part as friends*.

Except.

Except it's dark in the shed, and Eric's hands are a bead too sweaty. In my elation or exhaustion I made an error calculating my angles, and tokin', taxidermy-mad Dave left behind what feels, in the panicked second when my foot makes contact, like a Slip 'N Slide slicked with medical-grade lube and hidden in the shadows purely to sabotage my entire life's happiness, but which I learn later is only a scrap of Hefty bag.

I slip.

A stab in the back of my thigh as I slam into a corner of the bench, a kidney punch as the piece hits my stomach. But I hold on. There's a second where we can still recover.

I hear Eric's *oh, shit*, the sickening crack of Plexiglas on concrete, but I don't see him go down.

1:00 p.m.

Of the three accident survivors—me, the panel, Eric—I suffered the least damage. The back of my left thigh is tender, and there's an interesting star-shaped welt below my belly button.

Panel three's bottom-right corner chipped off, and it suffered a hairline fracture up the side.

Eric, in sandals, yanked off balance in his cluttered corner of the Dave Cave, stepped into the maw of a manual lawn mower. His foot is mercifully intact but his big toe is gashed from tip to web. He's soaked Lila's dish towel scarlet. His second toe juts straight out, like his foot is making a peace sign.

Lila, to her credit, became attentive as a candy striper after our fall. She draped Eric's arm over her shoulder and escorted him to the convertible, ran for clean rags and ice. Helped me cram our bags in the tiny trunk so we could shove the panel into the back seat. She insisted on giving me back some cash, tossing me a handful of twenties for our trouble. "You deserve some shots after that," she called.

Meaning whiskey, not tetanus, although the lawn mower blades were so rusty Eric should probably get a booster, too.

At Fort Bragg Emergency Services, Eric got seven stitches and a metal splint on his right toes. He has to wear an ugly blue Velcro boot.

My travel wardrobe, on the other hand, has been pared down.

I have my purse. I have my phone and driver's license. What I don't have is the floaty, bias-cut cerulean slip dress I planned to wear to the wedding. Or my wrapping paper for the wedding gift. Or even a change of underwear.

Lila left me a voice mail. "I guess this isn't exactly going to make your day," she said.

She found my suitcase by her juniper hedge. My World's Litest Carry-On! in the Fresh Pine color option.

Green on green, and we were rushing, focused on freeing space in the back of the convertible for panel three and getting Eric's foot looked at, so we forgot to throw it back in the car. Lila said I can pick it up or she'll ship it, whatever I want. And she hopes we're not too banged up.

Eric's asleep, his left leg on the dash and his right stuck out the window. It's not safe like that; if the airbag deploys he's toast.

So I'm driving carefully, under the speed limit. We're tracing the left edge of the continent, so near the water I can see white stripes of foam on the waves, a rocky island covered in a satiny, wiggling brown carpet of sea lions.

But the beauty of the scenery is lost on me; I want only to get to the wedding hotel. A few more hours of highway until I can eat, sleep. Buy a passable dress for tomorrow morning's ceremony. Regroup.

My new trip motto: *We can still regroup!*

I've never been this far north, so close to Oregon. I imagine we're flanked by a fairy-tale landscape. Giant mossy trees emerging from a sea of mist. Maybe those prehistoric redwoods are like the Ents, the kindly tree creatures in *The Lord of the Rings.* Maybe they're on my side, helping me on my quest.

Imagining Ents, I drift over the median.

*Pop-pop-pop-pop.* Heart hammering, jerked alert because the rumble strip sounds exactly like pistol shots, I overcorrect into the shoulder and swerve back into my lane.

Screw the Ents. I'll blast the AC on my face to wake up.

*It's fine. We're fine. Regroup and regrip, Becc.*

But Eric stirs. "What was that?"

"How's your foot?" I try to sound peppy, like my Colossal Quad espresso from the drive-through Java Hut thirty miles ago had any effect and I didn't almost crash us.

He grabs the box to pull himself up so he can examine me. "I think you need to rest. You look sort of...wild."

"I'm fine. Don't hurt yourself."

"How much sleep did you get last night? Tell the truth."

"Oh. Not my best sleep, but—"

"Becc. Give it up. Let's find a rest stop or something so you can take a nap."

## 54

### 360 Degrees

Saturday, 1:20 p.m.

I pull under the carport of Whistlin' Pete's Log Cabinettes: dark wooden boxes behind a cinder-block office and restaurant. There are signs in the window: KENO! and Kids Love Our World-Famous 360-Degree Log Run Play Table!! A plastic lumberjack guards the front.

It's not the Sea Whisper. But I'll take anything. A quick power nap and then we'll hit the road again.

The glass door is locked, but there's a button on the lumberjack's ax, and a placard: If Door Locked, Please Ring for Service. I buzz but the only answer is the *rip-crackle* of Eric adjusting his Velcro boot.

I peer in. "The restaurant's closed. They must be on their break."

Eric buzzes longer. "But it said Vacancy. And they have to be here for emergencies or ice or whatever, if people are staying in the cabins."

A woman emerges from the shadows in the back of the lobby and peeks out at us. She's tall and gray, seventyish, rubbing cream into her hands.

"We'd like a cabin, please!" Eric shouts through the glass.

"We're full up!"

"But it says Vacancy by the highway!" he yells.

"It's on the fritz. Sorry, hon."

She turns away but Eric knocks on the glass and she comes back.

"Is there any way you could let us rest in there?" He points at the ripped brown sofa behind her, next to the brochure rack. "Just for an hour? We'll pay your room rate!" Eric shuffles wearily on his crutch to show how desperate we are. He leans against the lumberjack as if he can't take another step.

"Laying it on a bit thick," I mutter, yawning.

"Ma'am?" he says. "We'd really appreciate it. I can't drive and she's so tired she nearly fell asleep at the wheel just now."

The woman approaches the glass, narrowing her eyes at Eric. His hair is sticking up at the crown and it could use a wash. She must think it's a scam, complete with a faux injury to tug at her heartstrings. That we'll break into her cash drawer and vanish when her back's turned.

"Let me try," I whisper to Eric and step forward. "I know it's a weird request, but the thing is... I'm sorry, we forgot to ask your name."

"Crystal."

"Crystal, we've been on the road all day, and my friend's hurt. What would it take to get us on that couch? We'll pay you more than the room rate, even. And you can hold on to our credit cards if you want. Whatever would make you more comfortable. It would be..." *Against all common sense?* "It would be a great kindness."

"Well, I don't know," she says.

"Please." My voice breaks. I want this now. I've dragged

Eric on this trip and thrown a pastry at him, busted his foot and nearly driven him off the road. An hour on a Naugahyde couch may not undo it, but it's right there, and I need this one thing to go my way. "I promise we're not con artists. I realize it's a lot to ask, and you have absolutely no logical reason to say yes. But I'm asking."

Crystal's face softens. She unlocks the door and opens it a few inches. "I just can't have you two napping in the lobby, hon. That won't do."

Damn.

Damn Whistlin' Pete, whoever he is, and damn whoever sold David Ratskeller the MowStriderDeluxe that ate Eric's foot.

"Well. We do have one cabin where the roof caved in last January. Big Doug fir limb broke off in the windstorm, so—"

"That's perfect!" I cry.

"That's fine!" Eric says.

"We're using it for storage. Toilet's working but the shower's busted, and—"

"We don't care! We love you!" I mean to say, *We'd love it!*

Though I do love her in this moment. I love her tattooed-on eyebrows and her smell of Pond's Cold Cream. I love her lumberjack statue, with his dapper red plaid shirt rolled up to his plastic biceps and his muttonchop sideburns.

"I'll get your key."

★

Cabinette Eight, deep in the shade of the fir trees, is an icebox. Our bathroom roof is a blue plastic tarp, and the floor is crammed with random motel gear: restaurant sandwich boards, a tetherball pole in a concrete-filled tire, a life-size plastic figurine of a female lumberjack (two ponytails, skimpy denim shorts, suspenders; I have many questions but now's not the time).

But the room has a working fireplace, and I've backed the car into a spot right outside the window so we can keep an eye on the gift.

Crystal drops off sheets and velour blankets, a Duraflame log, matches, and newspaper. She sets a tray of food on the TV. Biscuits, butter and jelly packets, two cafeteria milks.

"Sorry, they're stale," she says, though we're eyeing the gold-and-white rounds with unmasked desire.

I open my purse. "How much do we owe you?"

"Well. You can buy a meal here later, if you like."

"Thank you, Crystal."

As soon as she leaves I slide open the chain-mail fireplace curtain and get a good blaze going. We sit on the twin bed closest to the fire and devour our biscuits. Three apiece, slathered with all the butter and jelly we can scrape from the tiny plastic tubs. We drain our milks in one gulp.

Eric flattens his milk carton. "Hey. You were pretty great. *What would it take to get us on that couch?*"

"I sounded like a car salesman. *What would it take to get you in that S-Series?*"

"Nah. You were…"

"What?" I inspect the tray between us. Press my finger on the biscuit crumbs, collecting them.

"You were always good with new people. You're interested in them, and they sense it."

"That's… Thank you. You were pretty great, too. You really worked the crutch." I glance up at him, a corner of my mouth curled in a wry smile.

He looks pleased. "That's like winning an Oscar for…" a yawn overtakes him, his eyes closing completely until it's over "…for a crying scene where you used menthol."

His yawn is infectious and I answer with one of my own, my mouth stretching wide, like I'm singing an aria. "You should nap close to the fire so you don't go into shock."

"It's seven stitches, Becc, I think I'll survive."

But I'm already sliding the mattress off the other bed. "Please. It'll make me feel less guilty. About your foot."

"Let me help." Eric tosses his crutch on the floor and thumps over in the lurching, uneven gait he's adopted because of the boot. He grabs the bottom of the mattress and we hoist it, turn it on its side.

"Careful, this maneuver didn't end well last time."

"Now we have experience." He smiles at me from the other end of the mattress. "You got it?"

"Got it." I try to focus on our task, but his lower lip is shiny from butter. And his brown eyes are steady on mine, his face tense, concentrating. Like that afternoon at the Cielo-del-mar. Back then he'd been above me, holding himself up on the narrow bed in the sun. Both of us aching to remove the last thin barriers between us.

I know it's impossible now. My mind must have become porous from lack of sleep, to have let these images in.

"Still doing okay?" he asks. "We don't need two injuries."

"I'm fine."

The room's crowded with junk, but we move the mattress without anyone biting it, shove it next to the stone hearth.

We sit together on my bed, looking down at his.

"Nice work," he says.

"You, too."

"I like your hair this length."

"The professional look." I wear my hair just past my collarbone now. I can still get it into a ponytail, but just barely.

He brushes a stray lock of hair from my cheek and tucks it behind my ear. We're so close I can hear how his breathing has sped up a little from our task. I can see the rays of his irises, how they're every shade of brown. Fawn and maple and tan. And gold.

"Well. Any closer and I'll be in the flames." He scoots down onto his floor bed.

I throw him extra pillows so he can prop up his bad leg. He undoes his boot, places it on the mound. He rubs his eyes, reaches up and swats at the tetherball over his head with his right hand, spreading his long fingers, revealing the hairless length of skin on the underside of his arm. "Hey, so, I don't want you to feel guilty."

"But I do." I sit on the bed above him, take off my sandals. "And not just about your foot. About this whole fiasco of a trip."

I curl under my velour blanket, lulled by the crackle of the fire and Eric's soft breathing below me, the faint *bump-bump-bump* of the tetherball against its metal pole.

I close my eyes, and we're both quiet for a long time, listening to the bumps. Then it goes silent, and I think he's out.

I yawn, watching the lines of sun dancing in the cluttered room. The curtains behind me are closed but beams seep around the sides, lighting the framed painting on the wall above the TV. It's a dramatic oil of the ocean, viewed from the forest above. A slash of churning turquoise water between thick trees.

My eyelids are heavy, dropping.

"Becc," he whispers. "You asleep?"

"No," I whisper back, as if there is someone else in the room we don't want to wake.

"The trip hasn't been a complete fiasco. A few stitches are worth it for Serra's gift."

I'm so tired it just comes out: "You don't have to say that. I know why you really came."

"What?"

"I know why you're really here. And it's okay. I feel a little embarrassed about it, but it was beyond nice of you."

"I have no idea what you're talking about."

"What you said on the roof garden last night. About how your mom told you I've been having a rough time since last year, since… I know that's the real reason you came. So you can stop pretending…"

"You think I'm only here because I felt sorry for you?" he asks, hoarse.

"Basically."

"You're wrong."

I lie as still as I can.

Eric is only a few feet below me, and I want nothing more than to come down to him, curl into his chest. Before he remembers the hundred reasons we can't do that anymore.

"Eric?" I whisper.

But he's asleep.

# 55

### You and Me and the Open Road

Saturday, 4:00 p.m.

We have a nearly three-hour drive. I still have to get gas, clean and wrap the gift, buy a decent outfit for the ceremony tomorrow.

I'm not showing up at Serra's wedding, the grand gesture that was going to right all past mistakes and reunite the Three Mouseketeers, in Eric's long nylon Adidas basketball shorts and Dodgers T-shirt.

We eat at the hotel like we promised, and the restaurant's World-Famous 360-Degree Log Run is something to see. It's a trickling, toddler-height oval structure in the corner of the room, surrounding a play area. Crystal's late husband rigged it up out of parts from a train set and a Sushi Go-Round. Kids crawl in and out of the play area through a carpeted tunnel behind my seat to watch the replica of a sawmill behind a plastic barrier, the Lincoln Logs traveling around in an endless loop.

It is a beautiful thing to drink coffee and eat fresh buttermilk biscuits with a simulated river splashing by your elbow, but we eat quickly. We both want to get up to the Sea Whisper before sunset.

I check the car out the restaurant's front window again. It's become a habit as automatic as checking that my wallet's in my purse. The gift is there, of course, and as I stare out at it, I see not the utilitarian brown cardboard but the exotic world trapped inside. My body and mind are wrung out, soft, and there's a freedom in being too exhausted to control my thoughts.

Eric stirs his coffee, smiling. "What's funny?"

"It's so dopey."

"That's okay."

"I was thinking about how satisfying it would be to split open Serra's piece and…liberate the creatures. So they could float around on the play table, whoosh down that slope over there. We could make them little ponchos out of plastic bags." I can see it so vividly: little furred replicas of our younger selves cruising around.

"They totally deserve it. They've been trapped in Plexigas for a decade. But you don't believe in log-ride ponchos," he says. "You said so every single time we went to Disneyland and waited in line at Splash Mountain. You said that they take all the fun out of it and should be outlawed."

We hold each other's gaze for a few seconds, and I know he's remembering those long days at Disneyland on school field trips, or with Serra. Once, just the two of us had gone. It was a late-August day before senior year, and a work friend of my mom's had given us discount passes. That time we'd stayed until the park closed at eleven, riding a whipping, many-armed attraction in Tomorrowland at least five times. Hip to hip in the dark, sliding back and forth in our car, helpless against its centrifugal force, laughing hysterically. We'd stepped off the ride shaky each time, linking arms so we wouldn't fall, running dizzily right back into the line. His face splashed in colored lights.

I clear my throat. "I remember."

He fiddles with our coffeepot lid, his voice good-natured. "I think we may be slightly punchy."

I match his playful tone—"*Slightly?* I think I passed punchy last night around one."

"Here, have the last of the coffee." He pours me the last inch and I down it.

"So do you think Serra's nervous?"

"She'd have to be, with the wedding…" he checks his watch "…a little less than twenty-four hours from now."

"But she's happy, I can hear it in her voice. He's a good guy."

"Yeah, they came to New York two years ago." With a note of finality, nodding. "He *is* a good guy." He pauses, then continues, his expression less serious. "Have you come close to… you know?"

I smile. "Walking the plank? No. You?"

He shakes his head. "Not really. A few years ago, I was dating this chef and she and I talked about it once, but…"

I carefully tune my expression to the appropriate, midrange level of curiosity. I freeze it there, waiting, for what feels like ages.

As if I don't have to concentrate on breathing.

But he's not looking at me anymore. He's staring at the play table.

I glance down to what's caught his eye. A spot in the trickling water jammed with Lincoln Logs. "What is it?"

He stands, rolls up his right sleeve. Dunks his arm into the play river like he's Tom Hanks fishing bare-handed in *Cast Away*. Pulls his dripping arm from the water and holds up his catch: one of Serra's metallic-blue hinges.

"What the…" I grab my purse from the floor and root through it. Wallet, keys, journal…

The bag of hinges is gone.

# 56

## Island

The log-run incident cost us an hour, and we only recovered two more hinges. Just enough to connect the last panel of the gift.

Some kid had crawled past my unzipped hobo purse, spied the bag of shiny bright goodness in it, and given the hinges a merry ride. We found one stuck in a clump of plastic trees and one jammed under a slide near the miniature sawmill.

We tried to give Crystal cash to make up for disturbing her dining room, but she wouldn't take it. Instead, she gave us a huge white bag of biscuits for the road. We are calling the biscuits *power pellets*. Like the coveted magic pills from old video games, which gave your character temporary superpowers if chomped. Something to fuel us on our homestretch to the wedding.

"Want the last one?" Eric asks, hanging over his crutch, rooting in the bag. We're in the parking lot of a lighthouse, outside a sprawling beach town called Gull City, walking to the public restroom fifty feet ahead.

"Let's split it."

"I don't know. You're dragging." But he breaks the last biscuit in two, lobs my half at me. I catch it one-handed.

As we make our way to the low cinder-block building, chewing the last of our power pellets, a Cub Scout troop swarms us, dueling with plastic lighthouse models, small versions of the real one two hundred yards away, down a long, rocky causeway. It's a red-and-white beauty, a giant's peppermint stick. Eric gets stuck behind them in the restroom line.

I lean against a bus shelter to wait until he emerges, his hair flopping, working his crutch with a graceful swing-hop.

"You've got the hang of that," I say. "Ready? We should get moving so we can clean up before Serra's post-rehearsal thing."

"Yeah, let's hit it. I'm dying for a hot shower."

"Me, too."

"The hotel looks amazing. I checked out the website, and it's close to the world's biggest natural collection of sea glass. If there's time maybe..." He trails off, his smile falling away.

"What?"

"Nothing. Let's go."

I turn. On the bus shelter is an advertisement for a grinning realtor. Billy Greppo, Denton Realty... List with the Best! Someone has given charming Billy black devil's horns, a curling mustache.

And a label across his broad, shiny forehead: FRAUD!

*He wrote me a note. Let's put it that way.*

*A little welcome-to-the-family note.*

*Fraud.* It's what Eric spray-painted on Cal's boat in high school.

I rub at the word with my thumb but the ink's permanent. I turn back to face him.

"Sometimes I think you plan these things," he says dryly.

"No." I shake my head.

"I should've written something else," Eric says.

"What?"

He stares past me at the graffiti. "Thief."

He gives me a sad smile and walks off across the parking lot. I think he's going to get in the convertible, maybe slam the door.

But he swing-hops right past the car. Heads straight for the narrow pebbled-concrete causeway toward the lighthouse.

Even when he's a hundred feet away, surrounded by other bodies heading back and forth from the point, I know his shape. A little taller, a little thinner, a little faster, even with the crutch.

I follow at a distance, glancing back at the convertible, hoping the gift will be okay. I should pay a scout to watch it, but the tall figure walking rapidly ahead of me across the pebbly land bridge to the lighthouse pulls me more. The matter-of-fact way he said that single, devastating word cracks my heart in two: *Thief.*

When Eric rounds the lighthouse I lose him, and for a moment I imagine him running up the inner staircase. Like Kim Novak in *Vertigo*, climbing the spiraling bell tower in the old mission before poor, dizzy Jimmy Stewart can catch up.

Reality is less dramatic. The lighthouse door is locked and the pointed red hands on the adjustable clock sign in the window say the next tour isn't until tomorrow morning at 11:30.

I find Eric standing on the grass ten feet down the steep slope from the lighthouse, leaning casually on his crutch, facing the ocean. He's staring at a spot far out, where waves crash over a dome-shaped rock.

I edge down the slope, feet sideways. It's tricky enough for me to navigate; I can't imagine how Eric managed it. I stop on his left side, well in his sight line so that I won't startle him and make him fall.

He raises his crutch to point at the gulls wheeling and diving over the rock. "Beautiful, aren't they?"

I bite back my *be careful.* "Yes. Do you get to the coast much, out there?"

He sets his crutch down. "Sure. Everyone's got *places.* Weekend places or summer places. Places on Long Island, in The Hamptons, Maine."

"That must be nice."

"It is. I'm thinking of getting a place. My accountant wants me to."

A big wave surges toward the dome-shaped rock and crashes over it in a corona of white foam. The water is sucked back to the horizon, and another wave gathers, a smaller one. There is no pattern, at least not one that I can see. Sometimes there are two big waves seconds apart, and sometimes a minute passes between them.

"You know when my mom called you up out of the blue and asked you to coffee? After..."

"Yes. We met at Il Fornaio—"

"I asked her to. Pathetic, huh? As if you needed checking up on."

I take his hand and lace my fingers through his. "Oh, E. No. No..."

"I was worried about you. I was furious, but..." He shakes his head, staring out at the sea.

We stand quietly for a while. I caress his hand, my pinkie moving slowly up and down the warm valleys between his fingers.

"Nobody stole me, Eric."

He turns to me.

"You said he was a thief. But he didn't steal me. I chose to be with him."

"Why?"

It's the question I've wanted to answer for him for ten years.

"I met him at the right time."

He shakes his head again, looks back at the rock. "It can't be that simple."

"It's not simple. It sounds like it is, but it's not. But I can't explain it any other way. I met him at the exact moment I was trying to break away from who everyone else thought I was supposed to be."

I think back to myself at twenty, scared that who I would become had already been decided—by my suffocating need to please, collecting my awards and approval.

*Rebecca consistently delivers stellar work.*

*I've rarely come across such an outstanding, reliable young woman...*

*Rebecca is a joy to have on the committee.*

*Rebecca is such a cheerful and dependable editor.*

*Attendance: 100%. Wow!!!*

"And I wanted..."

They thought they knew exactly who I was, because I'd done such a good job of pretending *I* knew. When I didn't have a clue.

Such *stellar work.* If you weren't vigilant, words like that controlled you. Kept you from seeing yourself.

Like what we did at Newzly. People searched for answers to important questions, and we lured them toward what was easier and simpler in the moment. Until they forgot what they'd been searching for, or even that they'd been searching at all.

"I was allowed to be someone different with him. To try out another version of myself. And I needed to figure out who I was. Instead of letting everyone decide for me."

He offers the faintest of nods.

"So I can't be sorry it happened." I touch his elbow. "But I'll always be sorry that I hurt you. And that I lied."

5:40 p.m.

We make it back up to the top of the hill without further injury.

Our problem is not boot traction or balance, but timing.

It's always timing with us.

The lighthouse is now on an island. The center of the concrete causeway is submerged under a good foot and a half of water. While we were taking in the ocean, the tide washed in and surrounded us.

The causeway is still manageable. There's a family, two men and a little girl of about eight, sloshing through the water back to their car, yelling, and laughing. One dad carries the girl on his shoulders over the deep part.

"There should be a sign," Eric says.

"There is, look." We'd walked right past it: Caution! Causeway May Be Impassable at High Tide.

"We'd better run for it."

"Get on my back."

"What? No way."

"The doctor said you can't get your stitches wet. You want jungle rot or gangrene or whatever?"

"I'll hop."

"You'll fall."

"I'll find a plastic bag." He looks around wildly for a trash can.

"It's getting deeper, climb on." I stand in front of him, bend my knees.

"I weigh fifteen pounds more than—" I back into him, reaching behind me for his legs so he has no choice but to hop onto me and, good God, he is heavy. I carried him around often in his pool and the pool at Serra's, in chicken fights, but without water I can barely lift him. He's an awkward burden, long limbed and unsure what to do with his crutch; instead of wrapping himself around me properly he drapes one arm around my neck, leaning back, his right hand holding the crutch clear of my body like he's jousting. I can barely balance us, and though the shorts I borrowed from him are slipping, I can't yank them up.

I slog through cold water, trying not to splash Eric's Velcro boot.

"Becc, I'm sliding. And squashing you. Seriously, put me down, this isn't going to end well. Becc? What's a little jungle rot—"

"It's. Fine." I can barely grunt it out; Eric's weight is compressing my diaphragm. I wish I could ask him to check that

my shorts are in place and I'm not accidentally mooning passing boats or the lighthouse keeper; the wet hem is weighing
the fabric down, and maybe I'm paranoid but below the band
of warmth where Eric's body circles mine, I feel a cool breeze.

A man in a red windbreaker is coming toward us, crossing
the causeway ten yards ahead. He's wearing rubber waders and
an official-looking neon-yellow windbreaker, and he takes his
time on the flooded section. Unfazed.

And clearly entertained by our frantic piggyback.

We're only ten feet into the tide-wash when I know I can't
make it across. The water's cold, getting deeper and dragging
my shorts lower. It's either dump Eric or turn around, so I turn
around.

"What are we doing?"

"Can't." I just make it back, set Eric down on dry grass, pull
up my shorts. The relief is intense.

"Have I wrecked your spine for life? Are you permanently
five-two?"

I force myself to stand straight. There's a twinge in my lower
back but I resist rubbing it. "Five-eight again. Is your foot dry?"

"Yeah. Thanks." He gazes back at the choppy gray ocean,
where a small white tour boat has stopped so passengers can
photograph the candy-striped lighthouse.

We'll be in their pictures. Two damaged, weary bodies.

The man in the boots smiles as he sloshes closer. "You've got
a strong girlfriend there," he yells.

Now I'm positive he saw most of my butt when we about-
faced.

I jump in before Eric has to deal with the *girlfriend* mistake.
"When will it be clear again?" I call.

"This time of year?" The guy is close enough now that I can
read his jacket: USCG. Coast Guard. He turns to survey the submerged causeway. "Twelve hours. Peak is five feet. You're not
the only tourists to get caught, but we haven't lost anyone yet."

"Glad we're keeping the locals amused," Eric says under his breath.

"Do you have some plastic garbage bags we can borrow?" I ask. "He can't get his stitches wet."

"Sure thing. Or you could borrow a dinghy. Or..." He rubs his beard, considering. "It'll be dark pretty soon. You're welcome to spend the night here, if you can manage a few stairs. You two look pretty beat."

"That's nice of you, but we can't leave our car. We have a package in it." I point to the convertible, now the only one in the lot.

The Coast Guard man turns. "Oh, I could radio security to keep an eye on it for you. They chain up the parking lot at eight. Doubt anything'd happen to it anyway. Well, you two think about it. Plastic bags or the dinghy or a couple of warm beds. The room's not much, we just keep it for training and such, but it works. Take your pick, I'm not going anywhere." He saunters off.

"I'm exhausted and you're exhausted," Eric says. "I can't take you swerving around the highway again. Serra will understand. I'll text her and explain. Let's just stay here and start fresh tomorrow."

"You got eleven hours of sleep Thursday and eight Friday, plus the nap. And I'm totally fine, I'll grab a big coffee in a drive-through—"

"I got three hours of sleep Thursday and two Friday. That's why I've been crashing in the car."

His voice isn't just tired. It's aware that he's giving me something with this statement. Acknowledging something. And though I'm still shivering because my legs are still soaked, the fact that he has only slept for eight hours since Thursday morning warms me.

It gives me hope.

I'm stubborn; I have courageous stubbornness. Someone told me that once.

## 57

### Minor Miracle

August 1998
The morning after Eric ran away from me at the Fairmont
Orchard Hill

WHERE I WAS SUPPOSED TO BE | The all-company CommPlanet
wellness meeting at the *Liberty*
WHERE I WAS | Delivering a letter

"Well. At last." Mrs. Haggermaker opened the door, looking as
fresh and pressed as I was stale and rumpled.

It was 8:00 a.m.

After the Fairmont I'd gone to Cielo-del-mar. Eric wasn't
there, of course. The sheets were still rumpled from our bodies,
and I sank onto the bed where we'd been together only three
hours before.

"Are you all right, dear?"

I'd driven all night, pulling over only to leave messages for
Eric. Nine of them, none of which he'd returned.

When I got to my apartment he wasn't there.

I'd tried to drive to the paper for my meeting. But somehow I'd driven up Orchard Hill instead. To Francine's.

I still wasn't sure what I was doing there.

"Dear?"

"I'm sorry I haven't sent my last scholarship letter yet. Or answered yours. That's why I came. To say I'm really sorry."

"I so enjoy your letters, whenever they come. I realize that you're busy, dear."

"No. There's no excuse."

"It seems you might have an excuse. It almost seems like you've been crying."

"I'll get you your money back," I whispered. I turned to leave.

"Rebecca."

I looked over my shoulder.

"Come in the house."

★

I followed her through the entry to the hall. Eyes and nose streaming, exhausted, but trying to straighten my carriage to match hers. Even the bow in her hair was perfect: thin blue grosgrain, the tails exactly the same length.

In the living room she whipped her right hand up and back so that her pale blue handkerchief unfurled down her narrow shoulder blade.

I accepted it. Wiped my nose as she led me outside, to a bench by a sundial birdbath.

"I believe coffee is in order," she said.

Alone in her garden, I smoothed her linen handkerchief over my knee. Below her initials—an unfussy, block-lettered, FAH—was a single embroidered forget-me-not. Her signature flower, the one like the pin she always wore.

She returned with a tray of coffee and fruit and muffins, setting it on a wrought-iron table. "Cream or sugar? Or one of these horrid pink packets?"

"No, thank you."

"I didn't think so. On certain mornings, black coffee is a minor miracle." She handed me a cup. "My late husband used to say that."

I sipped, then drained the strong brew. I'd never had better.

She didn't say a word. Just sipped her coffee.

"I'll give you your money back. It will take a while, but I want to. I don't want to owe you anything."

"What are you talking about, dear?"

"The letter."

"Letters have been tardier, dear."

"*Your* letter about the museum board. The graffiti and the misuse of funds. How Derrek Schwinn told you I violated the morals clause."

"Pardon me, dear?"

"I'm admitting it."

"Admitting what, exactly?"

"How I protected Yvonne Copeland's vandals and embezzlers. Also, I cut classes. Drank. Smoked marijuana with my roommate. Twice. And played hooky from work. All the time. I'm playing hooky from work right now. And it turns out I'm a pretty bad reporter. Sloppy."

"What else?" She pursed her lips, her pale pink lipstick crinkling.

"You don't know that part? I slept with Devin McCallister for more than a year. You know, our *mutual acquaintance across the Bay*? I slept with him and lied about it. To people who deserved better. Add it to the list."

"Would you like a muffin, dear? Or strawberries? The last of the season."

"Did you hear me? I'm confessing. But you don't have to worry about broadcasting it and ruining my life because it's already ruined. I'm a liar and a coward. And I've hurt the last people in the world I wanted to hurt."

She nodded. Drank her coffee. Pressed a napkin to her lips.

"I've never smoked marijuana," she said, reaching over to touch the soil in a white stone planter of hollyhock near the table. "Needs water."

For a second, I didn't understand what she was getting at. Maybe her mind wasn't as sharp as it seemed.

But no, I was the slow one.

She had never smoked.

But she'd done everything else on my list. That's what she was saying.

"Yvonne Copeland is a friend, dear. She's the board member who called me. To tell me the truth about her liberal grant recommendations and her...private art projects. And the business with Schwinn. Who lives *across the Bay.*

"I think Yvonne's project is an excellent use of funds, don't you? I may find a way to contribute to it so it can continue."

"You—?"

"In fact, I once did something quite similar, myself. A long time ago. But you thought I'd side with that, pardon, rutting pig, Schwinn?"

"I—"

"Is that why you found it so difficult to write your letter?"

"I'm sorry, I—"

"You've said that three times now," she said. "I wonder why."

"I didn't realize I was saying it so much. I'm..." I stopped myself before I could make it a fourth.

She laughed. A surprisingly throaty, infectious burst. "All we're missing is the little wooden booth. And I'm not even Catholic."

"I'm sort of a mess today."

"I like it. Nobody tells you these things when you're my age. As if you haven't lived, yourself." She tilted her gray eyes up at me with a quick girlish smile, then looked down at her hollyhock again.

"So tell me." She picked a dry leaf from the bird feeder. "Do you wish you hadn't *violated the morals clause,* as you say? Truth, now."

I stared at the stone sailboat in the center of the birdbath, thinking about Cal. Not how it ended, not how confusing and messy it got in the middle, but how it started: that first golden summer.

"No."

"Good answer."

"But Eric hates me. Serra will, too."

She nodded, reached for my cup, and filled it with her perfect coffee.

Only after I'd finished the cup did she ask, "Do you hate yourself?"

"I should."

"Poor answer. You're a bright girl. I heard this expression once—*don't should on anyone and don't let anyone should on you.* I've always rather liked that. So try again. Do you hate yourself?"

"No," I said softly. She pressed her pale, wrinkled lips together slightly so I said it again, louder. "No."

"Good."

We sat quietly for a minute, and I asked her the thing I'd wanted to ask for years. "Why'd you pick me?"

She considered. "Your letter was...impenetrable. Like all the other application cover letters. But I liked what you wrote about Nellie Bly. It was touching, quite wise, the part about never giving up and how 'sometimes life required courageous stubbornness.' Now, may I show you something?"

★

When she walked me to the door two hours later, she said, "Will you email me sometimes? I appreciate your lovely stationery but my eyes aren't what they used to be, and your handwriting presents challenges."

"You have email?"

She smiled. "Of course, dear. But write only when you want to. We'll call this visit your fourth letter."

# 58

## Sundeck

2008
Saturday, 6:30 p.m.

Our host is Grigg Harris. He's been with the Coast Guard for thirty years. Sixteen at this lighthouse, living here full-time even in the off-season.

Eric and I sit at a small table in the tiny crescent-shaped kitchen tucked behind the gift shop on the first floor while Grigg heats tomato soup, opens a box of Cheez-Its for us to throw in our bowls.

With GPS the lighthouse isn't needed anymore, so it's maintained only for historical purposes. "It's quite a beauty, though. One of the finest on the West Coast, original astragal bars in the lantern room. The lamp was the first in the US to have an illumination radius greater than twenty miles. But you didn't come for the tour, look at you two."

Because though we're both listening attentively, trying to be polite, we're yawning behind our hands, and Eric looks like he's about to face-plant into his soup bowl. We pass up the pudding cups Grigg offers, hungry only for sleep.

Carrying Eric's crutch, Grigg leads us up the iron spiral staircase that carves its way through the center of each floor.

"How'd you hurt your foot?" he calls back.

"Lawn mowing accident."

I smile at this.

"Ouch," Grigg says. "One of the perks of not having a yard, I guess."

"How are you managing?" I ask Eric.

"Fine." Though his forehead is sweaty by the time we step onto the third floor.

"Well, this is it." Grigg hands Eric his crutch. "If you'd come last week you'd have shared with a maritime historian from Cal Poly and a trainee from the lighthouse gift shop at Cape Mears. We call it the sundeck."

Because there are no windows. It's a sparse, round whitewashed space with a bare wood floor. An iron bunk bed, a bookcase, a bulbous RCA TV/VCR on one side, and a jerrybuilt bathroom on the other.

"Sleep tight."

We take turns brushing our teeth with our fingers in the little bathroom. There's a sticker on the mirror, two crisscrossed anchors with the Coast Guard motto inside it: *Semper Paratus.* Always Ready.

"Well," Eric says, yawning from his bottom bunk below mine. "It hasn't been boring."

★

I've been lying awake for at least an hour under my scratchy, heavy wool blanket. I've reached a state of maximum alertness.

It's too dark. There are strange noises. Shudderings and creaks, a mysterious, rhythmic humming.

I imagine that the hum is from the light, that it's sweeping around and around like it did in its glory days. It's beaming across the ocean, toward land. I picture the great cone of light circling clockwise, with me and Eric in the middle. I count its revolutions, like counting sheep.

"Eric?" I whisper.

"Yeah?" he whispers back.

"I can't sleep."

"Me, either. This lighthouse is too dark. Except for that weird blue line up there. What the hell is that from?"

We watch the curve of blue light swim across the ceiling. A moment later, a smaller curve follows, and I lean over the bunk to track its source. "It must be coming through the staircase hole. Some fancy lighthouse equipment downstairs with a dig-ital readout. A...wave-scope. A marine-o-scope."

He chuckles sleepily. "Grigg'll tell us the official name in the morning."

"Now, what about that humming?" I ask.

"Generator, maybe?" A minute later, he asks, "Why aren't we sleeping?"

"Sleep begets sleep, I read," I say with a yawn.

"What does that mean?" Eric asks.

"That we're like overtired babies. We're too tired to sleep."

It's easy to talk, here in this room with the moving lines of blue light. It's like being underwater.

We talk about our work. The people we've dated and broken up with. Our parents. We talk about New York, California, get-ting older.

It rushes out, flies out like the day we first met, back in high school. The lovely surprise of being totally comfortable with someone from the first words.

"Your mom sent me all of your articles, when you were still writing. I loved them, Becc. Those profiles you wrote for *Coastal Weekly* were my favorite. That surf family who lives in the van, and the one on the old guy who's been picking up litter for fifty years?"

*Mom.* Once, this might have annoyed me. My petty judgment used to clash with her stifling worries like low- and high-pressure systems, creating a fog. But after college I grew to see her more clearly. Her kindness, her sacrifices. And I'm glad she did what I didn't have the guts to do.

"She never told me."

A blue line, scalloped like a wave, glides across the white boards. Then a warped infinity sign, which is probably from an 8 on the mystery machine, working hard below us.

"Eric?"

"Hmm?"

"You were right. I have had a hard time since Francine died. If you'd told me when I was a senior in high school that my closest friends would someday be my mom and Francine Haggermaker, I'd have thought you were insane."

"So Francine stayed in her house until the end?"

"Yes. And she was perfectly sharp. We had some of our best talks just a couple of years ago."

His voice is soft, like a gentle touch in the dark. "I'm so sorry, Becc."

"Thank you. I miss her." I clear my throat. "But she used to say she'd had *more than her fair share* of life. Eighty-nine, and… she did so much. She left me her journal, from when she was in her twenties. There's so much I wish I could ask her."

"I'd like to read that sometime," he says. Another yawn. "She must've seen a lot in Hollywood, back in the day."

"She did. Francine saw everything."

"The eyes watching over you. Remember?"

"Yes. I remember."

"My mom said they're making Crystal Cove into a hotel."

"I refuse to…" I yawn "…stay there."

"Me, too. No way."

We speak in fragments. Then single words.

At 1:00 a.m. we go silent. Spent, relaxed, I watch the curves of blue light above me. Soothing as a mobile.

But we're still rustling blankets, flipping pillows.

"Pudding?" Eric says into the darkness.

"Genius. Dairy sedative. Stay here."

I jump down from the top bunk and fumble in my purse for my flashlight keychain. I tilt my purse out on the floor and pat over the contents until I feel it.

I flick on the tiny LED flashlight and make my way down the cold iron staircase, clinging tight to the thin railing with my right hand, illuminating my bare feet with the other. On the second floor and below, windows make it easier to see, and from Grigg's quarters on the ground floor come the comforting sound of snoring.

Quietly, I grab two chocolate pudding cups, two spoons, and climb back up with our rations.

Eric has turned on the bare-bulb light over the bathroom mirror, leaving the door open a crack. He's on the floor next to the bookcase, in his boxers and T-shirt. Bad leg stretched out straight, sorting through VHS tapes.

"Anything good?"

"*US Coast Guard Boating Safety Tips for Kids.* No, thanks. *Historic Lighthouses of North America*... Ah, score. What do you say?" He holds it up.

"Two thumbs-up."

He shoves the movie in.

We pull our blankets and pillows to the floor, close to the screen. We keep the volume on three so we won't disturb Grigg, eat pudding, and watch *Easy Rider*.

"Eric?"

"Hmm?"

"I've missed you."

He stares at the screen intently. It's the diner scene. Jack Nicholson and Dennis Hopper getting grief about their long hair.

They joke nervously. Leave the diner, get on their bikes.

They fly down the highway.

Slow as I can, I lean forward, touch Eric's banged-up foot with my right hand. He's taken the boot off, so his foot is bare except for the thick white figure eight of gauze, which winds around his stitched, fractured toes and circles his ankle.

I touch him on the ankle lightly, tracing the line of gauze, careful not to disturb the tape or tiny silver clips. Back and forth.

"I'm not hurting you, am I?" Though my touch is a feather brush.

He shakes his head.

I brace for it: *Becc. Stop. We can't.*

Or the pained look in his eye that will hurt even more. But he doesn't stop me.

I'm so close to the screen that Jack Nicholson is reduced to dots, like pointillism. *Sunday in the Park with George.* I'm blocking half of Eric's view.

We both pretend to watch the movie as my hand ventures higher, up his taut inner calf. Slowly, until my hand is on his knee, then down to his ankle again. Up and down again, not going higher than his knee. Three agonizingly slow round trips. Four.

Eric clears his throat, shifts his other leg.

I leave my hand on his bare knee and turn to look at him, my back to the TV. It's like we're back in his closet screening room. Back in those theaters in San Francisco. Meeting up in the dark, setting our own schedules. Just the two of us, not because it was wrong, not because we were hiding. But because we were searching for something we couldn't find out in the light.

He covers my hand with his.

"I've missed you, too."

★

"Becc," Eric murmurs into my neck. "Becc. You taste the same. Like…"

"Like?" I laugh as his tongue touches my collarbone.

"Like Becc. Exactly like Becc."

I stop laughing as he rubs his face in the curving nook between the base of my neck and my jaw, his hands sliding up my shirt.

The smell of him, his hair and skin, is so familiar. He smells like all my favorite days.

"Careful. Your foot."

"It's fine."

On our sides, we kiss, long, sliding, effortless kisses. We're naked except for his boxers. I try to work them over his bad foot but we're not patient enough and leave them mid-thigh, a limitation we work around just fine. Beautifully, in fact, stuck together, lying on our sides.

Someone's rolled onto the remote and the volume's blasting, blaring the discordant jazz from the New Orleans cemetery LSD scene.

I fumble for it, for buttons, desperate for Off, settle for Mute.

We freeze, hot limbs locked together, him deep in me, waiting.

I'd been so close I can't stop completely, and I press against him, the smallest tilt of my hips against and away from his, as we wait for the terrible sound of a tread on the iron staircase below us.

But it's quiet. The only sound our hurried breathing.

# 59

### Better Time

Sunday, 10:34 a.m.

"Becc! We're late."

We are wrapped together in scratchy blankets on the floor and the TV is on the bright blue-and-white VCR settings menu.

The clock on the VCR says we've overslept. The light shooting up through the staircase opening is white, not blue. Everything in the room feels different.

Including us. Before we fell asleep, being together felt effortless, but now our bodies are weighed down, clumsy. Separate.

We're so late. The wedding's at four, 160 miles north, and there's so much to do.

Last night feels too big to talk about.

We dress quickly, not looking at each other. All politeness.

"Do you have your purse?"

"Here, I'll help with that. Your phone's down there."

"Thanks..."

56 minutes before the ceremony
Seal Beach, Oregon

Traffic up the coast is slow, and I've watched the minutes tick past with growing alarm.

I told myself Seal Beach would have at least one boutique where I could grab a dress, so we passed up a Target, two Walmarts.

But Seal Beach is a sleepy, wind-battered town with a one-block shopping district, and my only option is a resale store. Eric swing-hops to the druggist next door for cleaning solvent and wrapping paper. "And a bow," I call. "And tape and a card!"

I want a hairbrush and a razor, too, but we're running out of time, and maybe the hotel will have those desperation kits for forgetful guests.

"Dresses?" I ask the cashier.

"Back wall."

I attack the dress rack. Size 4 bronze lamé—*no way*—strapless cream velvet in my size, 8—but reeking of stale Obsession and bald across the seat. The Velveteen Rabbit of dresses, *please, no*, a green size 12 one-shoulder number with a busted zipper and deodorant stains down the sides...

I shove hanger after hanger across the rod. Maybe I can squeeze into a size 2 of Maggie's. Or beg random guests to lend me something or Serra's mom will help but she's petite, too, and it's so late, how rotten to waylay the mother of the bride minutes before the vows. Maybe Velveteen Rabbit won't be too tragic if I borrow a sweater.

Three hangers from the end there's a black knit in 10. Knee-length, short sleeved, an unfortunate diagonal ruffle across the skirt but at least it's not in contrasting fabric. It's got shoulder pads but I can rip them out, and it smells okay. We have a winner.

I reach the convertible at the same time as Eric. "Did you get everything?"

"Yeah, but they only had two dinky things of wrapping paper left. It's not the greatest. You found a good dress?"

I start the ignition. "In relative terms. What do you mean, *not the greatest*?"

He squeezes the top of the yellow plastic bag.

"Just show me."

He pulls a corner out. Pale pink, a block pattern spelling B-A-B-Y. "Sorry."

"We'll turn it inside out." I gun the gas.

3:56 p.m.

We're on time.

We're showered and changed. The front desk gave me a Kourtesy Kit—razor and comb, toothbrush and toothpaste. I kept the shoulder pads in my dress, worried that yanking them would tear the fabric, but I'm hoping they give me a Trekkie flair.

In the parking lot we scrubbed the white marks with Goo Gone, attached the third panel. We wrapped two-thirds in inside-out baby-shower paper and a third in USA TODAY comics.

We made a card from hotel notepaper, signed it, taped it to the top.

The porters rolled the present to the designated alcove of the *Indrijo-Fisher Wedding* private dining room, pushed it into the shadows behind the table bearing other white-and-silver-wrapped offerings. Maggie is in charge of seeing the gifts to Serra's house, two towns away, after the reception tonight, and I'll help. When Serra returns from her honeymoon in Friday Harbor, it'll be waiting.

I want her to open it in private. Not surrounded by drunk wedding guests, not pressured to overdo her thanks.

Now there's nothing left to do but sit, spent and a little breath-less, in white folding chairs in the sun, on the Sea Whisper's bright oceanside patio. I'm to the left of the aisle and Eric is next to me. It feels strange to have him on my left side; for most of our 904 miles he's been on my right.

Eric smells of lemongrass hotel shampoo, and his combed hair is damp. He has circles under his bloodshot eyes, purply-gray shadows so vivid they look painted on. Mine are worse, but I had time to dot on concealer.

"Well, you pulled it off," he says.

"We pulled it off."

"Yes."

He nods and turns to me, an expression of gratitude on his weary face.

I wait. This can't be all he wants to say.

I smooth the skirt of my secondhand dress. Read the back of the program. Set it on my lap and fold my hands over it.

He bends to adjust his pants cuff over his boot. Checks that his crutch isn't going to trip anyone. Though it's exactly where he stashed it one minute ago, under our seats.

"It's a nice thing, Becc. It'll make her happy."

"Thank you."

He nods and closes his eyes, lifting his tired face to the sun.

★

It's a casual, nondenominational service: no chuppa, no altar, no bride's or groom's sides. Just a bearded guitarist plucking out a Steely Dan medley and a professor friend of Serra's as officiant. She's standing in a flowy green pantsuit with her back to the sea, nervously reviewing three-by-five cards. So close to the edge of the patio I worry she'll topple back into the sea grass.

Someone bops my right shoulder pad. Maggie.

Eric stands, one steadying hand on his chair, and Maggie leans across me to hug him. Her hair, pure black at the moment, more versatile for auditions and go-sees, is pulled into a low knot, and she's wearing a vintage apricot swing dress. I helped her find it, in a funky shop in West Hollywood.

"Nice dress," she says to me.

"Don't even."

"How was the drive?" she whispers, looking meaningfully past me at Eric.

I shake my head subtly. *Not now.*

"You got the masterpiece here okay?"

"It's all set."

"I still think she should open it tonight."

"No. When she comes back, like we planned."

The guitarist downshifts to classical and Serra's fiancé takes his place up front.

I've never seen him without his sand-filled leather ball, never been near his body when it wasn't moving in a hypnotic rhythm of kicks and bounces within the hacky sack's flight patterns, the imaginary dotted lines that surrounded him like Pig-Pen's dust cloud.

Glenn teaches history at the community college where Serra works.

"Glenn looks good," I say to Maggie. "Have you seen her?"

"Yeah. She's nervous. Looks like it's showtime."

"Break a leg. Oops, sorry," I say to Eric, hoping he'll smile. But he's deep in conversation with the man on his left.

Maggie squeezes my shoulder pad and heads up front.

The guitarist starts "Canticle" and we all stand and turn and there's Serra walking toward us. She wears a long white sundress and her hair blows back in loose waves. She carries wildflowers tied with a scrap of old lace. She's smiling broadly, a little freaked out, a little giddy.

When she approaches our row I brace myself for her to pass without noticing me.

But she slows, turns her head to take both of us in, me and Eric, and her grin relaxes for a second into a subtler smile only for the three of us.

And it's enough, that brief *I remember.*

The tears that have threatened all weekend come quickly now. I watch the ceremony through a rippling, glassy curtain.

★

Eric and I are assigned seats next to each other, near the head table. The place cards are the one formal touch of the wedding, and I'm grateful Serra took the decision out of our hands.

It's a happy, lively reception. But I've been to twelve weddings, of varying budgets, and there are few surprises. Salad and rolls and butter shells and champagne—*fish or pasta, miss?*—knife clinks on glasses commanding the couple to kiss.

Then the toast-off, as guests battle to be funniest.

Glenn's father: *They were meant to be together, even though they were too stupid to realize it for years.*

Serra's cousin: *Sometimes love is right under your nose, except you're too damn stubborn to notice.*

Eric and I find plenty to do during these pronouncements. We sip, we observe the head table, we pass the salt and pepper and laugh with our tablemates.

We don't look at each other.

After the second off-color hacky-sack joke, I clink my glass and stand. When I'm on my feet I flush, blanking and wishing I could back out. But someone's handed me the mic.

I was going to say something about Plato House. But the words have evaporated.

I stall. "I'm so happy to be here today..."

Eric stares at his salmon en croute, probably worried that in my panic I'll hold forth on miniature log rides and Greek islands and second chances.

But I seize on an image: the Mary Cassatt print. I address Serra directly, fumbling at first. "Serra. You had a poster, back in the dorm, freshman year. Remember? It said, *With strangers we must try. With the ones we love, we lean back into the simple joy of being ourselves.*" My voice is firmer now. "And you and Glenn are a walking poster for that. You deserve all the joy in the world."

Glenn and Serra tilt their heads together affectionately. There's a smattering of respectful applause, a single *hear, hear*; my earnest speech goes over just fine. Sincerity always gets a more subdued reaction than a joke.

★

Serra and Glenn came to our table to say their thanks and she hugged both me and Eric, but she was pulled away quickly, and since then she's been busy or surrounded all night.

After the sweet dances, the Sinatra and Patsy Cline, the DJ badgers everyone into a bunny hop to liven things up.

He borrows Eric's crutch for a limbo contest and I do a couple rounds, easy ones requiring only a quick bend and a head tilt. Then I stand to the side next to Eric, watching as the bodies get lower, until only the truly flexible or delusional make the attempt.

Holding the back of a chair for balance, he shouts into my ear about his crutch, currently bobbing horizontally in the center of the packed dance floor. "Do you think I'll ever get it back?"

"I'll rescue it for you if I have to!"

I don't need to extricate the crutch from the dance floor. Glenn's brother hands it back to Eric right after the limbo contest.

We still haven't talked about last night.

I keep thinking that there will be a better time. A moment when it's just the two of us, and we're somewhere dark and otherworldly, like last night.

We'd found our way back to each other almost in a dream, in a strange room like the turret of an underwater castle. A room hidden from the world.

Maybe I did dream it. Or hallucinated it.

I've never been so tired in my life, but I dance to the next twelve songs. I do the Macarena and YMCA, every arm fling and jump. I throw my wrung-out muscles into the warm throng, staying close to the speakers, where conversation's impossible.

Eyes half-closed, I dance with anyone. Cousins, neighbors, artist or teacher friends.

Eric sits at a table near the back, his bad leg up on a chair. Deep in conversation with a pretty woman I don't recognize. I know he isn't trying to make me jealous. And I'm not. But the image of him sitting across the room with a stranger is so starkly different from what I pictured.

Last night, in the lighthouse, curled against his chest, I saw us dancing together.

★

It's a cash bar now. Two guys are lying flat on their backs on the patio, smoking cigars, making a spicy, leathery-smelling cloud. The seniors and parents with young kids have gone to bed.

It's time for me to leave, too. But I'm not ready.

I'm desperate for sleep, but the idea of retreating to my cool hotel room upstairs, to the quiet of my vast, soft bed, makes me ache. The party is a heart, sticky and messy but throbbing with life, and I want to stay near it until it stops.

Someone grabs my elbow. Serra. She's pink-faced, her professionally waved hair hanging in lank strips down her neck. "Come talk!"

She pulls me to the back of the room, to a deep windowsill by the gift table. She cranks the window open. "That feels so good. Eighty dollars for this do, and look at me," she says, laughing. "My mom paid for the stylist. She insisted."

"You look beautiful, Serr."

"You, too. Is that a vintage dress?"

"Serra."

"What? Okay, it's not the kind of thing you usually wear, but I like it."

"I lost my luggage. Long story. Let's just say this was the best among limited options."

"The *Least Hideous*?"

"Exactly."

She adjusts my shoulder pad. "Mags said you and Eric had a good time driving up together? That must mean…no?"

"Long story."

"Funny. That's what he said to me when I asked him."

"It went well. Considering."

"Yeah?" She waits for me. Even on her wedding day, she's interested in how I'm feeling.

I could tell her all about Eric, how I understood it was too complicated for him, and I wasn't upset.

We'd reconnected the triptych—beginning, middle, and end. And if Eric and I didn't find our new ending, at least we had the memory of what came before.

She'd make sure he got that message.

Serra's been so good to me. She didn't judge me for being with Cal. It was my lies that changed things between us. And the lies had been for nothing; she told me she and Maggie had known all along that I was secretly seeing someone.

"It was a beautiful wedding, Serr."

"It was pretty nice, wasn't it? The only bummer was that Yvonne couldn't make it. She has a big case in DC this week."

Yvonne is not an attorney, but she has three of them working at her nonprofit, trying sex discrimination cases. It was a comfort after Francine died, knowing that Yvonne's group would put her millions to good work.

Serra stretches, surveys her gifts. "Some haul, huh? Holy shit, what's that giant thing on the floor?"

"Where?"

"In the back corner. Wrapped in the funnies." She walks over.

"I'll bet it's one of those flat packs from Ikea. You should probably keep it wrapped so it'll be easier…"

She's already tearing at the paper before I can stop her. When she realizes, she sits on the floor and leans her forehead against it. "How…?"

"It wasn't that hard."

"Turn that light on?"

She crawls down the piece's length, brushing her hand against the outside, the gleaming silver-blue hinges, lost inside the world she created more than ten years ago. "Who had it?"

"A very attached collector. It took some persuading."

She looks at me over her shoulder, smiling. "Right. You probably had to hunt in every junk shop in Berkeley."

"No."

After a long silence, she says, "I haven't spent as much time on anything since. Or maybe I've put in the hours but... I haven't lost myself in them, not like back then. I'm not saying it's the best thing in the world. But...I *lived* in it. You know?"

"I do."

"I know right where it's going. In my studio, under the window. I have a studio now, did I tell you? We converted the garage."

"That's great, Serr."

"Becc. This is... I don't know how to..."

"You're welcome."

She stands and hugs me.

Then Glenn comes for Serra; she's needed for goodbyes.

"Will you come up again soon? So I can show you how it looks in the studio?"

"I'd love that."

# 60

## Working Vacation

The next evening, 8:00 p.m.

I'm staying a few extra days. I bought more clothes at the thrift store. Soft jeans and two T-shirts, a warm white sweater and a periwinkle scarf for walking on the beach at night. At the drugstore I bought books and magazines, a hairbrush, a toothbrush that's gentler than the one in my Kourtesy Kit.

I bought a stack of wire-bound notebooks and a pack of pens.

I'm going to take my time driving back. There's no rush.

I've accrued twenty-nine vacation days. *Unclaimed* days, HR calls them. I haven't taken time off in years, and the decision alone feels good. I'm going to claim those summer hours just for me.

Serra is off on her honeymoon. Maggie has flown home; she called to say her soap opera audition went well. She *killed* as Daphne, and Eliot misses me.

Eric must be home in New York by now.

He's having a late dinner in his high-rise apartment. Or sleeping. Probably sleeping. And that's okay.

I slept well last night.

I've worked feverishly all day. My hotel desk is buried in notes and outlines from Francine's journal. I took only one break around two, to devour a room-service club sandwich.

A little while ago I glanced up from my desk and saw kids down the beach to my right, running around, gathering wood. I've been aware of them all evening, vaguely monitoring their progress.

I set my pen down, rub my eyes.

I loop my scarf around my neck and head for the elevator.

And I realize that this whole day, productive and absorbing as it's been, has tilted toward this task.

I take the elevator downstairs to the lobby, follow the long, narrow wooden walkway to the beach. I unbuckle my sandals and hide them in the dunes, under a tuft of sea grass. I roll up my secondhand jeans.

The sand is still warm from the day, shifting and hard to walk on, but as I near the water, it's cool and packed.

There's a glow in the distance. A bonfire. Kids are pumping a pony keg, blasting the radio. It's a song I don't know, a techno beat, the woman's voice faultless but sterile from Auto-Tune.

I approach as close as I can without catching the kids' attention and sit on a washed-up tree trunk twenty feet back.

He left without saying goodbye, but I'm not angry. I'm only a little sad.

I know how hard it is sometimes to find the right words.

★

It's dark now, and getting chilly.

I'm ready to head back to my room. Maybe I'll order a pot of room-service coffee and stay up late working; Francine's notebook is calling.

The gray rubber knob of a crutch appears in front of me. I hold still as it digs a large circle in the sand. No, not a complete circle. The right side of a circle.

Then the tip of the crutch drags, slowly, straight down.
Lifts up.
Carves a dot below the vertical line.
He's scratched a message into the sand for me—
?

It could mean anything or nothing. It's not as easy to figure out his intended question as it would be in a movie.

But I pick the easiest one to answer, the one I want to answer—"Why am I still here?"

"Yeah," he says and steps closer.

I look up. "I'm staying here a few extra days. I'm using up my vacation time."

He nods. Shuffles around the log and settles next to me, stretches his booted leg.

"I'm glad," he says. "You deserve time off after this weekend."

"Correction," I say. "I should've said I'm taking time off *to* work."

"Interesting."

"It is to me. I have a lead on a story."

"Something juicy?"

"Francine thought it could be. And I think so, too, now. Why are you still here?"

"I got all the way to the airport. I was through security. The crutch was a nightmare, by the way. So I'm sitting in my airport chair waiting to board and I thought, I never said goodbye to Becc."

The kids at the bonfire are dancing, laughing, whacking the woodpile with sticks so sparks fly up in a glinting, whirling column.

"You came back to say goodbye?"

"No," he says.

He takes my hand and doesn't let go.

# Film Page

February 18, 2012
Briefly Noted section

A film about the life of Francine Haggermaker, wife of studio chief Lou Haggermaker, has been greenlit and is in preproduction at Everest/Northpoint.

The untitled production is based on the 2011 biography by Rebecca Reardon, *The Prop Girl*.

Reardon's research, along with that of her collaborator and film archivist, her fiancé, Eric Logan, uncovered how for a period of four years in the early 1950s, while a junior props assistant at Pacific Studios, Mrs. Haggermaker coordinated payment from her future husband to blacklisted screenwriters and devised a private scheme to mark their uncredited films with a blue forget-me-not ribbon in pivotal scenes.

The production is slated for an early 2015 release.

★ ★ ★ ★ ★

# Acknowledgments

Thank you to my wonderful agent, Stefanie Lieberman, for loving this story back when it was a messy draft without an ending. I'm so grateful that you believed in it, and in me.

My enormously talented, energetic, and sharp-eyed editor, Melanie Fried, never wavered in her support and made me a better writer. Thank you.

Thank you, Susan Swinwood, Lisa Wray, Pamela Osti, Gigi Lau, and everyone at Graydon House. I'm ridiculously lucky to be part of your imprint.

Kathleen Carter worked nonstop to get the word out, and Sarah Brody designed a cover so true to the novel that I can almost see Becc and her passenger in that tiny car. Molly Steinblatt has read multiple drafts of all of my manuscripts and her insight always strengthens the work.

Much love and appreciation to Carrie and Erin Higgins, all the Doans, and the Toronto Masons.

I scribbled early chapters of *Summer Hours* inside Powell's City of Books, surrounded by a fortress of pages. Thank you to Powell's, you miracle on Burnside, and to all my other beloved indies, including—Broadway Books, Rakestraw Books, E. Shaver Booksellers, Lido Village Books, Cloud & Leaf,

Books Inc., Compass Books, The Elliott Bay Book Company, Pegasus Books, and Roundabout Books.

I'd never have survived my debut year without Authors18, #Binders, and Novel Network. Huge thanks to the book bloggers, Facebook reading groups, and bookstagrammers who spread their love of reading every day.

Respect and gratitude to the gutsy journalists I've had the privilege of working with and those I know only from your bylines: the reporters and editors at the *Oregonian*, the *San Francisco Chronicle*, the *Orange County Register*, the *New York Times*, the *Capital Gazette*, the *Des Moines Register*, the *Washington Post*, and so many others. We need you. You do your jobs at great personal risk in the face of cowardly attacks from those who fear the truth.

Mimms—you're my most enthusiastic and cheerful reader, you're hilarious, and your heart is bigger than any.

Finally, and always, to Mike and Miranda: I love you. You matter the most. Let's go to the beach.

# SUMMER HOURS

AMY MASON DOAN

Reader's Guide

GRAYDON
HOUSE

1. The title *Summer Hours* has multiple meanings in the novel: in the 1990s thread, it's the name of Cal's boat and refers to the hours Becc and Eric play hooky from their jobs. In the 2008 thread, the title captures the carefree hours of youth. What does the phrase mean to you?

2. In the novel, characters like Becc and Eric are worried they might be "selling out." How does this notion of selling out shape their actions and decisions in positive or negative ways? What does the phrase *selling out* mean to you? Is it just an idealistic term, or do you think there is a way to balance dreams and professional realities in life?

3. Discuss Cal as a character. Did you understand why Becc was drawn to him?

4. Contrast Becc's relationships with Cal and Eric. How was Becc a different person in each relationship? Who did you feel was better for her?

5. Does Becc face more lingering consequences from the affair than Cal? Why do you think that is? Do you think she should have regretted their relationship more, or did she ultimately gain something from it?

6. Like the book/movie *The Graduate*, *Summer Hours* features a love triangle, but in this case, a woman is at the point. How does the author subvert gender tropes in both the 1990s and 2008 threads?

7. Why do you think Becc feels the need to lie or bend the truth in her letters to Francine Haggermaker? Does Francine give Becc any reason to fear her disapproval? Were you surprised by the revelation that Francine was also secretly subversive—much like the Feline Collective—in her youth?

8. Discuss the Feline Collective and its mission to expose sexual harassment on campus. Despite the '90s setting, did that element of the story resonate with you as a reader today? What has changed in society's approach to sexual harassment?

9. Discuss the older generation of women in the novel: Becc's mom, Eric's mom (Donna), Francine (scholarship granter), and Yvonne (Serra's art mentor and the force behind the Feline Collective). How did your view of these women evolve over the course of the story? How did these characters affect the younger generation of women in the novel?

10. Journalism, movies, and art play a big role in this novel. How do the changes we see in these fields in the 1990s narrative reflect the characters' own coming-of-age journeys?

11. *Summer Hours* explores the journalism industry both in the '90s, which was the beginning of the internet revolution,

and in 2008. Compare the journalism context we see through Becc's professional path to the ways people get news today. Do you think the changes have been positive, negative, or both?

12. Were you happy Becc and Eric ended up together, at least for the near future? Or do you think it's best to leave the past in the past?

**What inspired you to write *Summer Hours*?**

*My first job out of college was writing dry newsletters for a commercial real estate firm. I was so miserable that I used to sneak off to matinees in the middle of the day to meet a friend who was also in despair over his career. We knew we were lucky to have any paycheck, and we knew it was bratty and wrong to ditch work, but we got addicted to those covert movie outings. We even developed a complex secret email code like the one Becc and Eric use to plan their meet ups.*

*I still remember the movies we saw, the scorched-butter smell of the theaters, the nubby upholstery of the seats. And I remember how our subterfuge, childish as it felt, gave us hope and a sense of control when we desperately needed it. These memories were the seeds of the story.*

**Why did you choose the title *Summer Hours*?**

*Cal's boat was called the Summer Hours for a long time before I settled on the title. He thinks of himself as a rebel and that appeals to Becc. Summer Hours also fits the story perfectly because it all takes place in summer, and every chapter in the novel includes people playing hooky or, to put it charitably, setting their own highly flexible work hours.*

*Summer Hours ultimately means something bigger to Becc. She realizes near the end that it was in her secret moments, the times she slipped away from where she was supposed to be, that she was most free to define who she was. As an adult in 2008, she recaptures some of that exhilaration and is ultimately able to reconnect with her younger self.*

**In what ways did your own experiences as a newbie journalist in the '90s inform the novel?**

*I graduated from journalism school and started writing for print newspapers and magazines right when the internet started transforming the industry. It's hard to believe now, but back then web editors used to prowl the cubicles begging reporters to "file something for online" once they'd met their print deadlines. The internet was considered an extra and wasn't taken all that seriously. Then corporate takeovers and competition from free online media outlets made us wonder if print newspapers had any future at all.*

*Like Becc, I was extremely idealistic. I'd grown up in a household that subscribed to two daily papers, and I worshipped reporters like Nellie Bly and Edward R. Murrow, so it was hard for me to see veteran reporters getting laid off, to watch some sites blurring the line between news and advertising, and to hear that journalism was no longer a profession that required skills or standards—that anyone with a keyboard and an internet connection could do it.*

*Journalists aren't perfect, but when I see people today wearing T-shirts that say Rope. Tree. Journalist. Some Assembly*

Required, I want to ask them, Without reporters, would you know that smoking causes cancer? Would you know about Watergate? If your city council member was taking kickbacks? Certain politicians have vilified the media and weaponized the public's desire for simple, entertaining stories because, without the media to check them, they can lie with impunity.

But I remain an idealist. I see journalists doing extraordinary work—risking their lives and fighting to get the truth out there because it matters. And I think that Summer Hours is ultimately a hopeful novel, because Becc devotes her life to digging up facts that would otherwise remain hidden. She's still got that respect for the truth inside her.

### Why did you include so many movie references in the novel?

They're Eric's verbal tic and I'm as obsessed with movies as he is! The '90s movies give some texture to the story because they bring us back to that era.

But on a deeper level, movies give us a taste of other lives, so Becc and Eric escape into films when reality disappoints them.

### Were Francine's "activities" during the 1950s based on true events in any way?

The 1950s Communist blacklist is obviously real, and blacklisted screenwriters like Dalton Trumbo and Norma Barzman continued secretly working in the film industry via pseudonyms, fronts, or sympathetic producers. But the idea of someone systematically inserting secret messages into blacklisted writers' films via telltale props is fictional—at least as far as I know. I'd love to find out otherwise.

Francine is such a steely, wise character. She'd be part of the resistance no matter her age.

To me, her youthful actions are a form of graffiti that resembled the Feline Collective's. They both protest injustice and try to get the truth out via unconventional means.

**Why did you choose to include a plot that touches on sexism and sexual harassment?**

I wrote much of the book during the genesis of the #MeToo movement, but the Feline Collective was part of the plot for years before that. When I was in college we all read feminist zines, so it felt natural for Serra to be part of an underground feminist network. Feminism certainly became a bigger part of my characters' world as #MeToo took off and I grappled with the chauvinism and harassment I'd experienced throughout my life—like so many women are doing right now.

While Cal seems like a good guy and he and Becc are both adults when they get together, Becc ultimately learns he's not an ally. He laughs off Derrek Schwinn's behavior. That "boys' club" behavior, subtle and unconscious as it may be, is insidious. And I thought it was realistic that Cal would "sail away" while Becc would have to deal with the consequences of their affair for decades.

But as with the journalism themes in the novel, I think this part of the story is ultimately hopeful. Francine, who Becc is so sure will side with the powerful men, turns out to be a formidable ally. Women have each other's backs, and when they rise up together, they're a powerful force.